Textbook written according to revised syllabus of T.Y.B.Com.
prescribed by Savitribai Phule Pune University from 2015-2016.
Also useful for other Universities in Maharashtra.

Business Regulatory Framework

(Mercantile Law)

Dr. S. N. Kulkarni

Diamond Publications

Business Regulatory Framework (Mercantile Law)

Dr. S. N. Kulkarni

First Edition : June 2015

ISBN : 978-81-8483-630-1

© Diamond Publications

Type Setting :
Diamond Publications

Cover Page :
Sham Bhalekar

Published by :
Diamond Publications
264/3 Shaniwar Peth, 302 Anugrah Apartment
Near Omkareshwar Temple, Pune - 411 030
☎ 020-24452387, 24466642

info@diamondbookspune.com
www.diamondbookspune.com

Sole Distributor :
Diamond Book Depot
661 Narayan Peth
Appa Balwant Chowk
Pune 411 030
Tel. - 24480677, 66020282

PREFACE

This is my second book on Business Laws. Thanks to the teachers and students from commerce and management disciplines who have followed my earlier book and encouraged me to undertake the writing of this book.

In the context of globalization liberalization, persons involved in the business are expected to know various changes in the domestic and international legal regime. New avenues are open in the field of intellectual property and online transactions. It is advisable for the students, prospective businessmen and entrepreneurs to acquire basic knowledge of laws regulating business.

This book contains eleven parts comprising law of contract, partnership, companies, negotiable instruments, sale of goods, consumerism. Two new parts viz. Arbitration and Conciliation and Limited Liability Partnership have been inserted to broaden the scope of the book and to keep it updated in view of the changes in the syllabi of commerce and management courses. E-commerce dealt with by Information Technology Act finds place in the book.

I have made sincere efforts to update and improvise earlier writing on mercantile law. I have kept in mind the linkages between the law and other discipline. This book is designed for the students of T.Y.B.Com, B.B.A., B.B.M. (IB), M.B.A., PGDBM and who aspire to be CA, CS or undertake ICWA course. I have attempted to elucidate the legal concepts and elaborate the provisions in simple, lucid and precise manner keeping in view the commerce and management students. Illustrations, examples are provided and leading judgments are highlighted. I hope the students would find it easy to understand.

I am obliged by my senior colleagues who motivated me to continue to write and helped me by providing worthy suggestions. I acknowledge the intellectual and emotional support of my colleagues and well wishers, particularly Prin. Dr.Dileep Shinde, Chairman, Board of Studies for Business Laws and Prof. P.N.Choudhari from Pune. I am grateful to Shri D.G. Pashte, proprietor of Diamond Publications who allowed me to borrow novel ideas in making study of law interesting, simple and easy to grasp. I look forward for constructive suggestions and criticism for improvement of the next edition.

Dr. S.N. Kulkarni

INDEX

PART - IV

PART - V

PART - VI

PART - VII

PART - VIII

PART - IX

PART - X

PART - XI

INTRODUCTION TO BUSINESS LAW

Every person interacts with the other persons, groups, companies, society in general. In this interaction there is bound to be conflict of interests. Sometimes that leads to disputes. One's exercise of rights may trouble the others. If one is allowed to adopt a course of conduct of his choice, there would be chaos and anarchy. Law does not permit this. Law regulates the relationship of persons. Every legal system lays down the standards of behavior in given situation. The term ' Law ' denotes the principles or the rules regulating social conduct. It is a norm of social behavior, regulating the relationship. Few definitions of law, are given below.

Definitions of Law

> ***Austin -*** *'Law is a command of sovereign.'*
>
> ***Salmond -*** *'Body of principles recognized and applied by the states in administration of justice.'*
>
> ***Prof. Holland -*** *'A rule of external human action enforced by a sovereign political authority.'*
>
> ***Blackstone -*** *'Law in its most general and comprehensive sense, signifies a rule of action and is applied indisriminately to all kinds of actions whether animate or inanimate, rational or irrational.'*

The law, in simple terms, is a body of rules. Rules are imposed by some sovereign authority, say parliament. The government in many cases ensures that the law is followed. Law is enforced in courts. Family relationship, business relationship, citizens's relationship with the State is all governed by the law. Rights and duties are created in every kind of relationship and that is the subject matter of law.

Business Law - Meaning and Scope

This book confines to the discussion of business law, in india. Law and business are closely related. In business decisions, law cannot be ignored. Constitution of India guarantees every citizen freedom of carrying on business of his choice. But commercial activity should be lawful and within framework of law. Every manufacturer, dealer, distributer retailer and the consumer must know the related law of the land. Production, marketing, buying, selling and other incidental activities of the business enterprise should be according to law. Otherwise fine or imprisonment follows. Law in a way facilitates and promotes the trade and commerce. It protects individuals from being exploited.

Business law is also called as **commercial law or mercantile law**. This branch of law regulates business or commerce or mercantile transactions. Economic behavior is the domain of mercantile law. Mercantile transactions relate to merchandise or movable property or goods. Such transactions are carried on by mercantile men. Those may be a single individual or a proprietor, a sole trader or a company or a partnership firm. Business law is a type of civil law. Civil law basically deals with civil rights and obligations arising out of a transaction.

Mercantile law may be defined as that branch of law comprising law concerning trade, industry and commerce.

Prof. A. K. Sen defines the term as,

> *"Commercial Law includes the law applicable to the ordinary transactions of merchants, bankers, and traders and denotes the branch of law which relates to the rights of parties and the relations of persons engaged in commerce".*

K. Banerjee defines Commercial Law as,

> *"One ordinarily understands particular portions of law dealing with the rights and the liabilities or obligations arising out of ordinary transactions between people engaged in business or commerce, the merchants and traders".*

It generally includes the Law of Contracts, Sale of goods, Partnership, Negotiable Instruments, Copyrights, Insurance etc. These laws are dealt with by various enactments. The field of trading activity is ever-expanding. E-commerce, intellectual property regime and other new concepts are evolved. The scope of business law is also extended to cover new legislations. The basic principles mostly remain unchanged. This book limits to the study of these basic principles in major enactments regulating business transactions. This book highlights **legal framework regulating business or trade**.

Business Regulatory Framework

Indian Contract Act of 1872 is a general law dealing with business transactions. Sale of Goods Act, regulates sale of movable properties. Negotiable instruments embody monetary transactions dealt with by Negotiable Instruments Act of 1881. Partnership Firm is a business entity. Partnership Act of 1932, governs relationship of partners inter-se and with third parties. The contractual relationship between consumers and traders falls within the ambit of the Consumer Protection Act, 1986.

Intellectual properties like patents, copyrights, trademarks etc. involve large stakes in the market which is the subject matter of variant statutes like Patents Act, Copyright Law etc. All these statutes provide legal business regulatory framework within which business transactions should be confined.

> **"The law is the last result of human wisdom acting upon human experience for the benefit of the public."** – *Johnson.*

LAW OF CONTRACT
(INDIAN CONTRACT ACT, 1872)

INTRODUCTION

The law relating to contract is contained in the Indian Contract Act of 1872. It embodies certain basic principles and the law pertaining to special contracts. Business transactions are based on promises. Promises result in rights and duties. If the rights and duties were not enforced by law, business would be paralyzed. Law of contract gives legal sanctity to the commercial transactions.

On the utility of law of contract, Sir William Anson observes, "... *the law of contract is intended to ensure that what a man has been led to expect shall come to pass and that what has been promised to him shall be performed*". This branch of law brings a kind of certainty and definiteness in the business transactions and thus provides sense of security among the public.

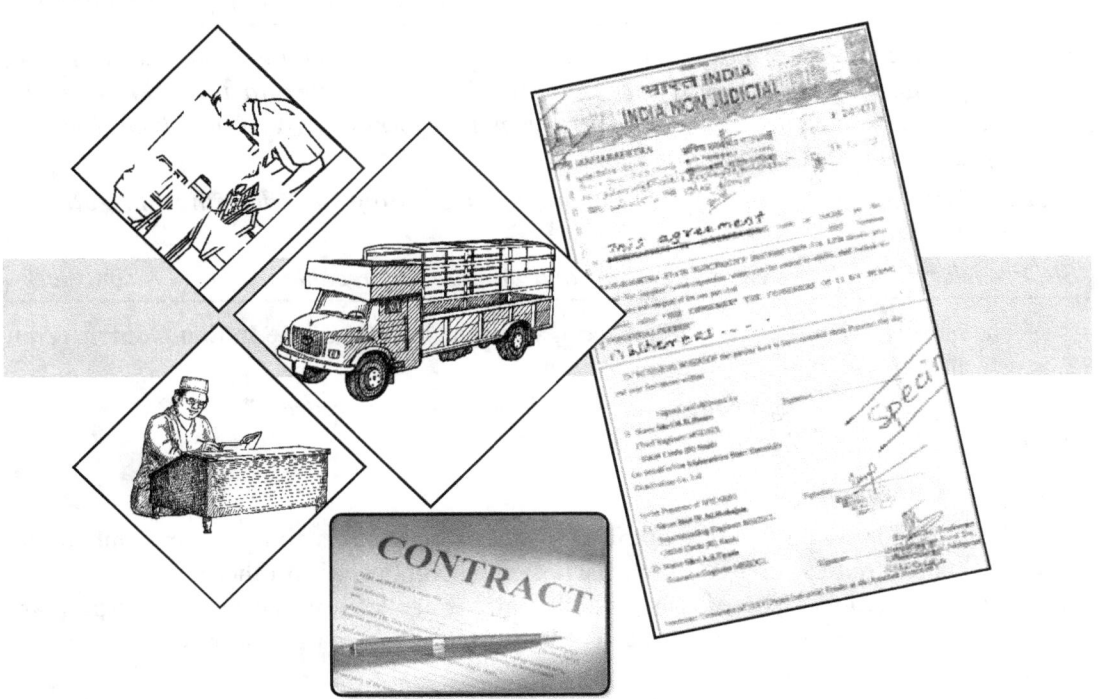

Chapter 1

CONTRACT : CONCEPT

Definitions, Meaning and Salient Features

Everyone, knowingly or unknowingly, enters into contracts with others to satisfy one's day-today needs. Sale or purchase of goods through shops, purchase of flats, lands, properties, travelling by locomotives, hiring services of doctors, builders, operating bank accounts, purchasing a book are all contracts. The traders, business entities, companies, trusts are required to enter into various transactions.Contracts are thus integral part of our life or business world.

1.1   Definitions of Contract

Some of the important definitions of the term given by experts are reproduced below:

Sir William Anson - 'A contract is an agreement enforceable by law, made between two or more persons by which rights are acquired by one or more to the acts done or forborne on the part of the other or others. It is that form of agreement which directly contemplates and creates an obligation."

Justice Salmond - 'A contract is an agreement creating and defining obligations between parties'.

Sir Fredrick Pollock - 'Every agreement and promise enforceable at law is a contract'.

The most relevant definition of the term, as given U/S **2(h) of the Indian Contract Act, 72,** is as follows :

"An agreement enforceable by law is a contract"

This definition is similar to that given by J. Pollock.

Concept of Contract

From the foregoing definitions it follows that a contract is an agreement embodying certain rights and duties. In a contract, parties enjoy rights against other at the same time subjected to obligations. These rights and obligations are legal in the sense that those are binding on the parties at law. Contract is thus is a legal nexus giving rise to rights and liabilities.

An analysis of the definitions further reveals that agreement and contract are two different concepts. For the formation of contract there must be —

1. An agreement, and

2. Legal obligation i.e. the duty enforceable by law.

1) Agreement

U/S 2(e) 'Agreement' is defined as *"every promise and every set of promises forming the consideration for each other"*. Section 2(b) defines promise as, *"A proposal, when accepted, becomes a promise"*. From these definitions together, it follows that a proposal is given by one party; it is accepted by the other party; proposal when accepted becomes a promise. In simple words and in ultimate analysis, an agreement is an accepted proposal.

2) Legal Obligation

A contract is an exchange of promises by contracting parties. In every contract a right is given to one and other is subjected to corresponding duty (obligations). These obligations are recognized and enforced by law and are called as legal obligations. These obligations are not social or moral obligations The concept of legal obligation is evident in various definitions given above.

Agreement is a bargain between two persons. It is the outcome of mutual consent between the two.

1.2 Characteristics of a Contract

From the definitions cited above and various sections from the Act, following characterstics of the contract emerge out.

1. **Plurality Of Parties -** There are at least two parties in a contract. One cannot enter into a contract with himself. The parties to the contract must be competent to enter into contract (S. 11).

2. **Proposal -** The first step towards creation of contract is 'proposal' or 'offer'. (Refer the definition given in chapter 3.)

   The proposal when accepted by other party becomes a promise.

3. **Acceptance -** To create contractual relationship, proposal must be accepted by the offeree. When the offeree responds to the offer by giving assent to it, proposal is said to be accepted.

   The rules relating to valid offer and acceptance are discussed in Chapter no.3

   The proposal or acceptance not according to law does not lead to a binding contract.

4. **Agreement -** The proposal when accepted by the offeree, it becomes a promise. As stated earlier, an agreement is a promise or set of promises. An agreement which creates legal obligation is enforceable and is termed as contract.

"The moral basis of contract is that the promisor has by his promise created a reasonable expectation that it will be kept." – *Prof. Goodhart*

5. **Intention To Create Legal Relationship** - Agreements which create or are capable of creating legal relationship are contracts. Parties must intend to be bound by contract. Intention is gathered from words or conduct of parties or facts and circumstances in a transaction. An invitation to a dinner, candidate's promise during election, husband's promise to pay money for pocket expenses do not create any right or duty, being moral or social or domestic promises. In commercial or business transaction there is a presumption that parties intend to create legal relationship.[1]

6. **Consideration** - (Refer definition of the term in chap. 4) "An agreement without consideration is void" (S.25) Consideration is thus foundation of a contract and agreement cannot be enforced if consideration is absent. For every promise there is "something in return". For example, price is consideration in sale. Consideration may consist of some act or abstinence or promise to do some act or abstain from doing something.

   Enforceability — S.10 -Further essentials may be discussed as conditions of enforceability of an agreement. According to S. 10 of the Act an agreement is a contract if it is made by the free consent of parties competent to contract, for a lawful consideration and with a lawful object and are not expressly declared to be void.

7. **Competency Of Parties** - Parties to the contract must be competent to enter into contract. Capacity to enter into contract is of vital importance as contract with incompetent person is void- ab -initio (from the beginning). According to S.11 of the Act, a person who is major, of sound mind and not disqualified by law has capability to form contractual relationship with other. A minor, an idiot, insane and persons prevented by law from entering into contract suffer from incapacity. (Refer Chapter 5 for details)

8. **Consent and Free Consent -** Parties to the contract must give consent to the contract and their consent must be free. Parties are said to consent when they agree over the same thing in the same sense. Absense of free consent makes the contract voidable (cancellable). Coercion, undue influence, fraud, misrepresentation, mistake in obtaining consent destroy free will of the party. Such a party can put an end to the contract. Thus for enforceability of the contract free consent is essential.

9. **Lawful Object & Consideration -** Refer point number six. A contract, therefore, must have consideration. It is a price of promise given by other. Further, the consideration and object of a contract should be lawful. According to S. 23, object and consideration is unlawful if it is forbidden by law, it defeats the provisions of law, it is injurious to third parties, it involves fraud or opposed to public morals or policy.

10. **Agreements Not Declared Void -** Void agreement is that which is not enforceable by law. (S.2-g) It has no legal sanctity. To constitute a binding contract, agreement should not be void. Ss.25 to 30, 36, 56 deal with such agreements. An agreement in restraint of marriage/trade/legal proceedings, uncertain or wagering agreement, agreement to do impossible acts are expressly declared void and hence inoperative.

---

1. *Balfour v/s Balfour — (1919) 2KB 571 An agreement of a purely social or domestic nature is not a contract — Jones v/s Vernon's Pools Ltd.(1938)2 AllER626*

Other Features

11. **Certainty in Contracts** - S.29 states that uncertain agreements are void. If the terms of the contract or the agreement as such is vague, ambiguous, its performance becomes difficult. The meaning of the agreement must be capable of being made certain for its enforceability.

12. **Possibility of Performance** - It is equally important that the contract must be capable of performance. S. 56 provides that an agreement to do an act, impossible in itself, is void. Due to physical or legal impediments contract may become impossible.

13. **Legal & Procedural Formalities** - The Contract Act does not provide for any formalities for entering into a contract. There is no specific format for any type of contract. Contract need not be in writing, it can be oral. However if a special law lays down some procedural formalities for making contracts enforceable, then those are to be completed. According to the Transfer of Property Act,1882,contract of sale, mortgage, lease, gift of immovable property should be effected by registered document. Documents transfering immovable properties need registration u/s 17 of the Indian Registration Act,1908. Registration of Memorandum and Articles of Association of company is compulsory under the Companies Act 1956, so also of arbitration agreements under arbitration laws. Attestation by two witnesses is necessary in case of gifts, leases or mortgages of immovable properties. — Certain documents require to be stamped as per the Indian Stamp Act,1894. S. 25 (1) & (3) of Indian Contract Act requires registration of certain contracts.

Every contract must satisfy all the above mentioned essentials for enforcement. If the contract does not possess any one of the characterstics, then the contract is either voidable or void or illegal and hence unenforceable. That would be only an agreement and not a contract.

1.3 Following statements throw light on the true relationship between contract and an agreement.

a) *"The Contract Act does not cover the whole law of obligations."*

Salmond has observed

"The law of contracts is not the whole law of agreements, nor is it the whole law of obligations. It is the law of those obligations which create obligations and which obligations have their source in agreements."

The Act is restricted to civil obligations but it does not encompass the whole range of civil obligations. It is applicable to those obligations which flow from agreements. Obligation is a very wide term and it arises under varied situations. Naturally, such obligations are dealt with by different laws and fall outside the purview of the Contract Act which confines itself to contractual relationship. Thus many relationships remain outside the field of contracts which are enlisted below :-

1. Status Obligations - Matrimonial obligations like duty to provide necessaries to near relatives, duty to maintain wife, children, trustee's duty to give effect to trust..;

2. Quasi-Contracts — Obligations which are similar to those created by contract (refer chapter no. 13);

3. Obligations imposed by the courts in their judgements/orders;

4. Obligations in law of torts — Law of torts is a general law dealing with civil wrongs and giving rise to liabilities. For e.g. duty to take care, to compensate other for violation of right..

These obligations, though not contractual in nature, are very much enforceable.

b) ***"All contracts are agreements but all agreements are not contracts".***
Salmond's observation, above cited, covers this statement also.

Which agreements are contracts?

From the perusal of S. 10 given above and various essentials of contract it can be stated that all contracts are ageements but all agreements are not contracts. This statement may be substantiated as follows :

A contract implies legal relationship i.e. a legal bond in which legal rights and obligations are created between parties. For that, intention to create such relationship must be present. An agreement with such intention and consequent legal relationship can only be the contract. Thus an agreement of social or moral nature is devoid of legal sanctity because parties never intend to have legal binding. For example, a promise to accompany a tour, etc. promise to fulfill assurances by a minister etc. lack legal binding.

An agreement is thus a wider concept than a contract. The Act restricts the term "contract" to legally binding obligations.

Chapter 2 — TYPES OF CONTRACTS

The Contract Act defines certain terms relating to contract but does not provide for any classification of contracts as such. This chapter however is useful in understanding certain important terms which are often used in the law of contract. Contracts may be catagorised according to their mode of creation, enforceability and extent of performance. Various types of contract are discussed below. Titles refer to the basis of classification.

Basis of Clasification and Types of Contracts

For easy understanding various types of contract are classified according to different criterion and explained under different heads :-

2.1A Mode of Creation

Contract can be created either expressly or impliedly and accordingly there are two types of contracts viz. *express or implied contracts.*

a) **Express Contract**

This type of contract is entered into by expressing words, either spoken or written. In express contract, intention of parties is expressed in words. Thus express contract can be oral or written. S. 9 states that insofar as the proposal or acceptance of any proposal is made in words, the promise is said to be express. Partnership Deed, Lease Deed, Sale Deed are in written form and are express contracts. A contract resulting from telephonic talk is oral but express. Though oral, contracts are perfectly enforceable.

b) **Implied Contract**

i) **Implied by Parties**

When contract is made otherwise than by words, it is implied or constructive. Sometimes no words are used for making a contract. In absence of words, contract is evidenced by conducts of the parties. The contractual relationship is inferred from acts, course of dealing between parties. Implied refers to tacit relationship. The assent to contract is manifest in some act and not in words. Circumstances prove that there exists a contract.

For eg. - A coolie at a railway station lifts the luggage of a passenger without being asked for by him. The passenger has to pay service charges to coolie as he has *impliedly* agreed to pay. Similarly, A enters and takes a seat in a bus going to his town. Law would imply a contract from the very nature of the circumstanses and A has to pay the fare.

ii) Implied by Law

Constructive or Quasi Contract

This type of contract is implied by law. There is no offer or acceptance or consent to contract by parties but contractual relationship is presumed/imposed by law. This relationship is similar (quasi) to regular contract by consent.

X, by mistake, leaves an article at B's house. B appropriates it. B has to pay for it. See for details chapter no. 12 on Quasi Contracts.

d) Classification of contracts under English Law-Formal and Informal Contracts

Indian law does not recognize this criterion. These contracts are found in English law. A formal contract is one to which law attaches validity because of formality or the special language by which it is created. Form is the basis of legality. eg. negotiable instuments which embody the contracts. Such Contracts are enforceable only when entered in prescribed format.

Formal contracts can be either ''Speciality Contracts 'or ''Contracts of Record''.A contract of speciality is a contract in writing, signed, sealed and delivered by the parties. It is also termed as **"contract under seal"**. This does not require consideration. A contract of record is one that is imposed on parties by court and entered in court's record. Strictly speaking it is not a contract as the consent is absent.The contract of record can be either a judgement or a recognizance. Recognizance is a written undertaking by a criminal that on default by him to appear in court or to keep peace or to be of good conduct, he is bound to pay to the State the sum under the recognizance.The contract which are not of the catagory in the above para are **simple contracts.**

The informal contracts do not require any formality or special language.The only requirement is that contract should satisfy the essentials of contract.

2.2B Extent of Performance

After entering into contract it is performed by the parties. It may be performed wholly or partially. According to the stage of performance contracts are catagorized as follows.

a) Executory Contract

When both the parties have yet to perform their part of contract, the contract is called executory contract. Contract implies obligations. When obligations of both the parties are outstanding, contract is in executory stage. In this case, as an initial stage, contract is entered into but something, either wholly or in part, remains to be done by both the parties. For eg. A builder agrees to build a house for owner who promises to pay constuction charges according to stage of construction.Contract is to be performed in future.

b) Executed Contract

When both the parties to the conract perform their part of contract, it is executed contract. The parties discharge respective mutual obligations and nothing remains to be done. This involves performance of reciprocal promises. For example, in the market, a consumer purchases an article and pays for it. Transaction comes to an end by its execution.

From the explanations of the above terms one can say that a contract is a contract from the time it is made and not from the time its performance is due. A contract can be performed as soon as it is made or its performance can be postponed.

Obligation (Duty) to perform - Who has performed Contract?

a) Unilateral Contract

"Uni" means one.It refers to a stage where one party preforms the contract and other's obligation is outstanding.When at the time contract made or even prior to that, one of the parties has already performed his part of duty and other party has yet to discharge his obligation, it is termed as unilateral contract. For example, a purchaser makes advance payment towards an air cooler. Seller has to deliver the cooler in future.

b) Bilateral Contract

Bilateral contracts are akin to executory contracts or contracts with executory consideration. In bilateral contract, when the contract is made both the parties are yet to fulfill their promises. Thus contract is to be perfomred in future by both.It is yet to be executed and contractual obligations are yet to be discharged by both.Through an agreement for sale, a manufacturer agrees to manufacture and deliver a product within one year from the date of agreement and other party promises to pay for the same. This is bilateral contract.

2.3C Enforceability of a Contract

According to the validity or enforceability factor, the contracts may be of the following types.

a) Valid Contracts

Contract is defined as an agrement enforceable by law. Validity or enforceability is, therefore, inherent in every contract. The term valid contract thus is a misnomer. Contract is always valid. But to contradict it from unenforceable contracts, the term valid contract is used.Valid contract satisfies all the essentials of contract, hence perfectly legal and enforceable in all respects.

b) Voidable Contract -

Definition - S. 2(i) of the Act -

"an agreement which is enforceable by law at the option of one or more of the parties thereto, but not at the option of the other or others, is a voidable contract".

In voidable contract, one party is having an option to affirm/continue with the contract or to put an end to it. Voidable simply means cancellable or which can be rescinded or repudiated by one party.

The Act provides three situations wherein a contract is voidable

i) -Ss. 19, 19-A - When the consent of the parties is not free.The consent is not free when is is caused by coercion, undue-influence, fraud etc.. (See chapter on free consent.) The party whose consent is not voluntarily given has liberty to continue with it or avoid it. The aggrieved party can exercise the option and cancel the contract. Till it is rescinded, it is a perfect and binding contract. The party has to repudiate the contract within reasonable time.

ii) -S.53 - Contract involves reciprocal promises, i.e. promises from both sides. If one party prevents the other from performing his promise, the contract becomes voidable at the option of the party so prevented.

iii) -S.55 - Sometimes the time of performance is the essence of contract. If a party under obligation fails to perform contract within time, contract becomes voidable. Other party can put an end to the contract.

c) Void Contract

The phrase "void" implies 'nullity', 'devoid of any legal effect' (infrctuous). Such a conract becomes futile, "not binding in law".

S. 2(j) of the Act defines void contract as -

> *"A contract which ceases to be enforceable by law becomes void, when it ceases to be enforceable."*

As the definition of contract goes, a contract is valid from its inception. Careful reading of this definition reveals that a contract is not void from the beginning. It may become void due to some changes after it is entered into. Its validity may be lost under peculier circumstances as mentioned below.

1 Supervening Impossibility/Legality - S.56-If, after the formation of contract, its performance becomes impossible, contract becomes void.

eg.-A agrees to sell his horse for 5 lakhs. The horse is killed in land slide. Transaction is void as it is impossible to complete sale.

2 Supervening Illegality-S.56-Similarly by reason of subsequent illegality, contract becomes void.

3 Voidable contract becomes void- When voidable contract is repudiated by the party entitled to cancell, it becomes void. As long as it is not recsinded, it is perfectly enforceable.

4 Contingent Contract - A contingent contract to do or not to do something on the happenning of an uncertain future event, becomes void when the event becomes impossible. (S.32.)

d) Unenforceable Contract

This type of contract is valid in itself as it satisfies the essentials of enforceabilty. The courts however will not give effect to it as it suffers from some technical flaw. Inadequecy of stamps, non payment of requisite stamps for a deed, non-registration of a document evidensing a contract, non-attestation of a document, absence of writing, bar of limitaton etc.. are the procedural defects which make the contract unenforceable. Once the defect is cured, it gains enforceability. (Refer point No. 13 in essentials of contract)

Void Agreements

The meaning of the word ''void '' is the same as given in void contract above. Void agreement is a nullity and it has no consequences. It is void ad-intio (from the inception). Agreement never takes birth in the eye of law. Agreement can be inpoerative if it lacks essential elements of enforceability. For example, an agreement with a minor or an agreement without consideration is void. An agreement may be expressly declared void. For eg.-agreement by way of wager, agreement in restraint of trade etc are by law, void. These are only agreements and not contracts. See chapter no.8.

Illegal Agreements

An agreement which is against the express provisions of law is termed as illgal agreement. An agreement prohibited or forbiden by law is illegal. Illustration-A agrees to let his bunglow for smuggling and share the smuggling profit from B. This arrangement is illegal as it violates penal laws.All illgal agreements are void but not vice-versa. Illegal agreement is wider in meaning than void agreements.Illegal agreement is void ab-initio but void agreements are not necessarily illegal. An illegal agreement is destitute of any legal consequenses but a void agreement is void when it is proved to be void. Transaction collateral to illegal agreements are also void.

These proceeding paras would clarify that agreement and contract with their types are conceptually different. These terms seem to be overlapping but there is a fine distinction between them.

"Ex turpi causa non oritur actio" i.e. "No action is allowed on an illegal agreement"

Chapter 3

OFFER and ACCEPTANCE OF OFFER

3.1 Offer (Proposal)

Offer and proposal are synonymous terms. Offer is the first step in the formation of a contract. Parties sometimes do not notice that they offer or accept offer in commercial transactions.

3.1.a Definition and Meaning

Prof. Pollock defines offer as-

> *"the expression of a person's willingness to become, according to the terms expressed, a party to an agreement is called an offer or proposal."*

Section 2(a) of the Contract Act defines proposal as follows

> *"When one person signifies to another his willingness to do or abstain from doing anything, with a view to obtain the assent of that other to such an act or abstinance, he is said to make a proposal."*

Example - X says to Y, " I am willing to sell my car for one lakh, are you interested?" Y agrees. Here statement of X is an offer. He has 'signified' his willingness to 'sell' (to do something) the car so that Y will buy it.

According to the definition under the Act, there are three *essentials of the concept.*

1. Signifying willingness by one person;
2. Willingness is to do or abstain from doing something;
3. Expression of willingness is with a view to obtain the consent of the other.

One who makes an offer is called as ' offeror' and to whom it is made is 'offeree'.

3.1.2 Essentials of (Rules for) Valid Proposal

Validity of proposal is one of the essential features of a contract. If the offer is not as per the law, contractual relationship does not result.

Rules regarding valid proposal are discussed below.

a. Signifying willingness

Signifying means communicating or making known. There must be *expression of willingness* to do or abstain from doing something. Proposal is the act of signifying or expressing desire to do something for the other.

b. Offer 'to do or abstain ...

Willingness must be 'to do something or abstain from doing something'. Offer thus involves either a positive act or abstinance.Offer to sell, provide services contemplate positive 'acts' hence it is called as **'positive offer'**. There can also be ' **negative offer'** in the sense that it is willingness to abstain from doing an act. To abstain means to refrain from or to keep away from doing a particular act. Offer, not to resign from the job, if salary is doubled, is a negative offer.

c. Object of offer

Object of making an offer is to obtain the assent of the offeree so as to reach to an agreement.Offer cannot be in the air. Proposal is communicated to other person so that he would respond positively.

d. Intention behind offer

There must be an intention to creat legal relationship through offer. A proposal should be such that it should give rise to legal consequenses and establish legal relations. A statement in jest, excitement or mere joking or otherwise casual does not amount to an offer. Promise to present a birthday gift, therefore, is devoid of any legality.

Rose & Frank Co. v/s JR Crompton & Brothers Ltd.[2] ℗ Parties agreed in their business transaction that ''..the agreement is not entered into..as a formal or legal contract..but it is only a definite record of the purpose and intention of the parties..'' Because of this derogatory clause it was held that no contract existed there being no intention to creat legal relationship.

Intention attaches seriousness to the proposal. Inq business transaction it is presumed that the parties intend legal consequences. Mere declarations of intention, however is not an offer.

e. Certainty of offer and Certainty as to terms of offer

Offer should be definite. An offer should be be clear, certain or should be capable of being made certain.If it is vague and confusing, intention cannot be gathered. In case of uncertainty performance of contract becomes very difficult.

Terms of offer must also be certain. If a term is vague, it cannot be given effect to. Rest of the agreement however stands.

---

2.   *(1923) 2KB 261*

f. Term as to non-compliance

Non-compliance of a condition in an offer cannot be considered as acceptance. A proposal should not contain a term that if offer is not accepted within a specified time, it would to be deemed to be accepted. Failure to respond cannot be treated as an assent to the proposal. The acceptance must be positive and burden of communication cannot be imposed on the offeree.

g. Communication of Offer

Offer must be communicated to the offeree. Though a person accepts it or does the act of acceptance without its communication to him, there is no contract. Offeree can accept only when he knows about the proposal or it is meant for him. Acceptance in ignorance of offer indicates absence of meeting of minds.

Laman Shukla v/s Gaury Datta [3] Gauri Dutta (G), a businessman, asked his munim, Lalman(L), to search his missing nephew. Afterwards G. distributed handbills offering a reward of Rs 501 to anyone who might find out the missing boy. Without knowing this, munim found the boy and handed over to G. Afterwords L was dismissed from services. Six months later he came to know about the reward and claimed it. The court held that the L was not entitled for reward because he searched the boy as a servant and in discharge of his duties and secondly, he did the act of acceptance (finding the boy and informing) without the knowledge the of offer. The acceptance of offer without its communication is not valid and hence no contract is concluded. The relationship between G & L was basically that of employer-employee and not contractual, to claim reward.

h. Communication of special terms of offer

A contract may contain special terms. On many occasions, a party knows the conract in general but is not aware of its special terms. E-contracts, web offers purchase receipt, journey ticket incorporate peculiar stipulations. Party's liability on such terms is decided as under.

a) If a party had no knowledge of special terms before or at the time of the contract, then he is not bound by the terms. [4]

b) If the party has the knowledge or presumed to have the knowledge of the special terms/conditions then obviously he would be liable on these terms. When one is bound to know something, whether infact one was knowing or not, that is irrelevant. [5]

This is important because now-a-days many orders are placed through e-mails and goods are delivered. Such transactions are subject to terms and conditions ('T/C apply')

i. Invitation to Offer

Invitation to make an offer is not an offer. Sometimes there are negotiations before a contract is signed. In these preliminary discussions, a party may propose certain terms on which he is willing to negotiate. He desires to negotiate by supplying some information.

---

3. *(1913) 13 ALL.L.J 489*
4. *Handerson v/s Stevenson (1875)2 HLSC APP 470.*
5. *Thompson v/s L.M.S. Railway Co.-(1930), 1 K.B. 41*

He thus invites the other to make a proposal on those terms. This is called as 'invitation to offer' and not actual offer. In judicial language it is called, 'invitation to treat'. If the person intends to be bound by his offer as soon as it is accepted by the other, then it offer. If he reserves himself any further act before becomes to be bound by it, it is invitation to offer.

     Illustrations - Quotations /catalogue of prices, price-lists, menu in a hotel, prospectus of a company, advertisement for tenders or for sale by auction, published time-table of a railway are invitation to offers. A statement as to a price made by a tradesman is not construed as an offer to sell.[6] In super markets/self-serviceshops, goods are displayed with prices. This is an invitation to the customers to buy at those prices. When the buyer picks up an article and takes it to the cash counter, he makes an offer. Acceptance of the cash amounts to acceptance of offer.Cash clerk may refuse to sell and turn down the offer.[7]

j. **Kinds of Offer**-Following are the kinds of offers.

i) Express and Implied Offers

An offer may be express or implied. An offer which is expressed by words either spoken or written, is called as an 'express offer'. Thus a telephonic talk, a letter, e-mail communication may contain an express offer.

An 'implied offer' is one which inferred from the conduct of parties, facts and circumstances of a case.

ii) Specific or General Offers

Specific offer means an offer to a particular person or identified party. In such offers, the person to whom it is addressed, should only accept it. A offers to sell his land to B, adjoining farmer. B only can accept it. "General or public offer" is that which is made to the public at large. Any member of the society may comply with the terms of public offer and accept it.[8] Offers of rewards (for lost article or providing information leading to arrest of a criminal etc.) are general offers.

iii) Cross and Counter Offers

When two persons are making the identical offers to each other but nobody knows about other's offer, those are called as 'cross-offers.'

In counter -offer, the offeree makes certain changes in the original offer and thus puts forth a new proposal. This is described as a counter-offer or bargaining in the market.

iv) Conditional Offers - An offer can be made subject to conditions or it may contain stipulations as to future compliances. Mode of acceptance can be such a condition. Contract comes into existance only when the proposal is accepted in that prescribed mode.

---

6. *Harvey v/s Facey, 1983 AC552*
7. *Pharmaceutical Society of Great Britain v/s Boots Cash Chemists-[(1952)2 QB 795]*
8. *Carlill v/s Carbolick Smoke Ball Co. -1893, 1, Q.B. 256 See in the next topic.*

v) Standing Offer

Standing offers are also called as 'Tenders'. Advertisement inviting tenders is an invitation to offer. Tenders submitted are actual offers. Usually it is an offer to supply commodity or provide services for a certain price/charges, for a particular period. Goods when advertised for sale at a fixed rate till stock is available, is a standing offer.

vi) Auction Sales

An advertisement of an auction sale is simply an invitation to offer. When prospective bidders bid, it is an offer. When the hammer falls for the third time, the offer is said to be accepted and the contract is concluded. The bidder can withdraw the bid at any time before it is accepted. If the auction is in persuance of court's order, contract entered is subject to court's confirmation. In such a case bid can be revoked before confirmation of the court. (See Auction Sale in Chapter 26) [9]

3.2 ACCEPTANCE

Acceptance is the second stage in the formation of a contract. An offer by itself does not lead to an agreement. It must be accepted by the other party and then only contractual relationship comes into existance. *Once the offer is accepted it is transformed into a binding contract. Definition of* **"Acceptance"**. S.2(b) of the Act defines the term in the following way

> *"When one person to whom the proposal is made signifies his assent thereto, the proposal is said to be accepted. A proposal when accepted becomes a promise."*

Acceptance thus means signifying assent to the proposal. It is the manifestation of the offeree's assent to the offer.

Important Provisions Regarding Valid Acceptance

An acceptance to be legally binding, must conform to the following rules.

1. Absolute and unqualified acceptance

Acceptance must be absolute and unqualified: S. 7(1) of the Act provides that.. "In order to convert a proposal into a promise, the acceptance must be absolute and unqualified".

Absolute acceptance means acceptance in total or as it is, in original form. It must be of the whole offer. Acceptor cannot assent to the favourable part and reject inconvenient part of the offer.

Sir William Anson commenting on the significance of the acceptance states — *"Acceptance of an offer is what a lighted match to a train of gunpowder. It produces something which cannot be recalled or undone. But the powder may have laid till it has become damp or the man who laid the train may withdraw it before a lighted match stick is set to it...."*

---

9. *The auctioneer is not liable to the prospective bidder for cancellation of auction and consequent loss of money, time or inconvinience to the bidder.*

Unqualified acceptance denotes unconditional acceptance. While accepting an offer, offeree should not change any term or attach a condition or put reservations. Such an acceptance is invalid. Acceptance with new terms in the offer or acceptance with conditions is a counter offer and cannot be regarded as an acceptance.

2. Mode of Acceptance

According to S.7(2) acceptance must be accorded in mode **prescribed** by the offeror. That manner should be followed even if it is unusual or unreasonable or funny. Acceptance in different mode is not good in law.

If the mode is **not prescribed**, then it should be in usual or reasonable manner. What is usual or reasonable manner depends upon the circumstances of each case. Acceptance by telephonic talk or by e-mail or through a messenger may be reasonable in the given situation.

3. Acceptance by performing the conditions of offer or receiving cosideration from the offeror also amounts to an implied acceptance (S.8).

Example - S offers to sell his laptop to P for Rs. 30 thousand and asks to pay Rs. 10,000 as an advance, if he accepts the offer. P pays the advance. It is a valid acceptance.[10]

4. Express or implied acceptance

S.9 - Acceptance may be **express** or direct i.e. by words spoken or written.It may be **implied** by conduct. Boarding a bus at a stop, consuming food in a hotel, enjoying benefit or availing services offered amount to implied acceptance of respctive offers. Acceptance referred to u/s 8 abovementioned, are instances of implied acceptance.

5. Silence is not a proper acceptance

Offeror cannot say, "..if you do not reply, I will presume that you have accepted my proposal." Such a failure to reply or silence is not deemed as an acceptance. Offeror cannot impose a contract on an unwilling recipient.

6. Time of acceptance

Acceptance must be communicated to the offeror within stipulated time or if time is not fixed, within reasonable time. Offer lapses or withdrawn if its acceptance is delayed beyond fixed time. If no time limit is fixed then it should be communicated within reasonable time. What is reasonable time is to be decided according to the facts of a case.

7. Who can accept?

Offeree to whom the offer is made can only accept it.A third person cannot accept it unless authorised. In case of public offers, any member of the society can accept it with the knowledge of offer and by fulfilling its terms. Similarly the offer to a class of persons can be accepted by any member of that class. (refer Carllil's case below mentioned)

---

10. **V. Rao. v/s A. Rao** (1939) 3 ALLER 566 An old lady desired her relation, R, to stay with her till her death and in consideration promised to give him all her property. R stayed with the lady till her death. It was held that R was entitled to claim the proprty as he had accepted the offer by fulfilling the condition in the offer.

8. Acceptance must succeed offer

First there should be an offer and then it should be accepted. Acceptance should not precede offer. There cannot be acceptance before communication of offer.

9. Offer once rejected cannot be accepted

This is because offer when rejected lapses. Renewed offer can be accepted afresh.

10. Acceptance must be communicated to the offeror

Acceptor after accepting the offer should communicate it to the offeree. Communication of acceptance must be by authorised person.That is necessary to conclude the contract.

Powell v/s Lee[11] Powell (P), was a candidate for headmaster's post. He was selected by school managing committee. A member of the managing committee, Dismore, informally told P about his selection. Subsequently, another candidate, Parker, and not P was appointed for the post. P filed a suit against, Lee, chairman of the committee for the breach of contract. The court held that in absence of official/authorised communication (say, a letter of appointment) of acceptance of offer, there was no binding contract between them. Hence the suit failed.

Advertisement for appointment is invitation to offer. Application for appointment in an offer of services and as in this case, appointment would have been the acceptance of offer.

11. Public offer and its Acceptance

Carlill v/s Carbolick Smoke Ball Co.[12] A company, proprietors of medicines, through an advertisement in a newspaper, offered a reward of £ 100 to anyone who contacted influenza after using their smoke ball as per the printed instructions. To show their sincerity, company had deposited £ 1000 with Alliance Bank. Mrs. Carlill, used smoke balls in the specified manner as instructed, but fell ill by influenza. On refusal to pay, she sued the company to recover the reward. Company defended the action on the ground that the offer was not made to the lady, she did not communicate the accepance of the offer to the company and hence there was no contract between company and the lady. (i.e. there was no privity of contract between the parties.)

The court in this leading judgement ruled that an offer can be made to the public at large and it is a valid offer. Such a public (general) offer may be accepted by any number of persons by satisfying the conditions mentioned in the offer.Contract can be concluded with anybody who came forward and performed conditions. There is no need of commnication of acceptance as it was dispensed within this case. Based on these principles, Carlill succeeded and got the award.

---

11. *(1908), 24 TLR 606*
12. *(1893)1 QB 256*

Chapter 4

CONSIDERATION

A subscriber pays Rs. 999 to a company which promises to provide internet services on mobile for a month. In this contract, the amount paid and the services to be provided is called "consideration".

4.1   Definitions of Consideration.

Few important definitions of the term are reproduced below.

> **Sir Frederick Pollock-** *"Consideration is the price of promise for which a promise is bought."*
>
> **Cheshire-** *"Price paid by the plaintiff for defendant's promise."*
>
> **Blackstone-** Consideration is *"the recompense given by the party."*
>
> **J. Patterson** *in Thomas v/s Thomas (1842- QB 851) - "Consideration means something which is of some value in the eye of law...It may be some benefit to the plaitiff or some detriment to the defendant"*
>
> **J. Lush** in Currie v/s Misa[13] *"A valuable consideration, in the sense of the law, may consists either in some right, interest, profit or benefit accruing to one party, or some forbearance, detriment, loss or responsibility given, suffered or undertaken by the other".*

The most relevant definition of **consideration u/s 2(d) of the Act,** reads as follows-

> *"When at the desire of the promisor, the promisee or any other person has done or abstained from doing something or, does or abstains from doing or promises to do or abstain from doing something, such an act or abstinance or promise is called consideration for promise."*

---

13.   *(1875) L.R. 10 EX 153*

General Meaning

From the perusal of the definitions given above it follows that consideration is **"quid pro quo"** i.e. **"something in return"** or **"price of promise."** What a promisor gets in return for his promise is consideration. If A sells his land to B for one crore, in this bargain, the money and the land are the considerations flowing from each side. It can take the form of money, property of various kinds or services. Consideration consists of benefit, profit, right, inretest, advantage accruing to one and detriment, loss, disadvantage or forbearance suffered by the other party.

Importance of Consideration

S.2(a) defines the agreement in terms of consideration. S.10 of the Act states that 'an agreement is a contract if made, ...for lawful consideration....' According to S.25 of the Act, "An agreement without consideration is void". Consideration thus is the foundation of a contract. In a contract, a party promises because there is a promise on the other side. Agreement in reality is an exchange of promises. Reciprocity is the basis of a contract. Consideration is the cause of promise. If it is absent, there is no contract. Hence it is said, **"no consideration no contract"**. A promises B to pay some amount for nothing on B's part. Such a promise is not enforceable by B because it is **"nudum pactum"** i.e. a bare or naked promise.[14]

Gratuitous promises do not give rise to any right or liability. Legal remedies are not provided for breach of gratuitous promises.This has been aptly described in the maxim, **"ex nudo pacto non oritur actio."** This means- **"out of a bare promise no cause of action arises"**. Contract is the result of offer and acceptance. These two provide outward semblance or appearance to the contractual relationship.But consideration is the evidence of seriousness or intention of contracting parties to establish real, legal relationship. Hence consideration is the backbone of every contract. A promise or an undertaking without consideration is null and void. It is purely gratuitous and however sacred or morally binding in nature, creates no rights or duties.

4.2 Concept, Essentials of Valid Consideration : (Rules of Consideration)

Various componants of consideration emerge from the above definitions. Those and other recquirements of consideration are discussed below. The Concept of consideration is developed mainly on the basis of its definition u/s 2(d) and various essentials directly flow from it.

1. Consideration must move at the desire of the promisor

The consideration in a contract must be provided at the desire or request of the promisor. If the act or abstinance regarded as consideration, is done voluntarily by promisee or at the desire of the third party, that act is not a consideration to support a contract. Whatever is supplied, if not needed by the other, is not a good consideration. Licensee repaires the premises without being asked to do by the owner. He cannot claim the charges from the owner.

Durga Prasad v/s Baldeo[15] - A builder, DP, at the desire of the collector of a town, built at his own expenses few shops in a public market. One of the shopkeepers, B,

---

14. *"...agreement, ... without any compensation ...will not, at law, support an action..." - **Blackstone***
15. *(1881)3 All. 221*

"Wealth in commercial age is made largely of promises." - Roscoe Pound.

who occupied a shop, agreed with DP, to pay commission on the articles sold through his shop. On refusal to pay commission, DP (promisee), filed a suit for recovery against B (promisor). The court held that as the consideration (shop) was not provided at the desire of the promisor but at the request of the collector, there was no consideration and hence the action failed.

To change the facts, slightly in the above case, suppose, a Chartered Accountant desires a commercial tenement for his office in the new building being constructed by the builder and builder provides it for some price, tenement (consideration) is provided at the resire of promiser and contract results.

2. Consideration may move from the promisee or any other person

Consideration need not be supplied by the promisee alone. A third person who is not a party to the contract (i.e. a stranger to contract) may also provide it. It is thus immaterial who furnishes the consideration. This is by Doctrine of Constructive Consideration. The leading case on this point is explained below.

Chinnaya v/s Ramayya[16] - An old lady gifted her property to her daughter R, through a deed of gift. The gift was with a condition that the daughter should pay an annuity to mother's brother, C. In view of this direction, R, on the same day executed a written promise in favour of maternal uncle, C. After accepting the property under the gift, R refuseed to pay annuity on the ground that C did not provide any consideration to support her promise. C filed a suit against R for annuity.The court ruled that C could successfully maintain an action because R had received consideration from her mother(any other person) though not from C(promisee). Referring *'the promisee or any other person'* in the definition of consideration, the court held that consideration need not be moved from promisee. Under the British law, however, consideration must be moved from the promisee.[17]

3. Privity of Consideration and Privity of Contract

Privity contemplates relationship either through consideration or contract. There is a privity of contract between two persons if a contact is entered between them. If parties provide consideration to each other, there is privity of consideration. In Chinnayya's case, there was a privity of contract but there was no privity of consideration between C and R. This is because C was a party to the writen promise(contract) but he did not give any consideration. Indian law thus recognizes the rule of privity of contract but not privity of consideration.In India stranger to the contract cannot sue. Only a person who is a party to contract can sue upon it. Privity of contract is essential to maintain legal actions. On the contrary privity of consideration is not recqired as a stranger to consideration has the capacity to sue as in case of Chinayya.

4. Consideration may be an act or abstinence

Consideration is "an act or abstinence" as indicated in the end portion of the definition. It is either a positive act or a negative act. To pay, to repair, to sell are the examples of

---

16. *(1882)4 Mad. 137*
17. *Tweedle v/s Atkinson 123 ER 762*

positive consideration. Promise not to sue for a particular period is a negative consideration. Consideration can be forbearance to sue: A party may have a right of legal action against the other, but he refrains from filing a suit in view of a promise by the other. This is called "forbearance to sue" and is regarded as a good consideration.

5. Consideration may be past, present or future

The specific phraseology used in the definition of the term u/s 2(d) indicates that the consideration may be past, present or future.

a) Past Consideration : (..has done or abstained from doing something..) Something done/suffered/forborne by the promisee, before making of a contract, can be the basis for a subsequent promise. However whatever has moved in the past should be at the desire of the promisor. Voluntary act cannot constitute consideration. Here consideration comes first and then contract.

Example-At father's request, a teacher has a special coaching of his son. Afterwords father promises teacher to pay the tution fees. Coaching is a past consideration.[18]

b) Present Consideration : (does or abstains from doing something..) This refers to the promises which are performed simultaneously. When we go to the market, we pay and the shopkeeper delivers the article (cash sales). It is also termed as "executed consideration" as in such transaction promises are performed.

c) Future Consideration : (promises to do or abstain from doing something..) When consideration from both parties is to move at a future date, it is called as "future consideration."

Example - A manufacturer agrees to deliver 100 refrigerators within a month's time and the dealer agrees to pay for on delivery. In this contract, consideration is to be supplied in future by both the parties.

6. Consideration must be real and not illusory

It is equally important that consideration is real to which law attaches value. Illusory consideration is no condideration. Illusory consideration gives an outward appearance of its existance but actually it is absent. Consideration would be real even if it is of slight value.

In the following circumstances the promises cannot be performed and hence unreal.

a) Physical impossibility-A promise to do something which is not phisically possible. For e.g. A promises B to discover trasure by magic for some consideration. This promise is not enforceable as the consideration is phisically impossible.

b) Legal impossibility-A promise to do an act which is legally not possible. For e.g.- A promise to supply ten tiger skins.

c) Uncertain consideration-If consideration in a contract is vague, uncertain, it cannot be real. For e.g. A agrees to provide construction material for B's house for adequate consideration or for 'whatever is right'. This agreement is unenforceable as consideration is vague. (See S.29)

---

18. *Lampleigh v/s Brathwait 80 ER 255*

7. Consideration must have 'some value'

Consideration should possess "some value" in the eye of law. Anything to which law attaches value would suffice for a reciprocal promise. Worthless act does not make a good consideration. Law should regard it having 'some value'. The benefit conferred or detriment suffered may be of trifling description or value but it should not be utterly useless.

8. Consideration need not be adequate

S. 25 (Explanation-2) makes it clear that- "an agreement to which the consent of the promisor is freely given is not void merely because the consideration is inadequate". Thus parties have liberty to decide the amount, nature of consideration and whether is commensurate with what is given and taken. Though the consideration is grossly inadequate, the contract is valid. Value of a property in the market may be in lakhs but can be sold for few hundreds.

Explanation - 2 further provides that "inadequecy of consideration may be taken into account by the court in determining the question whether the consent of the promisor was freely given".This means that though the inadequecy of consideration is immaterial as to the validity of a contract, inadequecy has evidenciary value. It can be a proof to show that the consideration is the result of fraud or coercion etc. and the consent of the party is not free.

9. Consideration must be something other than what the promisor is legally bound to do. Performance of a legal duty or a promise to do something under that duty, is not a valid consideration.The duty may be public or contractual.[19]

4.3 "An agreement without considearation is void."

a. **General Principle :** See importance of consideration.

This principle is recognized by well known exceptions. In the following situations the agreement is enforceable even without consideration and that is a valid contract;

Abdul Aziz v/s Mazum Ali [20]- MA promised AA (secretary of the mosque) to pay Rs. 500 for reconstruction of the mosque. Afterwards MA did not fulfil the promise. The court decided that as there was no consideration from AA/mosque, there was no contract between them. To donate money was a gratuitous promise and hence unenforceable.

b. **Exceptions to "No Consideration No Contract."**

The general rule that "No Consideration no contact" is subjected to following exceptions. (All the conditions of exceptions should be satisfied to bring a case within exceptions.)

---

19. **(Stilk v/s Myrick)** *(1809) 2 Camp 317 Two seamen deserted the ship during the journey. The master of the ship promised other seamen to pay wages of two errant seamen, if they brought the vessel home. Held that promise was not enforceble as the other seamen were otherwise bound to bring the ship home which act cannot be the basis for promise.*

20. *(1914) 36 All. 268*

1. **Agreement on account of love and affection. (S. 25-1)**

   An agreement made without consideration is enforceable if it is in writing and registered and is made on account of natural love and affection between parties standing in near relation to each other. **Conditions** of enforceability of such an agreement are-

   a - Agreement is between parties who are in near relation;

   b - Agreement is out of 'natural love and affection';[21]

   c - Agreement is in writing and;

   d - Agreement is registered under the law for the time being in force.

   Illustration - A grandfather promises grandson to pay ten lakhs of rupees. This promise is in writing and registered. Grandson can enforce the promise without any consideration from his part.

2. **Compensation for past voluntary services. (S. 25-2)**

   Sometimes a person does an act voluntarily for the other. The other later on promises to compensate for that act by which he is benefitted or which act, he was supposed to do. This promise is enforceable though there is no present consideration. **Conditions** for exceptions are -

   a) The promisee has already done something voluntarily (without a desire or request) for the promisor or

   b) The promisee does something which the promisor was legally compellable to do;

   c) The promisee promises to compensate for such voluntary act;

   d) The promisor must be in existance and competant when the services were rendered;

   e) Services rendered must not be immoral.

   It is to be noticed that no writing or registratuion is required for such a promise.

   Examples

   a) A finds a purse belonging to B, the owner and delivers it to B. B promises A to give a reward of Rs. 1000. This is a contract.

   b) A supports B's minor daughter. B promises to pay A, the expenses incurred in supporting. This is a contract.

3. **Promise to pay time barred debt (S. 25-3)**

   A debtor's promise to pay wholly or in part a debt barred by limitation is enforceable. When the debt is not enforced within limitation period, it is barred and no suit to recover it can be filed by the creditor. In such case a debtor's fresh promise is not supported by consideration from creditor but still enforceable if following **conditions** are fulfilled.

   a) There exists creditor and debtor relationship;

   b) Debt is otherwise legal, binding, certain and valid but not enforceable due to bar of limitation;

   c) Promise is in writing and registered. It is not a mere acknowledgement.

---

21. **Rajlukhee v/s Bhootnath** *(1900) 4 CWN 488 - Husband had strained relation with wife and they quarreled. He promised wife, by a registered document, to pay by way of maintenance. Wife did not provide any consideration. This exception did not apply because the agreement was not out of love and affection. Promise was unenforceable.*

Other exceptions

4. Completed Gifts

Explanation to S.25 provides that consideration is not needed for "gifts already made". Gift is a transfer of property without consideration. Hence it is a classic example of the exception. However gift must be executed one. Promise to gift is not coming within exception. Promise to gift a dimond ring on birthday is uneforceable. But once ring is gifted, it is covered in exception.

5. Remission

As per S.63 of the Contract Act, no consideration is necessary for an agreement to receive less than what is due under a contract. The party gives up claim over partial performance for no consideration.

6. Guarantee: (S. 127)

Contract of guanrantee also does not require any consideration, or benefit for the guarantor.

7. Contract of Agency

According to S.185, no consideration is necessary to creat agency. This affords a statutory exception to the principle.

8. Gratuitous promise acted upon

Contributions to charities are enforceable in peculiar circumstances.If the gratuitous promise is acted upon by the promisee and he suffers losses (or changes position), then even promise without consideration is enforceable.[22]

---

22. **Kedar Nath v/s Gorie Mohammad.** *ILR (1886)14 Cal. 64 - The promisor agreed to donate Rs. 100 for construction of a townhall. The secretary of the townhall, the promisee, relying on the promise asked a contractor to build and undertook liability to pay him. The promisor was held liable to the extent of liability incurred by the secretary. This is in contrast to the decision in* Abdul Aziz's *case already discussed.*

Chapter 5

CAPACITY TO CONTRACT

Competency or capabilities of Parties

Capacity of parties to contract is one of the conditions of enforceability and agreement is void if parties are incompetent. S.10 makes it clear that an agreement becomes a contract if parties are competent to contract. According to S.11 following persons are capable of entering into contractual relationship.

1. Person of age of majority i.e. Major;
2. Person of sound mind ;
3. Person not disqualified by law from entering into contract

To put it in negative way, following persons are **incompetent** to enter into a contract.

1. **Minor**
2. **Person of unsound mind**
3. **Person disqualified by law**

Incapacity may thus result from minority or mental deficiency or some disqualification under law.The law relating to competency of parties is discussed below.

5.1 Contracts By Minors

Who is major? Age of majority - Age of majority is to be determined with reference to the personal law applicable to the minor.

According to S. 3 of the Indian Majority Act, 1875, a minor is a person who has not completed 18 years of age. In the follwing two cases a person becomes major on completion of 21 years of age (i.e. minority is extended upto 21 years of age) -

a) Where a guardian is appointed under the Guardian and Wards Act, 1890 to lookafter the person or property (or both) of minor ;

b) Where the suprintendence of the property of the minor is assumed by Court of Wards under the Court of Wards Act.

This extension of the age from 18 to 21 years is to be considered while deciding on the validity of the minor's agreement.

The law relating to minor's agreements

Minor, because of his age, is incapable of understanding the nature of contract. His mental faculties are not developed. He does not possess the capacity to judge what is good or bad for him. In a contractual relationship he requires more protection of law than his counter part, particularly from uncrupulous parties. Minors can be pressurized, deceived, misled or influenced. In this situation *the judges are their counsellors, the jury their servants and the law is their guardian.* Keeping this in view, law protects infants, their rights, properties or estates.

1. **Minor's agreement is absolutely void — Mohoribibi v/s Dharmodas Ghose**

   S.10 lays down that parties to the contract must be competant and S.11 states that minor is incompetant. These two sections however do not state the legal consequences of minor's agreement i.e. whether it is voidable or void. The contraversy was resolved in a landmark judgement given by Privy Council in **Mohori Bibee v/s Dharmodas Ghose**[23] In this case, a minor(Dharmodas Ghose)) wanted a loan of Rs 20,000 from a moneylender(Bramhodutta). Out of Rs.20,000, minor received Rs.8000. Minor executed a deed of mortgage as a security for repayment of loan. Minor subsequently filed a suit for setting aside the mortgage on the ground that he was incompetant, at the time of execution of mortgage. Moneylender claimed refund of Rs. 8000 from minor. It was held that minor's contract (mortgage in this case) is altogather void and unenforceable. Moneylender, therefore, cannot recover the sum from minor.

   In this case it was held that minor's contract is absolutely void. It is **void-ab-initio** i.e. void from the beginning. Such a contract is null and void. No right is acquired nor any liability is created under it.Minor's agreement being void from inception, it devoid of any effect. Minor is not liable to fulfil any promise nor he can be compelled to return the benefit (here Rs. 8000) under such a contract.

2. **The rule of estoppel does not apply to minor — Minor can always plead minority.**

   Rule of estoppel- Estoppel is a rule of evidence.In the words of Lord Halsbury, estoppel means- "Estoppel arises when you are precluded from denying the truth of anything, which you have represented as a fact, altough it is not a fact." (Refer S. 115 of the Indian Evidence Act.)

   False representation by minor as to his age-Consequences.

   If a minor falsely states that he is of full age and thereby induces the other to enter into contract, such a contract is also void and not binding on minor.[24] Even if minor is guilty of false representation, in such a case, he can always plead minority and set up a defence of infancy when sued. Minor is not estopped from pleading infancy to avoid such a contract.The rule of estoppel therefore, has no application in case of a minor. There cannot be estoppel against a statute.

3. **Principle of restitution does not apply to minor — No restitution of benefit by minor**

   Restitution as incorporated under sections 64 and 65of the Act, implies that if a person,

---

23. *(1903) I.L.R.30 Cal. 539*
24. *Sadiq Ali Khan v/s Jaikishor 1928, 30 Bom.L.R. 1342-PC*

by false representation, obtains any property from another, he can be compelled to restore it to that other.

As a general rule, minor cannot be compelled to restore (return) the benefit or compensate for such a benefit obtained under the void agreement. S.64 and 65 of the Contract Act dealing with the restitution do not apply to minor's contract because S.64 applies to voidable and S.65 to contracts subsequently "becoming void". Minor's contract is neither voidable nor it subsequently becomes void. It is void from the beginning. On these grounds, in Mohoribibi's case, Privy Council refused to allow restitution-i.e. repayment of advance to moneylender.[25]

4. No specific performance of minor's contract

Specific performance means discharging obligations under the contract. There cannot be specific performance of minor's contract as it is void. The demand for specific performance of a contract is possible if it is enforceable at law.[26]

5. No ratification on attaining majority

Minor cannot ratify the contract on attaining majority. Ratification implies subsequent adoption and acceptance of an unauthorised act. It is post facto approval or confirmation. Ratification relates back to the date of act. Minor's agreement is a nullity, it never takes birth in the eye of law. Therefore there is no question of approving the contract which is void-ab- initio. Practically speaking, ratification is possible.For that a fresh agreement supported by fresh consideration is required.(*Shanmugan Pillai v/s K. S. Pillai, AIR 1973 SC.*)

6. No Compromise or relinquishment of any claim — Giving up any claim by any deed of Compromise/release by minor is not binding on him

7. Minor cannot be a guarantor to another. But someone can stand as a surity for him. In such a case, surity is liable and not minor.

8. Minor and insolvency

Minor cannot be declared as insolvent as he is incapable to contract debts. Minor is not a debter under the insolvency laws.

The points discussed above confirm the position that- "Minor's contract is absolutely void". In the following situations, however, minor is accorded some status in contractual relationship though maintaining that his agreement is void. The following situations under points no. 9 to 16 may be considered as a deviation of the rule. (exceptions)

---

25. *The minor would however be compelled to restore the benefit under the void contract when he himself wants to set aside the contract. Such a relief of restitution is available under S.33 of the Specific Relief Act, 1963 when a minor comes to the court as a plaintiff(and not as a defendant) to cancel the contract. S.33 is based on the principle of "he who seeks equity must do equity." If the minor has obtained a thing under the contract in which he makes a false representation as to his age and it is traceable in the hands of minor, the court may direct the minor to restore that thing to the other party.This relief is given to the other party on equitable consideration viz. "minor can have no privilege to cheat a man". Khan Gul v/s Lakha singh ILR (1928) 9 Lah.701.*

26. *(In Leslie v/s Sheill) (1914)-KB-707 A minor (defendant) had taken a loan from plaintiff. The plaintiff brought an action against minor for recovery under quasi-contract. Action failed because if such a suit is allowed, it would amount to indirectly enforcing a void contract.*

9. Contracts for minor's benefit are valid

Contract entered into by the guardian of minor and for minor's benefit can be enforced by or against minor. Guardian must however act within his authority. Minor can insist on specific performance, if contract is in his favour.

Contracts through guardian - The guardian can enter into contracts on behalf of minor and such a contract can be enforced if the contract is made-

a) for the benefit of minor;

b) within the scope of the guardian's authority and

c) guardian himself is competant to enter into a valid contract.

Liability of parents for minor's contracts - The parents of a minor are not liable for minor's contracts.Parents are not liable even if the contract is for necessaries. If a child acts as an agent of parent, then parents are liable.

Though minor cannot enter into contract, a contract can be entered for his benefit. Minor thus can be a beneficiary under a contract. As already stated, minor bears no personal obligation under such a contract.[27]

10. Contracts of service

An agreement by a minor to serve for money is not enforceable as minor cannot provide consideration to bind personally.

Raj Rani v/s Prem Abib [28] - A film producer assigned a role of an actress in his film to a minor.The agreement was made with her father. The producer terminated the contract with father and assigned the said role to another. The father and minor sued the producer. It was held that an agreement in which service of the minor is a consideration is void, consideration was yet to be supplied by minor and hence suit failed.- If he has served but not paid then he can claim the consideration (money) from the other party (not under the contract but under quasi-contract). A contract of apprenticeship is however valid under the Apprenticeship Act, 1961. The validiy is attributed to earning and learning policy incorporated in the Act. Under these contracts also, minor is not personally liable, his estate is liable.

11. Minor as a partner

Partnership results from an agreement. Being incompetant, minor cannot be a partner in the firm.But according to S.30 of the Partnership Act, 1932, a minor can be admitted to the benefits of the partnership. As a potential partner, he enjoys most of the rights of an ordinary partner.As far as liability is concerned, his share in the profit is liable. He is not personally liable. After attaining majority, he may elect to become the full-fleged partner.

---

27. *A minor is allowed to enforce a contract which is of some benefit to him.A promissory note executed in favour of a minor is valid and can be enforced in a court. Minor can purchase immovable property and can take legal acion to recover it. It is said that **minority is a personal privilege and only the minor can take advantage of it and bind the other party.***

28. *(1948) 51, Bom. L.R. 256.*

12. Minor as a shareholder

Generally speaking, a minor cannot be a shareholder in a company. If he inherits the shares, he becomes shareolder through the guardian. A minor can be a shreholder or member of the company if-

a) shares are fully paid up and

b) if articles of association do not prohibit him from becoming shareholder.

13. Minor as an agent

Accorging to S. 184 of the Act, minor can act as an agent. Principal is liable to third parties for minor-agent's acts. He is not liable for breach of the duty as an agent or negligence during the course of agency.

14. Minor can deal in negotiable instruments

He can draw, negoiate the instruemnts with no personal liability. He can be payee, promisee, indorsee. Negotiable instruments drawn in his favour can be enforced by him.

15. Minor's liability for necessaries

Minor though not liable under contract, his property is liable in quasi- contracts. Minor is liable to reimburse the expenses incurred by the supplier of necessaries furnished during his minority. The person providing necessaries to minor has a right to get compensated out of the property of minor for the expenses. (refer S.68 in quasi-contract) If the minor has no property then the supplier will have no claim against the minor.

5.2 Persons Of Unsound Mind

According to S.11 of the Act, a party to the contract must be of sound mind. Soundness of mind is thus essential to enter into a valid contract.

S.12 provides an explanation as to a **"person of sound mind"** which states –

"A person is said to be of sound mind for the purpose of making a contract, if, at the time when he makes it, he is capable of understanding it and of forming a rational judgement as to its effects on his interests."

S.12 thus lays down **two-fold test** for soundness of mind. The person is of sound mind if -

a) He is capable of understanding the nature of contract and

b) He is capable to form a rational judgement as to the effect of contract on his interests.

If one of conditions is not satisfied, the person would be unsound. Soundness of a person is to be determined with reference to the contract and that too his mental condition at the time of entering into contract and not before or afterwards.

S.12 further provides following two explanations -

1) "A person can enter into contract during **lucid interval** i.e. Interval of soundness (sanity) between two periods of unsoundness (insanity). Explanation provides - **"A person who is usually of unsound mind, but occasionally of sound mind, may contract when he is of sound mind."**

2) "A person can not enter into contract during a short period of interval of insanity between two periods of sanity. Simple rule is that when he is of sound mind then only he can contract.

Unsoundness of mind may be due to idiocy, insanity, lunacy or a disease. It may be permanant or temporary. Capacity of certain kinds of persons of unsound mind is discussed below.

1. **Idiots -** Idiocy is a permanant form of unsoundness (with no intervals of sanity) due to lack of development of brain. Idiot is completely deprived of his mental faculties and has no thinking power.He cannot enter into contract but can be a beneficiary under a contract.

2. **Lunatics (Insane) -** He is a person whose mental power is temporarily affected may be due to mental stress or malfunctioning of brain. Insanity is a mental disorder severe enough to affect understanding capacity. Insanity is a legal and not medical standard (Legal insanity, lunacy). He is sometimes sane and sometimes suffers from intervals of insanity (madness). Lunatic can be treated in lunatic asylum. Lunatic is incompetant to enter into a contract but can validly make a contract during lucid interval (explanation to S.12, above mentioned.) A patient in a lunatic asylum, who is at intervals of sound mind, may contract during those intervals.

3. **Intoxicated Person -** A person may be under the influence of a drug or liquor. He can enter into contract if satisfies the test under S.12.But if drunkenness or intoxication is severe so that he is unable to understand his acts, then contract is void.

4. **Person in delirium** or suffering from mental decay-A person in delirious state (due to fever, illness etc..) cannot enter into contract as he looses the power of understanding in delirium. Old age causes mental decay to make person incompetent.

5. **Person under hypnotism -** Hypnosis is artificially induced sleep and under hypnosis person cannot satisfy the condition u/s 12.

    Effect of Unsoundness of Mind - The agreement with a party of unsound mind is absolutely void and infructuous. In English law, a person of unsound mind is competant to contract. However the contract is voidable and he may, at his option, avoid the contract.

5.3 Disqualified Persons

Sometimes a party may be major or of sound mind but may suffer from third disability. S.11 of the Act gives this third catagory of incompetant persons who are **"disqualified from contracting by any law to which they are subject."** Following persons fall under this catagory.

1. **Alien Enemy**
    An alien whose country is at war with India is called an alien enemy. An alien enemy in India cannot contract. It is said that - *"Alien friend can contract but alien enemy can't contract."* Contract with alien enemy may harm economic interests of our country or promote economic interests of rival nation.

2. **Foreign Sovereigns and Ambassadors**
    These foreign dignitories including diplomats, employees of embassies can enter into contracts in India and there is no disability. They can sue for specific performance of

contract. However no suit for the performance of the contract can be filed against them except with the permission of the central government. Normally such a permission is not granted because these dignitories enjoy certain privileges and immunities as a matter of international protocol. If foreign sovereigns enter into contracts through agents, agents are personally liable to perform contract.

3. Company or Corporations

Companies are juristic persons, artificially created by law. Like natural persons, corporations can hold, acquire, transfer, sell or purchase property and for that can enter into contract. There is one restriction on this power. Scope of a company's activity is laid down by its Memorandum of Association.Companies cannot go beyond the Memorandum of Association and contract. Such a contract is "ultra-vires" and hence void. Companies also cannot sign a contract of personal nature.

4. Convicts

 A convict is a person who is undergoing a sentence (imprisonment) as a result of final order of the court. He is held guilty of a crime (offence) and convicted. Convict cannot contract as long as he is imprisoned. He can contract if he is out of jail on 'ticket of leave', 'parole, 'furlow' or his period of sentence expires or he is pardoned.

5. Insolvents

An insolvent is a person who is unable to discharge his financial, contractual liabilities. He cannot enter into contract relating to his properties as the properties vest in official receiver. However he can enter into certain contracts such as incurring debts, purchasing property, or contract of service. If he is discharged by insolvency court, he regains competency.

6. Married Woman

Under indian law, there is no discrimination between a man and a married woman as far as capacity to contract. Marriage puts no bar on a woman's contractual competence. She is free to deal with her absolute proerty like streedhan or self acquired property. She cannot enter into contract with respect to husband's property. However, if her husband fails provide her necessaries of life, she can in certain cases, pledge her husband's property for necessaries.

Chapter 6 | CONSENT AND FREE CONSENT

Consent and free consent lie at the foundation of a contract. An agreement without consent is not a contract. Not only there should be consent, the consent should also be free (S.10, chapter, 1). Absence of free consent introduces weaknesses in the contract.

6.1   Definition of Consent and Free Consent

CONSENT

S.13 of the Contract Act defines **"Consent"** as-

> *"Two or more persons are said to consent when they agree upon the same thing in the same sense".*

Consent thus is **"agreeing upon the same thing in the same sense"**. This in legal language is described as **"consensus-ad-idem"** i.e. meeting/unity of minds. Agreement contemplates mutual understanding of both parties. Consent means to concur, agree, acquiscence in.

FREE CONSENT : Acording to S. 14, consent is said to be free when it is **not caused by -**
  a)   **Coercion or**
  b)   **Undue influence or**
  c)   **Fraud or**
  d)   **Misrepresentation or**
  e)   **Mistake**

The consent in the contract should be given voluntarily. It must be real or genuine and must be the result of "volution" i.e. free mind.The factors mentioned in the definition, vitiate free consent. The party would not have entered into contract but because of these **'flaws in consent'**. Fear or pressure or some fraudulent trick may induce consent but it cannot be said to be free.

Legal consequenses of absence of consent and free consent : If there is no consent, there is no question of any contractual relationship. That agreement is just meaningless. If free consent is absent, contract is very much there but it is " voidable" (Ref. Secs. 2-j, 19 and 19 A). The party whose consent is not free can repudiate it at his option. Till that option is exercised, contract remains valid. According to Salmond, when the consent is altogather absent, there is **"error in consensus"**. In such a situation by lack of mutual understanding, no contract comes into exisatnce. **Cundy v/s Lindsey.**[29] But when consent is not free, Salmond calls it as **"error in causa" i.e.error in inducing the cause.** Such an error makes the contract voidable.[30]

The elements which destroy free consent are discussed below.

6.2 COERCION

Definition and meaning: S.15 defines the term as —

> *"Coercion is the commission or threatening to commit any act, forbidden by the Indian Penal Code or the unlawful detaining or threatening to detain any property, to the prejudice of any person whatever, with the intention of causing any person to enter into an agreement."*

Coercion implies fear, threat, pressure, or compulsion. It includes use of force directed against body or menace to property to induce consent. Consent obtained at the point of pistol, or by threatening to cause bodily injury or to burn one's property or slashing a valuable article fall within coercive techniques.

Characterstics of Coercion: The definition of the term given above sets out what constitutes coercion and other **essentials** of the concept. Those are explained in sequence.

1. **Commission of an act forbidden by Indian Penal Code (IPC)**

   Coercion is the commision of any act forbidden by the IPC. An act forbidden (prohibited and punished) by IPC is called as crime or an offence. Murder, kidnapping, decoity, extortion etc. may be employed to exert pressure on the other party.

   Example - A severely beats B and by the use of force obtains the signature of B on a deed (contract). B's consent is obtained by coercion.

   Rangnayakamma v/s Alwar Shetty[31] Husband died leaving behind a young widow. The relative of the widow threatened her that they will not allow the dead body to be removed for cremation unless she adopted a particular boy. The widow adopted the boy

---

29. *- (1878)3 App Cas 459 - Blenkiron & Co. was a well-known and respectable firm. Blenkarn was a fraudulent person. Blankarn took the advantage of the similarity of his name with that of Blenkiron & Co. and ordered goods from Lindsey & Co.(plaintiffs) Order papers had a printed heading. "Blenkarn & Co." Plaintiff believed that orders were from his firm and sent a bulk of handkerchiefs. Blenkarn after receiving the goods sold those to Cundy & Co. (defendant), bonafide purchaser for value. Plaintiff sued the defendant for recovery of goods.The court held that there was no contract between plaintiffs and Blenkarn. The reason being that the plaintiffs intended to contract with Benkiron & Co. and not with Blenkarn. It was a case of mistaken identity (though unilateral) destroying the consent for contract. There was no consent and hence no contract. Property did not pass to Blenkarn and defendant, therefore, could get no title in those. Defendant had to surrender goods to plaintiff (real owner).*
30. *Philips v/s Brook Ltd. (1919) 2 KB 243*
31. *(1819)13 Mad. 214*

but subsequently sought cancellation of adoption. The court held that the relatives obstructed the removal of dead body for creamation which was an offence u/s 297 of IPC. The act of threatening therefore, amounted to coercion. The consent of the lady was not free and hence the adoption was set aside.

2. Threat to commit an act forbidden by IPC.

Coercion also includes threat to commit an offence.

Example - A threatens to kill B if B does not sell his property at a prime locality. B, out of fear signs the deal. Killing and its threat, both are forbidden by IPC and hence amount to coercion.

Amiraju v/s Seshamma[32] Husband threatened his wife and son that he would commit suicide if they refused to execute a release deed (giving up a share) in his favour. As a result of that threat both of them executed the document. Later on wife wanted to cancell the release deed on the ground of coercion by husband.

IPC punishes only 'an **attempt** to commit suicide'. Neither 'suicide nor **threat** to commit suicide' is punishable. It was argued that threat to commit suicide cannot be said to be forbidden by IPC and hence not coercion u/s 15. The court observed that though suicide cannot be punished for obvious reasons, policy under IPC is to forbid suicide. This is evident from the fact that "attempt to commit suicide is punishable offence. Threat is deemed to be forbidden by IPCand it thus amounts to coercion.

3. Unlawful Detention of Property —

Unlawful detention of anybody's property (not necessarily that of contracting party) also amounts to coercion. Detention means withholding possesion of property or refusal to redeliver the property of another. If detention is authorised or lawful it is not coercion.

4. Threat of Unlawful Detention

Threat to detain unlawfully any property also constitutes coercion.

5. Applicability of IPC at the place of commision of coercion is immaterial

Explanation to S.15 provides- "It is immaterial whether the IPC is or is not applicable in the place where the coercion is employed."

Coercion may be employed outside the territorial jurisdiction of India. Once the act comes within the definition, coercion is constituted where ever it is committed. IPC may not be in force at that place. Coercion does not recognize territorial boundaries.

6. Object of Coercion —

Coercion must be exercised to induce the other party to enter into contract. If this purpose is lacking or if alleged act is for some different object, it does not amount to coercion.

7. Coercion by whom and against whom?

Coercion can be committed by the very party or by his agent or by a third person. Similarly coercion can be directed against the very party or his family member or against a stranger. It follows that who exersises it or who is the sufferer is not important. The gist of coercion is the act and its object.

---

32. *AIR(1917) 41 Mad. 33*

Examples-X kidnaps Y and thus forces him to sign a contract.

X kidnaps Y's son and obtains Y's consent for a contract.

X threatens to shoot Y if he does not sell his plot to a builder, Z.

In all these cases coercion is committed.

8. Burden of Proof

It is the duty of the aggrieved party to establish the fact of coercion and that it compelled him to give the consent to the contract.

9. Effects of Coercion

The following are the effects of coercion —

a) S. 19-The contract is voidable at the option of the victim of coercion ;

b) Rescission- The aggrieved party has a right to cancell the contract within a reasonable time under the provisions of the Specific Relief Act, 1963.

c) Restitution-S. 64-If the coerced party rescinds the contract, he must resore the benefit to the party from whom he received it.

d) S. 72 states that.. "A person to whom money has been paid or anything deliverded under coercion must repay or return it." (See Chapter on Quasi-Contract)

Railway company refused to deliver the goods to the consignee unless he paid illegal charges/carriage. To obtain the goods consignee paid those charges. Held that he had right to recover the excess amount from the railway.

10. Coercion and Duress

Coercion is a wider concept than duress in American law. Duress has been defined as causing or threatening to cause, bodily violence or imprisonment, with a view to obtain the consent of the other party to the contract. Duress does not include unlawful detention. Moreover duress can be committed only by or against the party to the contract. On these accounts duress differs from coercion u/s 15.

6.3 UNDUE INFLUENCE

6.3.a Definition and Meaning

The second element vitiating free consent is undue influence. Undue influence simply means influence execised unduly or improperly. Sometimes the parties stand in special relationship. One is influencial and abuses that influence to strike an unfair deal. Undue influence is unreasonable use of position. A party may not willing to enter into contract but he is persuaded to give consent to a contract. Party is morally influenced and hence it is called as moral coercion. Law does not allow to reap the benefits of such unfair persuasion.

16 (1) defines undue influence as follows -

> *"A contract is said to be induced by 'undue influence'where the relations subsisting between the parties are such that one of the parties is in a position to dominate the will of the other and uses that position to obtain an unfair advantage over the other."*

The concept of undue influence requires following conditions to be fulfilled –
a) There exists a special relationship between the parties;
b) The relationship is such that one party is in a dominating (influencing) position as regards other;
c) Dominating party uses that position to obtain unfair advantage.

The contract can be repudiated on the ground of undue influence only if above factors are proved.

6.3.b Law Relating to Undue Influence : Essentials of Undue Influence

The definition given above embodies concept of undue influence and sets out its conditions of applicability. These are explained below.

1. **Relationship Between Parties**

   The section is applicable only when there exists special relationship of inequality between the parties, i.e. one is in a position to dominate the will of the other party. Unless this relationship exists, undue influence is not applicable. The nexus may partake the character of blood relationship or professional ties or official links or relation of good faith.

2. **Position of Dominance**

   In peculiar situations, in a contract, one is a stronger and other is a weaker party. Because of superiority one is in a position to suppress the will of the party of inferior position and prevails upon him to obtain consent. Unequal relationship results in position of dominance. The aggrieved person is in full possession of all mental faculties but those are suppressed by other's dominating status.

3. **Presumption as to Position of Dominance**

   S. 16(2) of the Act lays down cetain circumstances in which one party is presumed to be in a position to dominate the will of the other.Mere status of a party is sufficient to presume the position of superiority. It is to be noted that the presumption is of position and not of actual exercise undue influence.

   One is presumed to dominate the will of the other in the following **three circumstances-**

   a) **Real or apparent authority over other**

      When one holds real or apparent authority over the other. A person yielding authority certainly can dominate other.

      For example - Master and Servant, collector and his clerk, income tax officer and assesee, a magistrate or a police oficer and an accused. In all such relations one has authority over other subordinate or the person of lower position. When a person by show of authority causes other's consnt, he holds 'apparent authority' over other.

   b) **Fiduciary relationship**

      This is relationship of mutual trust and confidence. One reposes confidence in other and other may betrey it. Trust is abused to obtain unfair profit.For example, a doctor and patient, advocate/solicitor and client, spiritual advisor, 'guru' and disciple, trustee and beneficiary.In these type of relationships, element of trust gives an opportunity to overcome the inner desire of the other.

A devotee, sufficiently old, donated all his property to his 'guru', spiritual adviser, with the object of securing benefits to his soul in the next world. This is a case of exercise of undue influence.

c) Mental incapacity

Where mental capacity of contracting party is affected either temporarily or permanantly due to age, illness or mental or bodily distress.

Age, illness and distress make persons vulnerable to all sorts of influences. One can understand the position of a very old bed-ridden person, a young one continuously ill, both requiring medical attendance. A person suffering physical pain in accident situation may succumb to the wishes of unscrupulous person nearby.

Example-A, a man enfeebled by disease or age is induced by B's influence over him, as his medical attendant, to agree to pay B, unreasonable sum for his professional service. B employs undue influence.

When there is no presumption?

Though there is a presumption in the above situations, the courts have taken a consistant view that the presumption as to position of dominance cannot be raised in cases of creditor and debtor, landlord and tenant,[33] husband and wife,[34] master and servant,[35] grand father and grand son even though the terms between these parties may be harsh. Each case is to be decided independantly by applying test under section 16.

4. Misuse of the position to obtain unfair advantage

Subsistance of relationship between the parties or its presumption is not sufficient. Actual exercise of undue influence is essential to prove that consent is not free. By the use of position, dominant party should obtain unfair advantage.

Illustration - A, having advanced money to his son, B, during his minority, upon B's coming of age, obtains by misuse of parental influence, a bond from B for a greater sum than the sum due in respect of advance. A employs undue influence.

5. Special Rule of Evidence

As a **general rule**, one who states something has to prove that. But as provided in S.16(2), this rule of evidence is deviated in special situations. The burden of proof lies on the party of dominance to prove that he has not used undue influence and the transaction is fair and honest. Thus there is a presumtion of exercise of undue influence against superior party.

However this presumption of undue influence is raised only when following **conditions** are satisfied-

a) Special relationship between parties and position of dominance;

b) Transaction apparently unconscionable - Unconscionable Bargains

The transaction should be, on the face of it, unconscionable. These are unfair and

---

33. *Laxmi Chand v/s Pt. Niader Mal, AIR (1961) All 295,*
34. *Howes v/s Bishop-1925-2 KB, 390),*
35. *Daulat v/s Gulabrao-1925- Nag. 369*

unreasonable transactions wherein one gets exorbitant profits of other's distress. A man of ordinary sence would not enter into such transactions. A property worth 10 lakhs rupees when sold for meagre sum of Rs. 100, is most unconvincing and hence unconscionable bargain.

c) **Shifting of onus/Rebuttal of presumption** - Once the above two conditions are fulfilled, then the onus is shifted on the influencial party to disprove (rebut) that undue influence was exerted. He has to establish that the other party had independant advice and with full knowledge and understanding the contract was signed.

A, a money-lender, advances Rs. 100 to B, an agriculturist, and induces B to execute a bond of Rs. 200 with an interest @ 16 pm. The court may set aside the bond, ordering B to repay Rs. 100 with such interest as may deem just.

The mere fact of charging high rate of interest cannot make the money lending transaction unconscionable.

6. Contract with Pardanashin Woman

There is no statutory or judicial definition of the term "pardanashin woman". A padanashin woman is one who leads a life in seclusion i.e. isolation from the outside world. Some degree of seclusion is not sufficient, complete aloofness is necessary to come within the term. This isolation is normally due to the custom in a particular community. Pardanashin woman is more open to the influences by the others. Law, therefore, provides them a 'special cloak of protection'. Special rule of evidence is applicable in case of pardanashin woman i.e. contract with her is the result of undue influence. To rebut the theory of undue influence the other party has to prove following-

— transaction was read over and explained to her; if it is not in her mother language, it was explained to her in her own language;

— she understood it;

— she had an independant, disinterested advice in the matter; such an advice should be given before the transaction, and with full knowledge of all relevant circumstances.

— it was her 'intelligent and voluntary act".

— her consent, therefore, was freely obtained.

The protection given to pardanashin woman is also extended to illiterate and ignorant women who are equally amenable to the pressures by other contracting party.

7. Undue Influence is a subtle form of coercion

Undue influence is often called as subtle form of coercion as it works on psychological plane. It is a sort of moral pressure. It impaires free thinking ability. Corecion however involves physical force, compulsion.

8. Effects of Undue influence

As in the case of coercion, legal consequences of undue influence are -

a) contract is voidable u/s 19-A; Courts have descretion to quash the contract either in part or in toto and upon such terms and conditions as court deem fit;

b) restitution of benefit u/s 64. See topic of coercion for details.

6.4 FRAUD

Fraud in General - Fraud is synonymous with deceit. Fraud is a false representation or concealment of a material fact with intention to deceive. Fraud denotes an intentional or wilful misrepresentation of material facts. Fraud involves cheating, deceiving tricks and unfair ways for inducing a party to give consent. The term includes all surprises, tricks, cunning and unfair ways adopted to cheat anyone. (Desai T.R. "The Contract Act" 18th Edn. 116)

Definition under S. 17 -

Fraud means and includes any of the following acts committed by a party to a contract, or with his connivance or by his agent with intent to deceive any other party thereto or to induce him to enter into the contract-

a) *the suggestion, as to a fact, of that which is not true, by one who does not believe it to be true;*

b) *the active concealment of a fact by one, having knowledge and belief of the fact;*

c) *a promise made without intention of performing it;*

d) *any other act fitted to deceive;*

e) *any such act or omission as the law specially declares to be fraudulent.*

Lord Herschell's definition of fraud in Derry v/s Peek- *"..a false statement made knowingly, or without belief in its truth, or recklessly careless whether it be true or false."*

Essentials of Fraud

(A) What constitutes fraud? (Catagories of Fraud – Points 1 to 5)

In order to prove fraud, the alleged act should be brought under any one of the following acts.

1. **Suggestio Falsi**

   Suggestion of falsity- False statement of a fact with knowledge of falsity or without belief in its truth amounts to fraud.

   Example - A falsely tells B that he is the owner of a car when in fact, C is the owner. Relying on A, B pays price and purchases car from A. B can cancell the transaction as it is the result of fraud.

   Essentials of suggestio falsi -

   a) There should be a statement of fact. Statement amounting to fraud must be of fact, must relate to a fact. It may be a term in a contract.It should not be a mere expression of opinion. Puffery or flourishing description, expression of commendation is not fraud as a party has liberty to use good words about his goods/property. The house is "very lucky", the land is "very fertile", our commodities are "number one in the market" are "commendatory expressions" and do not constitute fraud, though not absolutely true.

   b) Statement should be false. Truth destroys fraud.

c) False representation may be made in one of the following ways-
i) with the knowldge of falsity; or
ii) without belief in the representation; or
iii) with reckless disregard about its truth or falsehood.

Thus if the statement is true, or it is honestly believed to be true, though in fact untrue, is not fraud. A statement might be ill advised, stupid or even negligent, if it is made with the belief in truth, it is not fraud. What constitues fraud has been explained in the following landmark judgement.

Derry v/s Peek[36] A tramway company, through their directors, issued a prospectus inviting public to purchase shares. In the prospectus it was stated that the company had been authorised by a special Act of Parliament to use steam power instead of animal power to run trams. In fact, the company at that time had only applied for the permision of Board of Trade under the Act to use steam power. The directors honestly believed that the such a permision would be be granted in normal coure.Plaintiff, a shreholder, applied for shares considering better prospectus of the company. Later on Board of Trade refused permission to use of steam power. Company was sued by the plaintiff for playing fraud.

The court **held** that the directors were not liable in fraud as there was no intention to deceive the shareholders. Company made a false statement in good faith honestly believing that the consent to use steam power by the govt. authority was a mere formality and that would be granted. The statement however was negligently made and it amounted to "misrepresenation" and not fraud. Negligence is not fraud. The transaction was set aside on the ground of 'misrepresentation.'

2. Suppressio Veri

Suppression of truth – Active conealment of a material fact is fraud. It is different from "passive concealment". Passive concealment is mere silence as to material facts. Taking active steps to conceal important information is a type of fraud. In such cases a person takes positive steps to prevent material information from reaching the other party.

Illustration - B, having discovered a vein of ore on the estate of A, adopts means to conceal and does conceal, the existance of ore from A. Through A's ignorance B is enabled to buy the estate at an under-value. This amounts to fraud.

3. False Promises

Promise made without intention of fulfilling the same is fraud.

Illustration - X buys good from Y. X has no intention of paying for them. X plays fraud on Y. (Mere failure to pay without any dishonest intention is not fraud.)

4. Act fitted to deceive

This is a residuary clause. If any act is not covered under remaining catagories it can be fraudulent if it it is deceitful or is has the effect of deceiving. Catagories of fraud are never ending. Fraud cannot be confined by any exaustive definition. All kinds of intentional cheating would be covered in the concept u/s 17.

---

36. (1889) 14 AC. 337

5. Act or omission declared fraudulent by express laws

All acts or omissions which are expressly declared as fradulent by any statute are regarded as fraud for the purposes of contract. Under the Companies Act 1956, non disclosure of material information in the prospectus is fraudulent. "Fraudulent preferences" are covered by the company law and the insolvency laws. Non disclosure of defects in title(encumbrances) of immovable property by the seller to the buyer is regarded as deceitful u/s 55 of the Transfer of Property Act 1955 which nullifies fradulent transfers.

Example - A fraudulently informs B that A's estate is free from encumbrance. B, thereupon buys the estate. The estate is subject to a mortgage. B may either avoid the contract or may insist on its being carried out and the mortgage debt redeemed.

B-Essentials /Conditions of Fraud
(Discussion on 'what constitutes fraud' covers essential elements of fraud - which are continued further as conditions of fraud.)
The allegation of fraud is of serious nature. Standard of proof is obviously high.Before a contract can be avoided on the ground of fraud, following conditions should be fulfilled.

6. Fraud should be committed with intention to deceive

Fraud is an intentional wrong. Intention to deceive is the gist of this wrongdoing. As stated in Derry v/s Peek, negligence is not fraud.

7. Party must be deceived

"Fraud that does not deceive is not fraud." Attept to deceive is not fraud. *"Deceit which does not deceive is not fraud."* Fraud must have affected other party.
S. 19 States - "A fraud which did not cause the consent to a contract, of the party on whom such fraud was practisised does not render that contract voidable."

8. Party must have sufferred loss

Without damage, fraud is not actionable. The party deceived must act upon false statement and suffer loss, then only fraud is complete. Loss may be money or money's worth or some tangible detriment capable of assessment. It is said that there is '' No fraud without damages.''

9. Fraud may be committed by the party or with his connivance, by anybody or by his agent. Fraud by a stranger will not fix any responsibility on the contracting party.

10. Consent to contract may not be induced by fraud but fraud is practisised while carrying it out. In such a case contract cannot be rescinded. Only a claim for damages can be prefered.

11. Mere silence as to facts is not fraud in itself. However this is subject to certain exceptions. Where there is duty to speak or silence is equivalent to speech, silence amounts to fraud. This point has been discussed in detail in the following paragraphs-

Mere silence is not fraud

Explanation to S. 17 states -
"..silence as to facts likely to affect the willingness of a person to enter into a contract

is not fraud unless the circumstances of the case are such that regard being had to them it is the duty of the person keeping silence to speak or unless his silence is in itself equivalent to speech."

Normally silence does not amount to fraud. Law does not expect a party to disclose a fact which may affect the willingness of the other to enter into contract and there is no obligation to disclose the whole truth. Mere failure to disclose that information affecting other's judgement is not fraud in itself.

Illustration - Two traders, A and B, enter into a contract. A has a private information of a change in the prices which would affect B' willingness to proceed with the contract. Here A is not bound to inform B.
Refer **Ward v/s Hobbs** in "Sale of Goods."

Exceptions to the rule "Mere silence is not fraud".
In the following cicumstances silence is deceptive as provided in explanation to S. 17.

a. **Duty to speak**
S17-Explanation - "Silence is fraudulent, if in the circumstances of the case are such that is is the duty of the person keeping silence to speak." Sometimes in peculiar circumstances a person is under a duty to speak. Law imposes a duty of diclossure on one who has means of access to information or certain facts are within his special knowledge. If he keeps quite, it is fradulent. In the following contracts duty to speak arises.

i) **Uberrimae fidei contracts**.
These are the contracts of utmost good faith. One reposes confidence on the other contracting party. Naturally the party relied upon should disclose fully all the information which he has. When one is trusted, all material facts should be positively revealed to the other. Certain types of such cotracts are enlisted.

♦ **Insurance contracts** - Insured is under a duty to disclose full and complete information about the risk covered i.e. concernimg diseases, condition of health or property or of the relevant subject matter of insurance.

♦ **Contract of Guarantee/suretyship** - In this tripartite agreement, creditor must communicate to the guarantor all facts which he knows about the debtor. (S. 143)

♦ **Partnership** - Contract of partnership is the result of mutual trust among partners. Every partner owes a duty towords his fellow partners to disclose everything affecting the business of the firm.

♦ **Family Settlements** - As there is an element of good-faith in family relationship, in family arrangements, full disclosure is implied. If full facts are not known, such settlemnts can be set aside.

♦ **Fiduciary Relationhip** - As explained earlier in this topic, confidence reposed should not be betrayed. Party on whom confidence is placed is under an obligation to speak. For example such relationship exists between father and a son or doctor and patient etc..

Duty to speak also arise in contracts of marriages, purchase/allotment of shares through prospectus, etc. Strict and scrupulous accuracy is desired in such transactions.

ii) Statutory duty to speak

A statute may require a party to make disclosure of all material facts. S/s. 55 of the Transfer of Property Act, a seller is under a duty to disclose the defects in the title to the property(for example, a mortgage) to the buyer. Non disclosure amounts to fraud.

b) When silence amounts to speech

Fraud may be committeed by keeping mum when silence is euivalent to speech.

Illustration - A sells, by auction, to B, a horse which A knows to be unsound. A says nothing about horse's unsoundness. B says to A - "If you do not deny it, I shall assume that the horse is sound" A says nothing. Here A's silence is equivalent to speech.

c) Change of Circumstances

It may happen that when a statement is made, it is true. But due to the change in circumstances it becomes false when it is actually acted upon by the other party. In this situation, it is the duty of the representor to communicate about the change.

Rajagopala Iyer vs South Indian Rubber Works[37], A company in its prospectus stated that certain persons would be the directors of the company. This was true. But before actual allotment of shares, due to retirement, the body of directors changed. This should have been communicated to the public but company failed. As decided by the court, the plaintiff, an allotee, had a right to avoid the allotment.

d) Halftruths: "Everybody knows that sometimes half a truth is no better than a downright falsehood."[38]

Sometimes the person is not under a duty to disclose a fact and hence silence is justified. But if he chooses to speak, he should speak the whole truth. Disclosure of half truh becomes fraudulent.

12. Effects of fraud

Consent is not free when it is obtained by fraud. Following remedies are available to the party whose consent is obtained by fraud.

a) Contract is voidable u/s 19.

b) Rescission-Contract can be set aside by the party defrauded.

c) Restitution of the benefit under voidable contract u/s s. 64 of the Act..

d) S.19, para-2-The party can affirm the contract and insist on its the performance if it is beneficial to him and to put him in the position in which he would have been had there been no fraud. (i.e. restoration.)

e) Suit for damages for the loss suffered can be filed against fradulent party.

---

37. (1942)2 MLJ 228
38. Per Lord MACNAUGHTAN in Gluckstein v/s Barnes, (1900) AC 240, 250

6.5 MISREPRESENTATION

6.5.a Definition and Meaning. Misrepresentation means misstatement of a fact material to the contract. Misrepresentation is false statement made without ant intention to deceive. It is honest representation but wrongly made. Misrepresentation can be either deliberate with intention to deceive or unintentional. If it is intentional, it is dealt with by sec. 17 as fraud and the later is misrepresentation u/s 18.

S.18 defines and provides for the following **types of misrepresentation**

> A - Unwarranted False Assertion;
> B - Breach of Duty;
> C - Causing other (party) to commit mistake as to the subject matter of a contract.

A- **Unwarranted Statements** *(S.18-cl.1)*

> *"the positive assertion, in a manner not warranted by the information of the person making it, of that which is not true, though he believes it to be true."*

This clause covers innocently made unwarranted false assertions as misrepresentation. When a person makes a positive statement(assertion) that a fact is true, believing that it is true, but his information does not warrant truth in it, the statement is misrepresentation. A statement is warranted by information of a person when he has reasonable and trustworthy source to support it. In absence of that reliable source, it is unwarranted statement, a hearsay.

Example - A came to know from somebody that C would become the director of a company and told B so. B relied on and contracted to buy shares from A. C did not become director. Here consent of B is induced by misrepresentation.[39]

Essentials

> a. It is a positive assertion of material fact. Mere expression of opinion is not treated as misrepresentation even if it turns out to be wrong;
> b. Assertion is unwarranted by the information of the person making it;
> c. Maker has belief in its truth. The statement is made innocently;
> d. Representation is made with a view to induce other to give consent to the contract.

Refer Derry v/s Peek discussed in the topic of fraud.

B - **Breach of Duty** *(S. 18 cl. 2)* -

> *"any breach of duty which, without an intent to deceive, gains an advantage to the person commiting it, or anyone claiming under him, by misleading another to his prejudice, or to the prejudice of any one claiming under him."*

The second type of misrepresentation is found where a person is under a duty, say to disclose information. He commits a breach of it but innocently. Other is misled and thereby suffers losses. The person committing breach draws a benefit in the transaction. In the relationships like creditor-debtor, landlord-tenant, banker-customer, one owes a duty to the

---

39. *Facts based on-Mohan Lal v/s Shri Gangaji Cotton Mill (1900) 4 Cal. WN 369*

other to provide correct information. Failure may lead to the repudiation of contract. This clause covers the cases of "consrtuctive fraud" where the person derives the benefit but without any bad intention.

Essentials
    a - There is a breach of duty by one party which misleads the other party;[40]

    b - Breach is innocent;

    c - Breach results in a loss to one party.

Example - In contract of insurances, if an insured omits an important information, though inadvertantly, regarding health or gives incorrect particulars about age, illness etc., that is regarded as misrepresentation. When plaintiff reposes confidence, the defendant is under a duty to disclose fully the contents of a deed. The plaintiff had a right to cancell the deed if defendant commits a breach of duty to disclose.

C - Causing other party to commit a mistake *(S. 18-cl-3) –*

> *"..causing however innocently, a party to an agreement, to make a mistake as to the substance of the thing which is the subject of the agreement."*

It is a misrepresentstion if a contracting party induces other to make a mistake as to the subject matter of contract. For parties to the contract, subject matter possesses distinct value or quality. Mistake as to that is vital and contract can be rescinded. Causing mistake should however be unintentional.

Example - A company in its prospectus stated that it regularly paid dividends. As a matter of fact, company was running losses for the past few years and dividend could be paid only out of war time accumulated profits. Concealment of true state of affairs misled the purchaser of shares and afforded a ground for avoiding contract.

6.5.b Requisites of Misrepresentation

After perusal of the definition and essentials of the three forms of misrepresentation, following charactersics of misrepresentation, in general, may be enlisted.

1. There is statement/representation of fact-not of opinion.
2. Misrepresentation is as to a fact, material to contract. Statement as to unimportant (trivial) aspects of contract is not misrepresentation.
3. Representation is false. No dispute arises if it is true.
4. The statement is believed to be true by the representor.
5. Reprsentation is made without any intention to deceive. This factor distinguishes misrepresentation from fraud.
6. Misrepresentation is by the party to the contract and should not by the stranger.
7. Statement should be made before or at the time of entering into contract.

---

40. **Oriental Bank Corporation v/s John Fleming** - (1879)3 Bom.242 - *A plaintiff, due to want of time, signed a release deed in favour of defendant without reading it. He was given a belief by the defendant that the document contained formal matters previously settled between them. In this situation, the defendant was not under an obligation to inform about the contents of the deed.*

8. Misrepresentation should induce the other to give the consent to the contract i.e. misrepresentation must be the cause of consent.

6.5.c Effects of Misrepresentation

a) S.19- The contract is voidable at the option of the party misled.
b) Right of rescision is available to the aggrieved party.
c) Right to insist upon the performance and right of restoration to the original position can also be claimed.

When contract <u>cannot be cancelled</u> on the ground of misrepresentation?

In the following cicumstances, the party misled loses the right of repudiation of contract–

a) The aggrieved party had the means of discovering the truth.

Exception to sec. 19- "If such consent was caused by misrepresentation, the contract, nevertheless, is not voidable, if the party whose consent was so caused had the means of discovering the truth with ordinary diligence."

Illustration - A, by misrepresentation, leads B to erroneously believe that five hundred maunds of indigo are made annually at A's factory. B examines the accounts of the factory, which shows that only four hundred maunds of indigo have been made. After this B buys the factory. The contract is not voidable on account of A's misrepresentation.

b) The party had knowledge of truth before giving consent.
c) Party does not act upon misrepresentation.
d) Acceptance of benefit under the contract negatives the right of cancellation. (i.e. by estoppel)
e) Misrepresentation has not affected the judgement of the other i.e. consent to the contract.
f) If the third party who is a bonafide purchaser for value acquires a right in the subject matter of the contract, before the contract is cancelled by the party misrepresented.

6.6 MISTAKE

> *"Law relating to mistake is a comedy of errors."*

Mistakes do occur when parties enter into contracts. Certain mistakes are beyond rectification. Can parties put an end to contract due to mistakes? What are legal consequences of mistakes? **Sections 20 to 22** deal with law as to mistakes and their effects on contractual relationship.

6.6.a Meaning

Mistake is an erroneous belief regarding an aspect of a contract. It leads to misunderstanding of parties. Mistakes have a bearing on consensus (consent). But every mistake is not a justification for repudiation of contract. If mistakes are vital and strike at the root of an agreement, law assumes that there is no consent and consequently no contract.

The Contract Act neither defines mistakes nor any of its kinds. The relevant sections state the consequenses of mistakes, which are explained below.

6.6.b Kinds Of Mistakes

The mistakes basically are of two types -

A-Mistake of Fact and

B-Mistake of Law.

A) Mistake of Fact

Mistake of Fact again is sub-divided into two types viz.

1) Bilateral Mistakes and

2) Unilateral Mistakes

1. **Bilateral Mistakes** - S. 20 deals with bilateral mistake mistake which states -

   "When both the parties to an agreement are under a mistake as to a matter of fact essential to the agreement, the **agreement is void.**" (emphasis added)

   Ingrediants of section 20

   i) **Mistake is bilateral.** When both parties to the agreement are under mistake, it is bilateral mistake. This can also be described as common or mutual mistake.Mutual mistakes are same or identical mistakes. Each party undertands the contract in a different way.

   ii) **Mistake must relate to a fact**..and not to an opinion or judgement.

   Explanation to S.20-An erroneous opinion as to the value of the thing which forms the subject matter of the agreememt is not to be deemed a mistake as to a matter of fact.

   iii) **Fact is essential to the agreement**

   The mistake should strike a fact material (important) to the contract. The mistake as to collateral or trivial fact does not negative contract.

   iv) **Effect**

   Bilateral mistake makes the contract void. Bilateral mistake annuls the agreement.

Types (Instances) of Bilateral Mistakes :

Bilateral mistakes occure in differnt ways. (See - Cundy v/s Lindsey - supra note 29)

Bilateral mistakes may be divided into -

a) Mistake as to subject matter and

b) Mistake as to possibility of performance.

a) Bilateral mistake as to subject matter- Bilateral mistake relating to subject matter invalidates the contract.

Instances

i) **Mistake as to existence of subject matter**-Sometimes the parties at the time of entering into an agreement assume that the subject matter is in existence and that obviously so. But it may be revealed that subject matter either had never been in existence or it ceases to exist. Under such a common mistake the contract is void.

   Illustartion-A, agrees to buy from B a certain horse. It turns out that the horse was dead at the time of the bargain, though neither party was aware of the fact. Agreement is void.

Fact are stupid until brought into connection with some general law

- Louis Agnissiz

ii) Mistake as to the title of subject matter - There can be a wrong assumption by the parties as to the title (ownership right) subsisting in a property.

Illustration - A agreed to take a lease of fishery from B, though contrary to the belief of both the parties, at the time A was tenant for life by inheritance of the fishery and B had no title at all. It was held that the lease agreement was void [Copper v/s Phibbs-(1867), LR 2HL149].

iii) Mistake as to identity or quality of the subject matter -Quality or the description of the subject matter /property are the important attributes and attract consideration. Mistake by both parties as to these core elements vitiates the consent. Where the parties, on account of a reasonable mistake of fact, may have different subject matter in mind, there is no true consent and the agreement is void.

*Example-*A has two plots, one each on either side of the river. A agrees to sell plot on right side to B. B however, has, in his mind, plot on left side. Contract cannot be concluded due to mistake as to identity of the property.

iv) Mistake as to price of subject matter - Price assumes importance in almost every contract. Mutual mistake goes the root of the agreement making it void.

b) Bilateral mistake as to possibility of performance of contract.-Parties to the contract may be under a mistaken belief that contract would be performed at the proper time. Impossibility in performance may not be contemplated by both at the time of entering into agreement. This eventuality occurs in the following way-

i) Physical impossibility - Without the knowledge of both the parties, contract may be physically impossible to perform;

ii) Legal impossibility - Whatever is to be performed under the terms of contract, may be impossible by reason of legal obstacle. Rule prevails making the contract void. (see s. 56)

2) Unilateral Mistake

Mistake on the part of one of the parties is called is called as unilateral mistake. It is not an excuse to avoid the contract.

S.22 provides -

> *"A contract is not voidable merely because it was caused by one of the parties to it being under a mistake as to a matter of fact."*

Ingredients of S.22

a) Mistake is about a matter of fact ;
b) One of the parties is under a mistake in contrast to bilateral mistake ;
c) Effect - Contract is **not voidable**.

Exceptions - The general rule that a contract is not voidable due to unilateral mistake, is qualified by following exeptions. Contract can be repudiated by the party under mistake.

i) Mistake as to Identity of Parties

Identity of the party many times is the essence of the contract. One desires to enter into a contract with a particular person. In that case, mistake about identity is fatal and the contract is void though it is unilateral. The result is the same if the mistake is due to the fraud or misrepresentation by another party.[41]

In open market, where parties are face to face, ratio of Cundy is not to be applied.[42]

ii) Mistake as to Nature of Contract

An agreement is unenforceable even if there is a unilateral mistake as to the very nature and character of transaction. Nature of contract is its foundation. Any misunderstanding negatives the consent and the contract is void. Signature on the document should be a conscious act. It indicates application of mind. If it is not so, contract is devoid of any legal consequences as illustrated in the following case.

Bala Devi v/s Shanti Majumdar [43] An old illiterate lady appointed her nephew as her power of attorney to manage her estate. She signed a deed of gift in favour of nephew under the impression that it was power of attorney. She never intended to gift the property and the deed was not explained to her. The document was declared null and void as mind did not accompany the signature.

B) Mistake of Law

S. 21 lays down the law relating to mistake of law which is reproduced below-

> *"A contract is not voidable because it was caused by any mistake of law in force in India, but a mistake as to a law not in force in India has the same effect as a mistake of fact."*

Mistake of law as such is not defined but its effect is stated in the section. From the text of section it reveals that mistake of law is of two categories.

a) Mistake of Domestic (Indian) Law

Mistake of law of the country does not nullify the contract. It is said that **"ignorentia juris non excusat"** meaning thereby that **"ignorance of law is not an excuse."** If a person is allowed to say that law was not known or its meaning was not understood, that would lead to undesirable results. Therefore, everybody is supposed to know the law of the land.

Illustration - A and B make a contract grounded on the erroneous belief that a particular debt is barred by the Indian Law of Limitation, the contract is not voidable. The contract however may be repudiated if mistake of law is the result of inducement, intentional or unintentional.(i.e. fraud or misrepresentation)

---

41. *Supra note 29*
42. *"Mistake as to the identity" is to be distinguished from "mistake as to the attributes" of personality ''i.e. mistake as to solvency or credit or social status of a person has no effect on the formation of contract*
43. *(1956) AIR, cal. 575*

b) Mistake of Foreign Law - Mistake regarding law of the foreign country is equated with that of mistake of fact and the consequences u/s 22 follow. Mistake is then a question of fact.

Effects of mistake : As already covered under the relevant sections, effects are highlighted-

Unilateral mistake of fact - Contract not voidable, it is very much enforceable;

Bilateral mistake of fact - Contract is void;

Mistake of Law - Mistake of Indian law-contract is not void;

Mistake of foreign law - it is treated as a mistake of fact and hence above consequences follow.

Apart from this, Ss. 19, 64, 72 discussed earlier may be referred for legal consequences.

LAW OF MISTAKES

(Erroneous belief, Misunderstanding, parties agree in different sense.)

Kinds of Mistake

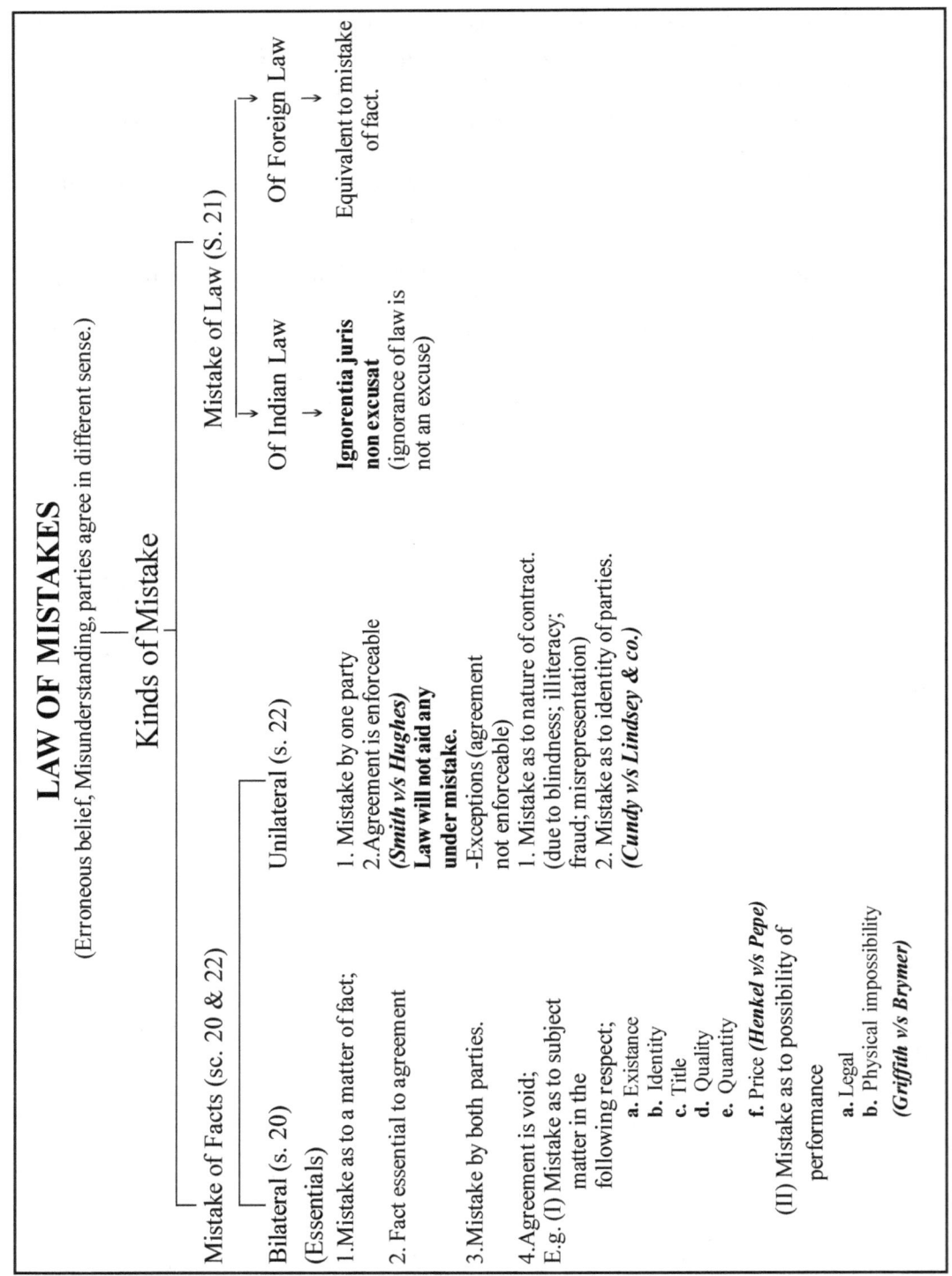

Mistake of Facts (sc. 20 & 22)

Bilateral (s. 20)
(Essentials)

1. Mistake as to a matter of fact;

2. Fact essential to agreement

3. Mistake by both parties.

4. Agreement is void;
E.g. (I) Mistake as to subject
matter in the
following respect;
   a. Existance
   b. Identity
   c. Title
   d. Quality
   e. Quantity
   f. Price (*Henkel v/s Pepe*)
(II) Mistake as to possibility of
performance
   a. Legal
   b. Physical impossibility
   (*Griffith v/s Brymer*)

Unilateral (s. 22)

1. Mistake by one party
2. Agreement is enforceable
(*Smith v/s Hughes*)
Law will not aid any
under mistake.

-Exceptions (agreement
not enforceable)

1. Mistake as to nature of contract.
(due to blindness; illiteracy;
fraud; misrepresentation)
2. Mistake as to identity of parties.
(*Cundy v/s Lindsey & co.*)

Mistake of Law (S. 21)

Of Indian Law

Ignorentia juris
non excusat
(ignorance of law is
not an excuse)

Of Foreign Law

Equivalent to mistake
of fact.

Chapter 7	LAWFUL CONSIDERATION AND OBJECTS

Legality of consideration and objects is one of the requirements for formation of a contract. Section 10 states- "All agreements are contracts if they are made for lawful consideration and with lawful object." Section 23 lays down that, "Every agreement of which the object and consideration is unlawful is void." These two sections emphasize the lawful character of both consideration and object as an essential element of enforceability of an agreement.

7.1 Consideration and Object

Consideration and object both should be lawful. If one satisfies the legality and other not, agreement is void. The Contract Act defines consideration, but not object. These two are usually different concepts. Object means 'purpose or design'. A commercial tenement is taken on lease in which rent is consideration but object is to earn money. In a transfer of property by an insolvent, consideration may be money or property but object may be to defraud the creditors. Section 23 declares certain consideration and objects as unlawful. Text of the section is reproduced below.

7.2 S. 23 — What considerations and objects are lawful, and what not -

S. 23 states that - The consideration and object of an agreement is lawful unless-
— it is forbidden by law; or
— is of such a nature that, if permitted, it would defeat the provisions of any law; or
— is fraudulent; or
— involves or implies injury to the person or property of another; or
— the Court regards it as immoral or opposed to public policy.

In each of these cases, the consideration and object of an agreement is said to be unlawful. Every agreement of which the consideration and object is unlawful, is void. Section 23 thus enlists the consideration and objects, which are unlawful, and states that the agreements are void. **The consideration and objects are unlawful in the following cases.**

1. **If it is forbidden by law**

   If the consideration and object is forbidden by any law then consideration and object is regarded as unlawful. 'Forbidden' means 'prohibited' by the law or 'punishable' by criminal law of the land. What is punishable is obviously prevented by the concerned law. Commission of a crime cannot be a consideration/object.

   Example- A promises B to pay one crore rupees if he kills his rival gangster. This agreement is void as killing is an offence of murder under s. 302 of IPC.

2. **If it is of such a nature that, if permitted, it would defeat the provisions of any law**

   Sometimes law does not expressly or directly forbid the consideration and object but if allowed, that has a tendency to defeat the intention of legislature. Such acts as consideration and object obliquely violate the law. Here the term "law" has the same connotation as given in earlier para. Pact between parties cannot frustrate legal provision.

   Example-1 An agreement between creditor and debtor wherein the debtor agrees not to set up a defense of bar of limitation, should a suit have to be filed, is void as that would undermine the statutory provisions as to limitation.[44]

   Example-2 A parent gave his son in adoption in consideration of an annual allowance. Held that suit to recover the allowance cannot be allowed as the adoption defeated the spirit of Hindu Law.[45]

3. **If it is fraudulent**

   Where parties agree to impose fraud on a third person, consideration and object would be unlawful. Fraud results in wrongful gain to one and wrongful loss to the other.

   Illustration - A, B and C enter into an agreement among them for distribution of gains acquired, or to be acquired, by them, by fraud. The agreement is void as its object is unlawful. Deceit taints otherwise lawful agreement.

4. **If it is injurious**

   An agreement whose consideration and object causes injury or harm to another person is unenforceable. It is also unlawful if it implies damage to the property of other. An agreement to commit a crime, or a civil wrong, (to assault or beat a person) to cheat one or to publish a libel is covered here.[46]

   In Clay v/s Yates also, it was held that an agreement to publish a libel (written defamation, by an article) is void.

---

44. *Rama Murthy v/s Gopayya- (1917) 40 Mad.701*
45. *Sitaram v/s Harihar, (1910) 35 Bom.169*
46. **W. H. Smith & Sons v/s C. Clington** *(1909) - A requested an editor of news paper to publish an article defamatory of B and agrees to indemnify editor against the consequences of publishing libel. Ruled that the editor cannot recover the amount under indemnity as the agreement was void which involved injury (by defamation) to B.*

Ex turpi contracts non oritur actio – No action arises on immoral contract

5. Court regards it as immoral

Agreements tainted with immorality are void. Law dislikes immorality as a foundation of any agreement. Morals cannot be laid down or defined. Immorality cannot be explained in precise terms. Morality is very much a relative concept. It depends upon the standards of morality of a particular time and place. Good conscience dictates us standard or ethical norms for our lives. Any departure may be violation of moral code. The courts have to decide the issue of immorality and lawfulness of object or consideration by applying prevailing standards. Immorality ordinarily refers to sexual immorality. For instance, illicit cohabitation or concubinage, services of paramour offend morality. Immorality is to be limited to sex outside marriage.

The Supreme Court in **Gherulal v/s M. Maiya**[47] pointed that the term "immoral" is comprehensive one and must be confined to sexual immorality. The apex court cited some instances of sexual immorality...settlements in consideration of concubinage, contract of sale or hire of things to be used in a brothel or by prostitute for purposes incidental to her profession, agreements to pay money for future illicit cohabitations, promises in regard to marriages for consideration or contracts facilitating divorce are held to be void on the ground that the object is immoral. Adultery is not only immoral but it is an offence and illegal. Adulterous cohabitation is highly immoral.

Example-1 A gift of property in consideration of illicit intercourse has been held to be void and inoperative, as its object was immoral. Ghumma v/s Ram Chandra- (1926), 47 All. 619

Example-2 A man knowingly let out his house for prostitution. He was not permitted to recover rent from tenant as letting was with the object in furtherance of immorality.

6. Court regards it as opposed to public policy

This clause lays down that any object or consideration "opposed to public policy" is unlawful. What is 'public policy" is a moot question. Generally if agreement harms public interest or works against public welfare, it is opposed to public policy. It is a flexible concept as it varies with social set-up, social problems, demands etc. It is an illusive concept and characterized as "unruly horse" or "untrustworthy guide". The agreements discussed below are opposed to public policy and hence void.

Interpreting "public policy" and as to how matters of public policy to be decided, Andhra Pradesh High Court has observed. "The twin touchstone of public policy are advancement of public good and prevention of public mischief and these questions have to be decided by the judges not as men of legal learning but as experienced and enlightened members of community representing the highest common factor of public sentiment and intelligence." - **Ratanchand Hirachand v/s Askarjung** - AIR (1976) AP112

---

47. *(1959) 2 SC 342*

"Law is nothing unless close behind it stands a warm living public opinion"
                                                              - Wendell Philips

Law does not assist a person to recover through his crime. **"The fruits of crime are irrecoverable."** *- Cheshire and Fifoot, Law of Contract, 333 (9th Edn by Furmston, 1976).* **"No person is allowed to benefit from his own crime."** *- Cleaver v/s Mutual Reserve Fund Life Assn, 1892) 1 QB 147*

7.3 Heads of Public Policy (Agreements against Public Policy)

a) Trading with alien enemy

The alien enemy is a citizen of a country at war with the State. Trading with alien enemy may advance the economic interests of enemy country. With special permission of Government, however, trading is possible. Business activity promoting a hostile action in a friendly nation is also against public policy.

b) Interference with Administration of Justice

If the consideration or object behind an agreement interferes in the course of justice, it is unlawful. Influencing a judge to procure a decision, inducing a witness to give false evidence are some of the examples of this sort of agreements. An agreement to delay the execution of a decree also falls in this class.

c) Stifling Prosecution

Stifling criminal prosecution is regarded as unlawful. Crime is a public wrong and the criminal should be brought to book by prosecuting and punishing him. Stifling prosecution simply means compromising a criminal case which is prima facie, inconsistent with logic of prosecution and punishment. Public offences (crimes) are either compoundable or non-compoundable. The former can be compromised through an agreement but latter cannot be the subject matter of agreement for the reason above stated. Any agreement, which foils this rationale and obstructs the administration of criminal justice is said to be opposed to public policy. Prevention or delaying prosecution amounts to an interference in the administration of justice. An agreement not to prosecute an offender or to withdraw a pending prosecution is a way to stifle prosecution. Law does not allow a person to extract a profit out of crime.[48]

Illustration - A promises B to drop a prosecution which he has instituted against B for robbery and B promise to restore the value of the things taken. The agreement is void, as its object is unlawful.

d) Maintenance and Champerty

Lord HALDANE explains "maintenance" as- "it is unlawful for a stranger to render officious by money or otherwise to another person in a suit in which that third person has no legal interest, for its prosecution or defence."[49]

Maintenance refers to maintaining a litigation by a person who has no legal interest in it. Providing financial or professional assistance to a litigant by a stranger (a third party) is undesirable. Maintenance implies encouragement to institute or continue the proceedings by a third party with no interest. It encourages speculative tendency.[50]

Champerty- Champerty is a species of maintenance. It is sharing the fruits of litigation.

---

48. *"You cannot make a trade of a felony" Lord Westbury in Williams v/s Bayley, (1866)1 HL 200*
49. *Neville v/s London Express, (1910) AC 368*
50. *Ram Sarup v/s Couirt of Wards, (1940) 67 IA50 "The uncertainties of litigation are proverbial; and if the financer must need risk losing his money he may well be allowed some chances of exceptional advantage. "*

An agreement to share the proceeds of a legal action in consideration of providing assistance (monetary or otherwise) by a third person is a champertous agreement. "Champerty in its essence means a bargain whereby one party is to assist the other in recovering property, and is to share in the proceeds of the action."[51]

Example-A agrees with B to provide financial help to B to recover a property from C by filing a civil suit. B promises to give half share in the property, if recovered. Because of the gambling or speculation involved in this arrangement, agreement is against public policy.

Legality of Maintenance and Champerty

Under English Law, both of these agreements are declared as illegal and void. Indian law treats maintenance and champerty differently. Maintenance and champerty as such are not illegal in India. In India many poor litigants do not afford to go to the court and cannot enforce their genuine claims. In such cases a stranger to the dispute may, out of charity, help the poor party. Agreement with reasonable terms to recover court expenses may be given effect to. Agreements on fair terms to provide financial help to the poor litigant and to get reimbursement out of money or property recovered in the suit is valid though champertous. Bonafide object of assisting a just claim would validate these agreements.[52]

The courts would refuse to enforce these types of agreements if those are found to be extortionate or unconscionable. Champerty is invalid if it is unreasonable, unjust or oppressive in nature. The courts would not allow exploitation of the person in financial distress. Gambling in litigation or encouraging unrighteous suits is unlawful.

Example - A agrees with B to financially help B in a court case. B promises to repay all the expenses incurred by A. This is allowed. But if B promises to pay after the case is won, one lakh rupees, for expenses of ten thousand rupees, the promise is void.

e) Trafficking in Public Offices

Public office cannot be sold or transferred for money. Agreements for sale or transfer of public office for monetary consideration are opposed to public policy. Appointment to public office cannot be sought by bribing. Inducing a public officer to adopt corruption methods is certainly unlawful. National awards, Honours like Padmbhushan, Paramvir Chakra or other public recognition cannot be bargained.

Illustration-A promises to obtain for B an employment in the public service, and B promises to pay rupees 1000 to A. The agreement is void as the consideration or object is unlawful.[53]

f) Agreement creating an interest opposed to duty

A person under a duty, particularly public, must discharge it faithfully. He by an agreement, cannot place himself in a position inconsistent with the discharge of the duty. If an agreement has a tendency to create a conflict between a person's right and duty, such an agreement is void.

---

51. *Hutley v/s Hutley, (1873)LR 8 QB 42 per Blackburn J.*
52. *Raja Venkata Subhadrayamma Guru v/s Sree Pusapati Vankatpathy Raju, 48 Mad. 230 (Privy Council)*
53. *Parkinson v/s College o Ambulance-1925-LKB.1*

Example-A, agrees to pay B, a lieutenant in the army, Rs. 50000 if he will assist her brother to desert the army. The object of agreement is opposed to public policy and hence illegal and void.

Illustration- A, being an agent for a landed proprietor, agrees for money, without the knowledge of his principal, to obtain for B a lease of land belonging to his principal. The agreement between A and B is void as it implies a fraud by concealment, by A, on his principal.

g) Agreement restraining personal liberty

An agreement by which a person is deprived of his personal freedom is void. To be void, restriction must be undue and oppressive in nature.

h) Agreement interfering with parental duties

Father or mother enjoys certain rights and subjected to some duties as regards their child. Neither a right nor duty can be assigned to a stranger, as it is derogatory to parental status. Right of custody or that of adoption cannot be the subject of transfered to anybody.[54]

i) Agreements in restraint of marital duties

These may take any one of the following forms.

1. An agreement to the effect that the wife would continue to stay with her parents after marriage and husband would also stay with in- laws.
2. Promise to lend money to a woman in consideration of her seeking a divorce from her husband and then marrying the lender.[55]
3. Promise by a spouse to marry another during the lifetime or after the death of the other spouse.[56]

j) Marriage Brokerage Agreements

Procuring a bride or bridegroom in a marriage for monetary consideration is certainly bad in law. In settlement of marriages, commerce cannot be introduced. However providing matrimonial information of for charges is a type of service agreement by marriage bureaus.

Agreements under sections 26 to 28, 30 are also opposed to public policy, those are explained in the next chapter.

---

54. *Giddy Aryanism v/s Mrs. Annie Bezant- (1915)38 Mad. PC. -GN, father, transferred guardianship of his two minor sons in favor of AB permanently and further agreed not to revoke transfer. Afterwards he filed a suit to regain custody of sons and to revoke guardianship. Held that revocation is possible as alienation of parental rights is opposed to public policy.*
55. *Tikyat v/s Manohar, 28 Cal.751.*
56. *Roshan v/s Mohamad-(1887) PR.66*

Chapter 8	VOID AGREEMENTS *AGREEMENTS EXPRESSLY DECLARED TO BE VOID AGREEMENTS*

S. 2(g) of the Contract Act defines "void agreement" as- "An agreement not enforceable by law is void." We have seen in the chapter on essentials of contract, as to when agreement is unenforceable and void. Void agreement is void-ab-initio i.e. void from inception, devoid of any legal consequences. A void agreement need not be illegal. So far, following void agreement have been dealt with in preceding chapters-

1. Agreement with incompetent party- S. 11(Refer chapter 5)
2. Agreement under 'bilateral mistake'-S. 20 (Refer chapter 6)
3. Agreement with 'unlawful object or consideration'- S.23 (Refer chapter 4)

One of the essentials of contract as mentioned in S.10 is that agreement must not be "expressly declared" to be void by the Act. These agreement may not lack any of the essentials of contract but still law specifically declares those as void.

Following agreements have been **expressly declared to be void** by the Indian Contract Act.

1. Agreements with object or consideration unlawful in part - S. 24 (Refer chapter 4)
2. Agreements without consideration, S.25 (Refer chapter 4)
3. Agreements in restraint of marriage, S. 26
4. Agreements in restraint of trade, S. 27
5. Agreement in restraint of legal proceedings, S. 28
6. Agreement with uncertain meaning, S. 29
7. Agreement by way of wager, S. 30
8. Agreement to do impossible acts, S. 56

First two categories of void agreements have been discussed in earlier chapters. Remaining catagories are explain below -

8.1 Agreement in Restraint of Marriage

S.26 of the Act states-*"every agreement in restraint of the marriage of any person, other than a minor, is void."*

Every person has freedom to marry and that too with a person of his choice. Any agreement incorporating a restriction on this freedom is void. Negative agreement like agreement not to marry at all, or to a particular person or to a class of persons are void. Agreement not to marry for a fixed period is also hit by s. 26. Promise to marry a particular person is however not in restraint of marriage and valid. Restraint may be general or partial, the agreement is void.

Illustration - A agrees with B for mmetory consideration that she will not marry C. It is void agreement.

Exception - Agreement restraining marriage of a minor is valid. The Child Marriage Restraint Act, 1978 - forbids child marriages.

8.2 Agreements in Restraint of Trade —

S. 27 states- *"Every agreement by which anyone is restrained from exercising a lawful profession or business of any kind, is to that extent void."*
General Rule-Constitution of India guarantees freedom of trade to every citizen of India. Every citizen has a liberty to carry on business of his choice in any part in India. One can enjoy fruit of his labor, skill or intelligence through various contracts. This freedom is subjected to "reasonable restrictions" provided in the Constitution. Apart from that, freedom of trade cannot be curtailed.[57] Neither the freedom profession can be curbed nor one can barter away his right. Sec. 27 of the Act is in consonance with this liberty and states the general rule that any agreement putting restrictions on lawful trade is void. Public policy protects freedom of trade and commerce.[58]

The restraint on trade may be absolute or partial, general or specific, unqualified or qualified, it is against public policy and hence void. The term incorporating restraint is inoperative, rest of the agreement stands.[59]

Exceptions-There are well recognized exceptions to the above mentioned general rule. Following agreements are not in restraint of trade and restrictions are held to be lawful.

i) Statutory Exceptions
These exceptions are provided in the statutes hence called as statutory exceptions.

a) Restriction on Seller of Good-Will
Exception-I to S.27- "One who sells the good-will of a business may agree with the buyer to refrain from carrying on a similar business, within specified local limits, so long as the buyer or any person deriving title from him, carries on a like business therein: Provided such limits appear to the court reasonable, regard being had to the nature of the business."
From this text, following points may be noted.

---

57. *"Liberty of trade is not an asset which the law will permit a person to barter away except in special circumstances."*
58. *Public policy requires that every man shall be at liberty to work for himself, and shall not be at liberty to deprive himself or the State of his labor, skill or talent by any contract that he enters into." Per JAMES VC in Leather Cloth Co. v/s Lovsont, (1869)LR 9 Eq 345-*
59. *"Every man should have unfettered liberty to exercise his powers and capacities for his own and the community's benefit."-Lord MACMILLAN in Vancouver Malt & Sake Brewing Co. Ltd. v/s Vancouver Breweries Ltd, AIR 1934 PC 101.*

1. Restriction is on the seller of the goodwill of a business;
2. Seller is refrained from carrying on business of which goodwill is sold and buyer would be carrying on;
3. Restriction is on the liberty to carry on similar business in a specified area and for a period for which buyer carries on the same business;
4. Restraint should be reasonable as far as local limits and its duration;
5. Reasonableness of restraint is decided by the courts considering above factors and the nature of business.

Example - L sells goodwill of his business in Pune to M. L is restrained from carrying on similar business in Pune for two years. This restriction is valid. But if L is refrained from conducting it anywhere in India and (or) throughout the life of M, this restraint would be unreasonable and void. Sale of goodwill is valid.

b) Restrictions on Partners-The Indian Partnership Act of 1932 legalizes following restrictions (as a part of Deed of Partnership) on partners on conducting business similar to that of the firm-

1. Restriction on existing partners-S. 11-All partners may agree that during the partnership, no partner would carry on a business similar to that of the firm;
2. Restriction on outgoing partners -S. 32-Outgoing partners may be restrained from conducting similar business within a specified locality or within a definite period within, of course, the limits of reasonableness;
3. Restriction in view of dissolution of partnership-S.54-In anticipation of dissolution of partnership, the partners may agree that they will not carry on similar business within a specified locality or within a period;
4. S.55 (3)-Agreement between the partner and the buyer of the firm's goodwill to the effect that the partner shall not carry on business similar to that of the firm within a specified period or within specified local limits, is valid. The restraint should be reasonable.

ii) Exceptions From Judicial Precedents —

a) Trade Combinations (Pooling Arrangements)

We find many trade associations of cotton manufacturers, grain merchants, sugar producers, sarafa union etc. working around us. Trade associations sometimes enter into voluntary agreements to carry on trade in an organized manner. These agreements (in the form of bye laws) regulate trading activity, fix up the prices of commodities, charges of services, and prescribe standards of qualities of goods or services. Working hours in a business, supervision and control of dealers, mode of transactions etc can be regulated. The traders/manufacturers may agree to bring all their profits/outputs in a common pool and distribute in agreed proportion. The primary object of such arrangement is to avoid cut - throat competition in the interest of all and assure equitable distribution of profits among all members. These agreements incidentally restrict member's freedom to carry on business in the manner he likes. If within the legal framework, the agreements are allowed. Such agreements working against public interest however would be declared null and void. For example, agreement attempting to create monopoly or to raise the prices of essential commodities prejudice public interest and hence is void.

b) Sole Selling (Exclusive Dealing) Agreements

Sometimes manufacturer appoints a single trader as his sole selling agent/distributor for a particular area. He thereby agrees not to appoint any other as his agent and the agent also agrees not to trade in other's goods in that area. Usually such arrangements are for a fixed period. The purpose is to assure market in certain area. Being negative in nature, agreement is in restraint of trade but still permitted. If the agreements were oppressive and lead to monopoly, those would be void.

c) Service Agreements

Contract of employment contains many negative stipulations in the nature of restrictions on employees. Employees are not allowed to work anywhere during the term of employment or compete with his employer directly or indirectly. Trade secrets cannot be disclosed by the employees to other employers. These restraints should not be oppressive in nature. A restriction on working beyond a period of service is prima facie, not fair. But if restriction is for protection of goodwill, then even after service it can be provided, for reasonable period.

Charlesworth v/s MacDonald[60] A agreed to serve B as an accountant at Zanzibar for three years. A agreed that he will not practice independently during the tenure of service. A left B's services after one year and started his own practice at Zanzibar. The court held that A has committed a breach of agreement and he could be prevented from practicing for the period of agreement.

8.3 Agreement in Restraint of Legal Proceedings

"an agreement purporting to oust the jurisdiction of the courts is illegal and void on the grounds of public policy." Rule of English law from Halsbury's Laws of England, Vol.9, 352.

S.28 of the Act states that every agreement in restraint of legal proceedings is void. Any right under the contract or in respect of contract can be enforced by filing a civil suit in the courts of law. An agreement if enforceable in this way can only be regarded as contract. Any agreement, therefore, providing that no party shall go to the court of law, even if its breach is committed, is void-ab-initio. Sec. 28 along with its exception can be summarized as follows

a) Section 28 renders void two kind of agreements, those are -

1) An agreement whereby a party is restricted absolutely from taking usual legal proceedings to enforce any right arising under the contract is void. Absolute restraint on preferring suits is void. Restriction is absolute when the parties are wholly precluded from pursuing their remedies in the regular courts.

2) An agreement, which curtails the period of limitation, prescribed under the Law of

---

60. *(1898) 23 Bom. 103*

Limitation, is also void. For example, normally three years period is available within which a claim under a contract can be filed in a court. If the parties reduce this period to one year, the stipulation is void.

b) The section applies to enforcements of rights arising out of contract and not to civil wrongs (torts) or crimes.

c) Exceptions 1 & 2 to S.28 - Arbitration agreement are not in restraint of legal proceedings -This section does not apply to arbitration agreement. Arbitration agreement is an agreement whereby the parties agree to refer their existing or future disputes (arising out of a contract) to an arbitrator. Once the arbitration agreement is executed, parties cannot agitate the disputes in courts as the jurisdiction of the court is ousted.

d) Absolute restraint on legal proceedings are void u/s 28, and not partial. Partial restraint does not make agreement void. The section does not affect the agreement preventing parties from "filing an appeal" in higher courts.

e) Many times we come across with term in a contract "subject to jurisdiction of Calcutta court only". Apparently such term does not offend Section 28 and are binding. Whenever two courts have concurrent jurisdiction over the same matter, the parties can select one court to decide the matter. When two courts are equally competent to try the suit, parties can limit the jurisdiction to one. This does not prevent parties from preferring legal action altogether.[60-a] However it is not open for the parties to confer jurisdiction on a court which it does not possess under the Civil Procedure Code.[60-b]

f) Forfeiture or Surrender of Rights- A clause providing for surrender or forfeiture of rights if no action is preferred within stipulated time, is valid.

Example - A and B enter into an agreement of sale of goods. A, seller, agrees that he will never file a suit against B for unpaid price in any court. This agreement is void.

8.4 Agreement with Uncertain Meaning

Sec. 29 provides *"Agreements the meaning of which is not certain or capable of making certain, are void."*

The agreement is uncertain when its terms are vague. In contracts, stipulations express intention to create relationship. If those are ambiguous, intention cannot be gathered and hence agreement looses its practical meaning. Terms in a contract need to be sufficiently clear and promises therein must be reasonably certain.

Illustration - A agrees to sell B 100 tons of oil. The agreement is void for uncertainty as to the kind of oil.

If the meaning is capable of making certain, the agreement is valid.

Illustration - A, who is a dealer in coconut oil only, agrees to sell B "on hundred tons of oil." The nature of A's trade affords an indication of the meaning of the words, and, therefore, impliedly, A has entered into contract for the sale of one hundreds tons of coconut oil.

60-a. *Hakam Singh v/s Gammon(India) Ltd.-(1971)1 SCC 286*
60-b. *Patel Roadways Ltd v/s Prasad Trading Co., (1991) 4 SCC 270*

8.5   Wagering agreements are separately explained in the next topic.

8.6   Agreement to do impossible acts —

"**An agreement to do an act impossible in itself is void.**" (Sec. 56, para-1)

Illustration- A agrees with B to discover treasure by magic. The agreement is void. (For details, see chapter on discharge of contract.)

VOID AGREEMENTS

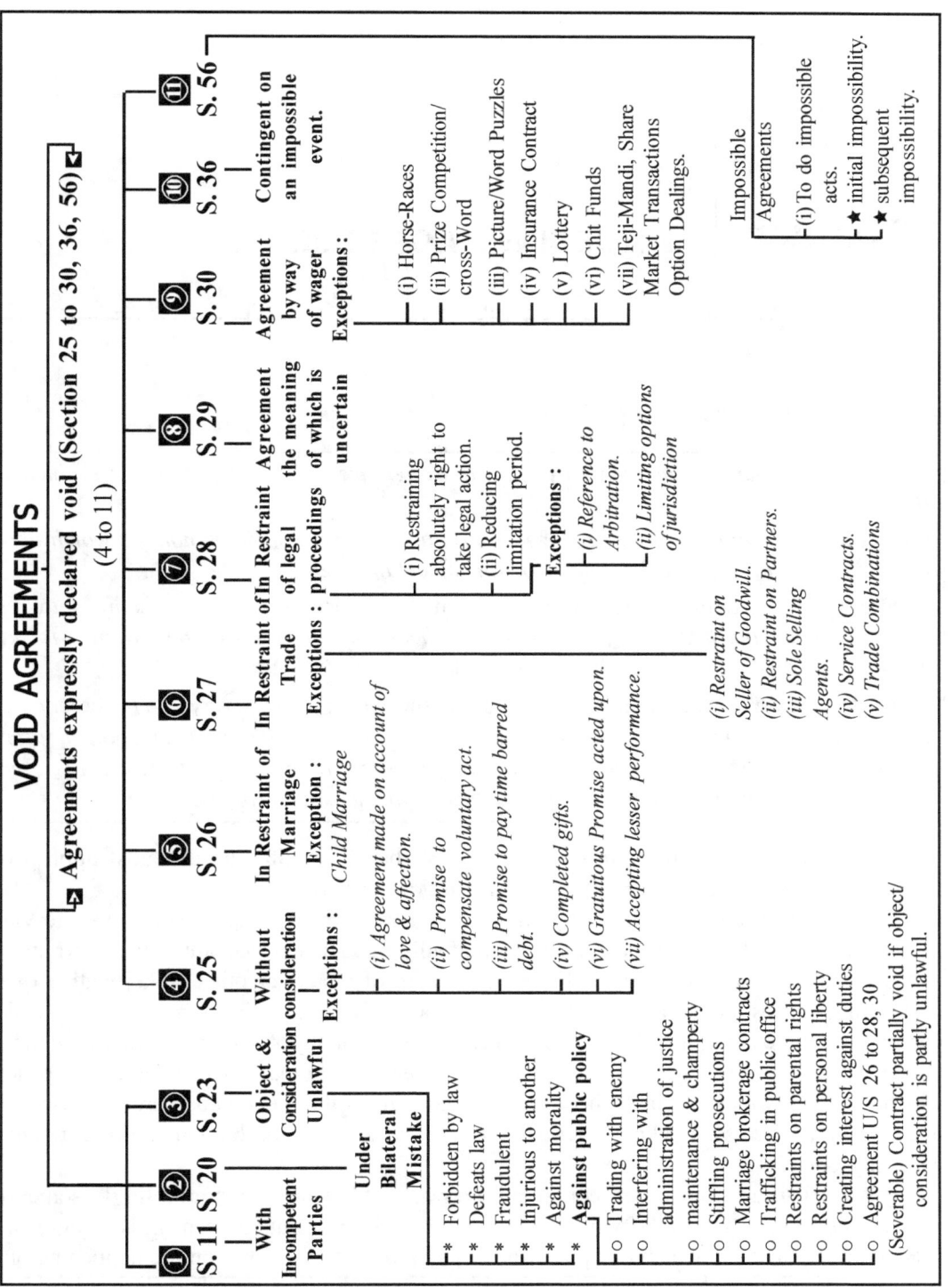

Agreements expressly declared void (Section 25 to 30, 36, 56)
(4 to 11)

① S. 11 S. 20 — With Incompetent Parties / Under Bilateral Mistake

③ S. 23 — Object & Consideration Unlawful

* Forbidden by law
* Defeats law
* Fraudulent
* Injurious to another
* Against morality

Against public policy

o Trading with enemy
o Interfering with administration of justice maintenance & champerty
o Stiffling prosecutions
o Marriage brokerage contracts
o Trafficking in public office
o Restraints on parental rights
o Restraints on personal liberty
o Creating interest against duties
o Agreement U/S 26 to 28, 30

(Severable) Contract partially void if object/ consideration is partly unlawful.

④ S. 25 — Without consideration

Exceptions :
(i) *Agreement made on account of love & affection.*
(ii) *Promise to compensate voluntary act.*
(iii) *Promise to pay time barred debt.*
(iv) *Completed gifts.*
(vi) *Gratuitous Promise acted upon.*
(vii) *Accepting lesser performance.*

⑤ S. 26 — In Restraint of Marriage

Exception :
Child Marriage

⑥ S. 27 — In Restraint of Trade

Exceptions :
(i) *Restraint on Seller of Goodwill.*
(ii) *Restraint on Partners.*
(iii) *Sole Selling Agents.*
(iv) *Service Contracts.*
(v) *Trade Combinations*

⑦ S. 28 — In Restraint of legal proceedings

Exceptions :
(i) Restraining absolutely right to take legal action.
(ii) Reducing limitation period.

Exceptions :
(i) *Reference to Arbitration.*
(ii) *Limiting options of jurisdiction*

⑧ S. 29 — Agreement the meaning of which is uncertain

⑨ S. 30 — Agreement by way of wager

Exceptions :
(i) Horse-Races
(ii) Prize Competition/ cross-Word
(iii) Picture/Word Puzzles
(iv) Insurance Contract
(v) Lottery
(vi) Chit Funds
(vii) Teji-Mandi, Share Market Transactions Option Dealings.

⑩ S. 36 — Contingent on an impossible event.

⑪ S. 56 — Impossible Agreements
(i) To do impossible acts.
★ initial impossibility.
★ subsequent impossibility.

Chapter 9

WAGERING AGREEMENTS

9.1 Definition and Meaning

> *Sec. 30 states that **"agreements by way of wager are void."** Wager is not defined in this section.*
>
> Sir **William Anson** defines "wager" as *"a promise to give money or money's worth upon the determination or ascertainment of an uncertain event."*
>
> **Cockburn,** C. J. defines wager in an illustrative manner as, *"A contract by A to pay money to B on the happening of a given event in consideration of B's promise to pay money to A on the event not happening."*
>
> **Lord J. Cotton**[61] highlights the essence of the wager in this way- *"The essence of gambling and wagering is that one party is to win and other to lose upon a future event, which at the time of contract is of an uncertain nature, that is to say, if the event turns out one way, one will lose but if it turns out the other way, he will win."*

J. Hawkins's statement in Carlill's case[62] has been cited as the most appropriate explanation of the term 'wager'. It goes in the following way-

A wagering contract is one by which two persons professing to hold opposite views touching the issue of a future uncertain event, mutually agree that, dependant on the determination of that event, one shall pay or handover him, a sum of money or other stake; neither of the contracting parties having any other interest in that contract than the sum or stake he will so win or lose, there being no other real consideration for making of such a contract by either of the parties. It is essential of wagering contract that each party may under it either win or lose, whether he will win or lose being dependent on the issue of the event, and, therefore, remaining uncertain until that issue is known. If either of the parties may win but cannot lose, it is not a wagering contract.

Wagering agreements are commonly known as **"betting"** or **"gambling"**, something stated to be lost or won on the result of a doubtful issue. Wagering agreement is an agreement between two parties in which one promises to pay money to the other on the happening of an

---

61. *Thacker v/s Hardy(1878) 4 O.B.D, 685*
62. *Supra note - 8*

uncertain event in consideration of other's promise to pay money on the non happening of that event. In other words, each party agrees to pay to money (or money's worth) to the other if an uncertain event does not occur or determine as per his view. Both parties have neither interest in it nor they have control over it. Their interest is to get the money i.e. the bet amount. Both have equal chances of winning or loosing.

*Example-*A promises B to pay Rs. 1000 if it rains tomorrow and B promises to pay A equal amount if it does not rain. Agreement is wager.

9.2 Essentials of Wagering Agreements

1. **Promise to pay money or money's worth**

   Wagering agreement involves a promise from each party to pay money or money's worth to his counter part.

2. **Uncertain event**

   As would be explained later, wager is a type of contingent contract. It is so because the promise is conditional upon happening or non-happening of an uncertain event. Payment depends upon the determination of an event in one-way or other. Uncertainty is to be understood as-uncertain future event or past event, not known to both parties. Wager is usually based on future uncertain occurrence.

   *Example-*M and N do not know the election result. M promises to pay N if candidate of his choice has won the election and N in turn promises to pay if his candidate has won. This amounts to wager because though the event is past, it is unknown to both the parties.

3. **Mutual chances of gain or loss**

   Each party must have equal opportunity either to win or lose. An important feature of wager is that one stands to win and other to lose. If one is to win but not to lose or vice-versa, it will not amount to wager.

4. **Neither party has interest in the event**

   Parties to wager should not have any interest in the very event. Their interest should be only the money (stake) to be won or lost. Insurance contract though akin to wager, is not wager as the insured has 'insurable interest' in the event contemplated. This factor distinguishes the two agreements.

5. **Neither party has control over the event**

   If one of the parties is having control or influence over the occurrence of the future event, transaction is not wager.

   *Example-*Two persons agree that if Rajdhani Express arrives in time on Sunday, one would pay Rs. 1000 to the other and if it were late, other would pay equal amount to the first. This agreement is void being wager. But if one of the two persons is the train driver of Rajdhani Express on Sunday, this is not a wager as one party has a control over arrival of the train.

6. Wager and Contingent Contracts

Wagering agreement is a contingent contract in the sense that payment of money i.e. performance of the contract, depends upon the happening or non-happening of an uncertain event. The big difference between the two is that contingent contracts are valid while wager is void.

7. Wager and Insurance Contracts

Insurance contract, though dependent upon happening of an uncertain event, is not a wager. Because of 'insurable interest' of the assured in the event, and other points of contrasts.[63] Both are contingent contracts.

8. Effects of Wagering Agreements

Legal consequences of wagering agreements may be summarized as under-

a) Wagering agreement is void-ab-initio, as declared by S.30. It is therefore, unenforceable.

b) **Stake not recoverable** - Sec. 30 makes it clear that no suit can be filed to recover the bet amount (stake). If it is deposited with a third person, stakeholder, it cannot be recovered from him by the winner. If stakeholder pays stake to the winner, he incurres no liability to the loser. Before actual payment to the winner, loser claim back the money deposited with stakeholder.[64]

c) **Effects on 'Collateral Transactions'-** If wagers are simply void, transaction collateral to wagers are not void, those are valid and enforceable. Borrowing of money to pay to the winner in betting is a transaction collateral to wager, but valid. If the wagers are 'illegal' and not merely void, the collateral transactions are also void and unenforceable. In the States of Maharashtra and Gujarath wagers are illegal.

Example - A borrows money from B to pay to C, who is the winner of a bet. Contract between A and B is valid.

9.3 Exceptions to "Agreement by way of Wager void"

In the following circumstances, transactions though similar to wager, are valid and enforceable.

1. **Horse Races** - According to the explanation provided to S. 30 subscriptions or contribution or any agreement to subscribe or contribute towards any plate or prize or sum of money of the value of Rs. 500 or more to be given to the winner of any horse race is not void.

2. **Crossword or Literary Competitions** - Crossword competitions require literary talent and application of skill are not purely speculative and hence those are not wager. In crossword competition where the best and skillful answer is rewarded, it is not betting. If merit of the solution is considered, it comes within exception.[65]

---

63. *in insurance contract, the assured is interested in protection of the life or property, it has public utility, social security, it is not speculative in nature, assessment of risk in it is based on the scientific method*

64. *Bridger v/s Savage(1885) 15 QBD 363*

65. Lord Heward *observed in Cole v/s Odhams press - "If skill plays a substantial part in the results and the prizes are awarded according to the merits of the solution, the competition is not a lottery. Otherwise it is."*

3. **Prize/ athletic competitions, games of skill, picture puzzles etc.-**As these involve skills, sports talent, are not regarded as gambling. An agreement to enter into a wrestling contest wherein the winner was to be rewarded the entire proceeds of tickets is not a wager. The Prize Competitions Act, 1955 legalizes the prize competitions in games of skill provided the prize money is not more than Rs. 1000.

4. **Lotteries or Raffle -** Lottery is a game of chance. Winner of a lottery gets the prize by drawing of lots. It amounts to a wager. Conducting lottery is also illegal u/s 294-A of IPC. As the position stands today, Government authorized /sponsored lotteries may be said to be legal and the winner of lottery can claim the prize money subject to payment of sales tax.

5. **Chit Fund -** Chit fund is a sort of investment scheme in which all the subscribers receive back their capital by a stipulated date. It is ruled that chit funds are not wager.[66]

6. **Share Market Transactions,** Teji-Mandi Transactions/Option Dealings-Sometimes demarcating line between genuine commercial transaction and speculative transaction is very thin. Honest dealings are to be protected. Intention is the deciding factor in such exchanges. Transactions for the sale of stocks, shares with intention of giving and taking of delivery of shares, are not wagers. Option dealings are speculative in nature wherein right to buy or sell goods at a fixed price is bargained at the time of entering into contract. Option dealings in securities are prohibited under Securities Contract (Regulation) Act, 1956. If intention is only to settle the price difference, and not effecting deliveries, transaction partakes the character of gambling.

---

66. *Narayan Ayyangar v/s K.Vellachami Ambalam-1927 ILR 50 Madras 696*

Chapter 10 | CONTINGENT CONTRACTS
(Sections- 31 TO 36)

Introduction

Contingent contract may be considered as a type of contract. This topic elaborates the concept of contingent contract and various circumstances in which such contracts are enforceable and when not.

10.1 Definition

> S.31-"A contingent contract is a contract to do or not to do something, if some event, collateral to such contract does or does not happen."

Contingent contract is like a conditional contract. A contract may be absolute or conditional. In absolute contract, the promise is performed unconditionally. In conditional contracts, the performance depends upon fulfillment of some conditions. These conditions may be either condition precedent or condition subsequent. 'Condition precedent ' is that condition which is to be satisfied first and then promise is to be performed. In 'condition subsequent', condition comes after the contract is entered into. By fulfillment of condition subsequent, effects of contract previously entered into are nullified. **The chapter** on contingent contract **deals with only conditions precedent** and not condition subsequent.

In simple words, contingent contract is a contract, the performance of which depends upon happening or non-happening of an uncertain event. The event is collateral to such contract. Contract of insurance; indemnity and guarantee are the known examples of contingent contract. Illustration - A contracts to pay B Rs. 10, 000 if B's house is burnt. This is a contingent contract.

10.2 Essentials of Contingent Contract

Following are the essentials of contingent contract.
1. Performance of contract depends upon happening or non-happening of an uncertain event-The peculiarity of contingent contract is that performance of contract is due only when a particular event happens or does not happen.

2. Event is future and uncertain- Contingency in the contingent contract is that the event may happen or may not happen. In this sense the event is uncertain.

3. Event is collateral -The condition specified in the contract must be collateral to such contract.

    According to Mulla, "-Collateral event is an event which is neither performance directly promised as a part of a contract, nor the whole of the consideration for a promise." Thus the condition should not be the part of the contract or the very performance of contract. It should not be the part of consideration.

    For example, A promises B a sum of money if B repairs his machine. Here that way condition for payment of money is repairs. But repairs is the very term in it. It is the performance of contract by B, and forms integral part of the contract. Such conditions are not collateral. Collateral means ancillary event, independent of contract.

4. If the performance of the contract depends upon the whim and pleasure of the promisor, it cannot be termed as a contract. If performance is dependant on the act of third party, that would be a collateral event.

    For example, A agrees with B to entrust the work of ship- building provided timber is made available by C. C's act is collateral to the contract between A& B.

10.3 Rules regarding Enforcement of Contingent Contracts

Sections 32 to 36 contemplate certain situations and lay down the rules as to when contingent contracts can be enforced and when those become void. The sections and the illustrations given below are self- explanatory. The chart may be referred for a better understanding of the subject matter.

1. **S. 32**-Enforcement of contracts contingent on an **event happening**. -If contingent contract (to do or not to do anything) depends upon the happening of an uncertain future event, it cannot be enforced unless and until the event happens. It becomes void if the occurrence of event becomes impossible.

    Illustration- 1 -A makes a contract with B to buy B's horse if A survives C. This contract cannot be enforced by law unless and until C dies in A's lifetime.

    Illustration- 2 -A contracts to pay B a sum of money when B marries C. C dies without being married to B. The contract becomes void.

2. **S. 33**- Enforcement of contracts contingent on an **event not happening.** -Contingent contract to do or not to do anything, if an uncertain future event does not happen, can be enforced when the happening of that event becomes impossible. Before that event becomes impossible, contract cannot be enforced.

    Illustration -A agrees to pay B a sum of money if certain ship does not return. The ship is sunk. The contract can be enforced when the ship sinks and not before.

3. **S. 34**- Enforcement of contracts contingent on **future conduct of a living person.** - Sometimes the contingency in the contract is the conduct (act) of a third person at future unspecified time. His act cannot be predicted at the time of entering into contract.

Therefore, how he will act is the uncertain event. This event shall be considered impossible when such person (by his act) renders the event impossible **within any definite time**. When the event thus rendered impossible, contract cannot be enforced.

Illustration - A agrees to pay B a sum of money if B marries C. C marries D. The marriage of B to C must now be considered impossible, although it is possible that D may die, and that C may afterwards marry B.

4. **S. 35-** Enforcement of contracts contingent on an event **happening or non- happening within a fixed time.** -This section covers two situations and can be treated as an extension of section 32 &33 with added feature of time.
    a) If the contingency is the happening of an uncertain future event within a fixed time, then the performance of contract is due when uncertain future event happens within that fixed time. It becomes void when-
        - The uncertain future event becomes impossible within the stipulated time or
        - The uncertain future event does not happen within that time.

Illustration - A agrees to pay B a sum of money if a certain ship returns within a year. The contract may be enforced if the ship returns within the year, and becomes void if the ship is burnt within the year.

    b) If the contract is contingent on non-happening of uncertain event within the fixed time, then contract is enforceable in the following two eventualities-
        - When the event does not occur within that time or
        - When the event becomes impossible within that time.

Illustration - A agrees to pay B a sum of money if a certain ship does not return within a year. The contract may be enforced if the ship does not return within the year, or is burnt within the year.

5. **S. 36-**Agreements contingent on impossible events. -An agreement dependant upon happening of an impossible event is absolutely void. Knowledge of parties about impossibility of event is irrelevant. Law will never support impossibility whether known or unknown.

Illustration - A agrees to pay B 1000 rupees if two straight lines should enclose a space. The agreement is void.

Chapter 11 | PERFORMANCE OF CONTRACT

The object of contract would be accomplished when a contract is performed. When parties undertake and complete their part of contract, those are discharged. Performance is the fulfillment of legal obligations and it is the natural and satisfactory mode of discharge of contract. This chapter explains the provisions relating to manner, time and place of performance, who can perform etc.

11.1 Offer of Performance

According to S. 37 of the Contract Act, the parties are obliged to perform their part of the contract. If the performance is dispensed with or excused under the Act or any other law, they need not perform the contract. Performance of the contract is possible in two ways-
a - Actual performance or
b - Offer of performance **(Tender of performance)**

When the parties act as per the terms of the contract, it is said to be performed actually. Attempt to perform is an offer of performance.

Importance of offer of performance / Effects of refusal to accept offer of performance. Though short of actual performance, valid offer of performance is equivalent to performance. When offer is made, it is for the promisee to accept it. If it is not accepted wrongfully (without any legal justification), S. 38 lays down the following consequences-
a - The promisor is not responsible for non performance and
b - He does not lose his rights under the contract.

Thus once the promisor tenders the performance, he is not liable for any breach. He can claim remedies if he suffers due to non-acceptance of offer of performance. But for this, tender should be legal and valid. S. 38 enlists the conditions of valid offer, which are discussed below. -

Conditions for Validity of Offer (Tender) of Performance.

1. **Unconditional Offer**
   The offer of performance should be unqualified and absolute. It must be as per the terms of the contract. If the dealer delivers the goods under a contract but demanding the

money at a rate more than agreed, the tender of goods is conditional. If the order placed is of 100 articles and the supplier sends 80, this is not a good tender as it is in violation of terms of contract.

2. **Tender of the whole obligation**

Offer should cover the whole obligation. It cannot be partial. Where the consumer expects the delivery at one time, then delivery of goods in instalment is an invalid tender.

3. **At proper time and place**

See sections- 46 to 50, 55

4. **By whom?**

The promisor or his representative can validly offer to perform the contract. Refer S.40.

5. **To whom?**

Offer of performance may be made to the promisee or his representatives. S. 38 clarifies that offer to one of joint promises is, in law, an offer to all of them. That means promisor need not offer to each one of them.

6. **"Ready and willingness to perform"**

The party offering to perform must be both ready and willing to perform the contract there and then only. He may be ready but not willing or vice-versa. In both the cases offer is bad in law. A debtor is ready with money but may not desire to pay off the dues or he is very much willing to pay all outstanding dues but has no money with him. What section 38 requires is that the performance should be offered in such circumstances that the offeror should be both ready and willing at the same time to perform the whole contract.

7. **Reasonable opportunity to ascertain**

The tender should be made under such circumstances that the other party must have reasonable opportunity to verify two things-

a) The offeror is "ready and willing to perform the contract there and then only"; and

b) The offeror is attempting to discharge the entire obligation under the contract.

The contracting party should be able to know whether the tender is as per the stipulations or not. There may be many terms as to the quality, quantity or even packing. Reasonable opportunity to ascertain is necessary to exercise the right of rejection of offer effectively.

8. **Form of tender**

Offer must be in the form as stipulated in the contract. Any deviation gives a right to refuse to accept the offer. If the mode of payment (cash or cheque or DD etc.) is suggested, it should be in that prescribed mode. Tender of money is possible with actual production of money. Again tender of money must be in legal tender, 'money' and not in foreign currency or promissory note or a cheque.

In connection with the performance of contract, following sections may be studied.

S. 39 - **Refusal to Perform** - If the promisor refuses to perform the contract, the promisee can put an end to the contract unless his acquiescence to continuance is signified. Disablement from performance has the same consequences. Refusal must be absolute with clear intention not to perform the contract.

11.2 S. 40 - Person by whom promise is to be performed

Following persons can perform the promise -

a) The **promisor himself,** should perform in case of contracts of personal nature. In such contracts parties intend that the very party should perform it. Where the personal skill, expertise is bargained, contract is of personal nature. For example, a pop star agrees to perform the show for one night or a dentist is engaged to make a denture. His performance cannot be assigned to any other person.

b) The **promisor or his representatives or agent,** may perform in case of non-personal contracts. Payment of money or delivery of goods is possible through the agents, promisee himself need not do that.

c) **Legal Representative-**Sec 37 states that "… Promises bind the representatives of the promisor in case of the death of such promisor before performance, unless a contrary intention appears from the contract."

*Illustration-*A promises to paint a picture for B by a certain day, at a certain price. A dies before the day. The contract cannot be enforced either by A's representatives or by B.

d) **Third person-**Ordinarily a third person cannot perform the contract between two others. But S. 41 provides that when promisee accepts performance of promise by third person, he cannot afterwards enforce it against the promisor. When the promisee is satisfied with the performance from Third person, the promisor is discharged. This section is based on the principle of estoppel.

11.3 Performance Of Joint Promises (Sections 42 to 45)

There may be more than one promisor or promisee in a contract. If there are more than one promisor those are called a joint promisor and if there are more than one promisee, those are called a joint promisees. Joint promisors are subjected to joint liabilities and joint promisees are entitled for joint rights. In case of death of joint promisor or promisee who is to perform the contract or who has a right to performance assumes significance. The relevant provisions are explained below.

Devolution of Joint Liabilities and Rights.

The rules relating to the devolution of joint liability and rights contained in sections 42 to 45 are summarized below. These rules are 'subject to the contract to the contrary' meaning thereby that private agreement would override the rule. That arrangement between the parties would govern the situation and the rule would be ignored.

A, B and C jointly execute a promissory note in favor of D. ABC are joint promisors. A executes a promissory note in favor of BCD. Here BCD are joint promisees.

Devolution of Joint Liabilities

1. **S.42**-All the joint promisors, during their joint lives, must fulfill their contractual promises. If any one of them dies then the representatives of the deceased and the survivor or survivors (surviving promisors) are jointly liable to perform the contract. After the death of the last survivor, the representatives of all the deceased promisors must fulfill the promises jointly.

2. **S.43 — *Joint and several liabilities*** - The liability of joint promisors is joint and several. This means that they are liable collectively and at the same time independently to perform the promises. From this it follows that the promisee may choose any one of them and compel him to perform whole of the promise. Promisor cannot insist promisee to join other promisors to perform the contract.

   Illustration - A, B and C jointly promise to pay D 3000 rupees. A, B and C are collectively liable pay the amount to D or in the alternative, A or B or C are liable to pay. D may compel either A or B or C to pay him 3000 rupees.

   ***Right of Contribution among joint promisors*-**The promisor who alone is compelled to perform the contract has a right of contribution from other joint promisor or promisors. In the absence of contract to the contrary, the contribution is equal among the joint promisors.

   Sharing of loss(deficiency) by default in contribution. -Whenever there is a default in contribution by any joint promisor, that deficiency is regarded as loss which again would be shared in equal proportion.

   Illustration - A, B and C jointly promise to pay D 3000 rupees. C is compelled to pay the whole. A is insolvent and cannot pay 1000 rupees as his share. This loss is to be shared by B and C equally i.e. 500 rupees each. C is entitled to receive 500 from B.

3. **S.44-*Effect of release of one joint promisor*** - The promisee can release (discharge) one or more promisor as the case may be, and hold other liable to perform. Release has two consequences. -

   a) Other promisor or joint promisor (who are not released) remain liable and are not discharged;

   b) Released joint promisor is responsible to(contribute) other joint promisor or joint promisors.

Devolution of Joint Rights

4. **S. 45** - In the case of joint promises, all the joint promisees, during their joint lives have right to claim the performance from the promisor. If any one of them dies then right to claim performance rests with the representatives of the deceased person and the survivor or survivors (surviving promisees). After the death of the last survivor, the representatives of all the deceased promisees can claim the performance jointly.

   Illustration - A, in consideration of 5000 rupees lent to him by B and C, promises B and C jointly to repay them that sum with interest on a day specified. B dies. The right to claim performance rests with B's representatives jointly with C during C's life, and, after the death of C, with the representatives of B and C jointly.

11.4 Time and Place of Performance. (Ss.-46 to 50, 55)

The provisions governing the time and place of performance are briefed in the following paragraphs. The provision is explained by laying down the rule and the circumstances (conditions of applicability of the relevant section) in which rule applies. Refer the chart.

1. **S.46** — The contract must be performed within reasonable time,
   — when time for performance is not specified and
   — promisor has to perform without request/application by the promisee.
   What is a reasonable time, in a particular case, is a question of fact.

2. **S.47** — The promisor may perform the promise at any time during the usual working hours of business on a fixed day,
   — when promisor has to perform without request/application by the promisee and
   — when he has to perform on a certain day (on a fixed day).
   In this situation, the place of performance would be the place at which the promise ought to be performed.

3. **S.48** — The promisee has to apply for performance at proper place and within usual working hours of business,
   — when promise is to be performed on a certain day and
   — the promisee is under a duty to apply for performance.

4. **S.49** — The promisor is under duty to apply to the promisee to appoint a reasonable place of performance and to perform the promise at that place,
   —when the promise is to be performed on application by the promisee and
   —no place for performance is fixed.

5. **S.50**-The section provides- The performance of any promise may be made in any manner, or at any time which the promisee prescribes or sanctions. Law gives liberty to the parties to decide the terms as to time, place and manner of performance as per their convenience.

6. **S.55**-*When 'time of performance is the essence of contract...*
   Many times the time of performance gains significance. The parties are keen on either the period within which the promise is to be performed or they fix up a specific day for performance of contract. In such contracts, time schedule is to be strictly followed. Failure gives rise to remedies like cancellation of contract or compensation.

The law contained in section 55 may be summarized as under.

a) When **time is the essence** of contract –
   If the party fails to perform at or before a stipulated time, the **contract is voidable** at the option of the promisee.

b) When **time is not the essence** of contract –
   The **contract does not become voidable** if the promise is not fulfilled within or at a specified time. However, the promisee is entitled to compensation for the loss he suffers on account of failure. It is to be noted that though the time is not made the essence of contract, the contract must be performed within reasonable time.

c) When compensation is not available?

If the contract is voidable at the option of the promisee but instead of putting an end to it, accepts the performance after the fixed time, he cannot claim the compensation for the loss caused due to promisor's failure. To claim compensation he has to give a notice to the promisor, at the time of acceptance of delayed performance, of his intention to reserve such a right.

d) Intention as to treat time as the essence of contract –

Whether the time would be essence of contract or not, depends upon the intention of the parties. It may be made express by including specific clauses in the document as to time factor. Intention may be implied and gathered from the conduct of parties or course of dealing between them. A surgeon orders life saving drugs for operation in his hospitals. Drugs should be supplied without delay.

11.5 Performance of Reciprocal promises

Definition of Reciprocal Promise u/s 2(f)- "Promises which form the consideration or part of consideration for each other are called reciprocal promises."

Provisions regarding performance of reciprocal promises –

a. **Simultaneous performance of reciprocal promises - S.51 -** When reciprocal promises are to be performed simultaneously, the promisor need not perform his promise unless the promisee is ready and willing to perform his reciprocal promise.

b. **Order of performance - S.52 -** If the order of performance of reciprocal promises is expressly fixed in the contract then that order is to be followed. In case the order of performance is not expressly stated, those are to be performed in the order which the nature of transaction permits.

Illustration- A and B contract that A shall build a house for B at fixed price. A's promise to build house must be performed before B's promise to pay for it.

c. **Consequences of prevention of performance (S. 53) -** Where a party prevents performance by other party, the contract turns voidable at the option of party prevented. Loss as a result of prevention must be compensated by party preventing.

Illustration – A transporter contracts to carry and deliver merchandise to B for Rs. 10,000/- as transportation charges. B himself prevents the carriage. A may cancell the contract and claim damages from B for losses he suffers due to cancellation.

d. **Performance of promise depends upon other's performance (S. 54) –** Sometimes promisor can perform his promise only when other party does certain act. Unless such act (or other's part performance) is performed, performance of promise can not be claimed.

Illustration – A agrees to build a ship for B who promises to provide necessary timber and pay the charges for ship construction. B can not claim construction of ship unless and until he supplies timber to A. Not only that, B must compensate A for his losses if he does not supply timber.

e. **Contract involving legal and illegal activities – (S. 57)** – Section applies when under a contract consisting reciprocal promises, parties agree to do legal things first and then illegal things. The first set of reciprocal promises covering legal things is valid and enforceable while second set is void. It is however necessary that sets of the promises (legal and illegal) are separable.

Illustration – X contracts to sell Y, a drug for medicinal purposes at Rs. 1000/- per gram. They also agree that if Y uses drug for purposes prohibited under the Act, rate would be Rs. 5000/- instead of Rs. 1000/-. First part of contract is valid, second void for illegality.

Chapter 12	QUASI - CONTRACTS

12.1 Relations Resembling Contractual Relationship-Sections- 68 to 72

General Explanation-The term "quasi-contract" is neither defined nor used in the Contract Act. The title of the chapter in the Act dealing with quasi-contract is **"Of Certain Relations Resembling Those Created by Contract." "Quasi" means "similar" or "resembling".** There are certain situations wherein the persons do not enter into contract but there exists some kind of legal nexus between them. Their relationship is similar to contractual relationship. In contracts, rights and liabilities are created. In this type of relation, rights and duties are created by of law. If you forget a valuable at someone's house you feel that he should return it to you. That is exactly law implies in terms of duty to return forgotten article. Quasi-contract thus is a creation of law. It is also described as ''constructive contract'' in English Law.

Principle-The concept is based on the principle of **"unjust enrichment"**, i.e. no one should grow rich at the cost of other. In other words, no person can enrich himself unjustly, at the expense of other.[67] The principle of equity, good conscience and fairness lies at the foundation of this relationship. If someone gets the benefit from other to which he is not entitled, justice requires that he should either return it or pay for it.

12.2 Provisions regarding Quasi-Contracts

Sections 68 to 72 embody the law relating to quasi-contract. These sections contemplate situations and lay down the rule governing that situation. The sections are explained in that fashion.

1. **Sec. 68-Supply of necessaries to incompetent person-**''If a person, incapable of entering into contract or anyone whom he is legally bound to support, is supplied by another person with necessaries suited to his condition in life, the person who has furnished such supplies is entitled to be reimbursed from the property of such incapable person.''

---

67. *Lord Mansfield is considered as the real founder of such sort of obligations who offered explanation for the term, in Moses v/s Macferlan- (1760) 2 Burr 1005, All ER Rep 581.*

Conditions for invoking the section -

a) The person benefited must be **incompetent** to enter into contract. (Ref. Sections 11 & 12.) Section applies to necessaries supplied to minor, insane or other category of incapable persons. It also applies to those, whom these incompetent persons are bound by law, to support. (Refer illustration-ii, below)

b) Other person supplies him **necessaries suitable to his condition in life**. **Necessaries**-Necessaries are those things which are required to maintain one's life. Those include expenses incurred for food, clothes, medical treatment, and upbringing of a child. The concept also extends to cost of performance of religious ceremonies, marriage or funeral expenses, cost of maintaining or defending suits etc.

c) **Right of reimbursement**-The person who supplies the necessaries has a right to be compensated for the expenses incurred. These expenses would be recoverable only from the property of incompetent. He has no remedy against his person.

Illustration - i) A supplies B, a lunatic, with necessaries suitable to his condition in life. A is entitled to be reimbursed from B's property.

Illustration - ii) A supplies to the wife and children of B, a lunatic, with necessaries suitable to their condition in life. A is entitled to be reimbursed from B's property.

2. **Sec. 69-Payment by interested person**
   S. 69 states - "A person who is interested in the payment of money which another is bound by law to pay, and who therefore pays it, is entitled to be reimbursed by the other."

   Example - T is a tenant of agricultural land belonging to B. As the land revenue is in arrears, land is advertised for sale by the government authority. As per the land laws, such a sale annuls (cancels) the tenancy and tenant loses possession of the land. T, to prevent the sale and consequent annulment of his own lease, pays to the government the sum due from B. B is bound to make good to T the amount so paid.

   To exercise the right of reimbursement under this section, following are the **conditions of liability. -**

   a) **A person is under a duty to pay**- There should be a legal duty to pay money under law or under contract. The section relates to obligation to pay only and not other kinds of obligations.

   b) **Other is interested in making payment**. -The payer must be interested in making the payment. His intention in making the payment due by other should be to protect his interest in the subject matter.

   c) **Payment should not be voluntary** in the sense that it should be made to safeguard his interest.

   d) Payment should be made to third person and not to himself.

3. **Sec. 70-Liability to pay for non-gratuitous acts**-"Where a person lawfully does anything for another person, or delivers anything to him, not intending to do so gratuitously, and such other person enjoys the benefit thereof, the latter is bound to make compensation to the former in respect of, or to restore, the thing so done or delivered."

Illustration - i) A, a tradesman, leaves goods at B's house by mistake. B treats the goods as his own. B is bound to pay A for them.

Illustration - ii) A saves B's property from fire. A is not entitled to compensation from B, if circumstances show that he intended to act gratuitously.

Many times a person is benefited by the voluntary but non-gratuitous acts of another. Section vests a right of compensation or restoration of benefit in the doer of such acts.

Conditions of liability to compensate or restore[68]

a) **A person lawfully does something for another or delivers something to him-** Whatever is done non-gratuitously, should be rendered lawfully. Section does not compensate non-gratuitous but illegal or unlawful services.

b) **He does so not intending to do gratuitously-**The person does the act or delivers something voluntarily but it is not a gratuitous act. While doing so for another, he must have thought of some return, or of money being paid. What section requires is a non-gratuitous act. Every one comes across with such acts for example, services offered by tradesmen, say, banker, overstay in the premises by a tenant, extra work done during continuance or after termination of contract etc. In the cases of this sort, there is no mentioning of consideration but law implies it in this kind of relationship.

c) **Other person must derive benefit from non-gratuitous act or services.**[69] If there is no 'enrichment', case falls outside the scope of quasi-contract.

d) The person benefited is under duty to compensate the former or restore/return the thing delivered.

4. **Sec. 71-Responsibility of finder of goods-**A person, who finds goods belonging to another and takes them into his custody, is subject to the same responsibility as a bailee. **Position of finder of goods-**By this section the finder of lost article is placed at par with bailee. Section reflects contract of bailment between the finder and the true owner of the goods. His rights and duties are discusses in the chapter on Bailment.

5. **Sec. 72-Money paid or thing delivered under mistake-**This section states- "A person to whom money has been paid or anything delivered by mistake or under coercion must repay or return it."

Illustration - A and B jointly owe 100 rupees to C. A alone pays the mount to C and B not knowing the fact pays 100 rupees again to C. C is bound to repay the amount to B.

---

68. *J.Gajendragadkar in State of West Bangal v/s B. K. Mandal-AIR (1962) SC779*
69. *Upendra v/s Naba (25 - BAL W. N. 813)*

Chapter 13 | DISCHARGE OF CONTRACT

Discharge of contract means termination of contract. In discharge, contractual relationship comes to an end. The rights and obligations of the parties, which is the result of a contract, are extinguished. After discharge, right and liabilities do not exist. 'Discharge of party' implies termination of one party's relationship with other parties. In that case contract very much subsists. In discharge of contract, the whole relationship is dissolved.

Modes of Discharge : A contract is discharged in any of the following ways. (For various modes of discharge at a glance, see the chart.)
   1 - By performance,
   2 - By Agreement,
   3 - By Operation of Law,
   4 - By Lapse of Time,
   5 - By Subsequent Impossibility, and
   6 - By Breach.

13.1 Discharge by Performance

Performance of contract is the natural, usual and satisfactory way of discharge of contract. By performance (by both the parties), the object of contract is fulfilled and the relationship comes to an end happily. The parties are no more under obligation to do anything under the contract. Nothing remains to be done. As we have seen in the topic of performance, it can be either actual or offer of performance. (Refer the chapter on 'Performance of Contract')

13.2 Discharge by Mutual Agreement

An agreement leads to a contract; similarly it may lead to its termination.

Discharge by agreement may take the form of novation, rescission, and alteration, remission and waiver. Sec. 62 covers first three modes of discharge viz. novation, rescission, and alteration while sec. 63 provides for remission.

Sec. 62 states - "If the parties to a contract agree to substitute a new contract for it, or to rescind or alter it, the original contract need not be performed."

a) **Novation-**This phrase originates from **'novatio'**, meaning **'change'**. Novation implies substitution of existing contract by a new contract.[70] "Novation occurs when a new contract is substituted for an existing contract, either between the same parties or between different parties, the consideration mutually being the discharge of old contract." The essence of novation of contract lies not in the dissimilarity of the terms between the old and the new contract, but in the intention of the parties to supercede the old by new.

Novation may be by –
i) Substitution of old contract by new one or
ii) Change of parties.

i) Substitution-Here the parties replace existing contract by a new contract. Between the same parties a new contract is entered into by which original contract is discharged.

ii) Change of parties-When a party to the contract is substituted by a new one without change in the nature of contract, novation occurs. Contract continues but with changed parties. When new partners are introduced in the existing firm, new team takes over the liabilities of the old firm, which illustrates novation. Arrangement by way of composition in bankruptacy can also be its example.

Illustration- A avails a loan from bank for purchase of a flat. Loan is outstanding. B agrees to purchase the A's flat and repay the outstanding dues of the bank. Banker accepts B as a new borrower instead of A. This is novation by change of parties.

Illustration- A owes B Rs. 10000. A enters into an agreement with B, and gives B a mortgage of his (A's) estate for Rs. 5000 in place of the debt of Rs. 10000. This is a new contract and extinguishes the old.

Conditions for valid novation-For validity of novation following are the prerequisites.
i) Original contract must be subsisting, enforceable;
ii) Novation should take place before the expiry of period fixed for performance of contract.
iii) Breach of contract should not occur because that changes the legal position altogether;
iv) New contract should be valid and enforceable; if it is not so original contract is treated as subsisting.
v) Novation contemplates concurrence of all parties to the contract.

b) **Rescission-**Rescission simply means 'cancellation of contract'. It is highly important that it is cancelled before it is performed or discharged in any recognized way. Rescission is possible in the following situations-
1) Rescission by mutual consent all parties; respective parties abandon mutual promises/rights and the parties are released from mutual obligations.
2) Rescission by one party when other fails to perform his part of contract. A party has a statutory right to repudiate the contract if other commits a breach, in addition to the right of damages;
3) Rescission by the party whose consent is not free i.e. when the contract is voidable u/s 19 and 19-A.

---

70. *Scarfe v/s Jardine (1882) 7 APP Cas 345*

c) **Alteration-**Alteration involves changes in the terms of the contract. New stipulations may be inserted or few deleted from the original deed. That changes contract in material particulars. It should be noted that the alteration should be of material (important) terms. For example, amount of consideration, subject matter or time of performance, which assume importance in a contract. Material alteration changes the legal position/relationship between the parties.

Alteration differs from novation in the sense that alteration is restricted to major changes in the terms while novation substitutes the old contract.

d) **Remission-**Sec. 63 of the Act lays down that "Every person who accepts a proposal may dispense with or remit wholly or in part the performance of the proposal made to him which he has accepted, or may extend the time for such performance....."

Sec. 63 refers to three contingencies when performance by a party is due, which are enlisted below-

i) Remission or dispensation of performance or

ii) Extension of time for performance or

iii) Acceptance of some other satisfaction in lieu of performance.

Remission is a sort of concession or rebate given to the party who is under a duty to perform the contract. Remission is "the acceptance of a lesser sum than what was contracted for or a lesser fulfillment of the promise made." A party may treat non-performance or part performance of a contract equivalent to full performance or discharge of a contract. Remission may be total, or partial. In total remission, party is completely exempted from performance by the other party who can demand it.

Illustration -A owes B 15000 rupees. A pays B and B accepts 12000 rupees in full satisfaction of the whole debt. The whole debt is discharged.

e) **Accord and Satisfaction-**Truly speaking this is a mode of discharge recognized in English Law. Accord means agreement to accept lesser performance than what is due under a contract. Satisfaction is the consideration for such agreement. Accord is a promise while satisfaction is the actual fulfillment of the lesser performance. Accord followed by satisfaction discharges the contract.

An accord without satisfaction is unenforceable under English Law. For the discharge of a contract accord and satisfaction should be made simultaneously.

Accord and satisfaction as such is not followed in India. Sec. 63 makes it clear that for remission and subsequent discharge, consideration is not necessary. Promisee may remit a part of his claim for which no consideration is necessary.

Illustration -A owes B Rs. 10,000. B agrees to accept Rs. 7500 in full satisfaction. The agreement to pay 7500 is an accord and actual payment is the satisfaction.

f) **Waiver-**Waiver means **'giving up'** or **'abandonment'** of a right or claim. When a breach of contract is committed, the party injured has a right to take legal action against the defaulter. If he does not insist on this right, the defaulter is discharged from performance. Waiver thus releases one party from performance of contract. Waiver in fact does not require agreement but as relinquishment of a right is voluntary and deliberate, and the consequence is the discharge, it is taken up as an independent mode of discharge. Consideration is not necessary for waiver. It should be an intentional act with knowledge of attending circumstances.

*Example-*A promises to provide catering services for B. Afterwards B himself forbids A from providing that service. B has waived his right to claim performance.

g) **Merger-**Merger is the union of inferior and superior right. When the rights of two different quality coincide and meet in one and the same person, merger is said to occur. The right of inferior quality loses its existence as it disappears into the right of superior quality. In merger, while rights combine, parties and the subject matter remain the same.

*Example -*T is the tenant of a house under a lease agreement. He purchases the very house from his landlord and becomes the owner by virtue of a sale deed. Tenant's inferior right of possession is merged into superior right of ownership and that is vested with one person i.e. tenant. Here old contract of tenancy is discharged by new contract of sale through merger.

13.3 Discharge by Operation of Law

In certain circumstances parties may not be willing to terminate the contractual relationship, but the relationship comes to an end by operation of law. In the following cases the contract is terminated by implications of law.

a) **Death -** In case of contracts of personal nature, contract is discharged by death of a party. Contracts involving personal skill, expertise, are discharged on the death of the promisor. A promises to paint a picture for B. A dies before painting. Contract is discharged.

b) **Insolvency-**When a person is adjudged insolvent by insolvency court, he is discharged from all his liabilities and obligations under the existing contracts. An adjudicated insolvent is not liable to pay his debts. His property, assets are apportioned amongst the competing creditors by the official assignee/receiver appointed by the court.

c) **Unauthorized Alterations-**Alterations in the contractual terms by one party without other's knowledge or permission discharges the contract. These alterations should be material and made without other's consent. Changes in the important terms of the contract are material alterations. Alterations to give effect to the common intention of both the parties or to rectify the trivial or clerical/typographical mistakes do not discharge the contract.

13.4 Discharge By Lapse of Time

When promisor commits a breach of contract, the party suffering by breach has a right to take legal action (suit) against the promisor. Such a suit must be filed within the period of limitation fixed by the Law of Limitation. (Normally it is three years from the day of breach) If the suit is not preferred within that period, the aggrieved party loses judicial remedies under the contract. That way the contract becomes unenforceable and law regards it as discharged.

13.5 Discharge By Breach

Contract can also be discharged by its breach by one of the parties. Default in performance may put an end to contract. According to section 39, the breach of contract means-
i) Refusal to perform the contract or
ii) Disabling oneself from performing the promise.

Thus breach occurs due to refusal or negligence or disablement from performance of contract. Breach is a failure to perform the contract or non-complianceof contractual stipulations. Refusal to perform should be absolute, without an intention to perform the contract in its entirety. Non-payment of price, non-delivery of goods, failure to provide services are few examples of breach. The party renounces his liability to perform contractual obligations.

How the breach may be committed? **(Kinds of Breach)**
The breach may be committed in the following ways-
A) Actual Breach and **B)** Anticipatory Breach.

A) **Actual Breach** -According to section 55, when a party fails to perform a contract when the performance is due, the breach is committed. The aggrieved then can persue the remedies provided under the law. Actual breach can be better explained from following points of view. -
   i) Breach when the performance is due – When a promisor refuses or fails to perform his part of contract at the time when the performance is due, the actual breach take place.
   ii) Breach during the performance of contract – Sometimes the party commences his work under the contract but afterwards discontinues or violates the terms and conditions agreed upon. Promisee in such cases also may treat it as a breach for the remaining part of the contract.

B) **Anticipatory Breach** - Breach of contract may be foreseen or anticipated in peculiar circumstances. One party may realize before the time of actual performance that the other party is not going to perform his part of the contract. Anticipatory breach of contract occurs in the following way —
   i) Repudiation of contract – Before the day of performance arrives, a party repudiates his liability under the contract. It's a case of renouncing the contract before performance. Anticipatory breach may be express or implied.

   Example - A agrees with B to supply electronic equipment on 1st of May. On 10th of April, A informs B that he will not be able to supply it. B is entitled to sue A immediately for breach of contract.

   ii) Making the performance of contract impossible – Before the performance falls due, if a party makes the performance of contract impossible, anticipatory breach results. By doing some voluntary act, promisor may render his performance impossible on the due date.

   Example - A promises to marry B in the month of December. But prior to that in April he marries C. marriage between A and B becomes impossible.

Legal implications of anticipatory breach -The promisee has following two options in case of anticipatory breach –

i) In anticipatory breach he need not wait till the day of performance arrives. He may treat anticipatory breach as actual breach. Promisee can cancel the contract and in that case, he is discharged from his contractual obligations. He can immediately sue promisor for legal remedies.

ii) In the alternative, promisee may ignore the anticipatory breach (in whatever way it is communicated to him) and may prefer to wait till the due date of performance. If the promisor fails to perform the contract on the due date, then promisee can take legal action against him for breach of contract.

If the promisee prefers **second option**, the **legal position** would be as follows-

— The promisor may change his mind or on reconsideration perform the contract on the due date and the promisee will be bound to accept the performance;

— The contract is kept alive and subsisting for the benefit of promisor till the date of performance.

— The promisor can take the advantage of any supervening impossibility, which discharges the contract. The promisor would be relieved of his liability due to earlier breach, in case of discharge by change in circumstances subsequently. The promisee thus loses the right to sue for damages in spite of initial anticipatory breach.

Example

Hochster v/s De La Tour[71] H engaged D as a courier on a tour from 1st June 1852 for three months at 10(British) pounds per month. Before the expiry of three months, H informed D in writing that he no more needed his services. In the suit instituted by D for breach of contract, it was held that H expressly repudiated the contract and D was not required to wait till the day of performance as he was having immediate right to take action for reliefs.

13.6 Discharge By Supervening Impossibility

Law does not recognize impossibility. Impossibility creates no obligations. Impossibility seriously affects the contractual relationship. S.56 of the Contract Act states, *"An agreement to do an act impossible in itself is void.... A contract to do an act, which after the contract is made, becomes impossible, or by reason of some event which the promisor could not prevent, becomes void when the act becomes impossible or unlawful..."*

Section 56 thus covers two situations of impossibility of performance —

1) **Initial (Existing) Impossibility**-This is impossibility existing when an agreement is entered into. This initial or absolute impossibility makes agreement void-ab-initio. It is void whether such impossibility is known or unknown to the parties.

*Example-*An agreement to discover treasure by magic or to put life in dead man etc. is impossible in itself and hence void. Such acts are obviously impossible.

---

71. *(1853-2E& B 678)*

2) **Subsequent or Supervening Impossibility** -Section 56 embodies the doctrine of supervening impossibility. Sometimes performance of contract is possible when it is concluded or entered into but it becomes impossible afterwards due to some event or changes in the circumstances. Subsequent impossibility is non-obvious by nature. In such cases the contract will be void and the parties are discharged.

On account of intervening events (events occurring between conclusion of contract and actual performance) parties cannot perform the contract. For example, natural calamity, war, emergency laws may hit the foundation of contract. These supervening circumstances are outside the knowledge or control of the parties. Impossibility does not mean literal or physical impossibility but it is practical impossibility. Supervening impossibility also covers those cases where, due to subsequent event, performance is impractical and useless considering the object in contemplation of parties.

Illustration - A and B contract to marry each other. Before the time fixed for marriage, A goes mad. The contract becomes void.

Conditions of applicability of the doctrine-The doctrine of supervening impossibility applies if following conditions are satisfied-
1) There should be a contract subsisting between the parties.
2) Intervening event or change in circumstances takes place after contract is entered into.
3) The supervening event is beyond the knowledge or control of the parties.
4) The performance of contract becomes impossible due to the supervening event.
5) Impossibility should not be self induced by negligence or act of the promisor.

Discharge of contract by supervening impossibility – The principle of supervening impossibility applies to variety of contracts. Following grounds of impossibility as a mode of discharge are well established.

a) **Death or personal incapacity of the promisor**-When the personal skill or qualification of the promisor is the basis of the contract, the death or physical incapacity of the promisor discharges the contract.

Example-A agrees with B to play piano at a concert on a fixed day. On account of illness, A could not perform his promise. Held that contract becomes void.

b) **Destruction of subject matter**-When specific property or goods are the subject matter of the contract, its destruction results in discharge of contract. The destruction need not be total. It is sufficient if destruction prevents the performance.

Taylor v/s Caldwell [72] - A let out a music hall to B for series of concerts. Before the date of first concert, the hall was destroyed by fire. It was ruled that contract had become void due to destruction of subject matter of contract (hall).

c) **Change of Law**-An agreement which is forbidden by law is void(S. 23). An agreement may be legal when it is entered into but later on, on account of changes in law, it may become illegal. In the altered legal position, contact is discharged, as its performance is made legally impossible. Subsequent alterations of law may prevent the performance altogether. Recently Maharashtra Government through a new law has banned cow

---

72. *(1863) 122 ER 299*

slaughter. All contracts involving slaughtering, storing, distribution and sale of cow flesh, made before the Act came into force, would become void and inoperative.

d) **Outbreak of War-** One cannot enter into a contract with an alien enemy. Contracts entered into with foreign nationals before the outbreak of war are either suspended or declared void by the government. If suspended, those can be revived after the war is over. If those are made void, the contracts stand discharged.

*Illustration-*A contracts to take in cargo for B at certain port. A's government afterwards declares war against the country in which the port is situated. The contract becomes void when the war is declared.

e) **Non existence of particular state of things as a basis of contract**
Doctrine of frustration in *English Law-* Contracting parties may assume certain state of things (circumstances) for performance of contract. The existence of state of things is the basis of contract. If the state of things ceases to exist or change, due to some subsequent event, the contract is discharged. There is no destruction of subject matter and the contract is capable of performance in literal sense but the object of the contract fails owing to supervening event. The following case would explain the position.

Krell v/s Henry[73] - H hired a room from a lodger, K for two days to view a coronation procession of King Edward 7th. Contract was silent as to object of hiring but K was knowing it. Procession was postponed due to King's illness. K sued H for the rent. It was held that contract is discharged, as viewing of procession was the foundation of contract, which did not occur. H was not required to pay the lodging charges.

Origin of doctrine of frustration can be traced back to the ruling in Taylor v/s Caldwell, already referred. The English courts applied this doctrine implying the term in the contract to the effect that parties shall be absolved from contractual obligation if performance is impossible by reason of intervening event. Intrusion of the event or change in the circumstance is so fundamental that it strikes at the very root of contract and the object of the contract is frustrated.

13.7 Exceptions to Doctrine of Supervening Impossibility

"He that agrees to do an act must do it or pay damages for not doing it". This statement embodies a general rule that there is no excuse for non-performance. Parties must perform their respective contractual obligations howsoever onerous, unprofitable, expensive, risky or even difficult. Law however absolves the parties from duties when performance is absolutely impossible i.e. by invoking the doctrine of supervening impossibility in the cases discussed above.

This **principle of supervening impossibility is not applicable in the following cases** and the contract is not discharged.

a) **Difficulty of performance-**Difficulty of performance, increased or unexpected difficulties in performing contract is not an excuse for non-performance.

*Example-*A agreed with B to send goods from Madras to Mumbai in November.

---

73. *(1903) 2 KB 740*

Transporters went on strike in October due to which transport rates went at a very high rate. Ruled that increase in transport charges is not a ground or discharge, though performance was difficult.

b) **Commercial impossibility**-Sometimes performance of contract may not be commercially profitable as expected or it may result in losses instead of profits. Here impossibility must be physical or legal and not to be viewed from ability or a situation point of view. Scarcity of raw material, difficulty in import-export may make the performance commercially impossible but that cannot be an excuse. This is not a ground of discharge.

c) **Strikes, lock-outs or civil disturbances**-The doctrine of supervening impossibility does not extend to the situations created by strikes, lock-outs or civil disturbances. The rationale is that the situation arising out of strike is manageable while lockout is self - induced act of employer. S. 56, therefore, does not cover these contingencies.[74]

d) **Impossibility due to failure of third party**.-For performance of a contract, promisor may rely on the act of third person. Failure/ default or behavior of that person however will not terminate the contract. Such a failure cannot be regarded as impossibility of performance.

Example-A wholeseller agrees with a retailer to sell goods 'to be manufactured by the producer'. Producer fails to manufacture the goods. Wholeseller must supply the goods of the same quality or pay damages for breach.

e) **Partial impossibility**-There may be several purpose for which a contract is executed. Non-fulfillment of one of the purposes does not discharge the whole contract.

13.8 Legal consequences of Supervening Impossibility-

Effects of supervening impossibility are enlisted below.

a) *S.56,* Para-2-Contract becomes void. Parties need not perform remaining contract.

b) *S.56,* Para-3-Where the promisor knew or with reasonable diligence might have known and which the promisee did not know that the act promised was impossible or unlawful, such promisor should compensate the promisee for the loss sustained through non performance of the contract.

Illustration-A contracts to marry B, being already married to C, and being forbidden by the law to which he is subject to practise polygamy. A must make compensation to B for the loss caused to her by the non-performance of his promise.

c-S.65-Restoration of benefit/advantage received under void contract to the other party or compensating for that benefit if restoration is not possible.(see chapter on violable contract)

---

74. *Jacob v/s Credit Lyonnais (1884)*-One supplier agreed to supply certain goods to his customer. The goods were to be imported from Algeria. Supplier could not procure goods due to riot and civil disturbances in Algeria. Held that supplier is liable for non- performance.

"Circumstances are beyond control of man; but his conduct is in his own power."
- Benjanin Disraeli.

MODES OF DISCHARGE OF CONTRACTS

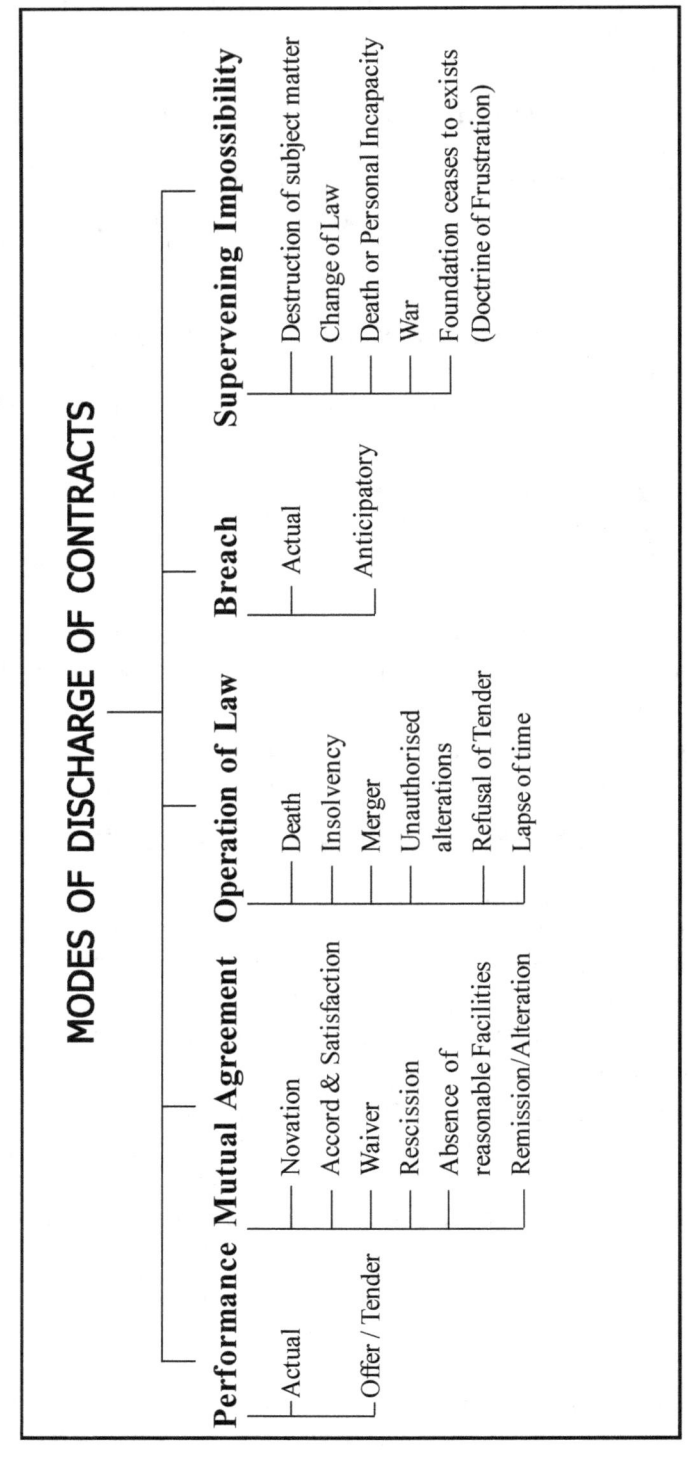

Performance
- Actual
- Offer / Tender

Mutual Agreement
- Novation
- Accord & Satisfaction
- Waiver
- Rescission
- Absence of reasonable Facilities
- Remission/Alteration

Operation of Law
- Death
- Insolvency
- Merger
- Unauthorised alterations
- Refusal of Tender
- Lapse of time

Breach
- Actual
- Anticipatory

Supervening Impossibility
- Destruction of subject matter
- Change of Law
- Death or Personal Incapacity
- War
- Foundation ceases to exists (Doctrine of Frustration)

Chapter 14

REMEDIES FOR THE BREACH OF CONTRACT

There is a popular saying in law that where there is a right there is a remedy. Remedy contemplates means of enforcing a right or redressing a wrong. If connotes legal, equitable relief or remedial action by the victim of wrong. Breach of contract violates a contractual right causing losses to the other. The injured party (aggrieved party) has following legal remedies-

1. Rescission of contract
2. Injunction
3. Specific Performance of Contract
4. Quantum Meruit
5. Suit for Specific Performance

14.1 Rescission of Contract

(See chapter on voidable contract.) Rescission means repudiation or cancellation of contract. It is setting aside of contract through court's order. The injured party can file a suit for setting aside the contract in the following circumstances-

— Breach of contract is committed or
— Contract is voidable or
— Due to defendant's fault the contract is unlawful.

The remedy of rescission is **not available** in the following circumstances-

— Express or implied ratification of contract;
— Contract is liable to be set aside in part but it is indivisible;
— Restoration of parties to original position is not possible by termination of contract by the court
— Acquisition of interests by third party in the subject matter of contract in good faith and for value;

As per section 64, the party setting aside the contract should restore the benefit to the other party from whom he received it. Section 75 gives the aggrieved an additional right of compensation for losses suffered by breach. The party rescinding is relieved from his obligations as he is discharged.

14.2 Injunction

Injunction affords a common, timely and significant remedy in the given situation. Injunction is simply an order of the court either to do something or to refrain from doing an act. The purpose of Injunction is to enforce a contract. According to its content and the time, for which it is operative, the injunctions may be categorized as follows-

— **Prohibitory Injunction -** When the court restrains a party from doing an act particularly breach of contract or an act in violation contractual terms;

— **Mandatory Injunction -** Mandate means command. Here the court orders a party to do a particular act under the contract or otherwise in fulfillment of contract;

— **Temporary Injunction -** It is normally granted during the pendency of litigation/ suit.

— **Permanent Injunction -** The court may forbid the party from committing an act in future and forever. Such an order has a perpetual effect.

Example - A builder, A has agreed to sell a flat to a purchaser B. A, in breach of earlier agreement to sale, attempts to sell the same flat to C. In a suit against A by B, the court may order A not to deal with that flat till the case is decided (temporary injunction). A may be ordered to complete the conveyance (transfer) of flat in favor of B (mandatory injunction). Court may prohibit the builder from selling it to C (prohibitory injunction).

14.3 Specific Performance of Contract

The Specific Relief Act of 1963 grants this remedy to the party in special circumstances. Specific performance implies performance of the promise in pursuance of court's order. The court may direct the party guilty of non-performance to specifically carry out the obligations under the contract. Suit for specific performance cannot be preferred in every case of breach. It is a discretionary remedy and granted only when it is just and equitable. It may be ordered if the court feels that-

— Monetary compensation is not an adequate remedy in the circumstances.

— Damages cannot be calculated by any satisfactory criterion.

The remedy of specific performance is generally **refused** considering one of the following factors-

— Damages is an adequate remedy.

— Contract is revocable by nature.

— Contract as a whole is uncertain or its terms are vague and unenforceable.

— Contract involves personal service e.g. contract to paint, marry, entertain etc.

— Court cannot monitor (supervise) the execution of contract i.e. compliance of its orders(mining operations, construction works..).

— Ultra-vires contracts entered into by the companies.

— Contract is frustrated in view of s.56

— Party against which specific performance is sought is (or becomes) incompetent (Insanity, Insolvency).

14.4 Quantum Meruit

(Sections- 65 & 70) Literal meaning of quantum meruit is "as much as merited" or "as much as deserved" or as much as earned' or "in proportion to the work done". Quantum meruit may be considered as a remedy in itself or as a tool to determine amount of compensation. Sometimes where work is done under the contract, which is discharged later on, or goods are delivered non- gratuitously, the party doing the work or sender of goods deserves something in return. Whatever is awarded in such situation is quantum meruit.

In the following situations quantum meruit is granted –

a) When contract becomes void or discovered to be void u/s 65. The court can order restoration of benefit under void contract or compensation if restoration is not possible;

b) Where some work under the contract (discharged) is done or services provided under the contract (which is discharged) but for which remuneration is not fixed. It covers the cases where contract is partly performed and other party prevents remaining performance and contract is thereby discharged.

   Example - On publisher's proposal, an author prepares a manuscript in part and afterwards the publisher abandons the idea of publication. Author has right to get compensation for his writing.[75] Similarly an advocate unable to prove special contract for payment of his fees, may recover the value of his services based on quantum merit.

c) Where something is done or anything delivered (not under express contract) without intention to do so gratuitously (refer section 70, quasi contract).

d) Where a party incurs liability under the contract and other abandons the contract to the prejudice of the former.

14.5 Damages

Law Of Damages

A) Meaning and Concept

Damage and damages are not synonymous. Former implies legal injury while later is a remedy when legal injury results. 'Damages' and 'Compensation' are used interchangeably. Damages are a monetary compensation awarded to the aggrieved party for the loss suffered by him as a result of breach of contract. It is a pecuniary equivalent of the loss suffered by breach. Objective of this remedy is to put the plaintiff in the same financial position as far as money can do it in which, he would have been, had there been no breach and consequent loss. Damages are paid to make up the losses due to breach by the defaulter. In commercial transactions every breach of contract entails loss of profit, money, loss of goods, inconvenience, damage to reputation etc.

B) Kinds of Damages :

The damages are of following kinds.
1. Ordinary or General Damages.
2. Special Damages.

---

75. *Based on planche v/s Coleburn - 1831 - SC & P - 58.*

3. Nominal Damages.

4. Exemplary Damages.

1) Ordinary or General Damages

These are also called as "**Substantial or Compensatory**" damages. These are awarded, as a general rule, to the injured party. According to S. 73, this kind of damages arise —

a) **Naturally** and

b) **directly in the usual course of the things** from the breach of contract. Such loss should be natural and usual result in that kind of breach. Those are awarded for direct, proximate, natural and probable consequences of the breach of contract and not for indirect, non-natural, unusual and impossible consequences. Ordinary damages are fair and reasonable compensation for the loss sustained as a result of breach.

In case of trading transactions like selling and purchase of goods, measure of the damages is the difference between contract price and the market price on the day of breach. Market rate is considered as the true value at which purchaser could obtain similar goods in open market.

Illustration

A contracts to buy B's ship for 60, 000 rupees, but breaks his promise. A must pay to B, by way of compensation, the excess, if any, of the contract price over the price which B can obtain for the ship at the time of the breach of promise.

2) Special Damages :

As the phrase indicates, special damages are awarded in special and unusual circumstances and for special losses. According to S. 73, party committing the breach may be asked to pay those damages, which were in contemplation (in mind) of both the parties at the time when they entered into contract as the likely result of the breach. Thus parties at the time of making contract know the special circumstances. They also know beforehand that breach would result in special loss to the injured party. If this is so, the defaulter should make up actual loss though such a loss may not occur ordinarily. Unless special circumstances and extent of loss are made known, special damages are not awarded.

For e. g. A, a manufacturer, agrees with B to manufacture and deliver an equipment for Rs. 20 lakhs . B makes it clear at the time of signing contract that if delivery is not made within 6 months time, he would be required to import it which would cost him 35 lakhs. If breach is committed, Rs. 15 lakhs is the special loss suffered by B, which A must pay.

Special damages cannot be claimed as a matter of right. Those are estimated considering the circumstances prevailing on the day of breach.

3) Nominal Damages*

Nominal Damages are awarded as a token amount and for namesake only. It is usually a very meager amount. It is neither compensation nor a penalty. Many times the plaintiff is not subjected to real loss by breach but his right is infringed. Breach may be very technical in nature and trivial.

For e. g. delay in delivery of goods may not actually harm the purchaser but breach of

---

* De minimis non curatlex - The law cares not for small things.

contract is committed. The court may award Rs. 5 or 50 as compensation in recognition of plaintiff's right or to vindicate his honor.

4) Exemplary or Vindictive or Punitive Damages

Exemplary means 'serving as a warning or deterrant'. Whenever heavy or excessive or exorbitant amount is sanctioned, the damages are termed as exemplary damages. Exemplary damages are punitive in nature acting as a deterrent to prevent the breach. If idea of damages is to compensate the aggrieved party for his loss, under the law of contract exemplary damages cannot be awarded. In the following cases however court may consider awarding exemplary damages –

— Breach of a contract to marry or
— Dishonour of a cheque by the banker in spite of having sufficient funds to apply for the cheque.

C) Rules for Assessment of Damages.

Actual amount to be paid in a suit for damages is always a moot question. Theoretically consequences are endless. Hence the defaulter's liability to pay damages should be delimited. He cannot be made be liable for all the consequences of his breach as there can be consequences of consequences. Cardinal principle underlying damages is "recompense", " restitution" or "restoration" if the injured is to be restored to the original position in which he would have been, had there been no breach.

(The courts consider following guidelines for calculation of amount of damages).

First 8 rules are laid down by S. 73 to S. 75, remaining are settled though the decisions of the courts in India.

1) In case of breach of contract and consequent loss, only those damages "which naturally arose in the usual course of the things from such breach" can be recovered. As a general rule the court awards ordinary damages. (S. 73, Refer the concept of **'Ordinary Damages'**)

2) Special Damages for special losses may also be recovered if "parties knew, when made the contract, to be likely to result from the breach of it" (S. 73; refer the concept of **"Special Damages"**)

3) Remoteness of Damages

Compensation for too remote consequences is not awarded. If the loss were not too remote i. e. proximate and directly flowing from the breach, plaintiff would succeed. For indirect losses sustained, damages are not awarded. Remoteness of damages is decided not on the basis of physical proximity but national proximity. If the injury is the direct result of the breach, loss is proximate and not remote. [S. 73(2)]

The first three rules are laid down and applied in a leading case of Hadley vs. Baxendale which is explained below

Hadley Vs Baxendale[76] Plaintiffs (H) were the mill owners in Gloucester. They had a broken crankshaft due to which mill was closed. They delivered the crankshaft to the

---

76. *(1854) 9 EX 341*

defendants (B), who were firm of carriers, with instructions to deliver it to manufacturer at Greenwich for copying it and to make a new shaft. While delivering the shaft the plaintiff told defendants to send the shaft immediately to manufacturer as the mill was stopped. It did not tell that delay would result in loss of profit. Defendants were negligent in delivering the shaft to manufacturer beyond a reasonable time. Plaintiff could not get new shaft for many days and as a result the functioning of mill could not be resumed. The plaintiff filed suit for damages for -

- Loss of profit during the days of delay;
- Wages of workers and
- Depreciation of factory.

Defendant pleaded that the damages claimed were too remote and hence are not liable to pay for loss of profit.

The court held that B was liable to pay only for the ordinary damages and not for loss of profit claimed as a special damage. That loss was regarded as too remote. The remedy of special damages was refused on the ground that —

- H did not disclose to B that delay would cause loss of profit;
- In the usual course of the thing H might have had a substitute shaft in reserve to avoid stoppage of mill.

4) **Duty to mitigate the loss**

The injured party is under a duty to mitigate (reduce) the loss as a result of breach. He should take reasonable steps to minimize possible loss. If he fails to do so or his negligence attributes to losses, the amount of damages would be reduced to the extent of loss, which he could have lessened. He should act like a man of ordinary prudence and take that much care which a person in similar circumstances would take in his own case. (Explanation to S. 73)If the aggrieved party increases the loss by his unreasonable conduct or fault, no question of damages arises for such increased loss.

Ramkumar V/s Shankar - A undertook the repairs of B's wall. A failed to repair it. B did not get it repaired through others and the whole wall collapsed due to rain. B claimed the entire loss from A. The claim was rejected as B failed to minimize the loss. He could have got it repaired through others and avoided the collapse.

5) **Damages for the breach of quasi contract** would be the same as the damages for breach of ordinary contract. (S. 73, stated earlier)

6) **Liquidated Damages and Penalty**- (S. 74, see below)

7) Difficulty in determination of amount of damages is not a ground for denial of damages. (S. 75)

8) As stated earlier, object behind awarding damages is restoration and not punishment. Barring exceptions, therefore, exemplary damages are not granted.

9) **Quantum Merit**

Already discussed as a kind of remedy. (S. 65 and 70)

Other rules.

10) When there is no loss actually suffered, nominal damages are awarded.

11) Damages may be recovered for physical inconvenience, discomfort. Motive or manner of breach of contract is irrelevant factor for measure of damages.

12) The court normally grants cost of suit in addition to the damages.

Illustration

A contracts to pay a sum of money to B on a day specified. A does not pay the money on that day. B, in consequence of not receiving the money on that day, is unable to pay his debts, and is totally ruined. A is not liable to make good to B anything except the principal sum he contracted to pay, together with interest up to the day of payment.

Liquidated Damages and Penalty-S. 74

A contract may stipulate a specific sum payable by the party in default to the injured party. The amount thus may be prefixed contemplating the breach. This sum may be either liquidated damages or penalty, depending upon the interpretation and the sum so predetermined is relevant to some extent in assessing the damages.

English Law on liquidated damages and penalty - The sum so fixed by the parties is **liquidated damages** if it is reasonable and fair estimate of actual loss as a probable result of the breach. Liquidated damages thus are a genuine pre-estimate of the damages. Liquidated damages are near equivalent of actual loss.

Penalty on the other hand is not based on the actual loss. It is exorbitant, disproportionate to the damages likely to result from the beach. The amount by way of penalty is obviously high, much greater than the possible loss. If the stipulated amount is unreasonable, extravagant, unconscionable, it is penalty. The penalty thus acts "in terrorum".

English law thus distinguishes liquidated damages from penalty. If the sum mentioned were liquidated damages, the English courts would allow that full sum as damages in case of breach. If it were in the nature of penalty, courts would grant reasonable amount commensurate with the actual loss, ignoring amount of penalty.

Indian law

Indian law does not distinguish liquidated damages or penalty. Indian courts would independently measure the amount of damages by following above rules. S. 74 provides limitations to the effect that courts would not award damages more than the sum named in the contract.

PART - I

Questions and hints for answers

(References to courses and year are from Pune University)

1. Define the term 'Contract'? What are the essential elements of valid contract? TYBCom 2012, 2008, MBA 2014, BBM (IB) 2012

2. Explain the concept of contract. Explain the nature and kinds? ✓ Ans. 1.1 & 2.1 to 2.3 TY B.Com 2012, BBA 2013

3. All contracts are agreements but all agreements are not contracts." Discuss fully. (TYBCom 2006, / MBA 2003) BBA 2011, BBM (IB) 2010 ✓ Ans. Chapter 1.1 & 1.2

4. "An agreement enforceable by law is a contract" Explain the statement in the light of conditions of enforceability of a contract. (PGDBM 2004, PU) ✓ Ans. 1.1 & 1.2

5. "No consideration no contract". Comment on this statement with exceptions. BBA 2012, 2010, 2008

   Or

   "An agreement without consideration is void" Elaborate the rule with exceptions, if any. (TYBCom 2004 & 2006, 2009, PU / MBA 2003 PU /PGDBM 2004 PU) ✓ Ans.

6. Give the definition of 'Proposal'. Explain the legal rules as to the proposal, (TYBCom 2004, 2013, PU) BBA 2012, BBMIB2013 ✓ Ans. 31.1 & 31.2

   Define Acceptance of a Proposal. Explain the legal rules as to acceptance of a proposal - TYBCom, 2010, BBA 2013, 2010, 2008

7. Define and explain the concept of consideration by setting out its essential elements? (MBA 2003, 2014) TYBCom 2009, ✓ Ans. 4.1 & 4.2

8. Who is competent to enter into contract? Discuss the law relating to minor's contract. (MBA 2004 PU, PGDBM 2005 PU) BBA 2011, 2009 ✓ Ans. 5.1, 5.2 & 5.3 in brief

9. State and explain the law relating to "competency of parties" BBM(IB) 2012, 2011 ✓ Ans.   Chapter 5 in brief

10. "Minor cannot enter into contract". Critically explain this statement. ✓Ans. 5.1

11. "A minor binds others. But is never bound by others" explain this statement
   ✓ Ans. 5.1

12. Define 'Consent'. When is the consent said to be a free-consent? Explain various factors affecting on free-consent. (TYBCom 2005, 2012, PU) BBA 2012, BBM (IB) 2013
   ✓ Ans. Chapter 6

12(a) Define, explain and distinguish 'Coercion' and 'Undue Influence'. (PGDBM 2004, PU)
   ✓ Ans. 6.2 & 6.3

13. Define, explain and distinguish 'Fraud' and 'Misrepresentation'. ✓ Ans. 6.4 & 6.5

14. Define & explain the concept of 'Fraud'? How far mere silence is fraudulent? Explain. BBM(IB) 2012 ✓ Ans. 6.4

15. State briefly the law relating to 'Mistakes' as embodied in the Indian Contract Act- 1872.
   ✓ Ans. 6.7

16. Define & explain the term "Contingent Contract". Enumerate the rules relating to performance (enforcement) of contingent contracts. ✓ Ans. Chapter 10

17. Elaborate the concept of 'Consideration'. What objects and considerations are unlawful as per the provisions of Indian Contract Act, 1872? (MBA 2005, PU) 2009, BBM (IB) 2012 ✓ Ans. 4.1 & 7.2

18. Discuss in brief "agreements expressly declared to be void" under the Indian Contract Act. BBA 2013, 2011, BBM (IB) 2011 ✓ Ans. Chapter 8 in brief

19. "Agreement by Way of Wager is Void" Comment. Are there any exceptions to this rule?
   ✓ Ans. 9.3

20. Define the term 'Contingent Contract' and 'Wagering Agreement'. Explain the rules of contingent contract (TYBCom 2003, PU) ✓ Ans. 10.1 & 9

21. What is "Tender of Performance"? What constitutes a legal tender? Explain the relevant law. BBA 2013 ✓ Ans. 11.1 & 11.2

22. Discuss in brief the various modes of discharge of contract. (MBA 2004) BBA 2011, BBM(IB) 2011 ✓ Ans. 13.1

23. What is doctrine of 'Supervening Impossibility'? When it applies & when not? Discuss.
   ✓ Ans. 13.1 (6th point)

24. Explain the law relating to 'Anticipatory Breach of Contract'. (PGDBM 2004) ✓ Ans. 13.1 (5th Point)

25. Discuss in brief the various remedies available in case of breach of contract. (PGDBM 2005 PU) BBA 2012, BBM (IB) 2010 ✓ Ans. Chapter 14

26. Explain in brief the rules for assessment of damages as a remedy in breach of contract.
   ✓ Ans. 14.2 (c)

27. What are 'Quasi-Contracts'? Discuss the provisions relating to quasi contracts under Indian Contract Act 1872. TYBCom, 2012, (PGDBM 2005, PU) ✓ Ans. 12.1 & 12.5

28. Short Answer Questions (For 2 and 4 marks)

(1) Define the terms Offer, Acceptance, Void contract, Voidable contract, Consent, Coercion.

(2) Explain in very brief Quasi contract, Wagering agreements, Fraud, Mistake of fact, Consideration unsound mind person, Contingent contracts, Merger, Anticipatory breach.

(3) Answer the following Question in 50 words.

   a.   What constitutes fraud ?

   b.   When consent is not free ?

   c.   When object & considerations are unlawful ?

   d.   What type of wagers are enforceable ?

   e.   How contract can be discharged by operation of law ?

   f.   What is doctrine of supervening impossibility ?

   g.   Enlist the remedies in breach of contract ?

PART - II

SPECIFIC CONTRACTS

Introduction

So far the general principles of Contract are discussed in Part - I. Those principles are applicable to every contract under special law unless special law overrules the general principles.

This part of the book deals with special contracts. The subject matter of this part is of practical significance. Indemnity bonds, guarantees are executed as a matter of necessity as a cover to losses or ensuring performance of contracts. We sometimes get the other's goods for use or give our movable property for repairs or other purposes. People are selling, purchasing variety of goods on enormous scale. Goods are subject matter of e-commerce and online shopping is our new culture. New Products including electronic goods are launched daily and consumers are going for those even without physical verification. These market transactions appear to be very easy but risky also. Buyers are to be watchful. Properties are hypothecated, deposited for loan. Trading concerns, companies even private individuals get the work done through agents. Knowledge of the provisions about these special contracts is therefore important.

Chapter 15 | LAW OF INDEMNITY AND GUARANTEE

CONTRACT OF INDEMNITY

15.1 Definition & Essentials

Definition - Sec. 124 of the Act defines the Contract of Indemnity in the following words.

> *"A contract of indemnity is a contract by which one party promises to save the other from loss caused to him by the conduct of promisor himself or by the conduct of any other person."*

Illustration

A) A agrees to indemnity B against the consequences of any proceedings which C may take against B in respect of a certain sum of Rs. 200. This is a contract of indemnity.

Indemnity means 'to save harmless from loss'. It is a promise to one to reimburse the loss suffered due to promisor's conduct or due to conduct of any person. Indemnity serves to make good the future loss.

Important features of Contract of Indemnity.

1) **Parties** - The promisor in contract of indemnity is called as 'indemnifier' and promisee is 'indemnity holder'. Indemnifier indemnifies the 'indemnified' i.e. indemnity holder.

2) **Object of indemnity** - Object of indemnity is to provide a sort of security against anticipated / future loss. The indemnity holder is assured of being compensated for the loss which he may suffer.

3) **Indemnity is a type of contract (contigent contract)** Contract of indemnity is a special type of contract and as such must prossess all the characterstics of a valid contract Indemnity for illegal purpose is unenforceable. Contract of indemnity is a 'contingent contract' because liability of indemnifier depends upon "loss suffered by the indemnity holder"

4) **Express or Implied Indemnity** - Contract of indemnity may be express by words or implied, by conduct.

5) **Indemnity by contract or by operation of Law** - Indemnity is usually the result of a contract. It can be annexed by operation of law. For example, principal's duty to indemnify the agent, partner's duty to indemnify fellow partners transferee's liability to indemnify transferor of shares under company law etc.

6) **Commencement of indemnifier's liability** - There is no provision in the Act as to the time of commencement of indemnifier's liability. There had been conflict of opinion of various High Courts. The issue was whether the indemnity holder should first suffer the loss and then ask the indemnifier to indentify or ask him directly to discharge the liability. Settled view is that if indemnity holder incurres a liability which is absolute (final), indemnity holder can call upon indemnifier to pay it off or discharge that liability and in that case he need not be damnified first.[77]

7) **English law and Indian law on indemnity** - English law of indemnity is wider than Indian law. English law covers the losses due to death, disability, destruction or natural calamities, act of God etc. Indian law is restricted in the sense that indemnity is executed to save the indemnity holder from the loss occasioned by the conduct of promisor or any other person. Sec. 124 apparently does not apply to the loss caused by accident or events without intervention of human beings. Indian courts however have followed English law to apply Sec. 124 to insurance contracts. i.e. losses caused by accidents or events beyond human control.

B) Rights of Indemnity Holder When Sued (Sec. 125)

This section contemplates a litigation (suit) in a court. Indemnity holder may be dragged in court or represent indemnifier in a suit. In such court matter he may incur monetary losses in conducting suit, arriving at a compromise or required to pay to the other party. In that eventuality, Sec. 125 vests the indemnity holder with the right to recover following sums from indemnifier.

1) **All damages** - which the indemnity holder was compelled to pay in any suit in respect of a matter covered by the indemnity.

2) **All costs** - which indemnity holder was compelled to pay in bringing or defending suit. For bringing or defending suits authority of promisor is necessary. Costs in the litigation should be such that a prudent or a reasonable man would incur. Indemnity holder should not contravene the express instructions of the promisor in this behalf.

3) **All sums** which the Indemnity holder was compelled to pay as per the terms of the compromise in a suit. To entitle for these sums —
— The indemnity holder must be authorised to compromise;
— or Compromise should have been a prudent act in the civil proceedings.
— The compromise should not be contrary to the orders of indemnifier;
Besides the right to recover above sums, the indemnity holder can file a suit for specific performance of the contract of indemnity if his liability is absolute as stated earlier.

---

77. ***Osman Jamal & Sons Ltd Vs Gopal Purushottam*** *(1928) ILR 56 Cal. 26 ...Indemnity is not neccessarily given by repayment after payment. Indemnity requires that the party to be indemnified shall never be called upon to pay ..."*
Gajanan Moreshwar Vs Moreshwar Madan - *AIR - (1942) BOM 302*

Rights of Indemnifier - The Act is silent as to indemnifier's rights. Rights of indemnifier are analogus to that of surety U/S 141 of the Act.

15.2 CONTRACT OF GUARANTEE

Many times a person wants a loan or goods from other or he seeks employment with somebody. Other party is willing to consider his desire if a third person is ready to bear the personal responsiblility as security for payment of loan or performance of a promise. Contract of guarantee meets the requirement of the situation. Banks, financial institutions for repayment of their loan or Govt. for ensuring completion of work with high stakes are usually demanding guarantee. This contract is therefore, of immense practical significance.

A) Definition and Characterstics
Definition (Sec. 126)

> *"A contract of guarantee is a contract to perform the promise or discharge the liability of a third person in case of his default."*

Illustrations -
   i)   A lends money to B and C promises A that in case B fails to pay, he will pay the money. This is a contract of guarantee.
   ii) On A's request, B promises A's employer that if A makes a default during his employment, he shall make good loss caused to him. This is a contract of guarantee.

Object of providing guarantee
The contract of guarantee is entered into for the purpose of -
   –   getting a loan, or goods on credit or an employment;
   –   to secure performance of a commercial engagement;
   –   to assure the honesty, fidelity of a person;
   –   to indemnify against the consequences of somebody's failure to discharge obligation.

Salient features of Contract of Guarantee
1) Parties
There are three parties in contract of guarantee.
   –   Principal Debtor – The person in respect of whose default, the guarantee is given;
   –   Creditor - The person to whom guarantee is given and
   –   Surety - The person who gives guarantee, also called as guarantor.

2) Tripartite Agreement
Guarantee is a triangular relationship comprising three agreements. An agreement between-
   i)   Creditor and Debtor - Original or primary agreement;
   ii) Creditor and Surety - The very agreement of guarantee;
   iii) Surety and Principal Debtor - This is in the nature of indemnity. The principal debtor impliedly undertakes to indemnify the surety if he is required to pay or discharge his liability.

There need not be tripartite agreement in the sense that - above agreements need not be entered into simultaneously. Contract of surety is not collateral to contract between creditor and principal debtor which may not be in existence on the date of guarantee. Though concurrence of three parties is essential for guarantee, guarantee may be executed before or after the contract between creditor and principal debtor is entered into.

3) Nature of liability

Principal debtor is primarily liable to discharge his duties. Surety's liability is secondary and conditional. It arises only after default is comitted by principal debtor. The liability of surety commences from the date of default of principal debtor and not from date of guarantee.

4) Legality of debts

Guarantee presupposes primary agreement to be legal. The debt or the liability to perform under the contract between principal debtor and creditor should be existing and legal, enforceable. If original agreement is illegal, guarantee is meaningless.

5) Consideration

Guarantee is an exception to S.25. Anything done or any promise made for the benefit of a principal debtor is a sufficient consideration for surety to provide guarantee. Benefit to principal debtor is a good consideration, personal advantage to surety, is not necessary. Past consideration also supports a contract of guarantee.

Illustration - A sells and delivers goods to B. C afterwards, without consideration, agrees to pay for them in default of B. The agreement is valid.

6) Formalities

No formalities are suggested for contract of guarantee. It can be oral or in writing.

B) Kinds of Guarantee

The contract of guarantee is of two types viz Specific Guarantee and Continuing Guarantee.

1) Specific or Ordinary Guarantee

Guarantee for specific debt or for performance of a particular obligation is called as specified guarantee. It is for a single transaction or a debt.

Example - A contractor agrees to constuct a farm house for Owner. Z, guarantees contractor's performance. This is specific guarantee.

2) Continuing Guarantee

S.129 defines Continuing guarantee as a guarantee which extends to a series of transactions. This type of guarantee covers independent and several transactions over a specific period. Continuing guarantee involves repeated activities, usually of similar type, to be carried out by the principal debtor. A tea dealer guarantees supply of coffee (regularly for one year) by a coffee dealer to a coffee shop. This is continuing guarantee.

Example - A in consideration that B will employ C in collecting rents of B's zamindari, promises B to be responsible to the amount of Rs. 5000, for the due collection and payment by C of those rents. This is a Continuing guarantee.

Revocation of Continuing Guarantee - Continuing Guarantee is revoked in the following circumtances.

i) By notice of revocation by surety - (Sec. 130)

Continuing guarantee as to future transactions can be withdrawn, by surety by notice to the creditor. His liability for future transactions then comes to end. However he continues to be liable for transactions prior to notice.

ii) By death of surety (Sec. 131)

By death of surety, the continuing guarantee is revoked automatically as to future transactions. No notice to creditor is necessary. Surety's estate is not liable for any transactions entered into after death even without the knowledge of death by creditor.

iii) Discharge of Surety (Sec. 133 to 139)

The continuing guarantee is revoked in the circumstances in which a surety is discharged from liability. (Discussed later is this chapter)

C) Rights of Surety

As stated earlier, the contract of guarantee is a tripartite relationship. As such surety has certain rights against principal debtor, creditor and co-sureties, if any. Those are discussed below.

1) Rights against Creditor

a) Right to security - (Sec. 141) A surety is entitled to the benefit of every security (for e.g. goods pledged or hypothicated) which the creditor has against the principal debtor at the time of entering into the contract of guarantee. Surety's knowledge of such security is irrelevant for the exercise of the right.

b) Right of set-off - Meaning of set-off - If surety is sued by the creditor to enforce guarantee, surety can claim set off or counter claim which principal debtor might possess against the creditor. He can avail the defences which the principal debtor can plead against the creditor.

c) Right of exoneration - Exoneration means getting exempted from liability. Before the debt under guarantee becomes due or before the surety is called upon to pay, the surety may require the creditor to sue the principal debtor and recover the guaranteed debt. If creditor fails to take proper steps, surety can claim exoneration. The surety is entitled to this remedy when he could show, that the debtor is likely to remove his property out of jurisdiction (of the competent court) so as to defeat the claims of the creditor. If property is removed outside the jurisdiction of the court, there are difficulties in recovering debt through the sale of such property under court's directions.

2) Right against Principal Debtor

a) Right of Subrogation (Sec. 140) - When surety pays off or performes the obligation on the default of principal debtor, the surety steps into shoes of creditor. Surety takes the legal position of creditor vis-a-vis principal debtor. He acquires all the rights and entitled to all remedies of creditor against debtor. Surety may claim securities, dividend in case of insolvency of the debtor. The surety stands in the place of creditor, not only through contract but by whatever securities are available to creditor.

Example - A sells goods to B. Payment is guaranteed by C. A has a lien over the goods as unpaid seller. C pays price on default of B. C is entitled to lien over the goods.

b) **Right to claim Indemnity (Sec. 145)** - In every contract of guarantee, there is an implied promise by principal debtor to indentify surety. Surety has a right to recover from principal debtor whatvever sums he has 'rightfully paid' to the creditor. He can recover principal amount with interest, costs of the suit (when defence is justified). He cannot however recover the sums wrongfully paid. Amount more than what is actually paid cannot be recovered.

3) **Right of contribution against co-sureties.** - There can be more than one surety for the same debt or performance of duty. These are called as cosureties. Generally the co-sureties are liable to contribute equally. If one is compelled to pay the entire debt or more than his share of debt, he has a right of contribution from other co-surety or cosureties.

Rules of Contribution

i) **Co-sureties liable for similar-sum under the same debt** - (Sec. 146) when the cosureties guarantee the payment of same debt for similar amount, they are liable to share outstanding debt equally and entitled to share securities equally.

"As between co-sureties, there is equality of burden and benefit".
This rule is subject to the contract to the contrary.

Illustration - A, B and C are co-sureties to D for Rs. 6000 lent to E. E fails to pay. A, B, C are liable to pay Rs. 2000 each. If A is compelled to pay Rs. 6000, he has right to receive Rs. 2000 each from B and C.

ii) **Co-sureties bound for different sums under same debt** - (Sec. 147) Co-sureties who are bound in different sums are liable to pay equally as far as the limits of their respective obligation permit.

Illustration - A, B and C as sureties for D, enter into several bonds each in different penalty, namely, A in penalty of Rs. 10,000, B in that of Rs. 20,000 and C in that of 40,000 conditioned for D's duly accounting to E.
If D makes a default of Rs. 30,000 A, B and C are liable to pay Rs.10,000 each.

D) Discharge of Surety – Modes of Discharge

A surety is discharged from his liability under contract of gurantee in any of the following ways.

1) **Revocation of continuing of guarantee** (see Sec. 130)

2) Death of Surety in continuing of guarantee : (Sec. 131) These sections are covered in continuing guarantee.

3) Novation : Existing contract of guarantee may be substituted by a new contract between same or different parties. Result of such a novation is the discharge of old contract of suretyship.

4) Changes in the terms of contract (Sec. 133) Concurrence is the basis of every contract. If the terms of contract of guarantee are changed without surety's consent, the surety is discharged as to transactions subsequent to such change. Variations whether beneficial to surety or disadvantageous, surety is absolved from liabilities.

5) Release or Discharge of Principal Debtor (Sec. 134) - Principal Debtor's liability is primary, while surety's liability is secondary. If principal debtor ceases to be liable, surety also is no more liable. Discharge of principal debtor may occur under the section in following two situations.

   i) Whereby the contract between creditor and principal debtor, principal debtor is released. Release of principal debtor releases surety or

   ii) Principal debtor is discharged as a legal consequence of any act or omission of the creditor.

It is to be noticed that discharge of principal debtor by operation of law would not discharge the surety. Insolvency of principal debtor or release of one co-surety does not discharge a surety.

Illustration - A contacts with B to build a house for B for a fixed price, within a stipulated time, B supplying necessary timber. C guarantees A's performance of the contract. B omits to supply timber to C. C is discharged from his suretyship.

6) Arrangement by creditor with principal debtor without surety's consent — Sec. 135 states that principal debtor is discharged if creditor makes a composition with principal debtor or creditor promises to give more time to the promisee (to discharge his liability) Creditor promises not to sue him. The surety however **will not be discharged** in the following eventualities.

   i) Where the contract to give time to the principal debtor is made by the creditor with a third person and not with the principal debtor.

     Illustration - C is the holder of a overdue bill of exchange drawn by A (drawer) as surety, for B and accepted by B (acceptor). C contracts with M to give time to B. A is not discharged.

   ii) Mere forbearance by creditor to sue the principal debtor or to enforce any other remedy against him, does not discharge the isurety unless otherwise agreed.

   iii) Release of one co-surety by the creditor does not discharge other co-surety or co-surities. Released co-surety remains liable to other co-surety to contribute as explained earlier. (Sec. 138)

7) Creditor's act or omission impairing surety's eventual remedy (Sec. 139)
Surety is discharged if his eventual remedy against the principal debtor is impaired by the creditor's act or omission. Such an act must be inconsistent with surety's rights or

omission must be of an act which must be undertaken by the creditor. Creditor is under a duty to do every act necessary for protection of surety's rights.

Illustration - A puts M as an apprentice to B and gives guarantee to B for M's fidetity. B promises on his part that he will, at least once in a month, see M makeup the cash. B, omits to see this done as promised and M embezzles. A is not liable to B on his guarantee.

8. **Loss of Security (Sec. 141)** - If the creditor loses or parts with any security that was given to him at the time of contract of guarantee, the surety would be discharged to the extent of loss of security. Surety would be discharged even if he does not know about the security. Section does not apply to the loss of security by the events beyond creditor's control. For example earthquake, fire etc.

9. **Invalid Guarantee -** Surety is discharged if the contract of guarantee between creditor and surety is invalid and uneforceable. The contract of guarantee, would be invalid due to following reasons.

   i) Guarantee is obtained by creditor (or with creditor's knowledge and assent) by mispresentation or fraud. However if guarantee is procured by mispresentation or fraud by principal debtor then contract of guarantee, remains valid. (S. 142)

   ii) Guarantee obtained by the creditor by keeping silence as to material circumstances. (S. 143)

   iii) Where a person gives a guarantee upon a contract that a creditor shall not act upon it until another person has joined in it as co-surety, the guarantee is not valid if that other person does not join. (Sec. 144)

   Example : A agrees with B to stand as a surety for C's payment only if D is also made party as a co-surety. D is not made co-surety. A is not liable under his contract of guarantee.

E) Nature and Extent of Surety's liability –

"A surety is undoubtedly and not unjustly, an object of some favour both at law and equity" - *Lord Sellborn*

The law as to nature and scope of surety's liability is summarized below.

1) **Liability of surety is secondary and conditional** - Surety's liability is secondary in the sense that principal debtor is principally liable and if he commits a default then only surety comes in picture. Surety's liability is contigent on the default of principal debtor and not before.

2) Liability of surety is co-extive with that of the principal debtor.
   Sec. 128 states -
   "The liability of the surety is co-extensive with that of the principal debtor unless the contract otherwise provides." This means that as long as and to the extent proncipal debtor is liable, surety is liable.

3) **When surety is liable ?** - Surety's liability arises only on the default on the part of principal debtor and not before. Creditor need not give notice of default to the surety.

Creditor is not bound to proceed against the principal debtor before filling a suit against guarantor. In a suit against surety, principal debtor need not be made a party. This is because the contract of guarantee between creditor and surety is independant and not a collateral one. Further, the creditor need not exaust his remedies against the principal debtor before taking legal action against surety. Creditor need not first enforce securities against principal debtor before suing surety.

4) Surety liable even if principal debtor is not liable - The word 'co-extensive' in Sec. 128 refers to quantum of surety's liability. There are cases where, principal debtor may not be successfully sued but surety is held liable for his bebt. In the following cases the liability of surety is diffferent from principal debtor.

i) When the original contract between creditor and debtor is void or voidable, surety remains liable. (Where principal debtor is minor or goes mad) This is not applicable to original illegal agreement.

ii) If the debt is time-barred, principal debtor may not be sued. If action under contract of guarantee is within time, surety may be proceeded against.

iii) If principal debtor is adjudged insolvent, surely remains liable.

In the following cases **surety is however discharged** from his liabilities when **principal debtor remains liable.**

i) Variance (changes) of the terms of contract without surety's consent. (Sec. 133).

ii) Guarantee is obtained by fraud or misrepresentation or by coercion (Sec.142 & 143).

iii) Failure to join co-surety. (Sec - 144)

5) Surety is a favoured debtor - From the above discussion it can stated that both law and equity favours the surety to some extent. He is that way a favoured debtor.

Chapter 16

CONTRACT OF BAILMENT

16.1 Definition — *Sec.148* of the Contract Act defines bailment as follows —

> *"A bailment is the delivery of goods by one person to another for some purpose, upon a contract that they shall, when the purpose is accomplished, be returned or otherwise disposed off according to the directions of the person delivering them."*

The person delivering the goods is called 'bailor' and to whom the goods are delivered is called as 'bailee'.

Examples – A delivers his car to B for repairs. A to pay repair charges and B to return it after repairs.

– A keeps his golden ornaments in a banker's locker for safe custody.

There is a bailment of goods in above examples.

16.2 Characteristics of Bailment

i) **Subject Matter of Bailment**

Subject Matter of contract of bailment is 'goods'. Goods means movable property. 'Money' (currency) is not goods. But old coins are goods.

ii) **Delivery of Goods**

Delivery of goods is the chief characteristic of bailment as it creates relationship. Delivery implies transfer of possession of goods. It is handing over possession by bailor to bailee.

In bailment, there is a change of possession for a temporary period. Entrusting goods to a servant is not bailment as legally speaking there is no change of possession. Ownership of goods remains with bailor.

How delivery is made? Sec. 149 of the Act providing the answer states, "The delivery to the bailee may be made by doing anything which has the effect of putting the goods in the possession of the intended bailee or of any person authorized to hold them on his behalf."

Delivery of goods may be 'actual' or 'constructive'. Actual delivery is the physical transfer of possession. Sometimes actual delivery may be impossible due to size or quantity of the goods. In such cases delivery may be effected by symbols. (Symbolic delivery). In constructive delivery, physical possession is not transferred. There is no change in physical possession. The possession is transferred by transferring control over the goods. For e.g. When goods are at sea, those are delivered by transferring bill of lading or goods in railway are delivered by transferring railway receipt.

Exapmple – A sells a LED TV to B. B requests to keep TV with him for a week and thereafter to be taken by B. Sale operates as constructive delivery of goods and A's position is that of a bailee without change in actual possession.

iii) Purpose of Delivery

In bailment the goods are delivered for a specific purpose. Hiring an article for use, delivery for repairs, workmanship, safe custody, service etc. is with specific purpose. If the goods are delivered without purpose or unintentionally or by mistake, that does not constitute bailment.

iv) Return or Disposal of Goods

Bailment is a delivery of goods upon a condition that —
— The goods would be returned to the bailor after the purpose is accomplished or
— Disposed of according to the directions of bailor.

The recipient should restore the possession of goods to the bailor. Borrowing a book from the library is redelivered to a librarian. (Delivering a parcel to a post office for onward delivery to the addressee, clothes given to a tailor for stitching purposes constitutes bailment who returns in altered form.)

16.3 Kinds of Bailment

Contract of bailment may be classified keeping in view either remuneration or benefit flowing from the contract.

a) Remuneration (reward) as a basis of classification

i) **Gratuitous Bailment -** If neither bailor non bailee receives any remuneration or reward, the bailment is gratuitous. 'A' delivering his horse for safe custody to his neighbour during his travel is a gratuitous bailment. Absence of reward does not mean there is no consideration in bailment. Bailor, when parts with possession of goods suffers detriment, or loss and bailee's promise to return is a sufficient consideration in bailment. A neighbour takes your silver utensils for some function and returns those to you is a gratuitous bailment. There is no commercial element in such give and take.

ii) **Non-Gratuitous Bailment or Bailment for Reward -** When eigher bailor or bailee receives remuneration or reward, it is a non - gratuitous bailment. Reward may be described as charges or fees or subscription.

b) Benefit as a basis of classification

i) **Benefit to Bailor only :** Benefit accrues to bailor exclusively. A villeger leaves a cow with B during his piligrimage wih no reward to B. Here A is the only beneficiary.

ii) Benefit to bailee only : Here benefit accrues to bailee exclusively. For eg. A takes B's car for 2 days for joy-ride. B gives it without any expectation.

iii) Benefit to Both : When bailor and bailee both are benefitted by bailment, the bailment involves mutual benefit. An equipment is hired in a hospital for operation purposes on payment of charges. Hospital gets the benefit on the article and the other gets the charges.

16.4 Rights and Duties of Bailee and Bailor

Rights and duties of parties in a contract are reciprocal. One's right has corrosponding duty on another. Subject matter of a right and duty in similar situation is common and rights and duties are two sides of the same coin. Duties are discharged and corrosponding rights are enforced. In that context, duties of bailee are rights of bailor and vice versa. Duties and rights of bailor corrospond with rights and duties of bailee. There is a logical connection between these duties and rights of parties in bailment. Hence overlapping is avoided.

16.4.1 Duties of Bailee

1) Duty to take reasonable care of goods (Sec. 151)

The bailee is under a duty to take reasonable care of goods bailed. The standard of care is that of a prudent man. He should take care of goods in possession 'as a ordinary prudent man would take of his own goods.' In similar circumstances what an average prudent man would do is expected of a bailee. If he is negligent and the goods are damaged / lost, the bailee would be liable to compensate bailor. The degree of care may be varied by special contract by the parties.

2) Bailee should not make unauthorised use of the goods - (Sec. 154)

Bailee should use the bailed goods strictly as per the contractual terms. If the goods are put to use inconsistent with conditions in the bailment, bailee is liable to bailor for eventual loss. Bailor has a right to terminate the contract on the ground of unauthorised use.

Example - A goldsmith had certain ornaments of his customers. He carried some of the ornaments with him to be worn by his wife in a marriage ceremony. Robbers robbed off those ornaments from the goldsmith. He was held liable to customer for the price of ornaments for unauthorised use.

3) Bailee not to mix his own goods with goods bailed (Sec. 155 to 157)

S.155 Mixing with consent - If the bailee mixes the goods with bailor's consent, then both would be the owners in proportion to their shares in the mixed product (Mixure);

Mixing without consent –

i) **S.156 – Separable mixture -** If the mixing is done without bailor's consent and the mixture is seperable, the bailee is bound to bear the expenses of seperation and the damage arising from mixing.

ii) **S.157 – Inseparable mixture -** If the mixing, without consent of bailor and mixure is inseparable, the bailee must compensate the bailor for his loss.

The above rules apply whether mixing is intentional or accidental.

Illustration - A bails a barrel of cape floor worth Rs. 45 to B. B without A's consent mixes the floor with country floor of his own worth only Rs. 25 a barrel. B must compensate A for the loss of his floor.

4) Duty to return the goods (Sec. 160)

When the purpose of bailment is accomplished, the bailee should –
– return the goods to the bailor even without his demand;
– dispose off goods as directed by him.
If he fails do so, he is liable for loss, destruction or deterioration of goods thereafter. He remains liable even if goods are damaged without his negligence, say by natural calamity.

5) Duty to deliver any accretion (natural increase, growth...) to goods (Sec. 163)

"In the absence of a contract to the contrary, the bailee is bound to deliver to the bailor or according to his directions, any increase or profit which may have accrued from the goods bailed."

Illustration - A leaves a cow in the custody of B to be taken care of. The cow delivers a calf. B is bound to deliver cow as well as calf to A.

6) Duty not to set-up adverse title (Sec. 167)

The bailee cannot set up his own or title of a third party in the bailed goods. Once he accepts the bailor's goods in bailment, he is estopped from claiming title adverse to bailor. As per Sec.117 of Indian Evidence Act, bailee cannot deny bailor's title to the goods or authority to bail. According to Sec. 167 if a person other than the bailor, claims goods bailed, he may apply to the court to stop the delivery of the goods to the bailor, and to decide the title of the goods.

16.4.2 Duties of the Bailor

1) To disclose faults in goods - Sec. 150 lays down two principles in view of gratuitous and non-gratuitous bailments.

i) In gratuitous bailment, bailor is under duty to disclose those faults in goods which he knows . In case of non-disclosure he is responsible for the loss resulting to bailee directly from such faults. The faults covered in this section are those which materially interfere with their use of the goods or expose the bailee to extraordinary risks.

ii) In case of non-gratuitous bailment, the bailor should disclose all faults in the goods whether he is aware or not.

Illustration

i) A lends a horse which he knows to be vicious, to B. He does not disclose the fact that the horse is vicious. The horse runs away. B is thrown and injured. A is responsible to B for damage sustained.

ii) A gives his carriage to B, gratuitously. The carriage is unsafe but A is ignorant about it. B is injured. A is not liable under the circumstances.

2) To pay necessary expenses in gratuitous bailment : Sec. 158

The bailor should pay to the bailee necessary expenses for the purpose of bailment.

Those include expenses for keeping the goods in safe custody or for carriage or work done on them. A cow is bailed, without reward, by A to B. A should reimburse B for expenses incurred in feeding the cow.

3) To pay extraordinary expenses in non-gratuitous bailment

But is in non-gratuitous bailment bailor has to bear extra-ordinary expenses incurred by bailee in respect of goods bailed.

4) Duty to indemnify bailee

a) For premature return of goods - According to Sec. 159, if bailor of goods lent gratuitously for a specific period or purpose asks the bailee to return the goods before expiry of the period or accomplishment of purpose, he must indemnify the bailee for the loss caused to him in excess of benefit from the goods.

b) For defective title (Sec.164) If the bailee sustains losses due to the defect in title of bailor, bailor must compensate for such loss.

5) Duty to receive back goods

Where the bailee tenders the goods to the bailor after bailment, he must accept those. If he wrongfully refuses to accept, he should bear the expenses required for preservation, safe custody of goods.

16.4.3 Rights of Bailee

As stated in the introduction, rights of bailee are the duties of bailor as subject matter of rights and duties is the same. Hence bailees rights are enlisted without elaboration.

1) Right to claim compensation in case of loss due to non-disclosure of faults - Sec. 150.
2) Right to receive necessary expenses u/s 158.
3) Right to receive extra-ordinary expenses u/s 158.
4) Right of indemnity case of premature demand goods (Sec.159)
5) Right of indemnity for loss due to bailor's defective title. (Sec. 164)
6) Right to redeliver goods to any one of joint owners (bailors) is vested with bailee U/s 165 of the Act. In this way he would be discharged in his duty to return the goods.
7) Right to deliver goods to bailor - Sec. 160 - If a third party sets up a little adverse to the bailor, then bailee would be justified in returning the goods to bailor.
8) Right against third party (sec. 180) - Bailee can resort to remedies as the owner of goods if a third person interferes with his possession or use of goods or damages those goods.
9) **Right of Lien -** (Ss.170 and 171) The bailee can enjoy statutory right of lien in the circumstances mentioned below. Lien is a right to retain the possession of other's goods till payment is received or debt is satisfied. Lien is possessory lien because factum of possession vests this right. Lien can be statutory or contractual or it may be available by usage.

Lien is of two types viz Particular or General Lien.

Particular Lien : Particular lien is a right to retain only that particular property (goods) in respect of which some claim exists. Other goods, though in possession in respect of which payment or debt or charges are not due, cannot be retained in particular lien.

Bailee's Particular Lien : Sec. 170 of the Contract Act vests bailee with statutory right of particular lien. This right can be enforced by bailee if following conditions are satisfied.

Conditions for exercise of particular lien.

i) Bailee must be is possession of goods;

ii) Bailee must have rendered some services involving labour or skill in respect of goods bailed;

iii) Bailee, by his services must have improved the value of goods;

iv) Bailee has not been paid remuneration for services inspite of being entitled to it; services are not credit based;

v) Bailee must have rendered the services in accordance with the terms of bailment;

vi) Lien u/s 170 is subject to the contract to the contrary;

vii) Lien cannot be exercised for charges for keeping goods for non-payment of extra-ordinary expenses :

Illustration - A, delivers a rough diamond to B, a jeweller, to cut and polish which is accordingly done. B is entitled to retain the stone till he is paid for the services A has rendered. (see condition - iii)

General Lien : It is a right to continue in possession of goods belonging to other untill all claims against the party are satisfied. General lien lawfully permits a person to retain possession of goods as a security for general balance of accounts. In general lien one can retain other's goods for payment of dues whether with respect to those goods or other goods. If between banker and debtor, there exist two separate loans secured by two distinct securities, banker can detain and enforce these two securities for any single loan.

Sec - 171 of the Contract Act recognizes general lien of bankers, factors, wharfinger, attorney of high courts and policy brokers. These persons can retain any security for the general balance of accounts. Banker has a general lies on all goods, cash, cheques and securities deposited by customer with him as a banker for any amount due to him as a banker.

16.4.4 Rights of Bailor - The rights of bailor are enlisted below.

i) Right to claim compensation from bailee for injury / damage to goods by bailee's negligence (Sec. 151)

ii) Right to terminate bailment (Sec. 153)

iii) Right to damages for unauthorised mixing and unauthorised use and consequencial loss / destruction of goods (Sec. 154 & 156)

iv) Right to demand the return of goods at any time in case of gratuitous bailment even if it is for a specified period or for specific purpose.

v) Right against third person - Sec. 180 In the circumstances described in Sec. 180 (explained earlier), the bailor, being the owner or a person having tittle, can also bring legal action against the third party for damage, injury to goods by wrongful interference in the possession of bailee.

vi) Right to share compensation received U/S 180 - The bailor has a right to claim share in the compensation along with bailee awarded by the court U/s 180.

vii) Right to claim increase in goods U/S 163.

16.5 Termination of Bailment – S. 154

A contract of bailment is terminated under the following situations.

i) Inconsistent use of goods : Bailee uses the goods inconsistent with the terms of the contract.

ii) Accomplishment of purpose : When the purpose of bailment is fulfilled or achieved.

iii) On expiry of the period : If the bailment is for a specific period, on the expiry of that period;

iv) Destruction of subject matter : When the goods bailed are destroyed or become unfit for the purpose of bailment (like frustration of contract)

v) Death of bailor or bailee : This is a ground for terminating gratuitous bailment.

vi) Termination of gratuitous bailment by bailor is possible at any time subject to his duty to compensate bailee for premature termination.

16.6 Finder of lost goods : (Sec. 168 & 169)

A person who finds goods belonging to other is a finder. Finder is not supposed to appropriate the articles found. Law subjects him to certain duties and confers on him certain rights. His position is like that of a bailee of goods. Sec. 71 States, "..a person who finds goods belonging to another takes into his custody is subject to the responsibility as a bailee"

Rights of Finder

1) **Right to retain goods** - He has right to hold goods against the whole world except true owner. He can retain the goods till the true owner is traced.

2) **Right of Lien** - He can exercise right of lien over the goods till reasonable expenses for finding true owner and preservation of property are paid by the owner. Suit for recovery of these expenses cannot be filed by him against the owner.

3) **Right to Reward** - (S. 168) Finder can file a suit for recovery of reward announced by the owner. Till reward is received, he can withhold the article found.

4) **Right of Sale (S. 169)** - In the following circumstances finder can sell the goods.
   i) Owner cannot be found even after searching him or
   ii) Owner refuses to pay lawful charges of the finder or
   iii) The goods are perishing in nature or in danger of loosing greater part of its value or
   iv) Lawful charges of the Finder amount to two-third of the value of goods.

Duties of Finder

As stated earlier, finder is placed in the **position of a bailee** and as such he has to discharge following duties -

i) To take reasonable care of goods. The standard of care is that of a man of ordinary prudence;

ii) Not to make use or appropriate the goods as he is not the owner;

iii) Not to mix the goods with his own;

iv) To take reasonable and necessary steps to find out the true owner of goods;

v) When found, restore the goods to the real owner;

Chapter 17 | PLEDGE (PAWN)

17.1 Definition and Essentials

Definition. (sec. 172)

> *"The bailment of goods as security for the payment of a debt or performance of a promise is called 'pledge'. Bailor is called as pawnor and bailee is called as pawnee."*

Illustration - X borrows Rs. one lakh from Y and keeps his diamond as a security for the payment of debt. The bailment of diamond is called a pledge.

Essentials of Pledge : The Act defines pledge in terms of bailment. If purpose of bailment is security of payment of debt or performance of promise, it is described as pledge. Pledge is thus a species or special form of bailment as a genus. It is a bailment with added feature of security. As a bailment it should possess all the requirements of a bailment explained in the relevant topic.

Pledge or pawn thus is a delivery of some goods (movables) for the purpose of securing repayment of loan or performance of a promise. 'Goods' include documents of title as railway receipt, bill of lading. Deposit of these documents as security with lender constitutes pledge. Pledge is not transfer of ownership (general interest) of property but of special interest with respect to goods. Pawnor retains the ownership of goods while possession and right to sell under certain circumstance is parted with in favour of pawnee.

17.2 Rights and Duties of Pawnee

Pledge being a branch of bailment, *the rights and duties of Pawnor and Pawnee are almost similar to that of bailor and bailee.*

Rights of Pawnee

i) **Right to retain the goods (sec. 173)**

The pawnee has a right to retain the goods until pawnor pays the debt with interest and the necessary expenses of preservation of pledged goods.

ii) Right to retain goods for subsequent advances (sec. 174)

Where the lends money to the same pawnor subsequent to the first debt and pledge, the pawnee's right to retain extends to the subsequent advances also continuation of possession however is subject to terms of contract between the parties.

iii) Right to extra-ordinary expenses (sec. 175)

Pawnee may be required to incur extra-ordinary expenses for preservation of pledged goods. Pawnee can file a suit for recovery of those expenses but he is not entitled to retain goods for the recovery.

iv) Right to sue or sell in case of Pawnor's default - (Sec. 176)

If the Pawnor makes a default in payment of debt or performance of promise in accordance with the contract, pawnee has following options : -

a) Suit for recovery of debt in addition to the right of lien over the goods as collateral security;

b) Suit for sale of pledged goods and appropriation of sale proceeds for realising debt;

c) He can himself sell the goods after serving a notice to the pawnor;

d) Suit for deficient amount (after sale) may also be filed by him.

v) Right against the real owner -

Pawnor's title to the goods may be defective if he procures those under voidable contract. If the pawnee accepts the goods in pledge in good faith (without notice of dedect in title), he gets a good title to the goods as against real owner.

Duties of Pawnee

i) Not to use the goods : The pawnee is not supposed to use the goods pledged.

ii) Not to purchase goods : When right to sell accrues to pawnee under Sec. 176, he himself cannot purchase the goods; third party can purchase in such sale.

iii) To return surplus - The pawnee must return the surplus in excess of debt in sale of pledged goods.

17.3 Rights and Duties of Pawnor

Pawnor's Rights

The pawnor is entitled to enforce the duties of pawnee listed above. He has the following rights.

a) Right in unauthorised sale :

If pawnor desires to sell pledged goods, he has to serve notice to the pawnor. Sale without notice is inauthorised. In such a case -

i) Pawnor can file a suit for redemption of goods by deposit of debt amount as if no sale has taken place ;

ii) Claim damages for conversion (wrongful use or dealing) of goods.

b) Right to redeem debt before sale :

Subsequent to his default in payment of debt but before actual sale by pawnee, the pawnor may redeen the goods by payment of debt with the additional expenses resulting from his default.

iii) Right to compensation :

Pawnor can claim damages from pawnee in case of damage to goods by default of pawnee.

17.5 Pawnor's Duties

Pawnor is under a duty -

1. To repay loan or perform the promise under pledge ;
2. To compensate pawnee for extra-ordinary expenses incurred by pawnee in preserving the goods pledged ;
3. To compensate the pawnee for any loss he suffers due to his defective title.

Chapter 18 | AGENCY

18.1 Concept of Agency

The Act does not define the term 'Agency'. The parties to the contract of agency are however defined.

Agent & Principal – Sec.182

> *"An agent is a person employed to do any act for another or to represent another in dealing with the third persons. The person for whom such act is done or who is represented is called the principal."*

Agent is a person
  i) Who is employed by another (principal)
  ii) He is employed to do the acts for another or represent the principal in dealings or transactions with third parties.

English law on contract of agency – "The employment of one person by another in order to bring the latter into legal relation with third persons."

Agent thus is appointed either to represent one or get certain things done for another. Agency establishes privity of contract between principal and third party. He acts like a connecting link or intermediatory between principal and third party. *Representative capacity coupled with the power to establish legal nexus is the gist of agency.*

Basis of Agency – The concept and the law of agency is based on a latin maxim **"Qui facit per alium facit per se"** which means –

"He who acts by another acts by himself"

or

"He who does an act through another is deemed in law to do it himself"

The act of the agent is considered in law as the act of the principal.

18.2 Creation of Agency

Agency is created in the following ways

1. **Express Agreement**

   Sec. 186 states that "The authority of an agent may be express or implied." Sec.187 further states, "An authority is said to be express when it is given by words spoken or written." Power of attorney is an example of express agreement.

2. **Implied Agreement**

   Sec. 187 states that authority of an agent may be implied when inferred from circumstances of the case, ordinary course of dealing. It can also be gathered from conduct of parties, usage or trade custom.

   Following ways of creation of agency are treated as various *forms of implied agency.*

3. **Agency by Estoppel**

   According to the principle of estoppel where a person by his words or conduct leads other to believe that certain facts or circumstances exist and induces the other to act upon it, he is estopped or precluded from denying the existance of such facts or state of things although such facts or state of things do not in fact exist.

   Incorporating this doctrine, Sec.237 provides that "When an agent has, without authority, done acts or incurred obligations to third parties on behalf of his principal, the principal is bound by his words or conduct, if he has induced such third persons to believe that such acts and obligations were within such scope of the agent's authority."

   Thus an agent does not possess authority from principal, but principal by his conduct causes third party to believe that agent had the authority. In these circumstances he is bound by agents's acts.

4. **Agency by 'Holding-out'**

   Holding out is an application of principle of estoppel. In this case person by his positive act or conduct holds other out as his agent. Later on the former is not allowed to deny that later is not his agent. By his prior active assertion or affirmative conduct, principal indicates that somebody is his agent.

   Example - X usually purchases goods from Y on credit through his servant Z. Once X pays money to Z for cash purchase from Y. Z misappropriates money and purchases goods on credit from Y. X should pay price of goods to Y.

5. **Agency by Necessity**

   Doctrine of Authority of Necessity – Sec.189 – Under some extraordinary emergent circumstances a person is required to act on behalf of the other to protect other's interest. Law in such circumstances assumes the consent of the other and confers an authority as an agent. Such an agency is called as agency by necessity[77-a]

77-a. Necessity knows no law

Conditions for implied authority by necessity –

i) There exist an emergency situation. The property or interests of other (principal) are in imminent danger and preservation or protection becomes necessary;

ii) The agent has no opportunity to communicate with principal within the time at his disposal and seek prior instructions;

iii) The agent should act bonafide to protect principal's interest;

iv) The agent mush have adopted reasonable and necessary course of action. He must observe ordinary prudence.

Instances of Agency by necessity

a) In the case of accident and emergency (Marine adventures) a master of a ship can sell or pledge the goods of the owner to save their value or he can borrow money to carry out necessary repairs of ship to complete the voyage.

b) The agent may exceed his authority in good faith in emergent situation.

c) Carrier of goods in the position of bailee may resort to necessary acts to protect or preserve goods.

d) Wife has implied authority by necessity where her husband fails to provider her means for sustenance. Under this authority she can pledge husband's credit for necessaries against his desire. However wife should not be responsible for the state of affairs.

Great Northern Rly Co. v/s Swafield [77-b] Railway Company kept the horse in a stable without owner's consent because nobody received it at its destination. Company was entitled for charges of stable paid.

Illustrations

i) An agent for sale may have the goods repaired if it be necessary;

ii) A consigns provisions to B at Calcutta, with directions to send them immediately to C at Cuttack. B may sell provisions at Calcutta, if they will not bear the journey to Cuttack without spoiling.

6. Agency by Ratification – Sec. 196-200

A person sometimes acts on behalf of the other without the other's authority. The other later on may approve that act. Such approval is called ratification. Ratification is post facto sanction of unauthorized act or transaction. Sec. 196 incorporates agency by ratification. Its ingradients are –

a) A person acts on behalf of other;

b) He acts so without other's knowledge or authority;

c) The other may elect

   i) to ratify the same or

   ii) to disown the act

d) The act performed will be deemed to have been authorised by the other (principal)

Example – A, without authority, buys goods for B. Afterwards B sells goods to C on his account. B's conduct implies ratification of purchase made for him by A.

77-b. *(1874) LR9 Ex 132*

Requisites of Valid Ratification : To borrow the theory of implied authority (agency), ratification must satisfy following conditions –

i) **Act should be done on behalf of the another** – The agent must contract for principal and not for himself. He must indend to act in the name of supposed principal. The principal must be ascertainable. The agent must purport to act as an agent for a principal in contemptation.

ii) **Supposed principal only can ratify** – The person on whose behalf act is done, only that person can ratify. If A acts in the name of B, B only can adopt the act and not C.

iii) **Principal must be in existence and capable of being ascertained at the time of contract** – Company can not ratify the transaction of its promoters before incorporation.

iv) **Act must have been done without knowledge or authority of the principal.**

v) **Ratification must be with full knowledge of all material facts** – S.199 – Ratification should be intentional acknowledgement or conscious act and knowledge is necessary for its validity. If the act is illegal and principal does not know about illegality, he is not bound by ratification.[78]

vi) **Ratified Act must not be void or illegal** – Ratification of voidable contract or tortious act is recognized. Something tangible or existing can be ratified. Renewal of a tenancy which is ceased cannot be ratified.

vii) **Ratification should be made within reasonable time after the contract is made.**

viii) **Ratifier must have been competent or power to authorize ratified act.** Ratification has retrospective effect. Act should be such that he could have performed it. A minor, person of unsound mind at the time of commission of the act cannot ratify the unauthorized act.

ix) **Ratification must be communicated to the other side (agent) within reasonable time so as to be complete.**

x) **The ratification must be of the whole transaction** (S. 199). Partial acceptance is deemed to be the ratification of the whole. Principal cannot reject burden and accept only benefit.

xi) **Ratification should not prejudice third parties.** Ratification is invalid if it results in deprivation of a right or interest of third party or subjects him to any liability or damage. (S. 200)

Example – T is a tenant of L (landlord). Tenancy is terminable by three months notice. A, without authority of L gives notice of termination of tenancy, such a notice cannot be ratified as T would loose tenancy.

Legal Consequences of Ratification

Authority to do an act may be given before or after the act is committed. Authority subsequently given is equivalent to authority given before[79] Act may be founded on contract or tort, to his detriment or advantage, once that is ratified consequences would follow.

---

78. *Marsh Vs. Joseph (1897) Ch 213*

79. ***Ominis ratihabitio retrotrahitur et mandato prior eaquiparatur*** = *Subsequent ratification is as good as prior authority. Ratification is adoption or acknowledgement of unauthorized act binding the principal.*

18.3 Kinds of Agents

Agents may be classified by applying different criteria. Agents can be general or special or mercantile or non mercantile agents. Various kinds of agents are explained as under.

1) **Special or Particular Agent**

   An agent employed to do a particular act or a transaction is known as special agent. He has a limited authority to complete the specific work. Power of attorney for sale of a flat is special agent.

2) **General Agent**

   He is entrusted with duties of general nature in a particular trade or business. Manager of a firm or director of a company are said to be general agents. General power of attorney, commercial agents are general agents. Till terminated, they continue as representatives of the principal.

3) **Mercantile or commercial agents**

   These agents are of following categories –

   i) **Commision Agent** – Agent working for commission is called commission agent He is not liable for non-performance of contract by third party. He may have possession of property of his principal. His lien is particular type of lien.

   ii) **Broker** – Broker is a mere negotiator and intermediatory. He finds either buyer for seller or seller for buyer. He acts for both. Broker does not have possession of property. He neither can sue third party nor can enter into contract in his name.

   His commission is called as brokerage. He keeps memorandum book and makes entries in terms of contracts.

   iii) **Factor** – Factor is an agent in possession of goods of his principal. He has authority to sell, sell on credit, pledge, fix price, make payments, receive goods. He can enter into contracts and sue in his own name.

   Lien is of particular type. He cannot part without authority.

   iv) **Auctioneer** – He is appointed to sell goods for price by auction. He has the possession of goods. Auctioneer works as agent of seller before sale and afterwards that of buyer. He cannot sell by private contract. Enjoys particular lien. He can sue third party in his name. Reasonable care of goods should be taken by him till those are sold.

   v) **Del Credere Agent** – This type of agent is an agent as well as guarantor. He guarantees or undertakes the performance of third parties and responsible for his failure. He guarantees solvency and payment of price. His liability is secondary. He is partly insurer and partly surety. For principal's default he is not liable. i.e. he is not liable to buyer for seller's performance. His principals are normally foreign entities.

   vi) **Pakka Adatiya and Kuccha Adatiya** – These agents work in adats and also known as dalal, sharaf or arhat. They work for brokerage called 'dalali'. They deal in transaction between upcountry constituents and Mumbai Merchants. They find cash for goods and goods for cash.

      – Pakka Adatiya – Pakka adatiya does not disclose name of parties to each other. He has a power to deal without reference to principal. He is not an agent in real sense. Acts like a principal with third party to whom he is personally liable. No privity of contract is established between two parties. He can himself perform the contract. He guarantees the performance to each other. His transactions are not wagers U/S. 30 of the Act.

      – Kachha Adatiya – He does not guarantee the performance of contract. Parties are responsible to each other and hence he establishes privity of contract. He is that way a perfect agent. His principal is 'unnamed principal'. He is personally liable to Mumbai Party.

vii) **Sub – Agent –** An agent appointed by an agent is sub-agent. He works under the direct control of original agent. Original agent has no authority to appoint sub-agent but custom/usage may necessitate his employment.

viii) **Substituted Agent –** Where the principal authorizes the agent to have other person in his place, the person so employed is called as substituted agent. He is directly responsible for the principal.

18.4 Agent's Authority

Extent and Scope of Agent's Authority.

      Authority of an agent is the power of agent to establish legal relationship with third parties. it is an authority to bind the principal. The agent can bind the principal only when his acts fall within the scope of his authority.

Express or Implied Authority

      Sec. 186 provides that the authority of an agent may be express or implied. Sec. 187. further states, express authority is said to be express when it is given by words spoken or written. It is said to be implied when it is inferred from the circumstances of the case.

The extent and scope of authority would be better understood by explaining types of agent's authority as - actual and ostensible authority.

1) **Actual Authority -** Authority which is confirmed by the principal upon agent is called as actual or real authority. It, therefore, includes express and implied authority.

2) **Ostensible or Apparent Authority -** Agent can also bind the principal for his acts within his 'ostensible or apparent' authority. What appears to the others as authority of an agent in a particular business is apperent authoriity. The persons dealing with him can assume such authority as necessary or incidental as to carry on business in question. Ostensible authority may coincide with actual authority or may exceed it. Apparent authority may be restricted by principal. An act of agent within apparent authority but exceeding actual authority would bind the principal, if the third party is unaware of such a restriction and acts bonafide.

Extent of agent's authority has been laid down u/s 188 in the following words.

Sec. 188 - "An agent having an authority to do an act or to carry on a business has

authority to do every lawful thing which is necessary in order to do such an act, or which is usually done in the course of conducting such business."

Illustration - A constitutes B, his agent, to carry on his business of a ship builder. B may purchase timber and other materials, and hire workmen, for the purpose of carrying on the business.

Extent of agent's authority thus depends upon –
- nature of business ;
- things which are incidental to the business or usually done to carrying it out.
- the customs and usages of trade.

Authority to recover debt includes authority to file a suit. Authority to deal in land includes to let out the land. Horse dealer can validly give warranty of fitness of horse if it can be usual in that kind of trade, under the authority to sell. An agent can negotiate, give notice, appoint advocate and describe property, sign the document and accept money. Sec. 188 confers in appropriate cases implied authority to borrow, to sell, to assign a decree. Power in the management of property business, implies authority to purchase, make payments, receive payments or to recover debts.

However power to dispose off property may not be construed as power to dispose off by mortgage, power to sell goods in one area will not be extended to sell goods in other area. Power of attorney is strictly construed.

18.5 Relations Between Principal and Agent

Duties, Rights, and Liabilities of Agent towards Principal –

A) Duties of an Agent

An agent has to discharge certain duties towards his principal. These duties are imposed by law and can be extended or restricted by special agreement between them. General duties of agent are explained as follows -

1. To follow principal's instructions (S. 211)

An agent should follow principal's mandate in conducting the business. He is bound to conduct the business according to the principal's directions. If there are no instructions, then he should follow custom prevailing in similar business. He is not supposed to follow illegal instructions.

2. To use skill and diligence in work (Sec. 212)

This duty is two - fold,
a) An agent should excercise skill which other agents possesses in similar kind of business. If the principal is aware of his want of skill, he is not under duty to use that skill.
b) He is always bound to act with reasonable diligence (care) and use the skill which he actually possesse. Amount of skill or care depends upon kind of profession of an agent, nature of business conducted.

3. To render proper accounts - (S. 213)

— An agent is bound to render proper accounts to his principal on demand.
— Duty to keep and maintain true and proper accounts is implicit in this duty.

— Agent should explain the accounts by vouchers.

Principal can file a suit for rendition of accounts if agents fails in his duty.

4. To communicate with principal - (Sec. 214)

In emergency situations, an agent should contact the principal and seek fresh instructions in the absence of prior instructions. On failure he is liable to consequential loss to his principal.

5. Not to deal in his own account (Sec. 215)

An agent cannot deal in his individual capacity in conducting principal's business. That is cantradictory to the the concept of agency. When he deals in his own accounts, principal can repudiate the transaction with third parties in flollowing situations-

i) Agent does not obtain his consent ;

ii) He fails to disclose all material circumstances within his knowledge pertaining to the transaction or

iii) He dishonestly conceals information from his principal.

iv) The dealings of the agent have been disadvantagous to him.

The principal has right to claim from the agent any benefit resulting from the transection in personal capacity. He can also claim secret profits earned by agent in the course of agency.

Illustration - A directs B, his agent, to buy a certain house for him. B tells A that it cannot be bought and buys the house for himself. A may, on discovering that B has bought the house, compell him to sell it to A at the price he gave fot it.

6. Not to make secret profit (Sec. 216)

Agent, as per agreement, may get commission or remuneration. Being in the fiduciary capacity, he cannot make secret profits or accept illegal gratification. If he receives, he has to account for it.

7. To pay sums received for principal (Sec. 218)

An agent is bound to pay to his principal all sums received on his account. He can deduct his remunerations, expenses incurred and advances made by him, while conducting principal's business.

8. Not to delegate authority (Sec. 190)

Agency is created by delegation of authority. Agent further cannot delegate his authority to anybody except in certain circumstances. (*Delegates non potest delegare* ie. One who is delegated cannot further delegate.)

9. Duty in case of death or insanity of principal (Sec. 209)

The agency is terminated on the death or insanity of the principal. In that case the agent should take all reasonable steps for the protection and preservation of the interests entrusted to him.

10. Agent, cannot set up his title or the title of third party against the principal in his property.

11. Agent should not use information obtained in the course of business of agency against the principal.

B) Rights of an Agent

The agent has the following rights against the principal.

1) Right to retain money for advances made or expenses incurred during the course of agency. (Sec. 217)

2) Right to remuneration - (Sec. 219).

Regarding claim for remuneration by him following points may be noted -

- Agent would get remuneration by way of right, if agreed.
- If not agreed, he would get reasonable remuneration.
- If payment of remuneration is subject to conditions, conditions must be fulfilled.
- If time of payment is mentioned in the contract of agency, at that time remuneration is receivable. If time is not specified, he will get it after his work is complete.
- Remuneration can be claimed when a transaction is the direct result of his efforts.

Sec. 220 States that, " An agent who is guilty if misconduct in the business of the agency, is not entitled to any remuneration in respect of that part of the business which he has misconducted."

3) Right of Lien (Sec. 221)

Right to retain the goods already possession is called as lien. Sec. 221 recognizes agent's right to lien. The law on lien can be summerised as under —

— Agent must be in possession of goods, other property (movable or immovable) or papers of the principal, over which lien can be exercised.

— Property must come in agent's possession in the course of business of agency and not by fraud or misrepresentation.

— Property held for special purpose cannot be retained.

— Property can be retained by agent until the amount due to himself as commission, disbursement and services in respect of the same has been paid or accounted for to him.

— Right of lien dose not imply right to sell, pledge or dispose off the property.

— Lien is subject to the principal's interests in the property which is retained.

— The agent's lien is generally a particular lien. Agreement may deprive the agent of his right of lien or provide a general lien. - Bankers, factors, attorneys of High Court, wharfingers or policy brokers enjoy general lien.

— Lien is lost if agent waives the right or parts with the possession.

4) Right to Indemnity

a) Sec. 222 - An agent has the right to be indemnified against the consequences of lawful acts done by him in exercise of the authority conferred on him.

b) Sec. 224 Clarifies that agent cannot claim indemnity in respect of unlawful or criminal acts.

c) Sec. 223 - Agent is entitled to be indemnified against the consequences of an act done in good faith though it turns out to be injurious to the rights of third persons.

It would be noted that indemnity is available for all authorised, lawful acts. It can also be claimed for unauthorised act provied it is done honestly.

Illustration - B, at the request of A sells goods in possession of A but which A had no right to dispose of . B does not know this and hands over the proceeds of sale to A. Afterwards C, the true owner of goods, sues B and recovers the value of goods and costs. A is liable to indemnity B for what he has been compelled to pay to C and for B's own expenses.

5) **Right to compensation**
Sec. 225. The agent can claim compensation for injuries sustained by him due to principal's neglect or want of skill.

Illustration - A employes B as a bricklayer in building a house, and puts the scaffolding himself. The scaffolding is unskillfully put up and B is, in consequence, hurt. A must make compensation to B.

6) **Compensation in case of premature revocation of agency** — If agency is for a fixed term and the principal revokes it prematurely without sufficient cause, the agent can claim compensation from the principal. (Sec. 205).
Agent also enjoys following incidental rights under various sections.
7) To do all lawful things to carry out the authorised act (Sec. 188).
8) To do all necessary things to protect the principal from loss.
9) To appoint substitute agent u/s 194.
10) To renounce agency by giving notice to the principal.

Rights and Duties of the Principal
Rights and duties of agents are principal's corrosponding duties and rights. Subject matter of these rights/duties is already covered while explaining rights and duties of agents.

Rights of principal
1. Enforcing various duties of agent.
2. To claim compensation in case of loss and profit under sections 211 and 212
3. To forfeit agent's remuneration when agent is guilty of misconduct while carrying out business. Sec. 220
4. He is entitled for extra (secret) profits earned by agent during course of agency (Sec. 216)
5. To receive the sums from agent which agent has received out of a void transaction entered into on behalf of the principal
6. To repudiate agent's transaction (Sec. 215)
7. To ratify or disown unauthorised acts of agent (Sec. 196)
8. To revoke agent's authority (Ss. 201, 203, 206)
9. To demand accounts (Sec. 213)

Duties of Principal
1. Payment of remuneration to agent (Sec. 219)
2. To indemnify agent. (Ss. - 222 and 224)
3. To pay compensation for injuries sustained (Sec. 205, 225).

18.6 Prinicipal and Agent vis-a-vis- Third Party

A) Principal's Liability to Third Party for Agent's Act - Principal's liability to third party for agent's act may be explained as under -

1. Lability for the acts of agent within scope of his authority
   Sec. 188 and 189 - See extent of agent's authority.

2. Liability by ratification - See agency by ratification.

3. Liability for agent's fraud or misrepresentation – Sec. 238 - Principal is liable to third party for agent's fraud or misrepresentation if,
   i) It is committed in the course of business or
   ii) It is within the scope of authority of an agent.
   Wrongs or torts of agent are regarded as that of his principal.[80]

4. **Notice to agent is notice to principal**
   Sec. 229 - Where an agent receives information while conducting business for principal, the principal is deemed to have constructive notice of such information affecting transaction. Agent may not infact communicate it to the principal, still, he is bound by agent's notice.

5. **Liability on account of 'Holding out' or estoppel - Sec. 237** (See 'Creation of Agency')

6. **Liability as 'Unnamed Principal'**
   When an agent discloses the existence of the principal but not his name, the principal is called as 'Unnamed Principal'. In this case the acts of the agent bind the principal as usual. When third party knows his name, he can hold principal liable subject to usage in that kind of business. If agent refuses to disclose name of the principal, he is personally liable to third party. If before disclosing name, agent dies, his estate is liable as if he was a contracting party.

7. **Liability as 'Undisclosed Principal'**
   Where an agent neither discloses the existence of principal nor his name to the third party, the principal is called as undisclosed Principal. The agent infact contract on behalf of the principal but makes an impression to the third party that he is personally contracting. Legal position between three parties is briefed as under.
   a) Agent is personally liable to third party.
   b) Between principal and agent, right and liabilities are not affected.
   c) In case of breach of contract by third party, principal may intervene but cannot exercise his right to prejudice him. In such a case third party has against the principal same rights as he would have had as against the agent if the agent had been principal. (Sec. 231, para 1)
   d) If the principal discloses himnself before completion of contract, the third party has option to refuse to perform the contract if he could prove that he would not have contracted with principal had he known about him. (Sec. 231, para 2).

---

80. *Briess v/s Wooley (1954) AC 333 — Company is liable for the wrongs of its directors and*
    Lyod v/s Grace Smith and Co. - (1912) AC 716 — principal is liable to third party injured by agent's torts committed during the course of agency.

e) Undisclosed Principal can demand performance of contract from third party subject to the rights and obligations subsisting between the agent and the other party. (Sec. 232).

B) Agent's liability to third party - Personal liability of an agent.

An agent is a connecting link between principal and the third party. After establishing contractual relationship between the two, he drops out of picture. Recognising this position, Sec. 233 states, "In the absence of any contract to that effect, an agent cannot personally enforce the contracts entered into by him on behalf of the principal, nor is he personally bound by them . " Thus neither he can sue nor be sued in respect of principal's contracts. There are exceptions to this rule and in the following cases an agent is personally liable to third party. (If there is a contract relieving him from liability, he is not liable).

1) Foreign Principal
An agent is personally liable to third party for the contracts on behalf of his Foreign Principal - Sec. 230.

2) Unnamed Principal
The existance of principal is disclosed but his name is not disclosed.

3) Undisclosed Principal
Refer the liability of these two principals. In unnamed principal, if he declines to disclose principal's identity, agent is personally liable. In case of undisclosed principal agent represents himself to be the principal and third party relies on his credit. Therefore agent is personally liable.

4) Incompetent Principal
If principal is incompetent and cannot be sued due to minority, insanity or he is ambassador or foreign sovereign, third party can hold agent personally liable. Promoters are held personally liable for pre-incorporation contracts entered into for a proposed non-existant company. (Sec. 230).

5) Where agent exceeds authority
Sec. 277-278. An agent incurres personal liability for the whole transaction if he exceeds his real and ostensible authority. (See scope of implied authority of an agent).

6) In agency coupled with interest,
to the extent of his interest, he is personally held accountable to third party.

7) Liability fixed by trade-usage
Agent can also be held liable personally in pursuance of usage or custom in a particular business for example, in stock exchange, jobbers hold brokers personally liable.

8) Money received by fraud or mistake
Where as agent receives money from third parties by means of fraud or mistake, he should repay back. Similarly agent can recover money paid to third party as a result of his fraud or mistake.

9) Liability of Pretended Agent
Where a person falsely represents to be the agent of a principal, he is called as 'pretended

agent'. Agent is under a liability to compensate for any loss to third party resulting in such transactions. Agent cannot compel performance of contract by third party. He is even liable for fraud for pretending as agent when in fact he is not.

It is worth mentioning here that when as agent is acting on behalf of principal, both principal and agent are jointly and severally liable to third party. Third party can sue both of them. *"The law which superadds the liability of an agent does not detract from liability of principal"*.

18.7 Termination of Agency

Agency may be terminated either by act of parties or by operation of law.

A) Termination By Act of Parties

1. **By agreement** –
Agency is the result of agreement which can be brought to an end by mutual consent between principal and agent.

2. **By Revocation** – Ss. 203 to 207
Revocation means withdrawal of authority of agent by unilateral act of principal. Agency is delegation of authority which can be revoked by principal (S. 201)

   Revocation can be express or implied (S. 207) Principal may revoke the authority any time before it is exercised (S. 203). Once authority is exercised, principal is bound by it. If agency is created for a fixed period and it is revoked without sufficient cause, the principal must compensate agent for premature termination. (S. 205)

   Principal can revoke the agency at any time when it is not for a specified period. But reasonable notice of revocation must be given. Failure to give notice entails liability of principal to compensate the agent for damage due to want of notice. (S. 206) Notice period should be reasonable. Length of notice depends upon length of agency.

   Irrevocable Agency – Under following circumstances agency can not be revoked.
   a) Where agent has partly exercised the authority, it becomes irrevocable so far as regards such acts and obligations, which flow from such partial exercise.
   b) Where an agent incurres personal liability, principal cannot revoke suddenly and unilaterally. Agent cannot be exposed to its risk and interfere with rights created.
   c) Agency coupled with interest (S. 202) - When an agent is created for securing or protecting his interest, agency is said to be coupled with interest. Agent thus has interest in the subject matter of contract. Agent should have interest at the time of creation of agency and during subsistence of interest agency is not revocable. Sec. 202 does not apply to interest developed afterwards or incedently.

      Illustration - A gives authority to B to sell A's land and to pay himself, out of the sale proceeds, the debts due to him from A. A cannot revoke this authority nor can it be terminated by insanity or death of A.

3. **Renunciation by Agent** – When an agent renounces the business, agency is terminated. (S. 201) If he is appointed for a fixed period and renounces before the expiry of that period, without sufficient cause, he must compensate the principal for the loss sustained.

(S. 205) Agent must give reasonable notice before renunciation. If notice is not given, he must compensate for consequential loss to the principal. (S. 206)

B) By operation of Law -

In the following cases, agency is terminated automatically.

1. **Death or insanity** – By death or insanity of principal or agent, agency is terminated (S. 201) – See Agent's duty on principal's death. (S. 209)

2. **Insolvency of Principal** leads to termination of authority. The Act is silent as to the insolvency of an agent and hence it would not terminate agency.

3. **Completion of Business** – Completion of business brings an end to agency.

4. **Expiry of Time** – Efflux of time puts an end to the agency for a fixed term. Though the business is not complete, by expiry of time, agency gets terminated.

5. **Destruction of subject matter** – Destruction of subject matter leads to termination as it frustrates the purpose of agency.

   Destruction of a house terminates agency for the sale of that house.

6. **Winding up of company** – As the company ceases to exist on winding up, the agency ipso-facto comes to an end.

7. **Principal or agent becoming alien enemy** – If either of the party to contract of agency becomes alien enemy, agency becomes unlawful. Consequently agency ceases to exist.

   Other ways of termination -

8. **Incapacity of agent or principal** – If some qualification is required for either principal or agent to carry on his business, by disqualification of either of the two, agency is terminated.

9. **Business or object of agency becoming unlawful** – See Sec. 56 of the Act.

   Time and Effect of Termination – Sec. 208 – As between principal and agent, termination is effective only when agent comes to know about the termination. As against third party, termination takes effect when he comes to know about it. (S.208). If agent is authorized to sell house and buyer buys it without the knowledge of termination, principal is bound by sale even after termination of agency.

Part - II

Questions and hints for answers

1. Define 'Contract of Indemnity' Discuss its salient features. MBA 2003, ✓ Ans.15.1.1

2. Define, explain and distinguish Contract of Indemnity and Contract of Guarantee. MBA-2004-PU, TYBCom 2009 ✓ Ans15.1.1&15.2.1
   Define 'Contract of Guarantee'. Explain methods of discharge of surety - TYBCom 2013

3. Briefly explain the rights of surety. Under I.C.A, 7 ✓ Ans.15.2.3

4. Under what circumstances a surety is discharged ? Explain. ✓ Ans. 15.2.4

5. "Liability of surety is co-extensive with that of principal debtor" Explain the statement in the light of nature and scope of surety's liability. MBA – 2005 – P. U . ✓ Ans.15.2.5

6. Explain the concept of Bailment What are its kinds? ✓ Ans.16.1, 16.2 & 16.3

7. Discuss in brief rights and duties of bailor vis-à-vis bailee ✓ Ans.16.4.2&16.4.4

8. Explain various duties of Bailee. ✓ Ans.16.4.1

9. Define & explain Pledge. Enumerate rights and duties of pawnor and pawnee ✓ Ans.17.1to17.5

10. Explain the concept 'Agency'. How agency is created ? ✓ Ans.18.1,18.2

11. What is 'Ratification' ? How agency can be validly created by ratification ? ✓ Ans.18.2(6)

12. What is Agency ? Discuss extent and scope of agent's authority ? ✓ Ans. 18.1 & 18.4

13. State various kinds of agents ? ✓ Ans. 18.3

14. State and explain in brief various duties of an agent towards his principal. PGDBM 2004 PU, MBA 2003 PU ✓ Ans.18.5.1

15. Explain in brief the rights and duties of the principal as against agent. (PGDBM 2004 PU) ✓ Ans. 18.5.3

16. Under what circumstances a principal is liable to third party for agent's act ? Explain ✓ Ans.18.6.1

17. When an agent is personally liable to third party for the acts during the course of agency? Explain. ✓ Ans.18.6.2

Part - III

LAW OF SALE OF GOODS
The Sale of Goods Act, 1930.

Introduction

The Act deals exclusively with sale of goods. Before passing of this Act, law relating to sale of goods contained in Indian Contract, Act 1872. The Act lays down specific principles and rules governing contracts of sale of goods. At the same time, contracting parties are not deprived of their liberty to requlate their relationship. In absence of express stipulation in a contract, law prevails. In this materialistic world, goods provide us comfort, convenience, pleasure. To cater the needs of people, goods are manufactured, stored, distributed and sold on large scale. Online shopping has added new dimension in sale of goods. Old goods are replaced by new, sophisticated, innovative articles and consumers are crazy to possess those. Replacement has also been made easy. All such transactions are subject matter of Sale of Goods Act. The Consumer Protection Act also deals with sale of goods but it is mainly concerned with protection of consumer rights. This Act lays down certain basis principles such as Contract of Sale, Conditions and Warranties, mode of delivery of goods, unpaid seller and buyer's rights etc. This part of the book covers almost all the chapters of the Act.

Chapter 19 | CONTRACT OF SALE

19.1 Contract of Sale

Definition [Sec. 4 (1)]

> *"A Contract of Sale is a contract whereby the seller transfers or agrees to transfer the property in goods to the buyer for a price ...."*

In simple language, contract of sale is a contract whereby ownership in goods is either transfered or agreed to be transfered by seller to the buyer. Perusing the definition, following special features of contract of sale may be noticed.

Characteristics of Contract of Sale

1. **Parties**

   Contract of sale is a bilateral contract between seller and buyer. Seller and buyer should be two distinct persons as seller himself cannot purchase his own goods. Seller can be the buyer in the following situations -

   — Owner can purchase his own goods in excention of a court sale (to save the dignity of family property)
   — One part owner can purchase other part owner's goods;
   — Pawner may purchase his goods sold by the pawnee in exercise of legal right to sell.

2. **Subject Matter**

   The subject matter of contract of sale is "goods." See definition of goods u/s 2 (7).

3. **Transfer of property** – This involves two concepts viz. 'transfer' and 'property'
   In contract of sale property in goods is transferred immediately or in future.
   'Property' means general property in goods and not 'special property'.
   [Definition U/S 2(1)]. General property implies ownership in goods. By sale, therefore, ownership is transferred. Special property cannotes a right in goods. Right of sale or lien over the goods vested in pawnee or bailee is an illustration of special property. Transfer implies 'passing' or 'making over' or 'conveyance.' It is the act of transferring ownership from seller to buyer.

4. Price

A contract should have consideration. For contract of sale, consideration is price. As per definition u/s 2 - (10), price means money only. If consideration is not money, the transaction is not sale. Barter (exchange) is different from sale because in that goods are exchanged while in sale, goods are exchanged for money. Consideration in sale however can be partly in money and partly in goods. Substantial portion of consideration should be money.

5. Form and Formalities - (Sec. 5)

There is no specific format to constitute a valid sale. No particular formalities are prescribed in the Act. Sec. 5 provides that contract of sale is formed by offer and its acceptance as in case of ordinary contracts. Contract may be express or implied, oral or written. Delivery of goods or payment of price may be effected immediately or postponed. Delivery or payment may be instalments. So it is left to the parties to execute and complete sale.

6. Essentials of valid contract

Contract of sale, being a contract should possess all the essentials elements of a contract under the Indian Contract Act, 1872.

7. Contract of sale includes 'Sale and Agreement to Sell'

From the definition it reveals that contract of sale is a generic term covering two Contracts - i) Sale and ii) Agreement to Sell, which are discussed in detail.

Sale and Agreement to Sell

> **Sale** - Definition. u/s 4 (3) - " Where under contract of sale property in goods is transferred from the seller to buyer, the cantract is called a sale .."

Sale is thus immediate transfer of property in goods at the time of making of contract. It is an absolute contract (like outright sale on a shopkeeper's counter) with immediate passing over of ownership from seller to buyer.

> **Agreement to Sell** - Definition u/s 4 (3) - "..Where the transfer of property in goods is to take place at a future date or subject to some condition thereafter to be fulfilled, the contract is called an agreement to sell."

In agreement to sell transfer of property takes place in future. It is a conditional sale as it is subject to expiry of time or filfillment of conditions.

Example

1) A pays Rs. 25000 for a smart phone and the dealer delivers phone to A. This is sale. Nothing is left to be done.
2) A takes musical system from B and agrees to purchase it if father approves sale. When they simply agree, it is agreement to sell subjects to father's approval. When fathers approves transfer is complete.
3) A farmer and Mahindra & Mahindra company agree today to buy and sell a tractor after 2 months. Today it agreement to sell and after 2 months it would be a complete sale.

When agreement to sell becomes sale? As provided in Sec 4 (4). agreement to sell becomes sale when —

i) The time lapses or

ii) Conditions are fulfilled.

8. Contract of sale and other transactions involving goods.

i) Contract of sale and Contract of Work and Labour

The Sale of Goods Act dose not apply to contact of work and labour. Sales tax is levied on the goods sold. Contract of work and labour is akin to contract of sale wherein goods are exchanged and delivered for monney. In contract labour, delivery of goods in incidental while in work and labour, service is the essence of contract. Contract of work and labour involves use of skill, labour, expertise in making a finished article i. e. goods. What is bargained in this type of contract is skill or labour and not the goods as such.

- **Lee V/s Griffin**[81] A dentist agreed to make a false set of teeth for a lady and to fit into her mouth. Held it was a contract of sale.

- **Robinson V/s Graves**[82] An artist was engaged to paint a portrait who was supplied with canvas and paint. Ruled that it was a contract of skill and labour in production of a portrait. If somebody purchases a portrait from shop, it is a sale.

ii) Hire - Purchase Agreement

In this type of agreements the goods are hired in the beginning with an option to purchase. If option is exercised, it is fruitified into sale. Following points in connection with hire purchase be noted which can be compared with sale or agreement to sell.

The Supreme Court in **K L Joher and Co. v/s Dy Commercial Tax Officer, Coimbator**[83] has thrown light on the substance of hire purchase agreement in these words

i) The goods are delivered on the hire basis.

ii) The consideration is 'hire - charges' paid in instalments. The understanding is that if instalments equal to the price of goods are paid, hire - purchase would ripen into sale. Ultimate object of hire purchase is transfer of ownership wherein price is paid in instalments.

iii) Hirer has a option to return the goods till the payment of last instalment. He may return the goods at any time declining purchase. *This option to terminate the contract is the gist of hire puechase.*

iv) If default in payment of instalment is committed by hirer, owner can resume possession of goods.

iv) After payment of last instalment ownership is transferred to the hirer.

v) Position of hirer is that of a bailee. Till it is converted to sale, the transaction is bailment. Hire purchase is thus 'bailment + conveyance'.

---

81. *(1861), 30LJ0B252 I B and S 272*
82. *(1935), IKB 579*
83. *AIR 1965 SC 1082*

19.2 Distinction between Sale and Agreement to sell. (See the chart)

Agreement to sell and sale are two distinct terms covered in Contract of Sale. Definitional and conceptual difference is pointed out below. –

Distinction Between Sale and Agreement to Sell (Definitions u/s 4(3))		
Points of Distinction	**Agreement to sell**	**Sale**
1) Nature of contract	- Executory Contract yet to be performed - Pure Contract	- Executed - Contract is performed Contract + Conveyance
2) Nature of right created person. (seller or buyer)	jus in personum-Right against against the whole world	jus in rem-Right of buyer
3) Transfer of property;	To be transferred in future Ownership with seller	- Property is transferred - Ownership is transferred
4) Risk of loss ("Risk prima-facie passes with property - Sec. 26) Risk is always with owner	Risk with Seller, being still the owner.	Risk with buyer; Loss /damage to goods born by buyer.
5) Remedies in case of Breach of contract		
a) Breach by buyer (Seller's remedies)	Damages for non-performance of contract	Suit for price; Unpaid Seller's rights (Ref. S. 55)
b) Breach by seller (Buyer's remedies)	Damages for non performance of contract;	Suit for non-delivery, damages, Suit for specific performance, and conversion.
6) Insolvency - of Seller	Buyer can claim rateable divident if price is paid.	Buyer being owner, can recover goods from official assignees.
Insolvency - of Buyer	Seller may refuse to deliver goods to official assignee unless price is paid.	Seller can claim rateable dividend for unpaid price (Goods cannot be claimed back)

Chapter 20 | GOODS

Goods are the subject matter of contract of sale. If the subject matter is not covered within the definition of the term, this Act or sales tax laws are not applicable to the transaction.

20.1 Definition. U/S 2 (7)

> *"Goods means every kind of movable property other than actionable claims and money and includes stock and shares, growing crops, grass and things attached to earth or forming part of the land which are agreed to be severed before sale or under the contract of sale."*

The definition provides the meaning of the term and clarifies what is included in it and excluded from it.

20.2 Ingredients of the term

i) **Goods are movable properties** – The properties which can be moved from place to place are goods. Articles, objects, commodities catering our needs are goods. Goods are corporal (having body form), tangible (which can be touched) and visible (which can be seen). Goods have size and shape.

ii) **The term includes** - Goods include stock, shares, growing crops, grass are movables and sold. Grass is used as fodder for animals.
Things attached to earth or forming part of the land (for eg. trees etc.) may also be goods provided those things are to be separated from the earth in pursuance of the contract of sale. Trees are goods when agreed to be cut and sold as 'timber'.

iii) **The term expressly excludes** – money, and actionable claims. Money or 'currency' is the legal tender through which price is paid. Foreign coins, old antique coins however sold as goods as those are not currency.
'Actionable claims' are claims which can be enforced by legal action. For eg. a claim to a debt. Actionable claims are 'immovable property' under the Transfer of Property Act, 1955 and their assignment is regulated by that Act.

20.3 Kinds of Goods

The goods are classified as under.

1) **Existing Goods** – The goods which are in existence at the time of contract of sale are known as 'existing goods'. Existing goods can only be sold. Existing goods Can be further classified into —

   i. **Specific Goods** – "Specific goods means goods identified and agreed upon at the time a contract of sale is made." [Definition u/s 2(14)]. When a buyer selects a specific washing machine, that machine is not only identified but agreed to be sold and purchased and hence 'specific goods'. In shopping malls, specific goods are purchased.

   ii. **Ascertained Goods** – Ascertained goods are those goods which are identified and agreed upon by the parties after a contract of sale in made. This means that these goods are unascertained when contract is made. When the goods are in large quantity and out of that fewer number is agreed to be purchased, say one motor bike out of 10, the goods are unascertained. When the goods in species are separated from the bulk and assigned to a contract, the goods are 'ascertained'. When one bike in particular is labelled for a purchaser, it becomes ascertained. Same logic can be applied for certain quantity of liquid (say oil, paint, gas) is to be purchased out of a big container.

   iii. **Unascertained Goods** – These goods are defined by description and not specifically identified at the time of contract of sale. A big heap of wheat is lying on the field. Buyer desires to purchase only ten bags of wheat. His ten bags in the heap are unascertained goods.

2) **Future Goods** – [Definition u/s 5.2(6)] "Future goods means goods to be manufactured or produced or acquired by the seller after making of a contract of sale."
   The future goods may be –

   i. In existence at the time of formation of contract of sale but seller has yet to become the owner or acquire it.

   Example : A agrees to sell a machine to B after he himself procures it from manufacturer. The machine is in existence but A is not the owner at the time of cntract of sale.
   ii. Not in existence at all –

   Example : A farmer agrees to sell his grapes that his land would produce after two months. The goods are future goods at the time of agreement to sell.

3) **Contingent Goods :** [Sec. 6(2)] Contingent goods are those goods the acquisition of which by the seller depends upon a contingency which may or may not happen. Contingent goods are thus future goods because ownership of the goods is yet to be acquired by the seller. The sale takes place only when a particular event (contingency) happens. If it does not occur, agreement becomes void.

   Example : A agrees to sell a car to B if the car is gifted by A's relative. If A's relative gifts the car then only sale would be completed.

Chapter 21

CONDITIONS AND WARRANTIES

Stipulations in a contract

Seller while selling his goods may make various statements about goods. In negotiations statements of praise (commendatory representations), opinion are made but those do not support consideration and hence are not terms of the contract of sale. Statements which attract consideration and form part of the contract are called 'terms or stipulations'. Stipulations influence the buyer to purchase. Sale of goods usually consists of terms regarding quality, quantity, time and place of delivery, price etc. These terms in a contract of sale are not of equal impotance. Some stipulations are more important while other are of lesser importance. A stipulation which is significant is called a 'condition' while a stipulation of lesser significance is a 'warranty'. It should be noted that non-compliance of a term (whether condition or waranty) gives a right of action against the defaulter.

21.1 CONDITION

Definition and Essentials
Definition (Sec. 12-2)

> " *A condition is a stipulation essential to the main purpose of the contract, the breach of which gives rise to a right to treat the contract as repudiated.*"

Essentials of a 'Condition'

1) **Condition is a stipulation** (Refer introductory paragraph)
   Stipulations create obligations and if not followed, give rise to legal consequences.

2) **Condition is essential to the main purpose of contract**
   Condition is a vital or major term in a sale. It goes to the root of contract. Breach of such a term frustrates the purpose of sale. Condition is thus a core element in the contract and its fulfilment is essential for its performance.

3) **Breach of condition leads to repudiation of contract**
   Condition is of such a nature that its non-compliance is treated substantial failure to perform the contract. Non performance of condition causes irreparable loss to the other

party and his purpose of purchase is defeated. This justifies a right to put an end to the contract (repudiation). The party can rescind the contract and reject the goods.

Baldry v/s Marshall[84] B wanted a car for touring purposes. He consulted M. a car dealer, who suggested a 'Buggatti' car. Relying of M's advice B brought Buggatti car. He found that car was not suitable for touring purpose. B wanted to cancel the sale, return the car and get the refund of price. Held that B is entitled to get the reliefs as suitability of the car was 'condition' and its breach frustrated the purpose of purchase of car.

Examples
i) A orders a Notepad of a particular company with specific facilities and configuration to be delievred within a month. Here quality of a notepad is a condition while time of delivery is a warranty.

ii) A retailer orders 20 packets of canned fruits, each containing 10 tins (from a manufacturer), so as to directly dispatch these to a consumer. Manufacturer delivers 10 packets with 20 tins in each. Here term as to parcelling assumes importance hence retailer can reject the lot.

21.2 WARRANTY

Definition [Sec. 12 (3)]

> " *A warranty is a stipuation collateral to the main purpose of contract, the breach of which gives rise to a claim for damages but not to a right to reject the goods and treat the contract as repudiated.*"

Warranty in business world refers to time period within which goods are to be repaired or replaced free of cost in case of manufacturing defect. But warranty in law conveys a different meaning. Warranty simply is a term of lesser importance, none the less it is to be complied.

Essentials of Warranty

1) **Warranty is a stipulation** - This is a common element which is discussed earlier.

2) **Warranty is collateral to the main purpose of contract** - Warranty is a stipulation of secondary importance. It is of subsidiary significance. Warranty is an obligation which is collateral (running side by side, does not lay at the foundation) to the main purpose of the contract.

3) **Breach gives a right to damages and not to repudiation** - Breach of warranty causes loss or inconvenience which can be compensated by money (damages). As the breach is not fatal, right to cancel the contract is not available. Contract survives.

---

84. *120 (1925) 1 KB 260*

Example :

Distinction between Condition and Warranty

Basis of Distinction	Condition	Warranty
1) Importance	of Primary importance. Essential to the main purpose of contract.	of Secondary importance. Collateral to the main purpose of contract.
2) Breach	Breach gives rise to right of repudiation - Goods can be rejected.	Breach gives a right to damages only and not rescission. Goods cannot be returned.
3) Option in breach of Condition	Breach of condition can be treated as breach of warranty	Breach of warranty cannot be treated as breach of condition.

When breach of condition is treated as breach of warranty ?

According to Sec. 13, in the following circumstances, the breach of condition is treated as breach of warranty. The legal consequence of exercise of such option is that the buyer cannot rescind the contract or reject the goods but has to contend with damages only.

   i) **Waiver of Condition :** Buyer may voluntarily treat the breach of condition as breach of warranty and accept the goods. Waiver of right to repudiation can be exress or implied.

   ii) **Acceptance of the goods :** When the buyer accepts the goods and then discovers the breach of condition, he has no liberty to reject the goods. Consequences of acceptance are involuntary because breach of condition is treated as breach of warranty by operation of law. (For the meaning 'acceptance of goods' see Sec. 42 of the Act.)

   Example : A agrees to sell 'Basmati' rice (long, scented grains) to B. A sends 'Delhi rice (long grains) resembling Basmati. Quality of rice is a condition. B may accept it and pay at reduced rate. (Express waiver) If he keeps the rice without rejection or consumes it, that amounts to acceptance of the goods.

21.3 Express and Implied Condition and Warranty

Conditions and warranties may be either express or implied. Express by words, oral or written. When the parties imcorporate various terms in a written contract, those are express condition or warranty, as the case may be. Implied condition or a warranty is that which is implied in a contract of sale by law. Law presumes certain conditions and warranties in a sale though the parties do not expressly stipulate.[85] A shrewd trader may claim absence of a term and avoid responsibility for poor quality goods. But implied conditions/warranties protect buyers' interests in absence of express terms.

By implication of law there are various implied conditions and warranties which are explained below.

---

85. *Implied conditions or warranties may be changed or altogether negatived by express agreement or by usage or custom as evidenced by course of dealing between the parties.*
   "What is expressly done puts an end to what is tacit or implied" *Custom and agreement overrule implied condition and warranty*

Implied Conditions

In every contract of sale following conditions are implied by law. These conditions are subject to the contract to the contrary.

1) **Condition as to Title - Sec. 14 (a)**

   In a contract of sale on the part of seller there are following implied conditions.

   a) In sale, the seller has right to sell and

   b) In agreement to sell seller will have right to sell the goods when the property is to pass.

   In contract of sale seller has right to sell if he is either the owner or his agent. There is an implied condition that seller has title in the goods. If seller has no title or his title is defective, there is a breach of implied condition and buyer can reject the contract.

   Rowland v/s Diwall[86]

   A bought a motor car from B and used it for several months. It was stolen car belonging to C, true owner, Police siezed the car and returned it to C. Held A could recover the price of car from B as there was a breach of condition as to existence of title (ownership) in the car.

   Subsistence of title with seller is not sufficient. He should further have right to sell his goods. Ownership and right to covey title are two different things. Both are covered by sec. 14(a). A rickshawala may be the owner of autoricksha but cannot sell it if it is hypothecated to a Bank for loan.

2) **Implied Condition in 'Sale by Description' (Sec. 15)**[86(a)]

   Many times buyer may not have occasion to see the goods. He relies on description. Goods may be described by appearance, packing particulars, quality, quantity, brand or trade name Sec. 15 States "...Where there is a contract of sale of goods by description, there is an implied condition that the goods shall corrospond with description ..."

   Even if the goods are examined by buyer, what is delivered should not deviate from description. The goods with latent defect may result in a breach of term as to description.

   Shepherd v/s Kain[87] A bought a ship from B. It was described as 'copper fastened' to be taken with all faults without allowance for any defect whatsever'. The ship turned out to be partially copper fastened condition. A was entitled to reject the ship and compensation for breach of implied condition in sale by description.

3) **Implied Condition in a Sale by Sample - Sec. 17 (a)**

   Definition of Sale by Sample - (d)

   "A contract of sale is a contract of sale for sale by sample where there is a term in the contract, express or implied, to that effect."

   Sample means a symbol or representative of the bulk. In sale by sample, implied conditions are —

---

86.   *(1923) 2 KB. 500*

86(a)   *S.15 "If you contract to sell peas, you cannot oblige a party to take beans. If the description of the article tendered is different in any respect, it is not the article bargained for, and the other party is not bound to take it." - Lord Blackburn.*

87.   *182.5 All 240*

a) The bulk shall corrospond with sample in quality;

b) The buyer shall have reasonable opportunity of compairing the bulk with sample;

c) Goods shall be free from any latent defect, making them unmerchantable.

Opportunity of comparison is necessary to ascertain whether goods actually supplied resemble with the sample. The third condition applies to latent or hidden defect and not patent defect. Patent defect is a defect which can be discovered by ordinary inspection or revealed by necked eyes.

4) Implied Condition in a Sale by Sample as well as Sale by Description - Sec. 15 -

Where the good are sold by sample as well as by description the goods should corrospond not only with the sample but with description also. Buyer can reject the goods if those are not according to either sample or description.

Nichols v/s Godts[88] — 'N' agreed to sell 'G', oil described as "foreign refined rape oil" warranteed only equal to sample. The sample of oil itself was adulterated with hemp oil. The court held that G could reject the bulk of oil. Though the bulk matched with sample, it was not as per description. Condition as to description was not complied.

Caveat Emptor

Sec. 16 (1) of the Act, embodies the principle of **'Caveat Emptor'** i.e. **'buyer beware'** or **'let the buyer beaware'** It states –

> *"Subject to the provisions of this Act and any other law for the time being in force, there is no implied warranty or condition, as to the quality or fitness for any particular purpose, of the goods supplied under a contract of sale."*

(Detail explanation of Caveat Emptor is given at the end of this topic)

Though as a general rule, there is no implied condition as to quality or fitness for any particular purpose, in the following situations, buyer can claim the benefit of implied conditions.

Following implied conditions are therefore discussed as exceptions to carveat emptor.

Implied Conditions (Exceptions to Caveat Emptor)

5) Implied Condition when specific purpose of goods is made known to the seller. [Sec. 16 (2)]

There is an implied condition as to quality or fitness of goods for any particular purpose if following conditions are fulfilled —

a) The buyer makes known to the seller the particular purpose of goods;

b) The purpose is communicated to show that the buyer relies on seller's skill or judgement;

c) Goods are of a description which the seller deals in ordinary course of his business.

Purpose of goods may be made known either expressly or impliedly. If the good are meant for one particular known purpose only, purpose need not be stated to the seller.

---

88. *(1854) 10 E x 191*

Priest V/s Last[89] A draper asked for a hot water bottle to a chemist. Draper was ignorant about the bottle. Chemist showed American Rubber bottle which the chemist said would not stand boiling water but was meant for hot water. A bought the bottle which was used by his wife. While being used, it burst and injured the wife. Held that bottle was not fit for use as a hot water bottle. Seller committed the breach of condition as to fitness for special purpose. Particular purpose need not be intimated to seller when serves only one specific purpose.

— See **Baldry v/s Marshall**[90]

— **Grant v/s Australian Knitting Co.**[91] — Plaintiff bought underpants from a retail garment dealer. Due to the excess sulphites used in manufacturing garments, the plaintiff suffered from dermatitis, a skin disease. Seller pleaded that the purpose of sale was not made known to him. Court held that seller is presumed to know the only purpose of garments being worn next to skin. Seller was held liable for breach of implied condition to fitness.

Sale Under Patent or Trade Name -

Provision to Sec. 16 (1) makes it clear that if goods are sold under a trade name or a patent, there is no implied condition as to fitness for any particular purpose. In sales under patent or trade mark, therefore, caveat emptor applies. In such sales buyer relies on brand names, he is guided by good-will of a product rather than seller's skill in suggesting an article. Seller's responsibility is to supply patented article as per demand and nothing further.

6) **Implied Condition as to Merchantability - Sec. 16 (2)**

In sale by description, there is an implied condition that the goods should possess merchantable quality. Merchantable quality is that quality which makes goods saleable in the market. Those should have 'exchange value' or 'use value'. Goods should fit for the ordinary purpose for which those are produced.

Implied condition as to merchantable quality exists in the following situations.

a) Goods are sold by description.

b) Seller deals with the goods of that description in ordinary course of his business.

c) Buyer has not examined the goods.

This **implied condition cannot be evoked** in the following case ;

a) When goods suffer from patent defects - which would be detected by ordinary inspection. Seller, therefore, cannot be blamed for easily detectable defects.

b) Sale is under patent name or trade mark where in buyer does not rely on seller's skill.

Morelli v/s. Fitch & Gibbons[92] — M bought a bottle of Stone's ginger wine. While attempting to open the bottle, neck of the bottle broke off which injured M's hand.

---

89. *(1903) 2 KB 148*
90. *Supra note 84*
91. *1936 - 70 MLJ 513*
92. *(1928) 2 KB 636*

Men like convention because man made them. - George Bernand Shaw

Held that there was a breach of condition as to merchantability of goods and M had a right to get the damages. (This case can also be referred in implied warranty in dangerous goods.)

7) Implied Condition as to quality or fitness by Custom (Sec. 16)
Condition as to quality or fitness to any particular purpose may be annexed by usage or custom. Usage plays significant role when the contract is silent over a particular issue.

8) Implied Condition regarding Wholesomeness;
This condition applies in case of eatables or provisions. The food items would be wholesome if those are fit for consumption. Seller commits a breach of implied condition if eatables or provisions are not fit to consume. A consumer bought a beer bottle from a dealer of wine. Consumer fell ill after drinking beer which was contaminated with arsenic. Dealer was held liable for illness as the beer was not wholesome.

21.4 Implied Warranties

Implied warranties are those which are presumed by law to have been incorporated in every contract of sale. The express agreement may rule out any of those implied warranties. Following are the implied warranties in a contract of sale.

1) Warranty of Quiet Possession
Sec. 14 (b) states, — "In a contract of sale there is an implied warranty that the buyer shall have and enjoy quiet possession of the goods."
(This implied warranty can be said to be an extension of imlied condition as to title.)
Warranty as to quiet possession implies -
a) No person other than owner / seller has superior title in respect of goods;
b) Neither Seller or nor anybody claiming through him shall disturb buyer's possession. If buyer's possession is interfered with under any title, seller shall compensate the buyer for breach of warranty. If title is weak, possession would be threatened.

2) Warranty of Freedom from Encumbrance
According to Sec. 14 (c) of the Act, in a contract of sale there is an implied warranty that the goods shall be free from any charge or encumbrance in favour of any third party not declared or known to the buyer before or at the time when the contract is made.

Emcumbrance or charge is a right in other's property. Lien or hypothecation, mortgage are examples of third party's rights. If goods are sold with charge, the seller has to discharge that liability so that buyer's possession is not distrubed.

3) Warranty in case of Dangerous Goods -
Goods which are dangerous by nature or likely to be dangerous require special care in handling or use. If buyer while purchasing such goods does not know about the dangerous nature, then seller is under a duty to disclose or warn buyer about possible dangers. If seller fails to give a caution and buyer suffers injuries, the seller must compensate him.

"a buyer needs a hundred eyes, the seller not one." - *George Herbert*

4) Warranty as to quality or fitness of goods for a particular purpose may be annexed by the usage of trade. (See Sec. 16 -3)

CAVEAT EMPTOR

'Caveat emptor' is a latin phrase which means "**let the buyer beware**". The principle obliges a buyer to take care while purchasing goods. The purpose for which a buyer buys any article, its suitability is better known by him. If the goods turn out to be defective or unsuitable for the purpose he cannot blame the seller. While purchasing buyer should protect his interest by exercise of skill and judgement in choosing the objects. If the goods do not serve his purpose, he should blame himself for his bad choice. In general, therefore, buyer purchases goods at his own risks.

Seller's duty is to supply the goods as demanded by the buyer. He is not bound to disclose every defect in the goods. Buyer should examined, the goods and select. Seller should not be made responsible for buyer's wrong choice. There is no implied condition or warranty that the goods supplied shall fit for the buyer's purpose. This principle finds its place in Sec. 16 (1) of the Act, stated earlier.

Caveat emptor has been applied in a leading case of **Ward v/s Hobbs**[93] — Plantiff bought pigs from defendant in an auction. Defendant seller did not give any warranty as to quantity or description. In fact it was a sale "with all faults". The pigs were suffering from typhoid fever and all but one died. They infected plaintiff's own pigs. Held that in the circumstances, the seller was not under a duty to disclose the illness of pigs. Applying caveat emptor, buyer's claim for damages was rejected.

The rule of caveat emptor is not absolute. The Act recognises exceptions to caveat emptor which are explained below.

Exceptions to Caveat Emptor

1) Implied condition in a sale by description (Sec. 15)
2) Implied condition in a sale by description and sale by sample (Sec.15)
3) Implied condition as to quality and fitness for a particular purpose (Sec. 16-1)
4) Implied condition as to merchantable quality (Sec. 16 - 2)
5) Implied condition annexed by usage (Sec 16 - 3)
6) Implied condition as to wholesomeness
7) Implied condition as to merchantability .. [Sec. 17 (2)]In sale by sample if goods suffer from latent defect making those unmerchatable, seller is responsible to compensate the buyer.
8) Fraud or misrepresentation by seller - Caveat emptor does not apply when seller obtains buyer's consent for contract of sale by fraud or misrepresentation. If by fraud seller conceals the defect in goods, caveat emptor will not assist him. The contract is voidable and buyer can rescind it. A goldsmith sells a golden ornament with a Hallmark certificate of 24 caret to a purchaser which in fact is a gold plated ornament with fake certificate. Caveat emptor does not apply and purchaser can return it and ask for refund of price. Exceptions 1 to 7 have already been discussed as implied conditions in contract of sale.

---

93. *(1878)4 APP Cas 13*

Chapter 22 | TRANSFER OF PROPERTY

Transfer of property in goods means passing of ownership of goods from seller to buyer. By sale, the property in goods is made over or conveyed to buyer and that is the chief objective of a sale.

Significance of time of passing property

The time of passing property assumes importance in view of the following legal propositions.

i) Risk of loss or damage of goods is always with the owner. - **"Risk prima facie passes with the ownership"** (Sec. 26).

  The rule is subject to contract to the contrary between seller and buyer.

ii) Only the owner can sue the party causing damage to the goods.

iii) In case of insolvency of buyer or seller, fact of ownership would decide the issue of recovery of goods by official assignee.

22.1 Time when property passes –

Rules for Transfer of Property

Sections 18 to 26 provide the rules determining the time when property in the goods passes from the seller to buyer. The set of rules can be better explained by classifying those as under.

  A) Transfer of property in specific or ascertained goods.

  B) Transfer of property in unascertained goods.

A. 1 Transfer of property in Specific or Ascertained Goods - (Refer definition of specific or ascertained good in chapter - 20).

i) **(S. 19-1) - "Property passes when it is intended to pass."**
  Where there is a contract of sale of specific or ascertained goods, the property in them is transferred at such time as the parties intend it to be passed. As a general rule, the precise time of passing property depends upon intention of the parties. Transfer of ownership takes place when parties intend.

ii) How intention u/s 19 (1) is ascertained? — S.19 (2) -

For the purpose of ascertaining intention of the parties, terms of contracts, conduct of parties and the circumstances of a case are to be considered. This section sets out in a general way the factors determining intention. Following section lay down certain rules for determinig intention keeping in view the special circumstances.

Rules for ascertaining intention in specific situations. (For easy understanding, *situation i.e. conditions of applicability covered by the section* are explained first which is followed by the rule).

iii) Sec. 20 - When goods are in deliverable state —

Conditions of applicability of the section -
- Goods are specific ;
- Goods are in 'deliverable state' [Definition u/s 2 (3) - The goods are in deliverable state when they are in such a state that the buyer would, under the contract, be bound to take delivery of them.]
- Contract is unconditional.

Rule - The property in the goods passes to the buyer as soon as the contract is made. Delivery of property or payment of price may be postponed. Property passes with the making of contract.

Example - A selects a dining set from B's furniture shop. B agrees to sell it to A for 10,000. A pays advance of Rs. 1000 and delivery is to be made after 2 days. Property in the goods passes immedintely after contract is made. If B's shop with dining set is destroyed in fire, A has to bear the loss.

iv) Sec. 21 -When the goods have to be put into a deliverable state —

Conditions : The goods are specific; Seller is bound to do something to put the goods in deliverable state.

Rule - Property passes when the seller does that thing and intimates buyer about it.

Example - An agriculturist has 10 quintals of 'tur dal' for sale. B agrees to purchase @ of Rs. 90 per Kg and to be delivered in bags of 20 Kg each. Property does not pass untill A puts turdal in the bags as per agreement and informs B accordingly so that B can take the delivery.

v) Sec. 22 -When the price of goods to be ascertained —

Conditions -
- The goods are specific ;
- The goods are in deliverable state ;
- Seller is bound to weigh or measure or test the goods for calculating the price of goods to be sold.

Rule - Property does not pass untill seller weighs or measures or tests the goods ascertaining the price and buyer has notice thereof.

Example - A agrees to purchase the entire timber lying in B's godown. Rate is fixed. Property passes only when timber merchant, B, weighs the timber to know the price and gives notice to the buyer. If before that whole timber is burnt in fire, B has lost it and not A.

vi) Sec. 24 - Goods sent on approval —

When the goods are delivered to the buyer 'on approval' or 'sale or return' basis, the property in goods passes in the following way -

a) Buyer signifies his approval or acceptance to the seller; (Express approval) or

b) He adopts the transaction by doing some act, (Implied approval)

c) Estoppel - Buyer retains goods after lapse of period stipulated for approval or after lapse of reasonable period (when period is not mentioned) without any notice of rejection.

Elphic v/s Barnes[94] Owner, A, delivered a horse to B on terms "Sale or return" within 8 days. The horse died on the third day without any fault on B's part. Held that A was to bear the loss as the horse was still his property when it died.

B. 1 Transfer of property in Unascertained or Future Goods

Ss. 18 and 23 deal with the passing of property in unascertained or future goods. It would be recollected that unascertained goods are defined by some sample or description but exactly which goods in species are sold, that is uncertain.

i) **Sec. 18 -** This section states that the property in unascertained goods is not transferred to the buyer unless and untill goods are ascertained. Ascertainment means goods must be assigned to a particular contract. Only when goods are ascertained property in those passes to the buyer.

ii) **Sec. 23 (1) -** *Unconditional Appropriation*-Conditions for applicability of the section –
   - Sale of unascertained or future goods by description.
   - Goods of that description are in deliverable state.

Rule - Property dose not pass unless those goods are "unconditionally approriated" to the contract.

Appropriation or ascertainment is earmarking or setting apart the goods under the contract. It is identifying or assigning the goods with the contracts. Appropriation may be through separation from the bulk, counting etc., with the object of identifying and determining the goods to be delivered under the contract.

Essentials of valid appropriation

   - Appropriation should be unconditional [See S.23 (2) and 25)]
   - Appropriation may be made by the buyer with seller's assent.
   - Assent of appropriation may be express or implied and may be given either before or after appropriation is done.
   - Notice of appropriation must be given by the party appropriating to the other.

Example : A agrees to sell 50 bales of cotton to B, out of his 500 bales in his godown.In the presence of B, A separates 50 bales from the bulk and puts marking on those for B. Property passes to buyer in 50 bales of cotton.

---

94. (1880) 5 CPD 321.

Sec. 23 (2) – *Deemed Unconditional Appropriation* – This section explains a situation wherein unconditional appropriation is presumed. Where the seller in persuance of contract of sale

— delivers the goods to a carrier or a bailee for the purpose of transmission to the buyer and

— does not reserve the right of disposal, this delivery amounts to unconditional appropriation.

Thus delivery to carrier without reservation of right of disposal amounts to delivery of goods to the buyer and on delivery, the buyer becomes the owner. It goes without saying that if the right of disposal is reserved, property does not pass even by delivery to the carrier.

Example - Goods are loaded on a railway wagon ; Railway receipt is taken out in buyer's name and sent directly to him. Ownership passes when goods are delivered to Railway.

Reservation of Right of Disposal (S. 25) –

Right of disposal (transfer by sale etc.) may be reserved in the following way –

i) **S. 25 (1) -**

Where the seller, while delivering the goods to a carrier or a bailee, orders that the goods should be delivered to the buyer on fulfilment of certain conditions, say on payment.

ii) **S. 25 (2) -**

Where the goods have been shipped or delivered to the railway for carriage yet the goods are deliverable to the order of seller or his agent.

iii) **S. 25 (3) -**

Where a bill of exchange is attached with the railway receipt or a bill of lading and bill of exchange is required to be accepted, the property in the goods will not be transferred until the bill is accepted.

Example - A sends a ship -load of sugar to B from Mumbai to Kochi. A takes bill of lading in B's name and send it to B with a bill of exchange for his acceptance. B dishonours it by non-acceptance. A still is the owner of the goods even if B takes delivery of sugar at Kochi.

| Chapter 23 | TRANSFER OF TITLE BY NON-OWNERS |

23.1 Who can transfer title? - General Rule -

In sale of goods ownership or title in goods passes to the buyer. The pertinent question is who can validly transfer the title? Only two persons viz. owner or a person with owner's authority or consent (agent) can sell in the goods to buyer. As a general rule, non-owner cannot legally transfer the   property or title in goods. This has been expressed in a maxim.- **"Nemo dat quod non-habet"** which literally means – **"no one can pass a better title than he himself has"**. This principle has been incorporated in S. 27 of the Act which states that —

"Where goods are sold by a person who is not the owner thereof and who does not sell them under the authority or with consent of the owner, the buyer acquires no better title to the goods than the seller had..."

In other words, seller cannot convey a title which he does not have or cannot pass a title better than what he has in the goods. The rule prohibits passing of 'better' title which means what one has in the property can be transferred. If seeler's title is defective, person through him gets a defective title. This can be illustrated as follows.

Illustrations -

i) A sells a stolen camera to B. B pays for it without knowing that it is stolen. C, the true owner, can recover it form B. A has no title in the camera which he cannot pass to B.

ii) A sells stolen goods at public auction to B who takes those for consideration and in good faith. B does not become owner. True owner's right is paramount.

23.2 Exceptions - Transfer by Non- Owners

The general rule enunciated in S. 27 is subject to following exceptions. In the following circumstances non-owner can pass a better to the purchaser. These statutory exceptions are provided under this Act and other laws. The sections contemplate exceptional situations which are explained as conditions of applicability of a perticular section.

1. **Sale by Mercantile Agent - (S. 27)**

   A mercantile agent, though not authorised to sell his master's goods, can lawfully transfer goods in favour of a buyer in the following situation.

   Conditions of applicability of the section are —

   – Seller is a mercantile agent,[95]

   – Mercantile agent is in possession of goods with owner's consent;

   – Mercantile agent sells the goods in ordinary course of business as mercantile agent (not in other capacity);

2. **Sale by Estoppel (S. 27)**

   Sec. 27 states a buyer will get a goods title to the goods from a non-owner if "..... The owner of the goods is by his canduct precluded from denying the seller's authority to sell." This transfer is valid by the principle of estoppel. Sometimes owner gives an impression that seller has power to sell. Buyer relies and purchases goods honestly without notice as to absence of authority with the seller. By virtue of estoppel he becomes the owner of goods.

   Example : A sells B's motor bike, without his consent, to C and asks C to pay to B. B accepts the price from C. B cannot challenge the sale as he is estopped from denying C's title.

3. **Sale by one of the joint - owners (Sec. 28).**

   Goods may be owned by more than one persons i. e. joint owners. If one of them sell the property without other joint owner's consent, sale would be valid if following conditions are satified.

   - One of the joint owners is in possession of goods; - Such possession is with other joint-owners' consent;

   - Buyer acts in goods faith and without notice of defect in title.

4. **Sale by a person under voidable contract (Sec. 29)**

   Conditions of applicability are –

   – Person is in possession of goods under voidable contract,

   – The party, whose consent is not free has not rescinded the contract ;

   – Buyer acts in good faith and without notice of defect in seller's title. (absence of authority to sell).

   In the above circumstances, the person can validly pass a title to third party.

5. **Sale by seller in possession after sale (Sec. 30-1).**

   Where -

   – The goods are sold to buyer but

   – The person (seller) is still in possession of goods or document of title to be the goods;

   – He effects the sale to a second buyer as a seller and not as a bailee or hirer

   – Second buyer acts in and good faith without notice as to first sale.

---

95. *Definition of Mercantile Agent u/s 2 (9) of the Act - "Mercantile agent means a mercantile agent having in the customary course of business as such agent, authority to sell goods, or to consign goods for the purpose of sale, to buy goods or to raise money on the security of goods".*

Example - A sells a neckless to B. A promises B to deliver neckless after 2 days. Before delivery, A agains sells it to C for better offer, C gets a goods title as he buys it from seller and in good faith.

The logic for this rule is that the seller has antecedant (earlier) title and moreover he is in possession. The second buyer is justified in presuming title with seller.

6. **Sale by buyer in posseseeion after sale (Sec. 30)** -

This section contemplates following eventuality for passing ownership by owner with defective title.

– A person buys or agrees to buy certain goods;
– He obtains the possession of goods with seller's consent,
– Seller however has lien or other rights in respect of goods;
– The buyer sells the goods to third party
– The third party acts bonafide. The third party gets a better title than the buyer, free from his seller's equities (rights).

Example - B obtains the possession of a home theatre music system under agreement to sell from A. Before B gets ownership, he sells it to C who acts in good faith. C becomes the owner of the system.

7. **Sale by unpaid seller** - (See the chapter on unpaid seller.)

It is an exception to Nemo dat quod non-habet... Unpaid seller though ceases to be owner, can sell it giving a perfect title to the third party.

Exceptions under other laws

8. **Sale by the finder of lost goods – Refer Sec. 169 of the Contract Act -**

9. **Sale by the pawnee or pledgee – Refer Sec. 176 of the Contract act -** The sales under these laws are circumscribed.

10. **Sale by Official Assignee** - Under law of insolvency (Provincial Insolvency Act, Company Law), official receiver or assignee appointed by the court can execute sale of insolvent's property.

11. **Holder in due course** - Position of holder in due course is known as an exception to nemo dat good non habet (Sec. 9 of the Negotiable Instruments Act).

Chapter 24 | PERFORMANCE OF CONTRACT OF SALE

In our daily life selling and purchasing of household goods, equipments is not much complicated. Buyer pays cash or makes e-payment and goods are delivered at the counter or home delivery is made. Goods of large sizes like buses, trucks, ships, machines or goods in large quantity required by industries involve issues of time, place of delivery, inspection of goods and payment. This topic explains the provisions contained in the Sale of Goods Act relating to execution of contract of sale. Performance of contract of sale involves delivery of goods and payment of price. In connection with these aspects sec. 31 and 32 lay down general rules.

Duties of Seller and Buyer - (Sec. 31)

Seller is under a duty to deliver the goods and buyer is under a duty to accept delivery and pay for them. Delivery and payment should be as per the terms of contract of sale.

Time of delivery of goods and payment of price (Sec. 32)

Delivery of goods and payment of price are concurrent conditions. This means that these two acts are to be simultaneously performed. However the parties may agree on different terms as to time of delivery and payment.

Delivery of goods thus assumes significance in performance of contract of sale.

24.1 Delivery

a) Meaning -
Definition u/s 2(2)

> *"Delivery means voluntary transfer of possession from one person to another".*

Delivery thus has two elements - i] Transfer of possession. Possession connotes actual custody or control or ability to assume control over goods. ii] Transfer should be voluntary. If possession is obtained by threat, fraud, it does not amount to delivery.

b) Rules Regarding Delivery. (Sec. 33 to 43)

Modes of Delivery (Sec. 33) – Delivery should be made by doing any act which should have the effect of putting the goods in possession of the buyer. Alternatively if parties treat a particular act as delivery, that would be delivery u/s 33. Delivery can be made to buyer's agent. Delivery of the goods may be made in the following manner.

i) **Actual Delivery** - When the goods are physically handed over to another, that is actual delivery.

ii) **Symbolic Delivery** - Sometimes goods because of their size, shape, quantity, are not capable of physical transfer. In such cases their symbol is handed over.

For example. Delivery of a key of a car is the delivery of car or delivery of keys of a warehouse is the delivery of goods stored in the warehouse.

c) **Constructive Delivery** - There may be a change in the possession of goods without any change in actual or physical custody. The same person continues in possession but in different capacity. This change over is construed as delivery and hence called as constructive delivery.

Examples -

i) A sells goods to B. B, unable to accept immediate delivery, asks A to keep the goods for him. Before sale A was holding the goods as the owner and after sale he continues in possession as a bailee/agent for B.

ii) A's onions are lying in B's godown. A sells onions to C. C asks B to keep the goods as his agent. Here B's character of possession changes. Before sale he was agent of A and afterwards continues in physical custody as C's agent. This is also called as *delivery by attornment.*

2) **Effect of Part Delivery of Goods** - (Sec. 34) Delivery of a part of the goods in the process of delivery of the whole is regarded as delivery of the whole. This rule is applicable when delivery of goods has the effect of passing of property in goods. This rule is very much relevant as far as the risk of loss of goods during the process of delivery.

Example :

3) **Buyer to apply for delivery - (Sec. 35)**

The seller is not bound to deliver goods until buyer applies for it. Application means a formal request or demand for delivery. This rule is however subject to contract to the contrary.

4) **Place of delivery : Sec. 36 (1)**

Section 36 provides the rules for 3 eventualities.

i) When the place is fixed - The goods should be delivered at that place which is agreed between the parties expressly or impliedly.

ii) In the absence of contract - The place of delivery would be determined by usage of trade.

iii) In the absence of contract and usage - The place of delivery would be as follows.

a. In **sale** - delivery at that place where goods are there at the time of sale;

b. In **agreement to sell** – delivery at that place where goods are there at the time of agreement to sell.

c. In sale of future goods - The goods are to be delivered at the place of manufacture or production.

5) **Time of Delivery - Sec. 36 (2)**

Where under the contract of sale, the seller is bound to send the goods to the buyer, but no time is fixed for sending them, the seller is bound to send them within a reasonable time.

Demand for delivery and tender (offer) for delivery by buyer should be at reasonable hour. What is reasonable time or hour is a question of fact.

6) **Delivery by Attorment - Sec. 36 (3) (See modes of delivery)**

Where the goods are in possession of a third person (neither with Seller nor buyer), the delivery would be complete if the third person acknowledges to the buyer that he holds the goods on his (buyer's) behalf.

7) **Expenses of Delivery - Sec. 36 (5)**

Unless otherwise agreed, the expenses of and incidental to putting the goods in deliverable state shall be borne by the seller. In online shopping 'shipping charges' are mentioned which buyer should pay on home delivery.

8) **Delivery of wrong quality / quantity - (Sec. 37)**

Many times it happens that the seller delivers the goods but buyer finds that those are not according to the contract. On inspection after delivery buyer may realise that those are of different quality or quantity. The summary of rules u/s 37 explains various options to the buyer in defective delivery.

i) **Short Delivery -** i.e. delivery of goods less than contracted, for The buyer may –
   – reject the whole lot and claim damages or
   – accept and pay for them at the contract rate.

ii) **Excess Delivery –** i.e. Delivery of goods more than contract for - The buyer may
   – accept the quantity as per contract and reject excess or
   – accept the whole and in that case he will have to pay for excess at the contract rate.

iii) **Mixed Delivery –** i.e. Delivery of goods contracted for mixed with goods of different description (not included in the contract). The buyer may –
   – accept the goods which are in accordance with contract and reject the rest.
   (This is however possible when the goods are separable) He may claim damages for breach of contract by seller.

9) **Instalment deliveries - Sec. 38**

i) **As a rule, instalment deliveries are not allowed**

Unless otherwise agreed, buyer of goods is not bound to accept delivery thereof in instalments." (Sec. 38-1)

ii) **Effect of breach with respect to one instalment - S. 38 (2)**

If agreed between the parties, delivery in instalment is possible. When parties so agree and each instalment is separately paid for, seller or buyer may commit a breach with respect to one instalment. In this situation a question arises as to –

what is the effect of breach of one instalment over the remaining contract ? The answer is provided in S.38 (2). According to this section following factors should be considered to decide the issue.

a) Terms of the contract and circumstances of the case ;

b) If it can treated as 'severable breach' (separable breach i.e. dissociated from remaining deliveries), then whole contract cannot be terminated. Failure to pay for one instalment would not justify repudiation of entire contract.

c) The quantitative proportion of the breach with the remaining contract.

d) Degree of probability of repetition of the breach (If a factory is closed, future deliveries may not be effected or if buyer goes insolvent payment may not be there.)

10) **Delivery to carrier or wharfinger - (Sec. 39)**

   i) **Delivery to carrier etc is delivery to buyer**
   If as per contractual terms, seller delivers goods to carrier for the purpose of transmission to buyer, the delivery to carrier is prime facie deemed to be a delivery to buyer. The same rule applies in case delivery to wharfinger. (39-1)

   Example - A sends parcels of alphonso mangoes to B through Jet Airways. Delivery of parcels to airways for transmission to buyer is delivery to buyer.

   ii) **Seller's Duty : (S. 39-2)**
   When delivery involves transportation of goods through carrier or wharfinger then seller is under a duty to make contract of carriage with the carrier. If he fails and the goods are lost or damaged during transit (or whilst in the custody of wharfinger), the buyer may decline to treat delivery to carrier as delivery to himself. He may accept the delivery and hold seller responsible for damage, if any, to goods.
   In the abovementioned two situations, the seller must be authorised or otherwise required to deliver the goods through carrier or wharfinger.

   iii) **Sea Transit : (39-3)**
   If the delivery of goods from seller to buyer involves sea-transit, the seller has to inform buyer about sea transit so that buyer may insure the goods. This duty arises when insuring the good is usual in such journey. If seller fails to inform, goods shall be deemed to be at the risk of seller during the sea-transit.

11) **Risk of deterioration during transit - (S. 40)**
   Where the seller agrees to deliver the goods at his own risk at a place other than that place where the goods are when those are sold, the buyer shall nevertheless (unless otherwise agreed), take any risk of deterioration of the goods necessarily incidental to the course of transit.

24.2 Acceptance of Delivery by the Buyer

1) **Buyer's right of examining goods - (S.41)** When the buyer has not examined the goods before delivery, the buyer has a right of examining them on delivery. This right is available to ascertain and confirm that goods actually sent are as per the contract.

2) **When buyer is deemed to have accepted the delivery ? (S.42)** - The buyer is deemed to have accepted the goods in the following circumstances

    i) **Express acceptance** - Buyer communicates the acceptance of goods;

    ii) **Implied acceptance** - On receiving goods buyer does any act inconsistent with ownership of seller. Buyer transfers the goods to third party or appropriates seller's goods.

    iii) Buyer retains the goods without intimating about rejection within reasonable time. In the first two cases, buyer's acceptance is voluntary and in third case, it may be against his desire.

3) **(S.43)** - Buyer is not bound to return the rejected goods. If the buyer has right to reject the goods, he is not bound to return those goods to seller. If he informs seller about rejection, that is sufficient. This is subject to what they have agreed between them.

4) **(S.44)** - Buyer's Liability for refusing or neglecting to accept delivery of goods – When seller validly tenders the delivery of goods to buyer or requests the buyer to take the delivery, buyer must accept the delivery, he is liable to the seller for any loss resulting from such refusal or negligence.

Chapter 25

UNPAID SELLER AND HIS RIGHTS

25.1 Definition of Unpaid Seller [Sec. 45 (1)]

> *"The seller of goods is deemed to be an unpaid seller within the meaning of this Act -*
> a) *When the whole of the price has not been paid or tendered;*
> b) *When a bill of exchange or other negotiable instrument has been received as conditional payment, and the condition on which it was received has not been fulfilled by reason of the dishonour of the instrument or otherwise."*

The seller is thus unpaid in the following circumstances.

i) In cash sales, the price is not paid. Obvisouly in sale on credit, he is not unpaid.

ii) He would become unpaid even in credit sale when credit period has expired and price is not paid.

iii) The 'whole of the price' is not paid to him. This means that if part payment is made, for unpaid balance he is regarded as unpaid seller.

iv) When payment of price is arranged through negotiable instrument (promissory note, bill of exchange or a cheque) and it is dishonoured, the seller is unpaid.

iv) Term unpaid seller includes seller's agent (endorsee of bill of exchange, consignor or agent (who has paid price or who is directly responsible for payment).

Seller is not unpaid if -
- The price is tendered and he wrongfully refuses to accept it or
- 'Price' of goods is paid but 'other charges' are unpaid.

25.2 Rights of Unpaid Seller

Non-payment of price frustrates purpose of sale. Hence unpaid seller has significant statutory rights. Unpaid seller can exercise rights against the goods and rights against the buyer personally.

1) **Rights of Unpaid Seller against the Goods**

When the goods are sold i.e. when the property in the goods has passed to the buyer the unpaid seller enjoys following statutory rights against the goods.

a) - Right of Lien

b) - Right of Stoppage in Transit and

c) - Right of Re-sale

Each of these rights is explained in detail.

2) **Right of Lien**

A) **Meaning, nature and scope of lien :** Lien means the right to retain other's goods in possession untill certain charges/price due from its owner are recovered. According to S.46 (a), unpaid seller has a lien on the goods for the price while in possession of them. Unpaid seller can withhold the delivery of goods untill full price is paid. Lien presupposes that seller ceases to be the owner by passing of property in goods to the uyer. It is a lawful refusal to deliver the goods untill price due in respect of them is paid or tendered. Statutory right of lien is 'possessory' as unpaid seller can exercise it 'while in possession' of goods. This right is indivisible and non transferable one. Unpaid seller's lien is 'specific lien' (in contrast to banker's general lien) as it is exercised over those goods, the price of which is not paid and not over other goods.

B) **Conditions for exercise of lien - When unpaid seller can exercise lien? - S. 47**

i) Sale is without any stipulation as to credit or

ii) Sale is a credit sale but credit period has expired and unpaid seller continues in possession or

iii) Where the buyer has become insolvent within the credit period - Insolvency weakens the terms of credit and seller is justified in asking for payment.

Other Features of lien.

a) Fact of possession of goods with seller is the gist of lien. Unpaid seller can be in possession as bailee or agent of buyer;

b) Delivery of document of title to goods does not prevent seller from exercising lien if he is in actual possession;

c) Lien is exercisable for non-payment of price only and not for non - payment of other charges (Warehouse / dock or storage or maintenance or custody charges)

d) In part delivery of goods, seller can exercise lien over the remainder (S. 48)

e) Buyer cannot ask for proportionate delivery of goods for part payment of price as lien is indivisible.

f) Unpaid seller is entitled to lien even after obtaining decree for price.

Example : A sells some goods to buyer on a credit of 2 months. Buyer requests to keep those goods in his godown. Two months period expires and buyer does not pay the price. A can exercise lien over the goods.

C) **Termination of Lien – When lien is lost ? (S. 49)**

As stated earlier, unpaid seller's lien is possessory. If possession is lost, lien is also destroyed. Factum of possession governs the exercise of lien. In the following cases lien is lost by unpaid seller –

i) Delivery of goods by the seller to carrier or bailee without reserving right of disposal (See Sec. 25) ;

ii) When buyer or agent lawfully obtains possession of goods. (*Eduljee Vs John Brothers*)[96]

iii) Express or implied waiver (giving up) of lien;

iv) When the delivery of part of the goods to the buyer amounts to the delivery of whole;

v) Payment of price by the buyer;

vi) Wrongful refusal on the part of seller to accept payment of price;

vii) When buyer disposes off the goods (by sale or otherwise) with seller's consent; (S.53-1)

viii) Where document of title to goods is lawfully transfered to the buyer and the buyer transfers document of title by sale to second buyer (The second - buyer must act in good faith and for consideration) S. 53 -1

ix) By holding out (estoppel) seller looses lien. The unpaid seller cannot exercise lien against bonafide purchaser for value from first buyer.

Example : A agrees to sell 1000 bags of cement to buyer and delivers the same to the railway for transmission to B.Rly. Co. passess Rly.Receipt in the name of B. A cannot exercise lien.

Lien is not lost by –

i) Decree for price (which is passed in a suit for price) or

ii) Sale or disposition of goods by buyer (unless assented to by the seller) S. 53-1

3) Right of Stoppage in Transit

a) **Meaning - (S. 50) -** Stoppage in transit implies instructions to stop carrying the goods further with a view to stop transmission. It is a right to advise the carrier to stop further transit of goods and asking him to take back the goods to the seller.

When the seller has delivered the goods to the carrier for onward transmission to the buyer and while the goods are in transit, buyer goes insolvent, seller has right to stop further transit and resume the possession of goods. He can retain the possession till price is paid.

b) **Conditions for exercise of the Right of Stoppage**

i) Seller is unpaid seller within the meaning u/s 45 (1) of the Act;

ii) Buyer has becomes insolvent as defined u/s 2(8) of the Act - Insolvent is a person who is unable to pay his debts in ordinary course of business;

iii) The property in the goods has passed to the buyer. This goes without saying because as one cannot exercise lien or stoppage over goods owned by him;

---

96. *AIR (1943) Nag. 249)*

iv) Goods are in 'transition' i.e. in 'transitue'. Transition contemplates that goods are being carried by a carrier and yet not delivered to the buyer.

v) Position of Carrier - The goods are with a carrier as an independent middleman. The goods are neither in possession of seller nor buyer. If possession of seller is with seller or buyer, lien or stoppage cannot be availed. Carrier must hold the goods in his own right as a carrier, neither the agent of seller or buyer. (because in law, agent's possession would be the possession of principal.)

c) Duration of Transit (S.51)

Goods must be in transit i.e. a period between commencement of trasit and its ends.

i) Transit commences when goods are delivered to carrier, or bailee for onward transportation to the buyer.

ii) Transit comes to end when buyer or his agent takes the delivery from carrier or bailee.

d) When right of stoppage in transit is lost ? (S. 51)

The crucial factor in lien or transit is the possession. Change in this aspect may destroy the right.

If the goods are no more in transition, the right is lost. In the following cases in right of stoppage is lost –

i) Buyer or his agent takes the delivery of goods at the point of destination. (i.e. where delivery is to be made) (S. 51-1)

ii) Buyer or his agent obtains delivery of goods before their arrival at destination point. (S. 51-2)

iii) Attorment by carrier at the destination point - acknowledgement by the carrier that he holds goods on buyer's behalf. (S. 51-3)

iv) Wrongful refusal by the carrier to deliver goods to buyer or his agent. (S. 51-6)

v) Transit does not come to an end if buyer wrongfully rejects goods and as a result, the carrier continues in possession (Buyer should not be given benefit of his own wrong)

vi) When delivery of part of the goods to the buyer is deemed to be the delivery of the whole. In that case, notionally carrier looses the possession of the whole of the goods.

vii) If buyer lawfully obtains document of title to goods. (which is transferred in his name) and further sells the goods through that document of title to second buyer who takes in good faith and for consideration, the right of stoppage is lost. This is because the second buyer's title is perfected and seller has to surrender his rights.

viii) Right is not affected by sub-sale or other disposition (say, pledge) by buyer without seller's consent (S. 53)

e) Mode of exercise of right of stoppage.

In the following manner, the right is exercised -

i) By taking actual possession from the carrier or bailee or

ii) Notice of claim to carrier or bailee :-

Notice may be given to the person having actual possession (truck driver with a truck - load) or to his principal. If it is given to the principal, it should be in advance so that principal can communicate it to his employee / agent, before actual delivery.

Distinction between Lien and Stoppage in transit		
Points of distinction	Lien	Stoppage
i) When exercised ? non-payment of price	Exercised in all cases of goes insolvent	Exercised only where buyer
ii) Possession with...	Goods are in possession of seller	Goods are in possession of carrier - not with seller
iii) Possession	It is retaining possession	It is regaining possession
iv) Exercised by whom ?	Exercised by seller seller or bailee	Exercised through carrier by
v) Commencement & Termination	Lien ends when possession is given to carrier / seller	Commences when possesion is given to carrier
(That is why it is said that right of stoppage in transit starts where lien ends)		

4) Right of Resale (S. 54)

Exercise of lien or stoppage would be futile without right of resale. In lien, unpaid seller retains and in stoppage he regains possession. But unless he is allowed to realize his unpaid price by selling the goods, his rights would be meaningless. Hence the Act provides further a right of resale the goods. This right is supplementary to earlier two rights and completes the remedy of unpaid seller.

When and how unpaid seller can resell the goods ?

In the following circumstances unpaid seller is entitled to exercise resale –

i) Right of lien or stoppage is exercised and he is having possession of goods or

ii) The right of resale is expressly reserved by the seller in case of buyer's default in non payment of price or

iii) Where the goods are of perishable in nature

iv) Formality of notice - In case of resale of perishable goods, notice of resale is not necessary. When resale is in the background of lies or stoppage, unpaid seller has to serve a notice to the buyer. Notice should show intention to resell the goods. If the buyer fails to pay or tender the price within reasonable time, unpaid seller may resell the goods.

Serving of notice or its failure has following consequences –

i) If notice is given —

— Profit on resale would go to the unpaid seller.

— Loss on resale should be reimbursed by buyer.

ii) If notice is not given -

— Profit on resale would go to the buyer

— Loss on resale would be borne by the seller.

Consequences of Resale

i) On resale new buyer gets a good title to the goods.

ii) Original sale is rescinded and unpaid seller can claim damages for loss he suffers.

25.3 Unpaid Seller's Rights against the Buyer

In addition to the rights against goods, the unpaid seller has following rights against the buyer personally. The seller has to file a suit in civil court to seek reliefs below mentioned.

1) **Suit for Price - Sec. 55 (1&2) -**
When the buyer wrongfully refuses or neglects to pay the price, the unpaid seller, within reasonable time, can file a suit for price in the civil court. If on a stipulated day buyer undertakes to pay the price and on that day price is not paid, seller has a cause of action against the buyer, irrespective of transfer of ownership or delivery of goods.

2) **Suit for damages for non-acceptance of delivery of goods - Sec. 44 -**
Buyer may not repudiate the contract but wrongfully refuses or neglects to accept the delivery of goods. In such cases buyer must compensate that loss. Seller can also recover the charges for the care and custody of the goods.
Sec. 56 - When the wrongful refusal or negligence to accept the delivery of good amount to repudiation of contract, seller can sue him for damages occasioned due to such non-acceptance.

3) **Suit for Special Damages -** (S. 61) - (See 'kinds of Damages' in Law of Contract.)

4) **Suit for interests -** (S. 61) The court may award interest on the unpaid price from the due date for payment or from the date of tender of delivery of goods.

25.4 Buyer's Rights Against Seller

Seller may commit a breach of contract by non-delivery of goods or by defective delivery. In such and other cases, the buyer may resort to following remedies.

1) **Repudication of Contract (Sec. 12-2) -** If seller commits a breach of conditions, the buyer can rescind the contract and claim damages.

2) **Suit for damages for breach of warranty -** Sec. 52(1) - Buyer may file a suit for damages for the breach of warranty on the part of seller. If he treats breach of condition as a breach of warranty in that case damages is the only remedy for buyer.

3) **Suit for damages for non-delivery of goods -** Sec. 57 states that where the seller wrongfully neglects or refuses to delivers the goods to the buyer, the buyer may sue the seller for damages for non-delivery.

4) **Suit for specific performance -** Sec. 58 of the Act provides for special remedy of

specific performance of contract by seller. This is available when seller commits a breach of contract of specific or ascertained goods. Remedy of specific performance is at the discretion of the court. (See. Chapter on 'Remedies' in Law of Contract)

5) **Special damages for non-delivery of goods -** Sec. 61 - If the buyer suffers special losses due to non delivery of goods the buyer may claim special damages. However buyer has to prove that the seller knew, at the time of contract of sale, that the special loss would be the likely result of his breach.

6) **Suit for refund of price - See 61 -**

When the seller commits a breach, buyer may prefer a suit for refund of advance paid.

7) **Suit for interest - Sec 61 -**

In addition to the claim of refund, buyer may claim interest over the advance price paid, from the date of its payment.

8) **Buyer's Rights of Examination** (Refer chapter on Delivery of Goods)

9) Buyer is not obliged to return the rejected goods. (Refer above chapter.)

Chapter 26 | AUCTION SALES

Very recently Prime Minister Narendra Modi's suit was sold in auction for more than Rs. 2.40 crores in Gujrath. Many advertisements of 'auction sales' appear in news papers. In auction sale goods are sold publicly to one out of many intending buyers. Advertisement for auction sale is 'invitation to offer'. Various intending purchasers offer to purchase the goods. Their offers to purchase at a price are called 'bids' and offering in public auction is called 'bidding'. The goods are sold to the buyer of highest bid. To perfect the title of the buyer the auction sale must be organized in accordance with the rules, contained in section S. 64.

26.1 Rule Relating to Auction Sales.

1. **Goods in Lots [Sec. 64 (1)] -**
   When the goods are sold in lots in auction, each lot is prima facie, deemed to be the subject matter of an independant contract.

2. **Completion of Sale - Sec. 64 (2)-**
   The auction sale is completed by the fall of hammer and announcement of completion by the auctioneer. Auction sale can be completed in any customary manner. Till the announcement of completion of auction sale the bidder may revoke his bid.

3. **Reservation of Right to Bid - S.64 (3)**
   Seller may expresslly reserve the right to bid in auction sale. Without such reservation, seller cannot bid at auction.

4. **Fraudulent Bidding - Sec. 64 (4)**
   Bidding by the seller or by his agent, without reserving right to bid is termed 'fraudulent bidding ' and consequent sale would also be fraudulent. **Pretended bidding -** bidding by the seller himself, to raise the price of goods is pretended bidding. Seller sometimes employs a person to raise the price by fictitions bids. This person has no personal interest in sale and is known as 'decoy duck'. Sale as a result of such false bidding is viodable at buyer's option.

5. **Reserve or Upset Price - Sec. 64 (5)**
   The auction sale may be announced subject to reserve or upset price. Reserve price is

the minimum price below which the auctioneer will not sell the goods. If the highest bid is less than the reserve price, the auctioneer may refuse to accept the bid or accept it subject to conditions and confirmation by seller or he may postpone or cancel the sale.

6. **Knock Out Agreement -**

An agreement between the buyers not to bid against each other to avoid competition is termed as knockout agreement. This agreement is not unlawful.

7. **Damping -**

Damping occures where a bidder is dissuadded from bidding by pointing out the defects in goods or otherwise he is obstructed from estimating the price of goods or scared away from auction. Damping is illegal and auctioneer can revoke or withdraw goods from auction.

8. **Bids may not be accepted -**

Auctioneer is not bound to accept the highest bid.

Bids may not be accepted or auction can be cancelled by the auctioneer. Before acceptance of a bid, bidder can take back his offer.

9. **Warranties in an auction sale**

Following warranties in favour of buyer are implied in a sale by auction –

i) Auctioneer's authority to sell ;

ii) Absence of knowledge of defects in the owner's title on the part of auctioneer.

iii) Warranty of quiet possession of goods to be enjoyed by buyer.

Part III

Questions and hints for answers

1) Define 'Contract of Sale'. Distinguish between Sale and Agreement to sell. TYB.Com - 2012, 2010, 2004, 2003 - PU, MBA 2004, 2013, BBA - 2008, 2010, ✓ Ans.19.1&19.2

   Or

   Write notes on :
   (i)   Auction Sale
   (ii) Right of stoppage of goods in transit.

2) Define 'Goods'. What are its kinds ? 2013, BBA ✓ Ans- 20

3) Define and explain with illustrations 'Conditions & Warranties' in Contract of Sale. How Condition differs from Warranty ? PGDBM P. U. 2005 ✓ Ans. 21

4) Explain in brief the Implied Conditions & Warranties in a Contract of Sale. 5.1 (in brief) TYB.Com. 2011, 2006, PU, MBA 2003 (Imp. Warranties) ✓ 2012, 2013 BBA PU Ans. Chapter 21.3 and 21.4

5) "No one can pass a better title than he himself has". Comment on the statement with exceptions with reference to the provisions of Sale of Goods Act, 1930.

   Or

   Write exceptions to the rule that "no person can transfer a better title to the goods than he himself has in them." TYB.Com - 2008, 2005 - PU Chap. 23; MBA - 2004 - PU, BBA 2011, 2009 PU

6) Define 'Delivery of Goods'. Explain in brief Rules as to Delivery of Good from seller to buyer. BBA 2008, PU

7) Who is Unpaid Seller? Discuss his rights against the goods.

8) Elaborate the doctrine of 'Caveat Emptor'. What are the exceptions to his doctrine? 2013, BBA, MBA, 2003 - P. U. ✓ Ans. 21.3

9) Enumerate the rules regarding Tranfer of Property from seller to buyer in a Contract of Sale of Goods. TYB.Com 2006, PU, Chapter. 2.2

10) State & explain the provisions relating to Passing of Property from seller to buyer in case of -
    a) Sale of Specific Goods
    b) Unascertained goods   MBA 2003

PART - IV

THE LAW OF NEGOTIABLE INSTRUMENTS

Introduction

In old days in local markets barter system prevailed. Properties were exchanged. Afterwards idea of money or paper currency developed. Due to expansion of commerce and multiplicity of commercial transactions, inherent risk and inconvenience in the use of paper currency was realized. Negotiable instrument came to be handled as an alternative to paper currency. Tradesmen do not favor giving and taking money. It is neither possible nor practicable. The negotiable instrument is freely used in most of the transactions. Thus the negotiable instrument are basically instrument of credit that can be converted into money. These instruments represent money and possess all the characteristics of money i.e. Title by possession and free circulation. The negotiability is the peculiar aspect of these instruments which give them wide acceptability and usage.

A negotiable instrument is a piece of paper which entitles a person to a sum of money stated therein and which is transferable from person to person by mere delivery or by endorsement and delivery. The negotiable instrument is a document containing an order or a promise to pay a definite sum of money.

The law relating to negotiable instrument is contained in the Negotiable Instrument Act 1881. It is based on English common law regarding the negotiable instruments. The act extends to the whole of India. The chief object of the Act is to legalize the system under which the negotiable instruments get circulated. The Act regulates the issue and negotiation of negotiable instruments. The Act deals with three negotiable instruments viz. promissory note, bill of exchange and cheque and passing of those from hand to hand. Other negotiable instruments in practice by usage or custom (like treasury bills, share warrants, dividend warrants railway bonds are also treated as negotiable instrument by mercantile usage) are also the subject matter of the Act. The negotiable instruments are chose-in -action or actionable claims. The Transfer of Property Act, 1955 regulates their transfers (assignments, between parties or by operation of law).

Chapter 27 | NEGOTIABLE INSTRUMENTS

Meaning and Characteristics of Negotiable Instruments

27.1 Meaning of Negotiable Instrument

S. 13 of the Act defines negotiable instrument as –

> *"a negotiable instrument means promissory note, bill of exchange, cheque payable either to order or to bearer."*

This definition does not explain what negotiable instrument is. As it is an inclusive dentition other instruments satisfying the characteristics of negotiable instrument are also included in the definition.

Definition by Justice K.C.Willis *"a negotiable instrument is one, the property in which is acquired by one who takes it bonafide and for value notwithstanding any defects of title in the person from whom he took it."*

The word 'negotiable' means "transferable by delivery". 'Instrument' implies a written document. Thus negotiable instrument is "a written document transferable by delivery". A negotiable instrument is a piece of paper which entitles a person to a sum of money stated therein and which is transferable from person to person by mere delivery or by endorsement and delivery. The negotiable instrument is a document containing an order or a promise to pay a definite sum of money.

From the definition and the discussion above, instrument is negotiable instrument if it possesses following attributes.

1) It should be freely transferable. It must be capable of being transferred by delivery or endorsement and delivery;

2) The person possessing negotiable instrument can sue upon it to recover the sum specified in it;

3) The person who takes it bonafide and for value is not affected by the defect of the person from whom he takes it.

27.2 Characteristics of Negotiable Instrument

A negotiable instrument possesses following important characteristics. Because of these attributes, the instrument is 'negotiable' and works like money in commercial transactions.

1) **Free Transferability** – Transferability with ease is the peculiar feature of Negotiable Instrument. It can be transferred freely by one person to another by simple delivery or endorsement and delivery

2) **Transferee gets a good title** – If the transferee takes negotiable instrument in good faith, for value, his title is better than his transferor under certain circumstances. Negotiable instrument comes to holder in due course free from all defects in its title.

3) **Right to transfer** – The negotiable instrument can be negotiated number of times till the date of its maturity.

4) **Presumptions** – There are certain presumptions regarding important aspects of negotiable instrument which avoid unnecessary complications inherent in any document.

5) **Right to recover money** – The holder of negotiable instrument has "right to" possess and recover money from any of the prior parties to Negotiable Instrument.

6) **Right to sue debtor without notice** – A holder in due course can sue on negotiable instrument in his own name without giving notice to the debtor. This facility is not available in ordinary actionable claims. (Negotiable instrument is an actionable claim)

Concept and features of negotiable instruments can be better understood in the light of elaborate discussion on the kinds of negotiable instruments.

Chapter 28 | KINDS OF NEGOTIABLE INSTRUMENT

Definition of negotiable instrument u/s 13 cited above includes three kinds of negotiable instruments, viz. promissory note, bill of exchange and cheque. Those are discussed in detail below.

28.1 PROMISSORY NOTE

Definition. (S. 4) –

"A promissory note is an instrument in writing (not being bank note or currency note) containing an unconditional undertaking signed by the maker, to pay a certain sum of money only to, or to the order of a certain person, or to the bearer of the instrument."

Specimen of Promissory Note

Rs.50,000/-	Pune
	July 10, 2015

Six months after date I promise to pay 'X' or order the sum of Rupees Ten Thousands only, for value received.

To X

Address

Stamp

sd/-

Essential Characteristics of Promissory Note

The promissory note must possess following characteristics for its validity.

1. **Writing**

   Promissory note must be in writing. Oral promissory note is invalid. Promissory note is usually on a printed-paper. It may be in ink or pencil. Printing, cyclostyling, lithography, raised letters for deaf or dumb or like visual modes may also be used for writing. There is no specific format for a promissory note. Promise in a book or a letter would suffice provided is bears all the important features u/s 4.

Illustrations – Content wise following instruments are promissory notes –
"I promise to pay B Rs. 3000"
"I acknowledge myself to be indebted to B in Rs. 40000 to paid on demand."

2. Contents of Promissory Note

Promise or undertaking to pay – The definition of promissory note does not use the word 'promise' but it should contain a promise or an undertaking to pay. In absence of express words such promise should be implied. Mere acknowledgement of liability or indebtedness or a receipt of money is not sufficient.

Illustrations – "Mr. A, I.O.U. (I owe you) Rs. 10,000."
"I am liable to pay A Rs. 10,000 for which I am accountable".
These are **not valid** promissory notes as undertaking to pay is absent.

3. Unconditional Promise to Pay

Undertaking to pay should be absolute and unconditional. If it depends upon a condition, it introduces uncertainty. Liability to pay cannot be fixed when promise is subjected to condition. Condition obstructs negotiability. If promise to pay depends upon an event which is certain to happen though time of its happening is uncertain, the promise is not 'conditional' and promissory note is valid. (Sec.5, Para-2)

Illustrations – "I promise to pay Y Rs. 15000 one month after my marriage with Z"
"I promise to pay B Rs. 5 lakhs on C's death, provided C leaves me enough to pay that sum".
(Invalid promissory notes, promise being conditional)
"I promise to pay A Rs. 5000 ten days after the death of B." (Valid promissory note as death is certain though time is uncertain)

4. Signature of the Maker

Promissory note should be signed by the maker. Signature is important as it authenticates or adopts the contents above it. It reflects maker's intention to subscribe to the tenor of negotiable instrument. Signature should not be a mere physical act but conscious or intentional one. Signature may be writing one's name, putting initials or marks, thumb impression indicating approval of the instrument. Unsigned negotiable instrument is worthless.

5. Certainty of Parties

There are two parties to Promissory note, Maker and Payee.
Certainty in material particulars of the negotiable instrument is vital for enforcement of every negotiable instrument.[97] Who is to pay and who is entitled for payment must be specified.
   a) Maker must be certain as he is principally liable party on promissory note. He may be identified by name or designation. If not certain by name, he must be capable of being

---

97. *"where liability lies no ambiguity must lie."*

ascertained, say by their status as chairman, secretary of a named institution. More than one person (i.e. signing jointly) may make promissory note.

b) Payee must be certain – Payee is a person who is entitled to receive money under promissory note hence he should be certain by name or description. Designation would suffice. He should be known with certainty. If A has a daughter, then a promissory note 'payable to daughter of A' is enforceable. Alternative payees are allowed, for that the negotiable instrument must be payable to order originally.

6. Certainty of Sum

The sum mentioned in the promissory note must be certain and definite. Principle amount with interest rate may be specified. It should not be susceptible of additions or subtractions.

Illustrations *– Valid promissory notes –* "I promise to pay A Rs. 10,000 with interest @ 12 p.a."

"I promise to pay A Rs. 10000 in 5 equal installments per month."

Invalid promissory note – "I promise to pay B Rs. 10,000 and all other sums which shall be due to him." (Amount uncertain)

7. Promise to pay money only

Undertaking should pertain to money only and not anything else. If in addition to promise to pay, something more is promised, it is not a promissory note.

For e.g. "I promise to pay you Rs. one lakh and to deliver i-phone", this instrument is bad in law.

8. Bank note or currency notes are not promissory notes

The definition of promissory note excludes these two notes. Bank notes are in fact promissory notes issued by a banker payable to bearer on demand. RBI has prohibited issue of such bank notes. Currency notes also possess all the features of a promissory note. Those are promissory notes issued by the RBI. Sec. 31 of the Reserve Bank of India Act 1934, states that no person in India except the RBI or the Central Government can make or issue a promissory note payable to bearer. Private individual, therefore, cannot issue such promissory note payable to bearer.

9. Other Formalities

There is neither any form nor formalities prescribed for a promissory note. As a negotiable instrument, date, amount, place, parties appear on promissory note. "Value received" need not be mentioned in the pronote.

Promissory note should be stamped as per the provisions of Indian Stamp Act, 1899. Insufficient or improper stamps make the promissory note inadmissible in evidence. On payment of adequate stamp, it regains enforceability. It is advisable to cancel the stamp.

10. Other features

It is clear from the definition that promissory note involves two parties viz. maker and payee. Promissory note does not require acceptance. The maker is primarily and absolutely liable to pay the sum to payee.

28.2 BILL OF EXCHANGE

Definition (Sec.5) –

> *"A bill of exchange is an instrument in writing containing an unconditional order, signed by the maker, directing a certain person to pay a certain sum of money only to, or to the order of a certain person, or to the bearer of the instrument."*

Bill of exchange is thus a written order to pay a certain amount to a person or his order. The bill of exchange has three parties, **"drawer", "drawee" and "payee"**. The maker of the bill is drawer. Drawee is one who is directed pay. The person to whom or whose order money is to be paid is called as payee.

Normally the drawer draws the bill and sends it to the drawee for acceptance. When drawee accepts it, he becomes **"acceptor"**. He then endorses the bill to the drawer. Drawer or endorsee holds the bill till the maturity. On the day of maturity or afterwards the acceptor has to make the payment.

Specimen of Bill of Exchange

Rs.10,00,000	Kolhapur Jun 10, 2015

Six months after date pay to B or order the sum of Rupees One lakh only, for value received.

To A _____

Address _____

Stamp

Sd/- C

Essential Characteristics of Bill Of Exchange

The essential characteristics of bill of exchange are more or less similar to that of a promissory note. Those are explained below. (For common features see topic on promissory note)

1. **Writing** –
    Bill of Exchange must be in writing. No particular language or form is suggested. Verbal order is not a negotiable instrument.

2. **Parties** –
    Refer general explanation of the bill.

3. **Contents of bill of exchange** –
    Bill of Exchange should contain an **order to pay** a specified sum. Order may be express or imperative. "Credit in cash" or simply "pay" is construed as an order. Courteous expressions like "please pay" may also imply order. But words of excessive politeness or request will not make a valid bill. "It would be kind of you if you pay X sum of Rs. 10,000."

or "Mr. X, please pay Y Rs. 10,000 and oblige" cannot be considered as a bill of exchange[98]

4. **Unconditional Order to Pay –**
   Order to pay in the bill must be absolute and unqualified. Contingency introduces uncertainty, hampering negotiation.

5. **Signature of the Drawer –**
   Bill of exchange must bear signature of the drawer. Without signature it is incomplete and even if accepted, it would not create any right or liability.

6. **Certainty of Parties –**
   a) Drawee must be certain – Drawee after acceptance becomes principally liable party and hence he must know whether he is addressed or not on the bill. Payee should also know the person to whom it is to be presented for acceptance and for payment.

   b) Payee must be certain – Drawee should know the person entitled for the amount on bill. Drawee and payee should be indicated with reasonable certainty.

7. **Certainty of Sum –**
   See promissory note.

8. **Other Formalities –**
   Other particulars like date, place, consideration appear normally on a bill. Appropriate stamp should be affixed on the bill.

28.3 CHEQUE

Definition – (Sec. 6)

> *"A cheque is a bill of exchange drawn on a specified banker and not expressed to be payable otherwise than on demand and it includes the electronic image of a truncated cheque and a cheque in electronic form,"*

Specimen Form of Cheque

STATE BANK OF INDIA   10-04-15
Mumbai
Pay Mr. B.————————————————————or bearer
Rupee Fifty Thousands only.   Rs. 50,000/-
A/c No. 20003644   10   Sd/- A

---

98. *Little v/s Slackford 1826 – M&W-171*

The recent amendment has enlarged the definition of cheque by inclusion of electronic and truncated cheques. Original definition of cheque remains unchanged. From the definition one would notice that cheque is a species of bill of exchange. Cheque, therefore, should possess all the ingredients of a bill u/s 5 of the Act and must be drawn accordingly. It follows that all cheques are bill of exchange but all bills of exchange are not cheques. Cheque is a bill of exchange with two additional distinctive features –

a) It is always payable on demand and

b) It is always drawn on a specified banker.

Cheque is thus a demand instrument and drawee is always a banker. Cheque is a direction to the paying banker to pay the sum to the payee or the bearer. There is an implied contract between the drawer and the banker that whenever directed (through cheque), the banker will debit his account and pay the funds to the rightful person. A cheque does not create any right in favor of its holder against the banker. There is no privity of contract between the payee/ holder and the banker. The banker is liable to the drawer as there is a relationship of creditor and debtor between the drawer and a banker. If it is dishonoured, the holder of a cheque has no remedy against the banker. He may have right of action against drawer. Cheque does not amount to an assignment of funds of drawer to the payee or the holder.

Salient Features of Cheque

1. It must be in writing

2. It should contain an order to pay the specified sum

3. Order must be unconditional

4. Order should be to pay money only

5. Order should be signed by the drawer

6. The amount of money should be certain

7. **Cheque is always payable on demand**—As stated earlier, cheque is a demand instrument. If it is not so, it is not a cheque. It is mature for payment as soon as it is drawn.

8. **Formalities**—No particular form of words are prescribed for a cheque. To be called a cheque, document should adhere to the ingredients of a bill. No stamp is required to be affixed on cheques.

9. *Cheque includes "cheque in electronic form" and "truncated cheque"* – The amended definition includes these cheques. Inclusion of these terms is in tune with provisions of The Information Technology Act, 2002. This Act recognizes electronic transactions and provides for authentication of electronic record by digital signatures. The new definition provides explanation of these terms as follows.

   a) "a cheque in electronic form" means a cheque which contains the exact mirror image of a paper cheque, and is generated, written and signed in a secure system ensuring the minimum safety standards with the use of digital signature (with or without biometric signature)and asymmetric crypto system.

   b) "a truncated cheque" means a cheque which is truncated during the course of a clearing cycle, either by the clearing house or by the bank whether paying or receiving payment, immediately on generation of an electronic image for transmission, substituting further physical movement of the cheque in writing.

Other notable points in connection with cheque

- Cheque, though a bill of exchange, does not require acceptance due to the special relationship between the drawer and banker briefed earlier. Cheque is intended for immediate payment.

- Post dated cheques – Post dated or anti-dated cheques are valid. A post dated cheque is a bill of exchange when it is drawn and it becomes cheque on the date mentioned or afterwards. It cannot be presented or paid before that date.

- A demand draft drawn by one branch of a bank on its another branch is not a cheque. For the purposes of sec.131A of the Act however, it is regarded as a cheque.

- Countermanding – Countermanding is "stop payment " instruction by the drawer to the banker. It is the revocation of authority of the bank to pay on a particular cheque.

- Noting and protest are not required in case of dishonoured cheques.

- A cheque is valid for six months. After that it becomes stale and banker may dishonour it.

Crossing of Cheques

Cheque are of two types viz. Open cheques and Crossed cheques.

In open or uncrossed cheque the payment can be obtained by presenting the cheque across the counter. In crossed cheques the payment is possible only through the banker. The nature of cheque decides the mode of payment.

- **Meaning of Crossing** – Crossing is a direction to the paying banker to pay the money through a banker or to a named banker. By crossing, banker is instructed not to pay holder across the counter. The banker is supposed to credit the amount only in the holder's account and direct payment is thus prohibited.

- **Object of Crossing** – There is always a risk of payment of a cheque to a wrongful person and he may not be traced. To avert this risk, crossing is done. Object of crossing is to protect the true owner of a cheque because payment to rightful person is ensured through crossed cheques. As payment of crossed cheques is by operation of account, identity of wrongful person is identified. He can be traced and money can be recovered from him.

- **Types of crossing** – The crossing is basically of two types viz. General and Special crossing which is explained below.

  a) **General Crossing** – Sec. 123 states that "Where a cheque bears across its face an addition of the words and "company" or any abbreviation thereof, between two parallel transverse lines, or of two parallel transverse lines simply, either with or without the words "not negotiable", the cheque shall be deemed to be crossed generally."

After examining above section, following instances of general crossing may be given

- Two parallel transverse lines on the face of the cheque without anything in between them.
- Two parallel transverse lines with "and company" or any abbreviation thereof between them.
- Two parallel transverse lines with the words "not negotiable" between them.

Specimen of General Crossing

	AXIS BANK	30-08-15
Pay Mr. A. _____		or bearer
Rupee Sixty Thousands only.		Rs. 60,000/-
A/c No. 64430 20		Sd/- B

A/c payee	**HDFC BANK**	20-06-15
Pay Mr. XYZ _____		or bearer
Rupee Five Thousands only.		Rs. 5000/-
A/c No. 20003644 10		Sd/-ABC

Not Negotiable	**ICICI BANK**	10-09-15
Pay Mr. Pradeep Patil. _____		or bearer
Rupee Seventy Thousands only.		Rs. 70000/-
A/c No. 64430 20		Sd/- Ashok Gupta

b) **Special Crossing** – According to sec. 124 "Where a cheque bears across its face an addition of the name of a banker, either with or without the words "not negotiable" that addition shall be deemed crossing and the cheque shall be deemed to be crossed specially and to be crossed to that banker." Special crossing is direction to pay only through a named banker to whom it is crossed specially.

Specimen of Special Crossing

Business Bank   31-03-15

Pay Mr. B. ——————————————————————— or bearer

Rupee Six Thousands Five Hundred only.   Rs. 6500/-

A/c No. 64435   20   Sd/-A

UCO BANK   **UNION BANK**   20-04-15

Pay Mr. B. ——————————————————————— or bearer

Rupee Five Thousands only.   Rs. 5000/-

A/c No. 64435   20   Sd/-A

                              BANK OF BARODA   20-05-15
Not Negotiable

Pay Mr. Ram Sharan . ——————————————————— or bearer

Rupee Seventy Thousands only.   Rs. 70000/-

A/c No. 64435   20   Sd/- Sai Sharan

Other Types of crossing

c) **"not negotiable" Crossing** – These words may be inserted in between the lines in general crossing or special crossing. Negotiability of cheques is restricted by such additions. Negotiable instrument or holder in due course is an exception to the principle that no one can pass a better than he himself has. The transferee gets a good title than his transferor and enjoys certain privileges. If the transferee gets the cheque with "not negotiable" crossing, he will not get title better than his transferor. The transferee is put on alert by these words and supposed to enquire about his transferor's title.

d) **Restrictive crossing** – The words "A/C Payee" are also frequently added in general or special crossing. It is a direction to collect the money only for the account of the payee. Though legally speaking negotiability by these words is not restricted, in practice, the effect is so.

Comparison/Distinction Between Promissory Note, Bill of Exchange, Cheque

Sr. No.	Points of Distinction	Promissory note	Bill of Exchange	Cheque	Remark
1	No. of Parties	Two (Maker, Payee...)	Three (Drawer, Drawee and Payee)	Three (Drawer, Drawee and Payee)	(Cheque is a BOE)
2	Contents/Nature of Promise/order	Unconditional undertaking to pay	Unconditional Order to pay	Order to pay	--
3	Payable to...	Cannot be payable to bearer and on demand	Can be payable to bearer Cannot be payable to bearer and on demand	Payable to bearer or order	--
4	Time/Demand Instrument	Can be Time Instrument	Can be Time Instrument	Always payable on demand	--
5	Acceptance	Not required	Required	Not required	--
6	Principal Party liable	Maker	Acceptor	Drawer	
	Nature of liablity	Maker's liablity absolute	Drawer's liability secondary Acceptor's liability absolute	Banker not liable to payee/holder	--
7	Notice of dishonour	Usually required	Usually required	Not required	
		(Maker, Acceptor do not reqire notice)			
8	Protest for dishonour	Not required / optional	Not required / optional	Not required	
9	Grace period	3 days of grace Unless on demand	Unless on demand 3 days of grace	No grace period (Demand Instrument)	
10	Stamping	Necessary	Necessary	Not necessary	
11	Crossing	No Crossing	No Crossing	Crossing is possible	
12	Countermanding (stop - payment)	No question arises	Countermanding not Possible	Possible	

These points can be elaborated in the light of essentials of three instruments.

Chapter 29 | HOLDER AND HOLDER IN DUE COURSE

29.1 HOLDER

Holder of a negotiable instrument is an important party because he is the person who can obtain the payment as a right. Holder can sue upon for payment and give a valid discharge.

Definition Sec.8

> *"The holder of promissory note, bill of exchange or a cheque means any person entitled in his own name to the possession thereof and to receive or recover the amount due thereon from the parties thereto."*

In simple words the holder is the owner of negotiable instrument in law. Under the Act a person can claim to be the holder if he satisfies following two conditions or in other words if *he has following two rights*

1) He is 'entitled in his own name' to the possession of the instrument and

2) He has the 'right to receive or recover the amount due thereon' from the parties thereto. These requirements are explained below.

a) **Right to possession** – The phraseology 'entitled in his own name' in the definition implies a right to possession of the instrument in one's name. To qualify as a holder, he must have derived title in a lawful manner. Possession means possession in law (de jure) and need not be possession in fact (de facto). Actual or physical possession is not necessary; he should have right to possess the instrument. Holder means dejure holder and not necessarily de facto holder. In order to be called as holder, a person must be named as a payee or indorsee or he must be the bearer of instrument. An agent possessing the instrument in trust for his principal is not a holder as he is not 'entitled in his own name' to the possession and recover the amount. His principal is the holder.

b) **Right to receive or recover the amount** – To constitute a person the holder of instrument, possession is not sufficient. He must have legal right to recover the amount i.e. to take legal action against the party liable to pay and give a valid discharge. It implies a right to sue on instrument. Payee or indorsee is not holder if prohibited by a court from receiving the amount due on instrument. A guardian or a 'benamidar' or a trustee having the instrument in their name can sue upon it.

Persons who are holders – Payee, bearer, indorsee are the holders of negotiable instrument as these are having the rights mentioned above. The heir or legal representatives of a deceased payee can claim to be the holder by operation of law.

Persons who are not holders – A thief or a person taking the instrument by forgery is not holder. These persons have the possession but their possession is illegal. A finder of a lost negotiable instrument is also not a holder in spite of having possession, as he cannot legally recover the amount. Similarly indorsee under a forged endorsement is not a holder, as forgery conveys no title. An indorsee for collection has possession but he cannot hold it in his own name and recover the amout by taking the action.

Other rights of Holder – Besides above two rights a holder has following rights –
   (a) Holder has a right to obtain duplicate promissory note or bill or a cheque if it is lost or destroyed (S. 8)
   (b) He can negotiate the instrument further.
   (c) He has the capacity to cross the cheque.
   (d) He can convert blank endorsement in full endorsement or vice-versa.

29.2 HOLDER IN DUE COURSE

Holder in due course is one who enjoys privileged position in connection with negotiable instrument. Sec. 9 of the Act defines the term in the following words.

> *"Holder in due course means any person who for consideration became the possessor of a promissory note, bill of exchange or cheque, if payable to bearer or the payee or the indorsee thereof if payable to order before the amount mentioned in it became payable, and without having sufficient cause to believe that any defect existed in the title of the person from whom he derived his title."*

Analysis of the definition reveals that a person must possess following qualifications for becoming a holder in due course.

Important Features of Holder in due course.

Conditions for becoming a holder in due course.

   1) **He must be the holder of the negotiable instrument –**
      As per section 8, a person must have right to possession and right to recover the amount under the instrument. Refer earlier discussion on the point.

   2) **He should be the holder as –**
      • A possessor of the instrument if payable to bearer or
      • The payee or indorsee thereof, if payable to order.

3) **He must have obtained the instrument for consideration –**
Consideration is necessary to support the title of holder in due course. It can take any form. A person who takes the instrument without consideration cannot be holder in due course. For the same reason, donee of a cheque is not a holder in due course and he cannot bring an action on gift cheque. There is a presumption that every holder has paid consideration to his transferor. The consideration should be valuable and lawful and satisfy the requirements of section 3 (definition of consideration) and sec. 23 (lawful nature of consideration) of the Contract Act.

4) **He should have obtained the instrument before maturity –**
It is equally important that he must have received the instrument before maturity. If he takes it on or after maturity, he cannot come within the definition u/s 9. This is so because the instrument can be paid on or after it becomes payable i.e. on maturity and on payment, the instrument is discharged. If somebody takes it on or after maturity, his rights are not better than that of his transferor.

5) **He must have taken the instrument in good faith and with due care and caution**
Section 9 states that the person should take the instrument "... *without having sufficient cause to believe that any defect existed in the title of the person from whom he derived this title.*" This portion of the section involves element of "*good faith and due care and caution*" on the part of holder in due course. The person claiming to be the holder in due course must act honestly i.e. he should take it without notice of defect in the title of his transferor. If he knows that his transferor had no title or having weak title, (say, a thief, mere finder or indorsee for collection,) then honesty is lost.

Notice of defects implies knowledge of facts creating a doubt in negotiable instrument. Willful disregard of means of knowledge is also construed as notice. The time when such a notice affects the holder is when he takes the instrument. Notice of existence of defects after taking the instrument will not invalidate his title. Notice of defect in the title of any prior party does not affect the rights of holder.

When circumstances create suspicion? There are many circumstances by reason of which a holder taking the instrument may have sufficient cause to believe that there is something wrong in the instrument. Irregularity apparent on the face of negotiable instrument in date, amount, certainty of party, a bill without drawer's signature, existence of material defect, inadequate stamp on the instrument, irregular endorsements, alterations in date, amount etc., absence of material particulars, blank acceptance, incomplete instrument or endorsement etc. put holder on guard. In such a situation the holder must examine the form and content of the instrument and then only deal in it. If in spite of these defects one takes it, he takes it at his risk and responsibility. If an instrument is torn out and pieces are pasted, it shows an intention to cancel the instrument. If one takes it, in this tampered form, cannot claim the status of holder in due course. Rule of caveat emptor applies in all these circumstances.

Examples of Holder & Holder in due course

1) A draws bill of exchange in the name of B, payee. B indorses it to C. C is the holder of the bill.

2) A makes a promissory note in favor of B. B indorses it to C. C takes it before maturity, for consideration and in good faith, with proper care. C is holder in due course. C gives it to D who provides no consideration to C .D is not holder in due course but only holder.

3) If in the second example, D negotiates it to E and E satisfies the requirements of sec. 9 then E becomes holder in due course though D is not.

4) A makes a promissory note for B who endorses it in blank to C. It is lost from C .D finds it. D being finder is not holder in due course. If D delivers the promissory note to E for consideration, before maturity and E has no reason to believe that D is a finder, then E is a holder in due course.

5) B procures a promissory note made by A by fraud. B endorses it to C who is not aware of the fraud and fulfills other conditions for becoming a holder in due course. C is holder in due course of promissory note, though B is not.

Distinction between Holder and Holder in due course - These two concepts are overlapping to some extent. However there is a vital distinction between the two.

1) **Definition and nature**
Every holder in due course is a holder. Section 8 defines holder in terms of the rights. In addition to these rights holder in due course must take the instrument in good faith and before maturity.

2) **Title**
Holder's title is not better than his transferor. Holder in due course's title is better than his transferor. Holder in due course is an exception to 'nemo dat quod non habet'.

3) **Privileges**
Holder in due course has a privileged position. Holder does not enjoy the privileges of holder in due course explained in the forth-coming paras.

4) **Consideration**
A person can be holder without consideration. Holder in due course must obtain negotiable instrument for consideration.

5) **Maturity**
Holder in due course should have taken the instrument before maturity. If instrument is negotiated to a person after maturity he is only holder and not holder in due course.

6) **Recovery of the money from parties**
Holder can recover the amount in negotiable instrument from his transferor and drawer/maker and not from all prior parties. Holder in due course being privileged can recover amount from any prior party till it is discharged.

7) **Notice of defect in the title of transferor**
Sec. 9 requires that the holder in due course must take the instrument without notice of defect in the title of his transferor. One may know about such a defect and still a holder provided he is not a party to the defect.

29.3 Privileges

Privileges of Holder in Due Course

Holder in due course satisfying conditions under S. 9, enjoys following special rights under the Act.

1) Every holder is a prime facie deemed to be holder in due course. He has right to recover the amount in negotiable instrument from any party liable on it.

2) Every prior party remains liable to pay him till it is duly satisfied – Sec.36.

3) Holder in due course is an exception to 'no one can pass a better title than he himself has.' He gets a good title even if his transferor's title is defective. Not only that the negotiable instrument going through his hands is cleansed of (purged of) all defects. A person deriving a title from holder in due course gets title free from all defects (S. 53)

4) Holder in due course gets a good title to recover the amount filled in an inchoate instrument. The person signing and delivering an inchoate instrument cannot plead that the authority to fill in the amount is exceeded provided the stamp covers the amount mentioned (Sec. 20)

   Following defences are not available to the concerned party as against holder in due course in order to escape from the liability to pay.

5) Acceptor is prevented from asserting that the bill is drawn in fictitious name. (S.42) Drawer's signature and first indorser's signature must however be in the same handwriting.

6) When an instrument is negotiated to holder in due course, the parties cannot escape liability by pleading that delivery of the negotiable instrument was conditional or for a particular purpose only. (S.46)

7) A party cannot plead as against holder in due course that the instrument which holder in due course has obtained was lost, obtained (by earlier party) by means of offence, or by fraud or for unlawful consideration. (S.58)

8) Even if consideration is absent between two earlier parties or made/drawn without consideration, holder in due course can recover the amount from any prior party.

   ### Estoppels in favour of holder in due course –

9) The validity of the negotiable instrument originally drawn or made cannot be denied by the maker or drawer or acceptor of a bill for honour (S.120)

10) The maker of a note or acceptor of a bill cannot deny payee's capacity to indorse the same on the date of note or bill (S.121)

11) Indorser cannot deny the signature of any of his prior party or capacity to contract. (S.122)

    The defences mentioned in Ss.120 to 122 cannot be advanced in a suit by or against holder in due course.

| Chapter | NEGOTIATION OF NEGOTIABLE |
| 30 | INSTRUMENTS |

Negotiable instruments are very often used to make payments in commercial transactions. Instead of keeping it till maturity, it is passed to creditors to discharge financial olbigations in business. An instrument may be transferred from hand to hand till maturity. Such transfers effect transfer of ownership of the instrument. This process of transfer of ownership of the negotiable instrument is called as "negotiation". Transfer with ease is the chief characteristic of negotiable instrument.

30.1 Definition & Meaning

Definition of Negotiation – (Section 14)

> *"when a promissory note or bill of exchange or cheque is transferred to any person, so as to constitute that person the holder thereof, the instrument is said to be negotiated."*

Meaning of Negotiation

From the definition it can be seen that negotiation has two aspects

a) Transfer of negotiable instrument and

b) Transfer of (negotiable instrument) with the intention of making the transferee the holder of negotiable instrument.

Transfer thus is a deliberate act which vests transferee with rights of holder i.e. right to possession and right to recover the amount. It is a transfer with purpose. Negotiation in a way is a transfer of the title/ ownership of negotiable instrument.

Who may negotiate? (Sec. 51) Every maker, payee, drawer or indorsee can negotiate the instrument. If there are several makers, drawers, payees or indorsees, all of them can jointly negotiate an instrument. An instrument can be negotiated provided negotiability is not restricted or excluded.

Duration of negotiability. (S.60) An instrument may be negotiated until it is paid or satisfied at or after maturity by maker or acceptor. It cannot be negotiated after its payment or satisfaction. If it is not paid or satisfied at or after maturity, it still may be negotiated.

Effects of Negotiation –

When an instrument is transferred by negotiation to a person, he becomes the holder in due course. Negotiation passes a better title to the transferee than his transferor. Even if his transferor's title is defective by his fraud or coercion or misrepresentation, holder gets a good title, free from all defects.

30.2 Modes of Negotiation

An instrument is negotiated in two ways according to the nature of negotiable instrument.
1) Negotiation by delivery and 2) Negotiation by indorsement and delivery

1) Negotiation by Delivery

According to Sec. 47 an instrument payable to bearer is negotiable by mere delivery. No signature of indorser is needed to negotiate bearer instrument. By simple delivery the possessor becomes the holder.

Delivery - Delivery is an important formality in negotiation. Delivery is essential for creating rights under the instrument. Delivery is a voluntary transfer of possession of instrument by one to another. Delivery is a conscious act made with an intention of passing the ownership of the instrument. Mere delivery without specific intention of transfer does not convey title. Delivery of instrument to an office boy for safe custody will not effect negotiation.

Delivery may be actual or constructive or conditional.

Actual delivery is physical transfer of possession. Constructive delivery is a delivery in the eyes of law. Physical possession remains unchanged. Conditional delivery is delivery for special purpose or subject to some condition. Defence of conditional delivery can be taken only against the party taking with the notice of condition or purpose. This plea cannot be availed against the holder in due course.

2) Negotiation by indorsement and delivery

Section 48 states that an instrument payable to order is negotiable by indorsement and delivery. For negotiation of an order instrument two steps are essential viz. indorsement and delivery.

Indorsement – Indorsement is an important formality in negotiation which is defined in Sec. 15 as follows.

> *"When the maker or holder of a negotiable instrument signs the same, otherwise than as such maker, for the purpose of negotiation, on the back or face thereof or on slip of paper annexed thereto, or so signs for the same purpose a stamped paper intended to be completed as negotiable instrument, he is said to negotiate the same, and is called the indorser."*

Important features of indorsement – As per sec. 15, indorsement has following notable features.

a) **Signature** – Indorsement means the signature of the maker or holder. Signature connotes writing person's name. No form of words can be suggested for an indorsement. Signature should be in ink or left hand thumb impression of illiterate person, duly attested, would work. Signature on an inchoate instrument for negotiation is also a valid indorsement.

b) **Place of Signature** – Signature may be on the face or back side of the instrument. As instrument can be negotiated till satisfied or paid. Number of indorsement on an instrument may be unlimited. If no room is left for further indorsement, a slip of paper can also be annexed and used for the purpose. This slip of paper is called as "allonge" and it is treated as part of the instrument.

c) **Intention to negotiate** – Maker or holder must sign with the purpose of negotiation. Indorsement thus is an intentional act. "Animus transferendi" (intention to transfer the property) should accompany the signature.

d) **Effect of indorsement** – By indorsement followed by delivery, the property in the negotiable instrument passes to the indorsee. Indorsee gets right to negotiate furher. Right to negotiate may be restricted or excluded by indorsement (See restrictive indorsement.)

e) **Parties to indorsement** – One who indorses is "indorser" and for whom it is indorsed is called as "indorsee".

g) **Who can indorse and negotiate?** Following parties may negotiate the instrument by indorsement.
— Maker or holder of a negotiable instrument (otherwise than as such as maker – sec.15); If maker draws the instrument payable to 'Self', then he has to indorse it not as a maker but as an indorser.
— Sole maker or drawer when the instrument made or drawn is payable to his own order;
— Payee or indorsee; all Payees or indorsees (who are not partners). If one is authorized, he may negotiate. Partner has implied authority to indorse as a representative the firm.
— All of several joint makers, drawers, payees or indorsees;
— A stranger has no capacity to indorse as he is not a holder. His indorsement is infructuous.

Delivery – Concept of delivery is explained in the first mode of negotiation. Indorsement is completed by delivery. Indorsement without delivery or delivery without indorsement in order instrument is devoid of any effect. One may indorse and may revoke before delivery.

30.3 Kinds of Indorsements

1. Blank or General Indorsement.
Blank indorsement is an indorsement without indorsee's name. It consists of bare signature of the indorser.

Section 16(1) – If indorser signs his name only without specifying the name of the indorsee, the indorsement is described as blank indorsement. Blank indorsement obviously converts order instrument into bearer instrument. (S.54)

Example – A Cheque is payable to A or order. A merely signs on the back of it. Cheque becomes payable to bearer and can be negotiated by delivery.

2. Indorsement in Full or Special Indorsement. Section 16(2)

If the indorser, in addition to his signature, also adds a direction to pay the amount mentioned in the instrument to or to the order of, a specified person, the indorsement is said to be in full. No specific words are necessary for indorsement in full.

Example – A holder of promissory note negotiates it as "Pay to B or order. Sd/A." This is indorsement in full as the name of the indorsee is mentioned.

Conversion of blank indorsement into full indorsement : (S. 49) – A blank indorsement may be converted into indorsement in full. Holder of a negotiable instrument with blank indorsement may write a direction above his indorser's signature to pay it to next person. This is converting blank indorsement into full indorsement. Here the holder's name does not appear on the instrument and hence he is not liable as an indorser.

Example – A, is the holder of a bill indorsed in blank by B. A writes over B's signature the words "pay to C or order". A is not liable as an indorser and indorsement is treated as an indorsement in full.

3. Restrictive Indorsement — Indorsement restricting or prohibiting further negotiation is known as 'restrictive indorsement'.

Sec. 50 – As explained earlier, indorsement not only transfers the property in negotiable instrument but also vests indorsee a right to negotiate further. This right to negotiate may be totally prohibited or restricted by the indorser. In this type of indorsement, the indorsee has to follow the directions of indorser. It is a mere authority to deal with the bill as directed and not a transfer of ownership. Such indorsement does not deprive the indorsee the right to receive the amount on maturity but he cannot negotiate. The effects of 'restrictive indorsement' under this section are as follows

- Prohibition or exclusion of further negotiation or
- To constitute the indorsee an agent to indorse the negotiable instrument or
- To constitute the indorsee an agent to receive the amount for a specified person.

Examples – "Pay to A only." "Pay to A for me". "Pay to A for the account of B." "the within must be credited to A." These examples illustrate the exclusion of right to negotiate.

4. Conditional Indorsement — Conditional indorsement means an indorsement subject to some condition or a qualified indorsement.

Sec. 52 – When an indorser of negotiable instrument makes his liability dependant on the happenning of a specified event, the indorsement is termed as "conditional indorsement". To be covered by the definition, it should be by express words. The event mentioned in the indorsement may never happen. In that case the indorser incurs no liability on the negotiable instrument. Though the making or drawing of promissory note or bill of exchange should not be conditional, conditional indorsements are allowed. By such an indorsement, the indorser's liability arises only on happening of that event. However all other prior parties (maker, acceptor indorsers etc.) remain liable even though event does not happen.

Example - "Pay to A or order on the arrival of Tytanic-2006', a ship at Mumbai."
"Pay X or order after his selection as on IAS Officer"

5. Sans (frais) recourse Indorsement. (Sec. 52)

When an indorser expressly excludes his own liability on the negotiable instrument to the indorsee or to any subsequent holder in case of dishonour of the instrument, the indorsement is known as "sans recourse" indorsement. Usually the words like "sans recourse" or "without recourse" or "at his risk" are added in the indorsement to absolve from the liability to pay.

Examples – "Pay A or order sans recourse." "Pay A or order without recourse to me"; "Pay A or order at his own risk."

6. Partial indorsement. (Sec 56)

Partial indorsement is an indorsement which transfers part of the amount covered by the instrument. By this indorsement, the indorsee gets right to receive the amount mentioned in the indorsement and not the full amount. Such indorsements are not permitted and declared invalid. A partial indorsement does not operate as negotiation. An indosement must be of the entire amount. Partial indorsement is not desirable, as prior parties will have to satisfy different claims for amounts in part. Personal contract cannot be apportioned. Secondly such indorsement impedes further negotiation.

Example – A is the holder of a bill of exchange for Rs. 5000. He indorses it to B for Rs. 2000 only. Indorsement in B's favor is invalid.

Exception – As provided in section 56 itself, when the amount in the instrument has been paid in part and it is negotiated for the remaining amount, the indorsement is valid. The partial indorsement must clarify the earlier payment while negotiating for balance. The instrument may be further negotiated as if it is made for the residue.

Example – A bill is originally drawn for 10000 rupees. The acceptor pays 5000 rupees to A, the holder of the instrument. A negotiates it to B for the balance of 5000 rupees. This indorsement is valid.

7. Facultative Indorsement

When the indorser abandons any right or increases his liability under the negotiable instrument, the indorsement is termed as "facultative indorsement". In contrast to sans recourse indorsement, this indorsement assumes liability by giving up a right.

Example – "Pay A or order, notice of dishonour waived." Liability of a party to pay on negotiable instrument depends upon receiving notice of dishonour. By this indorsement the indorser undertakes to pay even without notice.

8. Forged Indorsement

When indorsement is effected by forgery of indorser's signature, it is a forged indorsement. It is an established rule that forgery conveys no title. Forgery is a nullity. No one acquires the rights of holder in due course under a forged indorsement, though he takes it bonafide and for value.

Example – A bill is payable to A or order. B steals it from A and forges A' indorsement and gives it to C who takes it in good faith and for consideration. C acquires no title to the bill.

Negotiation Back

In the process of negotiation if the last indorsee indorses it to the original holder or any previous indorser it is known as "negotiation back". The indorsee in addition to his right as former holder also acquires the rights of a holder by virtue of the last indosement. However he cannot hold intermediate indorsers liable to pay because the law does not allow circuitry of actions. The prior party is remitted to the original position and comes within the definition of the holder. This position is an exception to the rule that holder in due course can sue all prior parties. One cannot sue a person to whom he himself is liable. One cannot be a plaintiff and defendant at the same time.

When such an indorser indorses the negotiable instrument by striking off the indorsements of the previous intermediate indorsers, his action is termed as **"taking up of a bill"**. Whose names are struck off are discharged from liability to pay on though bill.

Example – A, the holder of bill indorses it to B; B indorses it to C, C to D and D to A. A is liable to B, C, D by first indorsement and B, C, D are liable to A by second indorsement. A therefore cannot sue B, C and D (negotiation back). A may again negotiate the bill by striking of the indorsements of B, C and D (Taking up of a bill).

Chapter 31 | LIABILITIES OF PARTIES TO NEGOTIABLE INSTRUMENTS (Sections 30 to 32 and 35 to 40)

Negotiable instrument is meant for payment. The parties to it are liable in different capacities. Nature of their liability is explained below-

1. **Liability of Drawer - S.39 -**

   Drawer of a bill of exchange or cheque is liable to compensate the holder if it is dishonoured by non-acceptance (by drawee) or dishonoured by non-payment (by acceptor). Liability depends upon notice of dishonour. If notice is not received, he is discharged. Untill accepted , his liability is primary and after acceptance his liability becomes secondary. Acceptor in that case becomes primarily liable. The liability of the drawer of a cheque however is primary.

2. **Liability of a Banker - S.31 -**

   As a drawee of a cheque , the banker having sufficient funds of drawer , must pay the cheque when duly required to pay. Wrongful dishonour entails his liability to compensate drawer for any loss sustained by him due to its default. It should be noted that banker in no case is liable to holder as there is a privity of contracts with drawer and not holder.

3. **Liability of a Maker or Acceptor - S.32 -**

   The maker of a note and acceptor of bill before maturity are under a duty to pay the amount at maturity. Maker becomes liable on signing the note while acceptor becomes liable on accepting the bill. They should pay according to apparent tenor of instrument. Acceptor must pay the amount at or after maturity to the holder on demand. In case of default , the maker or acceptor must compensate any party for the loss caused to him by default. It is clear that, liability of maker and that of the acceptor is the same. Sec. 32 is subject to the contract to the contrary between the parties.

4. **Liability of Indorser - S.35 -**

   Indorser before maturity is liable to compensate every subsequent holder for the damage / loss sustained by him due to dishonour of the instrument by non-acceptance or by non-payment. The liability is conditional upon receiving notice of dishonour. Indorser may absolve himself from liability by 'Sans recourse' indorsement.

5. Liability untill satisfaction - S.36 -

Every prior party to negotiable instrument is liable to holder in due course untill the instrument is satisfied.

Nature of liability of parties

The negotiable instruments embody and reflect contracts between parties. Contract of surety governs the liability on the negotiable instrument. Holder in due course is entitiled to get the amount on negotiable instrument while all other parties are liable to pay either as principal debtors or sureties.

S.37 -Principal Debtors — Maker of a note , drawer before acceptance of a bill and acceptor are liable as principal debtors. 'Other parties' are liable as sureties for prinicipal debtors (Sec. 37 applies subject to contract to the contrary whereby the liability may be reversed between parties).

S.38 -As between the two sureties, each prior party is liable as principal debtor and subsequent party as his surety. Thus 'other parties' are not 'co-sureties.' Sec. 38 is also subject to contract to the contrary.

Illustration - A is the drawer and B is acceptor of a bill (payble to order). A indorses it to C, C to D, D to E and E to F. Here F is the holder and all other (A to E) are liable to him. B is principal debtor and others (A, C, D, E) are sureties. Among A, C, D, and E, A is principal debtor and C, D, E are his sureties. Between D and F, D is principal debtor while E is surety.

S.39 -Any contract between principal debtors and creditor without surety's consent dischages surety (S. 134 , Indian Contract Act). Similarly any composition with principal debtors or creditor's promise to give more time to principal debtors discharges the surety (S. 135 of that Act). Sec. 39 of the Negotiable Instruments Act enables holder of a bill to enter into such contracts with the acceptor without relinquishing his rights against other parties. He has however to expressly reserve such rights against sureties.

Example - X, holder of a bill gives Y, its acceptor of more time for payment. Ordinarily, the drawer and indorsers are discharged. But X may reserve rights against any of the other parties and make him liable.

S.40 -Provides that where the holder of a negotiable instrument , without indorser's consent, destroys or impairs the indorser's remedy against a prior party, the indorser is discharged from liability to holder to the same extent as if the instrument had been paid at maturity.

Chapter 32 | DISHONOUR OF A NEGOTIABLE INSTRUMENT

A negotiable instrument is said to be dishonoured when it is either not accepted by drawee or remains unpaid on maturity. Refusal to accept or to pay by the concerned party is known as dishonour. Dishonour may be *"dishonour by non-acceptance"* or *"dishonour by non-payment'"*. A bill of exchange requires first acceptance and then it is paid. A bill therefore, can be dishonoured by dishonour by non-acceptance and dishonour by non-payment. A promissory note or a cheque does not require acceptance and hence these are dishonoured by non-payment only.

32.1 Dishonour by Non-Acceptance (Sec. 91)

A bill is said to dishonoured by non acceptance when the drawee or one of several drawees (not being partners) –
- Makes a default in acceptance upon being duly required to accept or
- Where presentment for acceptance is excused and the bill is not accepted.

A bill is said to be dishonoured by non-acceptance in any of the following circumstances.

1) The drawee refuses to accept it when properly presented for acceptance.
2) The presentement for acceptance is excused and the bill not accepted.
3) One of the several drawees (not being partners) makes a default in acceptance. This means generally all joint drawees should accept the bill.
4) The drawee fails to accept it within "drawee's time for deliberation."(i.e. 48 hours from the time of presentment for acceptance)
5) The drawee cannot be found after a reasonable search.
6) The drawee is incompetent to contract.
7) Drawee gives a qualified acceptance.

When drawee in case of need is also mentioned in a bill, the holder has to present it to him for acceptance if original drawee dishonours it. The bill is not regarded as dishonoured until the drawee in case of need also dishonours it. Thus both drawees should accept it.

Effect of dishonour- When a bill is dishonoured by non-acceptance the holder gets immediate right of an action against the drawer and the indorser. He need not wait till the date of maturity.

32.2 Dishonour by Non-Payment -

Two situations of dishonour by non payment are provided under the Act.

1. Sec. 76--An instrument is dishonoured by non-payment when presentment for payment is excused and instrument remains unpaid when falls overdue.

2. Sec. 92--A promissory note, bill of exchange or a cheque is said to be dishonoured by non payment when the maker of the note, acceptor of the bill or drawee of a cheque makes default in payment upon being duly required to pay the same.

32.3 Notice of Dishonour

Importance and object of notice of dishonour. As state previously, when instrument is dishonoured, the holder is entitled to sue the parties liable to pay thereon. The drawer of a cheque, maker of a note, acceptor and drawee of a bill and all indorsers are liable jointly and severally to the holder in due course. This liability is conditional upon receiving notice of dishonour. Notice of dishonour thus is a condition precedent for fixing the parties. The party receiving notice is also put on guard and is prepared to pay. It also enables him to protect himself against his prior parties.

Contents, form and mode of notice - Notice is formal communication of the fact of dishonour. No specific words or language or form is provided but it must convey about the fact of dishonour, its mode and that party would be required to pay the instrument. It may be oral or written. Notice may be sent in any reasonable manner. It should be served at the place of business if one has or at the residence of the party liable. Notice should be given within reasonable time after dishonour. Reasonableness of time depends upon the type and nature of instrument, usual course of dealing between the parties.

Notice to whom? Notice of dishonour should be given to all parties to whom the holder wants to make liable. Where there are more than one drawers or indorsers, jointly liable, notice to one of them is sufficient. If a party liable dies, notice should be served to his legal heirs/representatives. In case of insolvency of party, it must be given to the official assignee.

It should be noted that no notice is necessary in case of a maker of a note or an acceptor of a bill or drawee of a cheque (banker) as those are primarily liable to pay. Their liability is absolute as principal debtors (S. 93).

Notice by whom? According to section 93, notice should be given by holder or by a party liable on negotiable instrument. A party receiving the notice must give notice to all his prior parties to hold them liable to himself. If a party is in receipt of a notice from holder, intermediate subsequent parties need not give him notice as they can take advantage of holder's intimation. Knowledge of dishonour is important rather than its source. Notice by the authorized agent is valid.

When notice is not necessary? Sec. 98 provides that in the following circumstances the parties are liable without notice.

1) The party entitled to notice dispenses with it. i.e. he undertakes to pay without notice (facultative indorsement)

2) Party charged could not suffer any damage for want of notice. When a cheque is dishonoured due to insufficiency of funds or stop-payment instructions, notice to drawer is obviously not required.

3) Drawer is also the acceptor or he is one of the drawees/acceptors.

4) The party entitled to notice cannot be found after due search.

5) The party is unable to give notice due the situations beyond his control, for example, accident, illness or death.

6) When the promissory note is made "non-negotiable." Such a note cannot be negotiated by indorsements. In spite of this, if indorsed, holder cannot enforce liability against the maker or indorser as it is originally non negotiable. Want of notice would not put anybody to inconvenience/loss.

7) After the fact of dishonour, the party entitled to notice undertakes to pay unconditionally the amount under the instrument.

Legal consequences when notice is not given--As mentioned in the introductory Para, if notice is not given to the party entitled to it, he is discharged from duty to pay. No action can be taken against him for the recovery of the sum. Negotiable instrument is nothing but contract between the various parties and the parties are discharged if the terms (as to notice etc..) are not complied.

32.4 Dishonour of cheques for Insufficency of Funds in Accounts (Ss. 138-142)

Introduction - When a drawer issues a cheque without keeping sufficient funds in his account, the cheque would be dishonoured by the bank. This dishonour gives rise to a criminal liability u/s 138.

Issuing cheques without intention to pay amounts to cheating. Cheating is an offence u/s 420 of IPC. Many persons were acquitted on charges of cheating for want of proof inspite of issusing bogus cheques. Moreover every bouncing of cheques may not involve cheating. To fasten drawer with criminal liability for issusing worthless cheques, Chapter XVII has been introduced in the Negotiable Instruments Act by Amendment in 1988. This chapter applies principle of strict liability in the sense that once the cheques issued is dishonoured by the bank due to lack of sufficient funds in the account, offence is complete. *No intention or mens rea is needed to prove the offence as in the case of cheating.* The chapter aims to ensure the efficacy of cheques as mode of payment and curb the practice of issuing cheques without making proper arrangements.

Sec. 138 defines the offence, sets out **procedural requirements** and provides for punishment. Ingredients to constitute offence u/s 138 are explained below.

i) **Drawing of a Cheque -** The drawer should have drawn a cheque on his account with the banker for the payment of money.

ii) **Object of issuing -** Such a cheque must have been issued in discharge of a debt or other liability. The cheque must have been issued for the full or partial discharge of such debt or liability.

Debt is a liquidated amount of money owed and payable to another. Liability is a state of being liable. Debt or liability must be legally enforceable. Cheque issued by way of gift or for illegal purposes would not attract sec. 138. There is a presumption that cheque is drawn for legally enforceable debt/liability. The presumption can be rebutted. Drawer may issue a cheque to discharge some others debt or liability non necessarily his own.

iii) **Presentment of cheque within time** - Cheque should have been presented to the bank within a period of six months from the date of drawing or within the period of its validity (whichever is earlier) -

According to prevailing banking practice, a cheque should be presented for payment within six months from the date of drawing. Afterwards it is regarded as 'stale cheque'. Stale cheques can be justifiably dishonoured by the bank, a situation to which sec. 138 does not apply.

iv) **Dishonour of Cheque and Reasons thereof -**

The cheque should be returned by the banker due to one of the following reasons –

a) Amount of money standing to the credit of that account is insufficient to honour the cheque or

b) Cheque exceeds the amount arranged to be paid from that account by an arrangement with that bank.

Sec. 138 is applicable to the dishonour by above reason only and not due to other various reasons availiable to banker. In the first case (a) banker dishonours it with remarks *'refer to drawer'* while (b) covers overdraft or cash credit arrangement.

Closing of account after issuing a cheque amounts to an offence.[99] 'Stop payment' instructions is, deemed to be an offence u/s 138, if it is not justified.[100] Direction for not presenting the cheque will have the same result.[101]

v) **Demand for Payment -**

The payee or holder of the cheque should make a demand for payment of the amount of cheque by way of a written demand notice to the drawer. This notice should be served within 30 days from the receipt of intimation by him from the bank regarding dishonour. There is no specific form or language for the notice. Oral communication however will not suffice. Notice may be sent through power of attorney, an advocate. The purpose of notice is to offer an opportunity to the drawer to pay and protect an honest drawer. It can be sent by post, fax or through personal service.

vi) **Failure to pay within period of notice -**

The offence under Sec. 138 is complete, when the drawer fails to make payment of the amount to the payee or holder in due course within 15 days of the receipt of notice.

The notice of demand may stipulate any period i.e. less or more than 15 days for payment. Such a notice is valid. But the cause of action for criminal complaint aries only after 15 days.

---

99. *NEPC Micon Ltd V/s Magona Leasing Ltd (1999) 4 AD 453 SC.*
100. *ET & TD Corp. Ltd V/s Indian Technologies Business Pvt Ltd AIR 1996 SC 2339.*
101. *Modi Cement Ltd V/s Kuchil Kumar Nandi (1998) 2 CLJ 8*

vii) Punishment -

The drawer committing the offence u/s 138 shall be punished with imprisonment upto 2 years or a fine extending upto twice the amount of the cheque or both.

Offence by Companies - Sec. 141

Offenes u/s 138 may also be committed by the companies i.e. not only by natural persons but by body corporates. Firms, association can be criminally liable for issue cheques without keeping adequate bank balances.

If the offence is committed by a company, the person incharge of the company who is responsible for company affairs would be liable along with body corperate. He can take the defence of absence of knowledge or exercise of due care to prevent the commisssion of offence. The director, manager, secretary or other officer of the company is also liable if the offence is committed by their consent, connivance or occurs due to their negligence. In all such cases person in charge or director etc. can be prosecuted and punished u/s 138.

32.5 Payment for Honour (Sec. 113)

"When a bill of exchange has been noted or protested by non-payment, any person may pay the same for the honour of any party liable to pay the same; provided that the person so paying [or his agent in that behalf] has previously declared before a notary public the party for whose honour he pays, and that such declaration has been recorded by such notary public." (Refer Sec. 101 (f) in the Chater of Nothing & Protest)

A bill may be duly accepted but dishonoured by non-payment . When such a bill is protested for non-payment, any person may intervene and pay supraprotest for the honour of any party liable to pay on the bill.

Conditions for Payment for Honour.

1) The bill of exchange should have been noted and protested for non-payment;
2) The person paying (or his agent) must declare before a notary public, the name of the party for whose honour he pays;
3) Such a declaration should by the notary public.
4) Payment for honour must be effected for the honour of any party liable to pay the bill.
5) Any person, whether already a party to bill or not, may pay for honour;
6) Payment made in contravention of S.113 is not a valid payment supra protest. It is only a voluntary payment without any protection to the payer.

Position of the payer for honour - Sec. 114

The person paying for honour is treated as an indorsee of an overdue bill. He is subject to all equities, (defects in title of the bill) on the date of its maturity. All parties subsequent to party for whose honour it is paid are discharged. According to Sec. 114 payer for honour is entitled to all rights of the holder of the bill at the time of such payment. He has a right to recover from the party for whose honour he pays all sums so paid. He can also recover interest on that amount together with expenses incurred in making such payment. When bill is paid supra protest, it ceases to be negotiable.

Chapter 33 | NOTING AND PROTEST

Dishonour of a promissory note or bill of exchange gives a right of action to the holder to sue the maker or drawer for payment. He has to give a notice of dishonour and file a suit. In the court he has to prove the dishonour and the parties' liability on negotiable instrument. Noting and protest serve to lessen the burden of proof of dishonour.

Noting and protest afford an authentic evidence of dishonour. In a suit upon the dishonoured negotiable instrument, the courts shall presume the fact of dishonour relying on noting and protest. These two, therefore, have evidentiary value. Noting and protest is not mandatory. Failure to note or protest would not deprive the holder any rights but it is advantageous to adopt this method of securing evidence of dishonour. There cannot be noting and protest of a cheque when dishonoured by the banker. The banker, when refuses the payment, returns the cheque with reasons of dishonour on a printed slip. This provides evidence of dishonour.

Noting (Sec. 99) -

Noting means recording the fact of dishonour on the negotiable instrument. When a promissory note or a bill of exchange is dishonoured by non-acceptance or dishonour by non-payment, the holder has to take the bill or note to the notary public who makes a formal demand for acceptance or payment upon the drawee or acceptor or the maker. On refusal by these parties or if otherwise it is dishonoured, the notary public records the same. Noting is to be done on the instrument or upon a paper annexed to it or partly upon each. It should be done within reasonable time after dishonour. The notary should specify following particulars while noting.

Contents of Noting –

The fact of dishonour, type of dishonour, reasons of dishonour, if it is not expressly dishonoured, the reasons, why the holder treats it as dishonured and notary's charges, signature and seal of the Notary.

Protest -

Protest is a formal certificate of dishonour issued by the notary public. This certificate in a way attests the dishonour and is based upon noting. After the dishonour, the holder may cause the dishonour to be noted and certified by the notary public. Such certificate is called as "Protest". (Sec.100)

Contents of protest (Sec. 101)

The protest must contain following particulars.

a) The instrument itself or its literal transcript (copy) with everything written or printed (indrosement etc.) on it.

b) The name of the person for whom and against whom the instrument is protested.

c) The fact of dishonour and the reasons of dishonour, mode of dishonour, why it is treated as dishonoured.

d) The time and place of dishonour.

e) Signature of notary public.

f) In case of acceptance for honour or payment for honour, the names of the persons by whom, for whom and the manner in which such acceptance or payment was offered and effected.

Noting and protest of inland bills or notes is not compulsory. Sec. 104 provides that foreign bills must be protested for dishonour if required by the law of the place where they are drawn.

Protest for Better Security (Sec. 100, Para 2)

This type of protest can be made in bills only. When the acceptor of a bill has become insolvent, or his credit in the market is publicly impeached, the holder may cause the notary public to demand better security from the acceptor. For this protest, the holder should approach the notary within reasonable time after insolvency. On being refused to provide better security, holder may, within reasonable time, cause such a fact to noted and certified. Such a certificate issued by the notary public is called as "protest for better security."

Holder, however, has no immediate right of action against the acceptor, drawer or indorsers. He has to wait till the date of maturity of the bill. The main advantage of this protest is that it enables the bill to be accepted for honour after such protest has been drawn (Sec. 108)

PART - IV

Questions and hints for answers

1. Define the term 'Negotiable Instrument'. State the features of three types of Negotiable Instruments ○ TYBCom 2013, 2012, 2005 P.U. BBA, 2009 ✓Ans. 27.1 & 27.2

2. Define Cheque and Bill of Exchange. Distinguish between Cheque and Bill of Exchange. ○ TYBCom 2004 P. U., MBA 2004 P. U. ✓Ans. 27.1 & 27.2

3. Define and explain the terms 'Holder' & 'Holder In Due Course'. Enumerate privileges of holder in due course. TYBCom 2012, 2010, 2008, MBA 2004 P. U. ✓Ans. Chapter 29.

4. Define 'Negotiable Instruments' What are its characteristics? ○ MBA 2003, 2013 Ans. 27.1 & 27.2

5. Define 'Promissory note'. Explain its essential features. ○ MBA 2003 ✓Ans. 28.1

6. Define and explain 'Bill of Exchange'. How it differs from two other negotiable instruments. ○ MBA 2003, 2013 ✓Ans. 28.2

7. Define and explain the concept of 'Endorsement' on negotiable instrument. Explain with illustrations different kinds of endorsements. PGDBM2004 P. U. ✓Ans. 30.3

8. Define the terms 'Holder & Holder in due course'. How they differ? ○ BBA 2008, MBA 2003- 29.1, 29.2

9. What is 'Negotiation'? What are different modes of negotiations? Explain. ○ MBA 2003 P. U. ✓Ans. 30.1, 30.2, 30.3

10. What is an endorsement? Discuss different kinds of endorsement. TYBCom 2011, 2009 ○ PGDBM 2005 ✓Ans. 30.3

11. Explain the law relating to dishonour of negotiable instruments contained in the Negotiable Instruments Act 1881. ✓Ans. Chapter 32.

12. State and Explain the provisions relating to 'Dishonour of Negotiable Instruments' embodied in the Negotiable Instruments Act, 1881. TYBCom 2011 ○ MBA 2005 P. U. ✓Ans. Chapter 32.

13. Discuss the Nature of liabilities of various parties to negotiable instrument.

14. What is meant by 'Noting & Protest'? State their significance. Explain in brief the rules relating to 'Noting & Protest' ○ TY B Com. 2004, PGDBM 2004 ✓Ans. Chapter 32.

LAW OF PARTNERSHIP
INDIAN PARTNERSHIP ACT, 1932

Introduction

Many trading concerns around us are infact partnership firms. An individual finds it difficult and risky to carry on business as a proprietor. Company requires registration and has to work within legal framework. Business by firm is convenient that way.

Law of partnership is embodied in the Indian Partnership Act, 1932. This enactment came into force on October, 1932. Prior to that partnership was governed by old Indian Contract Act, 1872. Partnership is a special type of contract and the provisions of the Contract Act being the general law on contract still apply, unless inconsistent with the Act of 1932.

This Act defines partnership and kinds. Its provisions regulate the relationship of partners interse and with outsiders, by setting out rights, duties of par and authority of partners. The Act lays down the law governing changes in the constitution of the firm and various circumstances in which it gets dissolved.

Chapter 34 | PARTNERSHIP - DEFINITION AND NATURE

34.1 Definition

Sec. 4 of the Act defines 'Partnership' as follows .

> *"Partnership is the relation between persons who have agreed to share the profits of a business carried on by all or any one of them acting for all."*

Scruitiny of the definition reveals following salient features of partnership.

34.2 Salient Features of Partnership

1. **Agreement of Partnership**

   Partnership is a 'relationship' between persons. This relationship flows from an agreement (contract) between persons called as partners. Sec. 5 clarifies that relationship arises from contract and not from status or by operation of law or inheritance. Partnership. thus presuppoces existence of a contract. This contract may be express or implied. As a contract, it must satisfy all the conditions fo enforceability.

2. **Agreement of between two or more persons**

   Partnership is an association of persons called partners. Obviously there must be at least two partners in a firm. Act does not prescribe maximum number of partners in partnership.

   According to Sec. 11 of the Companies Act, 1956 partnership having more than ten persons carrying banking business and more than twenty persons in non-banking business must register as a body corporate, otherwise that association would be illegal. Thus the maximum number of partners in banking or non-banking business would be below the statutory limit of 10 or 20 respectively.

   Partners as parties to the contract must be competent. A partner may be natural or artificial person like company. Partnership is not a legal person and hence it cannot enter into partnership with others. (Whether individual or a firm). Two firms cannot have an agreement of partnership.

3. Agreement to carry on business

There must be an agreement to conduct a business. 'Business' implies any trade, occupation, calling or profession [Def- u/s 2 (b) of the Act] Business activity may be production or manufacturing goods, providing services dealing in goods etc. A charitable trust or a club or society do not carry on a business, hence not treated as a firm. 'Carried on ...' suggests business being conducted continuously for some period.

There can be partnership relationship between persons for developing a single plot and constructing a building, for working out a coal mine, production of a film, cultivating a crop in a single season. Though these involve single adventure, there exists a continuity of relationship.

4. Sharing of profits of a business

Business is carried on with the object of profit. Though it is not the only test to determine existence of partnership, the agreement must aim at sharing of profit. Agreement may not refer sharing of losses as it is not the test of partnership. If business is conducted with philanthropic motive and profit element does not exist, the relationship is not partnership. Where only one of the partners is to enjoy the whole of the profit and not others, partnership is not valid.

5. Mutual Agency

Besides the above essential features, business in partnership must be 'carried on by all or by one (or more) acting for all'. Agency is thus implicit in partnership. Every partner assumes a dual role - that of a principal and an agent at same time, in relation to other partners. This position enables every partner to carry on the business on behalf of others. Among others the mutual agency is one of the determining factors for partnership relationship. Law of partnership, as rightly stated, is an extension of the law of agency. (Refer Cox v/s Hickman, explained u/s 5 & 6 of the Act)

34.3 Test of Partnership

Analysis of definition of partnership u/s 4 reveals that all the essential elements of partnership must co-exist so as to creat the relationship of partnership. If one of the factors is absent, relationship cannot be called as partnership . There is no single test for existence of partnership.

Sec. 6 of the Act provides the test when its states —

"In determining whether a group of persons is or is not a firm or whether a person is or is not a partner in a firm, regard shall be had to the real relation between parties, as shown by all relevant facts taken together."

Every type of legal relationship rests on intention between parties. Intention is a crucial factor which determines whether a person is a partner or not or whether a group of persons is a firm or not. In determining the intention and ultimate relationship, all the facts, circumstances of the case must be examined. Their collective effect should lead to the conclusion as to its existence. The Courts must weigh all the relevant facts distinctly and collectively and then draw conclusion as to real relation. Sec. 6, Explanation II, in particular emphasizes that no single factor can be the sole criterion for existence of partnership.

Explanation II to Sec. 6 states that receipt of share in profits or receiving payments in a business by following persons, will not of itself, make them partners with others who carry on a business.

a) Lender of money sharing profits of business of his debtor.
b) Servant or agent receiving a remuneration, from employer or Principal.
c) Widow or child of a deceased partner receiving annuity out of profits of a firm.
d) Seller receiving share of profits in business carried out by the purchaser of goodwill.

Thus merely sharing of profits / receiving payments in some business without mutual agency and other essential factors of partnership, cannot be given undue evidenciary value in determining the existence of partnership. Profit sharing by itself does not creat partnership. Participation in profits is one of the evidence of partnership but not the conclusive proof of its existence. It has even not a presumptive value. One has to consider all the facts taken together reflecting the real relation among them.

Sec. 6 embodies a comprehensive statement of rule laid down by House of Lords in **Cox v/s Hickman.**[102]

S and S were partners in iron industries. On account of problems they entered into a compromise with creditors. In persuance of the deed of compromise, their property of the firm was assigned to a group of creditors called as trustees. Trustees were empowered to carry on the business and divide the profits / income among the creditors in rateable proportion. After the debts were satisfied, the business was to be returned to S and S. Cox was one of the trustees. The trust purchased certain quantity of coke from one Hickman. Towards payment, he was given a bill which remained unpaid by the trust. Hickman sued the trustees including Cox for payment. He pleaded that all trustees (creditors) are partners carrying on business for profit and everybody is liable for payment.

It was *held* that trustees were not partners and hence Cox is not personally liable for the payment of coke. The court ruled that the deed of compromise was not that of partnership. It was an arrangement by S and S to pay debts of creditors. Court opined that sharing of profits affords a cogent often conclusive evidence of partnership but in absence of 'mutual agency', conclusion as to existence of partnership relationship cannot be drawn. The suit was dismissed.

Mollow March & Co. v/s Court of Wards.[103]

Two British Merchants were running a business as W & Co. They wanted some loan from a Hindu Raja. They entered into an agreement under which in consideration of advances, Raja was to have control in their business and to receive a commission of 20 % on all profits made by them until the whole debt of Raja was paid. The court observed that Raja was not a partner in the firm by merely sharing profits in business in the absence of other relevant factors (particularly agency).

102. (1860)8 HLC 268
103. Mollow March & Co. V/S Court of Wards (1872)7 ER 495 PC

34.4 "Partnership is created by contract and not by status"

Section 5 states,

"The relationship of partnership arises from contract and not from status; and in particular the members of a Hindu undivided family carrying on a family business as such, or a Burmese Budhist husband and wife carrying on business as such are not partners in such business."

This section incorporates a general principle stating that the relationship of partnership emerges from agreement and not from status. This principle is emphasized by clarifying that Hindu Undivided Family (HUF) or Budhist husband and wife carrying on family business are not partners. Partnership is created by express or implied contract between partners. It is not created virtue of by status, or by operation of law. The status of partners is not obtained by birth.

Members of HUF are not partners ... Sec. 5 excludes members of HUF and Buddhist husband and wife carrying on family business from the perview of this Act. In Hindu Law business is a distinct heritable asset and inherited like property. It is jointly owned by members of the family. These members though enjoy the fruits of family business, are not partners but they are coparcerners. Their relationship arises from status (by birth) and not by any agreement. It is governed by Hindu law and not by the Partnership Act.

'Family business' is not defined under the Act. It means 'ancestral business' or business carried on by HUF with joint family property or funds / assets. Karta of a HUF may enter into partnership with others (outside family). In this firm Karta would only be a partner and members of his family would not ipso-facto become partners. Members of the HUF in their individual capacity and with their personal property are free to have partnership with others.

Distinction between Partnership, Hindu Joint Family Firm, Company and Co-ownership

Sr. No.	Basis of Distinction	Partnership	Hindu Joint Family Business	Company	Co-ownership
1.	Mode of Creation	By agreement	By operation of law	By operation of law (or by incorporation)	By agreement or law
2.	Legal Status	Not a legal person - firm means all partners taken together	Niether a firm nor a company	Legal, artificial person	Not a legal person
3.	Legal Status of Member	Not different from firm	Members with joint interest	Share holders different from Company	Ownership held jointly
3.	Minimum No.	2	No such limit	Private Company - 2; Public Company-7	-2
	Maximum No.	10 - in banking 20 - in non - banking	—	Private Company - 50; Public Company-unlimited	No limit
4.	Mutual agency	Exists - Partner is an agent of firm.	Does not exist Coparcener not an agent of joint family business.	Does not exist Share holders not agents of Company; Directors are agents of Company	Does not exist
5.	Liability of Member (constituents)	- Unlimited / Personal property is liable for firm's debts. - Joint and several	Karta is personally liable, not coparceners Coparcener liable to the extent of his share in HUF	Limited to share-holding	Jointly liable to the extent of share
6	Transfer of interest	Not possible without others' consent	Share in HUF can be transferred by a Coparcener	Shares freely transferable subject to Articles of Association	Transferable without others' consent

Sr. No.	Basis of Distinction	Partnership	Hindu Joint Family Business	Company	Co-ownership
7	Duration of existence	Untill dissolved continues	Family business continues till partition	Perpetual succession	Co-owners to decide
8	Registration	Optional-Advisable	Not registrable	Compulsory (by incorporation)	Not registrable
9	Minor Members	Cannot be a partner but admitted to Partnership Profits	Becomes Member/Coparcener by birth	Can be a share holder subject to Articles	Can be a Co-owner
10	Effect of Death or Insolvency of a member	Dissolution (Subject to contract)	No effect - continues	No effect Perpetual succession	Continues with legal heirs of deceased coowner.
11	Business Motive	Exists	Exists	Exists Company may be incorporated for non-commercial purposes.	Does not exist.
12	Nature of interest of constituents	Collective	Collective	Individual	Individual and collective interest
13	Role of Members in business	Right to take part in business	Karta manages business & not others	Share-holders do not manage	Business & agency does not exist.

Chapter 35

REGISTRATION OF FIRMS
(Sec. 58, 59 and 69)

The registration of the firms is not compulsory under the Act. It is optional. Section 58 lays down a simple procedure for registration of firm.

35.1 Procedure for Registration

i) Application
Application for registration in the prescribed format should be made to the Registrar of firms of the area in which the place of business of the firm is situated or proposed to be situated. The application should be accompained by proper fees. It can be sent by post or personally delivered.

ii) Contents
Following information should be furnished along with application.
- Name of the firm;
- Principal place of business of the firm;
- Other places where the firm carries on business;
- Names, addresses of the partners and their date of joining the firm;
- Duration of the firm.

iii) Signature and verification
The application must be signed and verified by each parter or their duly authorised agent.

iv) Registration (S.59)
The Registrar, on being satisfied that the provisions as to registration are complied with, shall make entries with respect to that firm in the register of firms.

v) Certificate of Registration
The Registrar then issues a Certificate of Registration to the firm. The certificate is the evidence of registration.

vi) Time of registration
There is no provision in the Act as to the period within which the firm is to be registered.

Firm can be registered at any time after it starts doing business. Even before filling a suit in court, it can be registered.

35.2 Consequences of non-registration - S.69

Though registration of firm is not mandatory, it is advisable to register it in view of some *disabilities associated with non-registration* u/s 69 of the Act. Section 69 thus ensures registration of the firms.*Firm cannot enforce its rights by filing suits due to non-registration or certain liabilities cannot be avoided by* pleading the non-exsitence of the firm. These disabilities are given below -

Sec. 59 A- 1

Accordings to Sec. 58 (1 A), the statement giving the particulars of firm (required to be filed alongwith application for registration), should be filed within one year from the date of constitution of the firm. For late registration of firm, S. 59 A-1 provides a penalty of Rs. 100 per year of delay or any part of, the year.

Sec. 69 - Bar to file certain suits.

Following suits cannot be filed in any court by alleged partner in a firm unless his name is shown in the register of firm as a partner and unless the firm is registered.

a) Suits against firm or any partner to enforce- right arising from a contract or under the Act-

   Exception : Above requiement of registration is not necessary in case of suits instituted by the heirs or legal representatives of the deceased partner of a firm for the accounts of a dissolved firm or to realise the property of a dissolved firm.

b) Suit for dissolution of firm or a suit to enforce any right or power to realise the property of a dissolued firm;

   Exception : as in (a) above.

c) Suit against third party by a firm cannot be instituted for the enforcement of a right under contract unless firm is registered or the partner suing is shown as partner in the register of firms. Above provisions also apply to a claim of set-off or other proceedings to enforce a right arising from a contract.

   It would be thus gathered from S.69 that a partner cannot enforce remedies against other partners or firm or firm as such finds it difficult to seek remedy against third parties if it is not registered. The rights of a partner or a firm may be genuine, their claims may be rightful but non-registration may defeat such claims.

Other exceptions - for disabilities on account of non-registration.

The provisions as to bar of suits without registration also do not apply in following cases –

a) Firm is constituted for a duration upto 6 months only or its capital is not more than 2000 rupees or

b) Suit for realisation of property of an insolvent by official assignee/receiver of the court or

c) Where firm has no place of business in the area in which the Act applies or it has place of business in the area to which this chapter does not apply, or

d) Claim of set-off or the suit is not exceeding rupees 100 in value.

Chapter 36 | KINDS OF PARTNERSHIPS

Partnership may be either for a fixed period or at will. It may be particular or general type of Partnership.

i) Partnership at will :

This kind of Partnership exists when there is no provision in the partnership agreement for

a) Duration of partnership **or**

b) Determination (end) of their Partnerships.

If these two conditions are complied, the Partnership would be at – will. If the duration is fixed, or the mode of termination is stated, it is not at will Partnership. If duration is fixed, after the efflux of time, it automatically dissolves. Thus in this type of partnership mode of determination is provided. In simple words, the life of partnership depends upon the will of the partners. At any moment of time, they are free to dissolve it.

ii) Partnership for a fixed period

As the title indicates, where a Partnership is for a definite period, it falls in this category. After the expiry of the period, it is dissolved ipso – facto. Partner may decide to continue after that period. In that case if period is fixed again, it is not at will. If without stipulation as to period it continues, it is converted into Partnership at-will.

iii) Particular Partnership

Partnership for a particular adventure or undertaking is known as 'Particular Partnership'. It is dissolved after completion of adventure. It continued after that adventure, it becomes at – will partnership. For example, a partnership for production of a film, publication of a book, construction of one complex etc.

iv) General Partnership

Where partnership carries on a business in general and it is neither particular nor for a fixed terms, it is called as general Partnership.

Chapter 37 | RELATIONS OF PARTNERS TO ONE ANOTHER (Sec. 9 TO 17)

Law of partnership has two aspects. First it deals with relationship of partners with each other and second, relationship of the firm as such with third parties. Rights, duties and liabilities of partners fall within the relationship of partners inter-se.

Sec. 11 of the Act states that mutual rights and duties of the partners may be determined by their agreement. Partners are thus free to regulate their relationship, subject however to few specific provisions under the Act. In absence of a specific term regarding a right or duty, Sec. 9 to 17 may be referred.

37.1 Rights of a Partner

1) **Right to take part in the conduct of business - Sec. 12 - (a) -**
   Every partner has a right to take part in the conduct of business of the firm. Business of the firm belongs to all and hence everybody has a right in the management of its affairs. In absence of special agreement, a partner cannot be excluded from business activity. Remedy in case of unlawful restriction or deprivation of this right is injuction, rendition of accounts or dissolution of the firm.

2) **Right to be consulted - Sec. 12 (c)**
   Majority rights of partners - A partner has a right to express opinion, right to be consulted and heard in a matter of difference/dispute.
   Ordinarily disputes over day - to - day affairs of the firm are settled by majority of the partners. How majority should settle the disputes ?
   i) All should act in good-faith;
   ii) Matter should relate to ordinary business of the firm;
   iii) Every partner should be heard and consulted (The very right u/s 12 - c)

   Matters which majority cannot decide
   (Unanimous decision is necessary to decide following issues)
   i) Change in the nature of business ;
   ii) Place of business ;
   iii) Sale of the whole business
   iv) Enlargement of the business.

3) Right to access to the accounts - 12 (d)

Every partner has a right to have access to and to inspect books of accounts. He can also copy any of the books of accounts. This is a personal right and can be exercised through agent. It cannot be exercised for hostile purposes or purposes injurious to the partnership. Partner cannot abuse this right. Right should be enjoyed bonafide.

4) Right to remuneration - Sec. 13-a

Generally a partner cannot claim remuneration as he shares profits. But if agreement provides, he is entitled for remuneration.

5) Right to share profits - Sec. 13 (b) -

The section provides that every partner has right to share. The profits equally and contribute equally to the losses. Ordinarily the partners determine the proportion in which profits and losses are to be shared among them. In absence of such an agreement, there is a presumption of equality.

6) Interest on capital – Sec. 13 (c)

If there is an agreement, a partner is entitled to interest on his capital contribution. Such as interest is payable out of profits only.

7) Interest on advances – Sec. 13 (d)

In order to claim interest on advance or payments made by a partner beyond his share capital, there must be –

i) Express agreement for payment of interest or

ii) Practice of a particular firm evidenced by facts, books of accounts etc. or

iii) Any trade or custom or

iv) Statutory provision giving him such a right.

Under Sec. 13-d, a partner is entitled to an interest @ 6% p.a. over the advances beyond capital subscription. Advance is treated as a loan to firm. No such interest is payable after dissolution and contract to the contrary exists during continuance of partnership.

8) Right to indemnity - Sec. 13 (e)

The firm shall indemnify a partner in respect of liabilities incurred or payments made by him -

a) in ordinary and proper of conduct of business or

b) during an act in emergency.

Basis of this right or firm's liability is agency. When a partner incurres personal liability with respect to payments, disbursements in proper execution of firm business, he should be indemnified. Where a partner acts in emergency for the purpose of protecting the firm from losses, the firm should assume responsibility for partner's acts. No right to indemnity exists if he is guilty of fraud or wilful neglect and consequent loss to the firm.

9) Power in emergency - Sec. 21

Every partner has authority to do all such acts for protecting the firm in emergency. To claim indemnity he should act like a man of ordinary prudence would act in similar circumstances.

10) **Right to retire** - See Sec. 32

11) **Right to carry on competing business** - See Sec. 36

12) **Right to share in profits after retirement - Sec. 37 -**
For above the rights, refer chapter on outgoing partners.

37.2 Duties of Partners

The partners of a firm are subjected to following duties under the Act. Some of the duties are absolute while others are qualified i.e. subject to the agreement between the partners.

1) **Duty to carry on business to the greatest common advantage - Sec. 9 -**
Sec. 9 of the Act enlists three duties of general nature. A partner should conduct the business in a manner to obtain maximum gain or profit and try to minimize losses or firm's liabilities. He should use skill, knowledge, expertise for common benefit and not for personal advantage.

2) **To be just and faithful to each other - Sec. 9**
A partner is bound to be just and faithful to his fellow partner. Mutual trust or confidence is the foundation of their relationship. Partner should exercise utmost good faith in every transaction of the firm. Personal interest should be kept aside and that should not conflict with interest of the firm.[104]

3) **To render accounts and give full information - Sec 9**
Sec 9 casts a third duty on partner to render true accounts and full information of all things affecting the firm. This duty also flows from fiduciary relationship between partners. Partner must keep or maintain accounts of all the transactions which he enters into. He should also explain the accounts when asked.[105]

4) **To indemnify for fraud - Sec. 10**
A partner shall indemnify the firm for any loss caused to it by his fraud while conducting the business of the firm. It may happen that a partner may defraud a third party which holds firm liable. The firm in turn can get indemnified from the guilty partner.

5) **To attend duties diligently - Sec. 12 (b)**
Every partner should attend diligently his duties in the conduct of the business. A partner is supposed to use skill or act prudently in business affairs. If other partners are required to work because of lack of his care, defaulting partner should compensate them.

---

104. *Dunne v/s English (1874) 18 Eq. 524*
105. *References u/s 9*
    a) *Law Vs Law (1905) 1 Ch. 140*
    A partner knew material facts regarding partnership assets. He did not disclose these to fellow partner and purchased his share. The transaction was held to be voidable and was set aside.
    b) *Gordon Vs Holland (1913) 108 LT Rep. 305*
    A partner violated terms of express agreement of partnership and concealed facts from his co-partner. He thereby sold firm property to a third person and re-purchased it from that person. He has no right to keep profits out of such dealing in breach of trust.

6) To indemnify for wilful neglect - Sec. 13

Where a partner causes loss to the firm by his 'wilful neglect' in the conduct of business of the firm, he should indemnify the firm for such a loss. 'Wilful neglect' is construed as intentional failure to take care while performing duties. Conduct of business honestly, in good faith absolves him from duty to indemnify.

(Note : For 'Liabilities fo Partners' refer next chapter)

7) To account for secret profits - Sec. 16 (a)

Where a partner obtains any advantage or profit without the consent or knowledge of rest of the partners, he should account for it. Partnership agreement is in the nature of 'uberrimae fidei' (Contracts of utmost good faith). Obviously personal profit or gain has no place in partnership business. This duty arises when secret profit is earned in the following four situations -

i) From the use of firm name ;

ii) From the use of firm property;

iii) From the use of firm transaction;

iv) From the use of firm business connection of the firm.

8) Not to compete - Sec. 16 (b)

A partner has freedom of carrying a business of his choice in his private capacity. But partnership agreement may restrict him from conducting a business similar to that of firm business and competing in nature. If he commits a breach, he is liable to account for profits in competing business and pay to the firm.

Chapter 38 | RELATIONS OF PARTNERS WITH THIRD PARTIES

Authority of a Partner

Mutual agency is one of the salient features of partnership agreement. A firm establishes its relationship with third parties through partners. Partners are thus agents of the firm. Sec. 18 of the Act states that —

"A partner is the agent of the firm for the purposes of business of the firm."

As stated earlier, partner is agent as well as principal in relation to the third parties. As an agent his acts bind other partners and as a principal he is bound by firm's acts. It is rightly said that law of partnership is an extension of law of agency. As an agent of the firm, a partner has either express or implied authority to bind the firm.

38.1 Express Authority

Authority expressly conferred on a partner to do certain acts on behalf of the firm is called as express authority. Whatever is done by a partner within express authority, binds the firm. An act may not be within the scope of partnership business but if that falls within the express authority, the firm is liable for such act. Sometimes his authority as a partner may be restricted. In that case if partner's acts falls outside his actual authority but well within his ordinary authority as a partner, the firm is bound by such act. If third party knows about restriction by express agreement then firm is not liable to third party if something goes wrong. Express authority in a way is restriction or extension of the ordinary authority as an agent/ partner. (Sec. 20)

38.2 Implied Authority

Law on implied authority of a partner is contained in Sec. 19 and Sec. 22 of the Act. These sections define the scope and extent of the implied authority of a partner.

Implied authority is also, known as *'Ostensible or Apparent or General Authourity'* of a partner. Authority which is apparent from one's position or which can be inferred from the facts and circumstances of a case, conduct of partners, course of dealing between parties is called as 'implied authority'. Partner is general or accredited agent of the firm **(Praepositus negotitis societatis)**. Acts of the partner bind the firm in all matters of undertaking of the firm. This authority to bind the firm by his acts is called as implied authority.

Sec. 19 states - "Subject to the provisions of Sec. 22, the act of a partner which is done to carry on, in the usual way, business of the kind carried on by the firm, binds the firm."

Thus to bind the firm, the act must be done in the following way -

- In the conduct of the business of the firm — Act must have connection with the business of the firm or done to facilitate the firm transaction.

- In the way usual in such a business — Act must be such which is usual in the business of the kind carried on by the firm. Whether usual or not or whether such an act is ordinarily undertaken in that kind of business is a question of fact, nature of and practice, usage in that business. In the business of land development, hiring landscape developers, architect, contractors is usual.

- Act must be executed in the firm name or in the manner implying an intention to bind the firm — The third requirement is laid down in Sec. 22 of the Act which gives 'Mode of doing an act of the firm'.

Mode of doing an act of the firm -
Sec. 22 Lays down that,

"In order to bind a firm, an act or instrument done or executed by a partner or other person on behalf of the firm shall be done or executed in the firm name or in any other manner expressing or implying an intention to bind the firm."

Act must be done in the capacity as a partner i.e. on behalf of the firm and not on his own behalf. If it is done in firm's name, firm is certainly liable. But if it is not in firm's name then difficulties arise. Settled view is that though the act is not in firm's name (principal not disclosed) but it is for the firm or firm is benefitted by that act, firm is bound by such acts with third parties.

Acts ordinarily falling within implied authority of a partner

i) To enter into contracts;

ii) To employ agents, servants;

iii) Drawing cheques etc;

iv) Adjustments, settlement of accounts;

v) Acceptance of debt amounts;

vi) Transfer, assignment of debt amounts;

vii) Bringing or defending suits;

viii) Pledging property of firm, taking a security (but not mortgage)

ix) Borrowing in trading concern.

1. **Exceptions to Implied Authority**
   (Acts not within the scope of implied authority of a partner)
   Sec. 19 provides statutory exceptions to implied authority of a partner. These restrictions

on implied authority are subject to trade, custom or usage prevailing in particular locality, markets, trades etc. Such a usage etc. is a question of fact and must be specifically proved. As per sec. 19(2), a partner cannot undertake following activities -

Sec. 19 (2)

i) Submission of a dispute relating to business of the firm to arbitration - A partner has no authority to bind the firm by arbitration award unless the submission to arbitration is expressly authorised or ratified by firm;

ii) Opening of a banking account on behalf of the firm in his own name;

iii) Compromise or relinquish any claim of the firm. Compromise even if without fraud or done honestly, would not bind the firm;

iv) Withdrawal of a suit or proceedings filed by the firm;

v) Admission of any liability in a suit or proceeding against the firm. Partner cannot give consent for injunction;

vi) Acquisition of immovable property (land, building etc) on behalf of the firm;

vii) Transfer of immovable property belonging to the firm;
Partner cannot bind the firm by mortgage, lease, sale of immovable property;

viii) Entering into partnership agreement on behalf of the firm;

Other limitations on implied authority

- Partner cannot bind the firm by guarantee for a loan on behalf of the firm.
- He cannot set-off his own debt against debt due to the firm.
- He cannot sell whole business or assign all goods/effects of the firm.
- Partner cannot acknowledge the debt due from the firm to bring it within limitation period.
- He cannot delegate his duties to another unless authorised. (because he himself is having delegated authority.)

It would be noticed that the acts which increase firm's liability or give up firms rights or which are otherwise detrimental and cause legal embarrassment to the firm, fall beyond implied authority.

38.3 Liabilities of a Partner towards Third Parties

The liabilities of a partner are discussed below.

1) Liability of a partner for 'acts of the firm' - Sec. 25

According to Sec. 25 a partner is liable for all acts of the firm done while he is a partner. 'Acts of a firm' are those acts which give rise to a right enforceable by or against the firm. Acts of a partner done in express, implied authority or in emergency bind the firm. Wrongful acts under Sec. 26 & 27 are also binding on firm. For all such acts a partner is liable.

To hold partner liable for act of the firm under this section, following **conditions**, must be fulfilled.

i) Act must have done in the name or on behalf of the firm and not in the personal capacity of the partner doing that act;

ii) Act must have been done in the ordinary course of business and

iii) Act should have been done while he is a partner in the firm.

The liability of partners is joint and several. The liability is based on the principle of agency.

2) Liability for wrongful acts of a partner - Sec. 26

If by wrongful act or omission of a partner, loss or injury results to third party or penalty is incurred by third party , then the firm is liable to the extent that partner is liable. Such an act or omission must be in the ordinary course of business of the firm.

If by misconduct (in carrying firm business) a partner causes loss to the third party, not only the guilty partner is liable to third party, but other partners are also liable.[106]

Firms have been held liable for offences / criminal acts of an errent partner if those acts fall within the scope of partner's authority.

3) Liability of the firm for misapplication of funds by a partner - Sec. 27

To fix the liability on the firm or other partners following circumstances must exist -

i) A partner receives money or property from third party;

ii) Such a receit is in his apparent authority or in the course of his business ;

iii) The partner misapplies the money or property when he himself receives it or partner misapplies while money or property is in his custody.

The firm is liable on account of the fact that firm has control or power over the property in its custody and presumed to have been benefitted by such money or property.

Other liabilities :

4) Liability to share losses - Sec. 13 (b)

Every partner should share losses equally with other patners. This liability is subject to contract to the contrary.

5) Liability for debt of the firm

Each partner is liable to satisfy the debts of creditors of the firm, incurred while he was a partner. This rule may be considered as an application of Sec. 25 of the Act.

6) Liability of incoming partner for old debts

(See. Sec. 31 in 'Reconstitution of the firm')

7) Liability for acts of a dissolved firm - Sec. 45

The partner shall continue to be liable to third parties for any act of a partner which would have been act of the firm if done before the dissolution. Such liability is continued till the public notice of dissolution is given. In this situation however, a dormant or insolvent partner or estate of the deceased partner is not liable for acts dissolved firm.

---

106. *Hurruck Chand v/s Govindlal - (1906) 10 Cal. 1053 - A partner was held liable to real owner of goods for receiving and selling stolen goods by another partner.*

Chapter 39

RECONSTITUTION OF FIRM

Changes in the composition of the firm are inevitable. Firm is reconstituted by changes like partners getting in the existing firm (incoming partners) or partners going out of it (outgoing partners). The law relating to such changes and their consequences is discussed below.

39.1 Incoming Partners

Admission of a partner

Sec. 31 of the Act deals with admission of a partner in the continuing firm. A partner is introduced in a firm in the following ways -

a) **Introduction with the consent of all the partners at a particular point of time -** Consent of all the partners is necessary for admission because harmonious working is essential in a firm. 'Delectus personae' is the basis of partnership.

Nomination of a stranger in a firm

Sec. 31 is subject to the contract to the contrary meaning thereby that without consent of all, a partner can be introduced. This is possible by power of nomination given to a senior partner in accordance with contract of partnership. A partner may name his successor after death or retirement. Nominee in case of death, has all rights of his predecessor.

b) **Introduction of a partner in accordance with the contract already entered into.** In such a case consent of all for introduction is not required. Minor may elect to become a partner on attaining majority.

Liability of Incoming partner

Legal aspects of Liability of Incoming partner can be summarized as follows.

i) Incoming partners will be liable to third party for all acts of the firm (debts or any other liability) from the date of his admission. i.e. Liability commences from the date of introduction.

ii) Newly introduced partner is not liable for previous acts of the firm i.e. acts prior to his admission. Creditor cannot hold him liable for past debts because introduction does not imply 'ratification'.

iii) New partner can be made liable to the outsiders / creditors for existing acts of the firm or debts in the following eventualities.

a) New (reconstituted) firm assumes the liability of the old firm and

b) The creditor has accepted the new firm as their debtors and discharges the old firm. This change (Novation) thus requires a tri-partite agreement between old firm, new partner and the third parties. (creditors)

39.2 Outgoing Partners (Ss. 32 to 38)

A partner's relationship with the firm is severed by retirement, explusion or insolvency. Death also has the same effect.

1. Retirement of a Partner

a) Meaning : Retirement is severence of relationship of a partner with that of the firm. Remaining partners continue to conduct the business of the firm without any dissolution. In dissolution the entire relationship comes to an end.

b) Modes of Retirement - Sec. 32 (1) provides following modes retirement of a partner -

i) With the **consent of all** partners at a particular time. Consent may be express or implied ;

ii) In pursuance of **previous**, express **agreement** among partners. This is retirement by exercise of right and no consent at the time of retirement is necessary.

iii) By giving notice of retirement in 'Partnership at - Will'. Notice must be in writing making clear the intention to retire.

c) Discharge of Liability of a Retiring Partner

i) Liability for previous acts - [Sec. 32 (2)]

The retiring partner remains liable for all acts of the firm / debts obligations done or incurred before his retirement. Liability continues for works began but unfinished. He may be discharged for past acts by an agreement between retiring partner, other partners and the third party or parties. This is an example of 'novation' (subsitution of old contract by new one).

ii) Liability for future acts

Sec. 32 (3) states that a public notice of retirement should be given. His liability as a partner comes to an end only when such a notice is given. Till the date of public notice, he continues to be liable for acts of the firm. Liability in absence of notice is based on 'holding out.' There is a presumption of continuance of relationship if public notice is not given.[107] Other partners also continue to be liable for his acts as a partner till the notice is given. As per Sec. 32 (4) public notice is unnecessary in case of dormat partner's retirement. There is no particular form of notice. If a third party in fact, knows that a partner has retired, he cannot hold that partner liable. Knowledge of fact is a sufficient notice.[108]

---

107. *Scarf v/s Jardin.*

108 . *ibid = Notice may be given by retiring partner or other partners.*

d) Rights of Retiring Partner :

The rights of a retiring partner are two fold -

i) Right to carry on competing business and

ii) Right to share subsequent profits

i) Right to compete (Sec. 36)

Retiring partner can carry on business competing with that of the firm. This right is subject to following restrictions.

- He cannot use the firm name;
- He cannot represent himself to be the partner of the firm or as carrying on firm's business;
- He cannot solicit customers of the firm who had dealings with firm when he was a partner.
- Additional restrictions imposed by the contract of partnership on the business of competing nature. The restrictions would be invalid if those are found to be unreasonable, unfair and harsh, depriving one's right to trade. Reasonable restrictions are premissible.

ii) Right to share subsequent profits (Sec. 37)

If a partner retires or dies and business of the firm continues without final settlement of accounts, then the retired partner or legal representatives of retired partner are entitled to claim —

- Share in profits earned after retirement or death attributable to the use of share of retired / deceased partner in the property.
- an interest @ 6 %. p.a. on the amount of his share in the property.

2. Explusion of a Partner

Explusion is an act of removing a partner. It is imposed against a partner's wish for his misconduct.

Conditions for valid explusion –

i) **Agreement** - There must be an agreement empowering the majority of partners to expell. Such an agreement may be express or implied. The right to expell is strictly construed.

ii) **Explusion in good-faith** - Power of explusion must be exercised in good faith. It cannot be abused by uscrupulous majority. Right to expell should be exercised in the general interest of the firm or for the benefit of all. Ulterior motive or undue advantage cannot justify explusion.

iii) **Notice of expulsion** - As a general rule, notice of expulsion to the expelled partner is not necessary. Right of hearing (opportunity to explain one's conduct) is generally not implied in expulsion cases. If partners are placed in the position of a tribunal (quasi - judicial body), then notice becomes a requirement.

Legal consequences of invalid expulsion -

If the expulsion is malafide or otherwise irregular, explusion is inoperative. Partner will not cease to be a partner and partnership continues with him.

Rights and liabilities of the expelled partner are similar to that of retiring partner. Public notice of expulsion is necessary.

3. **Insolvency of a Partner - (Sec. 34)**

   An adjudicated insolvent ceases to be a partner from the date of his adjudication. He ceases to be liable for firm's act from the date of adjudication. Public notice of adjudication is not essential as court proceedings are said to be public. Estate of the insolvent is liable for previous acts of the firm.

4. **Death of a Partner - (Sec. 35)**

   Death dissolves partnership unless there is contract to the contrary. If the firm is not dissolved on death, the estate of the deceased partner is not liable for the acts of firm after the death. His estate is liable for acts of the firm during his ties with partnership. Public notice of death is not required for the discharge from liability, as death is a notorious occurance.

Chapter 40 | DISSOLUTION OF A FIRM

40.1 Definition (Sec. 39)

> *"The dissolution of partnership among all the partners of a firm is called the 'dissolution of the firm.'*

Dissolution of the firm is the termination of relationship among all partners of a firm. That brings an end to the business and the existence of the firm. There is a complete break-down of or extinction of relationship between all the partners of a firm.

40.2 Modes of Dissolution

The firm may be dissolved in any of the following ways

1. **Dissolution by Agreement (Sec. 40)**
   A firm is the result of agreement. An agreement may put an end to the partnership relationship. A firm is dissolved -
   i) With the consent of all the partners at a particular time or
   ii) In accordance with a contract previously entered into.
   In the second situation (ii) partners may agree to dissolve the firm upon happening of an event. The partners may not be willing to accept the dissolution but they cannot avoid it once that eventuality occures. For example, if a firm runs a hospital and partnership provides for dissolution if one doctor settles in foreign country, firm would be dissolved if that happens.

2. **Compulsory Dissolution (Sec. 41)**
   Dissolution becomes unavoidable in certain situations mentioned in sec. 41. S. 41 is not subject to any contract which means that the dissolution occures automatically under all circumstances.
   Compulsory dissolution takes place in following circumstances —
   i) **Insolvency of all or all but one S. 41** (a) - If all the partners or all but one are adjudicated insolvent, the firm stands dissolved. This section is in consonance with Sec. 34 under which an insolvent ceases to be a partner in the firm.

ii) Business becoming unlawful - Sec. 41 (b) - When business subsequently becomes unlawful or partners cannot carry on their (lawful) business lawfully, the firm is compulsorily dissolved. By change in law, firm's business may become unlawful or that law may forbid partners to continue the business, dissolution occures. A firm of coal miners are engaged in coal mining. Court declares allotment of coal blocks illegal and hence firm cannot further continue mining. Firm gets dissolved.

Provision to Sec. 41 - Where a firm carries on more than one distinct adventures or undertakings, the illegality of one or more shall not of itself lead to dissolution of the firm in respect of its lawful adventure or undertaking.

Example - A firm of developers are developing four plots. Construction on one plot is illegal. Firm can develop and construct on remaining three plots.

3. Dissolution on the happening of certain contingencies (Sec. 42)

On the happening of certain events (contingencies), firm may be dissolved. Sec. 42 is made subject to the contract to the contrary. Dissolution u/s 42 is not compulsory and the partners may agree to continue inspite of the following contingencies.

Contingencies u/s 42

i) Efflux of time - S. 42 (a)

Where the partnership is for a fixed term (period), the firm is dissolved after expiry of that period. The partners may continue after the expiry of the term. Rights and liabilities of the partners are the same after the period unless otherwise agreed. After the efflux of the first period, firm may be continued for another fixed period. If period is not fixed it would be partnership at-will.

ii) Completion of adventure - Sec. 42 (b)

If the partnership is 'particular' i.e. for a specific adventure or undertaking, it is dissolved by completion of that adventure / undertaking. The date of dissolution would be the date of completion of the adventure.

iii) Death of a partner - Sec. 42 (c)

Death of a partner dissolves relationship. There is a presumption of termination of relationship on death of a partner. Date of dissolution would be the date of death. Partnership agreement may provide for nomination of a successor after death. Notice of dissolution on death is not necessary as death is presumed to be known.[109]

iv) Insolvency of a Partner - Sec. 42 (d)

When a partner in the firm is adjudged insolvent, the firm is dissolved. Notice of dissolution is unnecessary. Estate of insolvent is liable for acts of the firm and acts for winding up (and not for subsequent acts).

Death or insolvency before completion of adventure or expiry of fixed term -

It should be noted that if the partnership is for a fixed term and death or insolvency occurs before expiry of that term or before completion of adventure, the firm is dissolved, subject of course, to the contract to the contrary.

---

109. *Harmohan Vs Sundarson - AIR (1921) Cal. 538*

4. **Dissolution by Notice in Patnership-at-Will (Sec. 43)**

Partnership-at-will is dissolved by notice. The following points may be noted in connection with such dissolution –

- The dissolution by notice is possible in patnership at - will;
- Notice may be given by any one partners to all others. It must be in writing, certain and not vague. It cannot be in the form of a proposal.
- Notice must be explicit, effectual, and should reflect final and unequivocal intention of dissolution.
- Date of dissolution would be the date mentioned in the notice. If not mentioned it would be the date of receipt of notice. Notice should always be prospective.

Section is absolute. Notice once given cannot be withdrawn without the consent of all others. Reasonableness of notice is not a requirement under the section. The time of notice may be inconvenient to others. Filing of a suit and service of summons is treated an notice of dissolution in partnership at will.[110]

5. **Dissolution by the Court - Sec. 44**

Dissolution may be effected by court's order. A partner has a right to invoke court's power and the courts are under a duty to interfere in a fit case. Section is not subject to the contract to the contrary. Court 'may' dissolve the firm indicating unlimited discretionary power of the court to dissolve. A partner may file a suit for dissolution on any of the following grounds –

Grounds of Dissolution by Court

1) **Unsoundness of Mind : S. 46 (a) -**

If a partner becomes 'insane', suit for dissolution may be filed by -

i) Any partner of the firm or

ii) Next friend of an insane partner.

There is no ipso facto dissolution on insanity of a partner. Dissolution is at the instance (suit) or a partner. 'Unsoundness of mind' may be interpreted in the light of provisions of Contract Act or Lunacy Act. Insanity refers to madness or loss of mental capacity to understand. Permanent, confirmed or incurable insanity is not necessary. Order of dissolution is generally not passed in case of a dormant partner.

2) **Permanent Incapacity - Sec. 46 (b) -**

If a partner has become permanently incapable of performing his duties as a partner, the court may dissolve the firm. Such a suit is to be filed by partner other than incapacitated partner. Physical incapacity of permanent nature is a valid ground for dissolution.

3) **Misconduct - Sec. 46 (c) -**

When a partner, other than the partner suing, is guilty of misconduct, the court may dissolve the firm. The misconduct which is likely to adversely affect the business of the firm attracts the section. The misconduct need not be connected with firm's business. The partner guilty of misconduct cannot bring such a suit. Instances of misconduct u/s 46 (c) are –

---

110. *Shib Ram Vs Chinta Har AIR (1933) Lah. 1032.*

- Adultery by one partner.[111]
- Conviction for travelling without ticket.[112]
- Conversion of books of account of the firm.
- Breach of trust by partner...etc.

4) **Persistent Breach of Agreement - S. 44 (a)**
To obtain an order of dissolution on this ground following **conditions** must be satisfied-
- Wilful or persistent breach of partnership agreement. Innocent breach or occasional breach are outside the perview of this clause.
- Breach is committed in conducting the business of the firm or managing firm's affairs.
- The partner conducts himself in such a way that other partners cannot (reasonably) conduct the business with him.
- The suit is to be filed by the partner other than partner committing breach.
- Instances of breach or misconduct - Keeping fake accounts, taking away books of accounts, misappropriation of firm's money, continued quarrels with other partners, destroying mutual confidence and trust.

5) **Transfer of Interest - S. 44 (e) -**
This section is applicable in the following cases -
- Transfer of whole of share by a partner to the third party or
- Share of a partner being charged under Order 21 Rule 49 of the Civil Procedure Code or
- Share being sold in recovery of arrears of land revenue or recovery of dues as arrears of land revenue. Suit under this section can be filed by the partner other than partner whose share is transferred or sold.

6) **Continuous Losses - S. 44 (f) -**
When business cannot be carried on except at a loss, firm may be dissolved by preferring a suit. The ultimate purpose of business is to earn profit. Continued losses is, therefore, a just ground for dissolution. Partnership may be for a fixed period or for a particular adventure, firm can be dissolved before the expiry of term or completion of adventure.

7) **Dissolution on Just and Equitable grounds - S. 44 (a)**
The court may dissolve the firm on any grounds which appears to be just and equitable. Section vests salutory and necessary power to dissolve the firm in a fit case. Exercise of judicial discretion depends upon circumstances and exigencies of a case. No hard and fast rules are laid down for exercise for such a discretion. Courts enjoy wide, unfettered, uncontrolled power to dissolve the firm on the ground which renders dissolution just and equitable.
Instances - Frustration of the purpose of partnership agreement, loss of substratum, constant quarrels, partners not on speaking terms, deadlock in the administration of business etc.

---

111. *Abbort Vs Crumb (1870) 5 Bang LR 106.*
112. *Charmichael Vs Evans (1904) ch 986.*

Part V

Questions and hints for answers

1. Define Partnership. Explain its Essentials. BBA 2012, 2011, BBM (IB) 2012 Ans. 34.1 & 34.2

2. What is 'Partnership' ? What is the test for determination of existence of partnership ? BBA 2012, BBM (IB) 2010 Ans. 34.1 & 34.3

3. "Partnership is created by agreement and not by status" Discuss. Ans. 34.4 & refer the chart of distinction.

4. State the procedure for registration of Partnership. What are the consequences of non - registration of a firm ? BBM (IB) 2011 Ans. 35.1 & 35.2

5. Discuss various rights of a partner against his fellow partner. BBA 2013, BBM(IB) 2011, 2013 Ans. 37.1

6. What are the duties of a partner towards his fellow partner ? Explain BBA 2011, BBM(IB) 2011, 2013 Ans. 37.2

7. What is implied authority of a partner ?

   Explain with illustrations exceptions to implied authority. BBA 2013 Ans. 38

8. Under that circumstances a partner is liable to third parties ? Explain the relevant provisions. BBM(IB) 2012 Ans. 38.3

9. Explain in brief the provisions relating to admission, retirement and expulsion of a partner in a firm. BBA 2013, 2011, BBM(IB) 2012, 2010 Ans. 39.1, 39.2 (1) and 39.2 (2)

10. How a partner can retire from a firm ?

    Explain rights and liability of a retiring partner. Ans. 39.2

11. What is dissolution of a firm ? Explain in brief the modes of dissolution. BBA 2012, BBM(IB) 2012

12. Explain the provisions of Ind. Partnership Act. 1932 relating to the following modes of dissolution.

    a) Dissolution by agreement - 40.2 (1)

    b) Compulsory dissolution - 40. 2 (2)

13. Under what circumstances a firm can be dissolved by Court's order ? Explain - 40.2 (5) Sec. 4

14. Explain 'Dissolution of Partnership' & 'Dissolution of firm'. When dissolution of firm takes place without court's intervention ? MBA 2003 P. U. Ans. 40.1, 40.2 (1 to 4)

15. Explain types of partnership & partners. MBA 2003 P. U. Ans. Ch. 36

16. Define and explain essential features of Partnership Firm. How it is different from company? BBA 2013, 2011

PART - VI

THE LIMITED LIABILITY
PARTNERSHIP ACT, 2008

Introduction—Indian economy has taken a great leap in the first decade of twenty first century. Indian laws should not put unnecessary hurdles on economic growth. On the contrary those should boost economic progress. Technical and professional manpower is India's asset. Entrepreneurs with their expertise, knowledge, skill have great potential to provide impetus to India's growth. They should have adequate freedom to govern their lawful business. In traditional partnership partner's liability is unlimited while in a company, shareholder's liability is limited to the extent of his share holding. The need was therefore felt to find an alternative to traditional partnership on the one hand and statute governed corporate form. Concept of Limited Liability Partnership provides a practical, suitable format of governance for economic activity.

Limited liability partnership is viewed as an alternative corporate business vehicle which provides benefits of limited liability at the same time allows flexibility of organizing internal structure of partnership. This form is based on mutual agreement. This concept is aptly regarded as commercially efficient vehicle suited to requirements of entrepreneurs and professionals. It is essentially a partnership with the shades of corporate structure. Limited liability partnership is flexible, innovative and efficient structure for small investors.

This Act received the assent of the President on 7th January, 2009 and this Statute is called as The Limited Liability Partnership Act, 2009.

NATURE OF LIMITED LIABILITY PARTNERSHIP

1. Limited liability partnership is a body corporate—S.3— Limited liability partnership is a body corporate formed and registered under this Act. According to S.2 (d), body corporate means and includes...

    — Limited liability partnership registered under this Act;
    — Limited liability partnership incorporated outside India;
    —Company incorporated outside India.

    Body corporate however does not include—

    —a corporation sole;
    —a registered co-operative society;
    —any other body corporate notified by Central Government.

2. Limited liability partnership is a legal entity separate from its partners.
3. Limited liability partnership shall have perpetual succession.

4. Any change in the partners of limited liability partnership shall not affect the existence, rights and liability of limited liability partnership.

   Above features of limited liability partnership are very much similar to that of a company and elaborated in the chapter of company law.

5. Partners in limited liability partnership —
   a) Who can be partners? S.5— An individual or body corporate can be the partners in limited liability partnership. However a person of unsound mind, an undischarged insolvent, who has applied for adjudication as an insolvent and his application is pending are disqualified to be the partners in limited liability partnership.
   b) Number of Partners—S.6—Limited liability partnership must have at least two partners. If the number is reduced below two and with one partner business is carried on for more than six months, that partner is liable personally for the obligations incurred after six months. The liability depends upon his knowledge that he is alone carrying on business after six months.
   c) Designated Partners—S. 7—This seems to be the special feature of limited liability partnership—

Meaning—-Definition—S.2 (j) Designated partners means any partner designated as such pursuant to S.7.

Who can be Designated Partner?—Minimum two designated partners are required. One designated partner should be resident in India. If the group of designated partners comprises all body corporates or one or more partners are individuals and body corporate, then at least two individual partners shall act as designated partners.

How designated?—If incorporation document designates certain persons as designated partners then those would be designated partners on incorporation. Or in the alternative, if incorporation document states that each partner from time to time would be designated partner then every partner shall be designated partner. As a general rule, any partner may become designated partner or may cease to be designated partner in accordance with limited liability partnership Agreement.

Prior Consent—Qualified individual has to satisfy prescribed conditions and requirements to be a designated partner. Prior consent of a partner is a precondition to become a designated partner of limited liability partnership. Limited liability partnership shall file with the Registrar the particulars of designated partner who has given consent to act as such within thirty days of his appointment.

Liability of Designated Partner —S.8— A designated partner shall be liable—-

—-for all acts, matters, things of limited liability partnership in respect of compliance of the provisions of the Act. In particular, he is responsible for filing of document, returns, statement, and report pursuant to the Act and limited liability partnership agreement.

—-to all penalties imposed on limited liability partnership for contravention of statutory provisions.

Changes in Designated Partner—S.9—In case of vacancy, limited liability partnership may appoint a designated partner as per s.7 above explained within thirty days of vacancy.

Punishment for contravention of Ss.7 to 9—Punishment for contravention of the provisions regarding number, requirements of appointment, filing particulars of designated partner and liability and changes in designated partner attracts minimum fine of ten thousand rupees and maximum fine of five lakh rupees.

INCORPORATION OF LIMITED LIABILITY PARTNERSHIP—Ss.11 to 15

Provisions regarding incorporation of limited liability partnership are contained in Chapter *III* of the Act. Those are stated below.

1. Subscribers—Two or more persons shall subscribe their names to an incorporation document. (Herein after called as subscribers) They must be associated for carrying on a lawful business with a view to earn profit.

2. Incorporation Document—S 11—Incorporation document shall be filed along with prescribed fee to the Registrar of the State.

3. Statement of Compliance— Along with the incorporation document a statement to the effect that all requirements of the Act and the rules there under in respect of incorporation are complied with shall be filed by the subscribers and an Advocate or Company Secretary or a Chartered Accountant or a Cost Accountant engaged in the formation of limited liability partnership.

4. Incorporation document shall be in the prescribed form. It should state the name of limited liability partnership, its proposed purpose, registered address, names and address of each partners of limited liability partnership on incorporation, names and address of designated partners on incorporation and other information which is prescribed.

5. Penalty for false information—If subscribers or advocate etc who are signatory to the statement of compliance make a false statement which is knowingly false or made without belief in its truth, shall be imprisoned or fined. Maximum term of imprisonment prescribed is of two years and fine of minimum ten thousand and maximum of five lakh rupees may be imposed.

6. S.12 Incorporation by Registration—When Registrar is satisfied as to compliance of S.11, he shall retain incorporation document and within a period of 14 days register the incorporation document and issue a certificate of incorporation of limited liability partnership. This certificate would be signed by the Registrar and authenticated by his official seal. The said certificate shall be the conclusive evidence of incorporation of limited liability partnership. The Registrar may treat the statement of compliance u/s 11 as sufficient evidence as to compliance.

7. Effect of registration—Registration of limited liability partnership clothes it with chief attributes of a body corporate. S.14 enlists those as under.
   a Limited liability partnership can sue or be sued;
   b Limited liability partnership can acquire, own, hold, dispose off property. The property may be movable, immovable, tangible or intangible.

c   Limited liability partnership may have a common seal;

d   Like body corporate, it can do or suffer acts or things.

S.15. Name of limited liability partnership— Name of limited liability partnership shall have the words "limited liability partnership" or simply "LLP" as the last words of its name.

The name of limited liability partnership should not be undesirable or identical with the existing partnership or limited liability partnership or body corporate.

PARTNERS AND THEIR RELATIONS

This set of sections (22 to 24) regulate two fold relationship, namely relationship between partners inter se and between the limited liability partnership and its partners. Law gives liberty to determine relationship and in the absence of agreement law prevails.

1. **Eligibility to be partners**—S.22 Subscribers to incorporation document (at the time of registration) shall be the partners <u>on incorporation</u>. Any other person may become partner of limited liability partnership in accordance with the limited liability partnership agreement.

2. **Relationship of Partners**—S.23
    a) Mutual rights and obligations of partners of limited liability partnership and mutual rights and obligations of a limited liability partnership and its partners shall be governed by limited liability partnership agreement between partners or between the limited liability partnership and its partners.
    b) Limited liability partnership agreement and subsequent changes therein are required to be filed with the Registrar. Filing should be in the prescribed form, and manner accompanied by the fee.
    c) Written agreement between the subscribers to incorporation document may impose obligations on the limited liability partnership. However such agreement needs to be ratified by all partners after incorporation.
    d) In the absence of agreement referred in above para, the mutual rights and obligations of partners and mutual rights and obligations of limited liability partnership and its partners relating to those matters shall be determined by the provisions which are enlisted in the First Schedule of the Act.

3. **Cessation of partnership interest**—S.24
    a) By agreement or notice—A person may cease to become partner of limited liability partnership in pursuance of agreement with fellow partners. If the agreement is silent on this point then he may discontinue his association by giving notice to other partners of his intention to resign. Notice should be in writing and of not less than thirty days.
    b) In certain contingencies— A person shall cease to be a partner of limited liability partnership in the following circumstances—
    —His death or dissolution of limited liability partnership;
    —Declaration of a person to be of unsound mind by a competent court;
    —If he has applied to be adjudged as an insolvent;
    c) Liability of Former Partner—A person who ceases to be a partner in above

circumstances, is called a former partner. In relation to a person dealing with the limited liability partnership (say, a third person) he is still a partner of limited liability partnership if that third person has no notice of cessation of his partnership interest or if notice of cessation of his partnership interest is not delivered to the Registrar. This means that for discharge of his liability towards third person, either third person must have notice or such notice should be given to Registrar.

Cessation of person's partnership interest does not by itself discharge him from any obligation towards limited liability partnership or other partners or to any other person which he incurred while he was a partner. Former partner still remains liable for acts during his association as a partner.

Rights of Former Partner— Former partner or his successor (on death or insolvency) shall have right to receive the amount of his capital contribution made to limited liability partnership and share in accumulated profits of limited liability partnership (after deduction of accumulated losses). S.24 makes it clear that former partner or his successor has no right to interfere in the management of the limited liability partnership.

EXTENT AND LIMITATION OF LIABILITY OF LIMITED LIABILITY PARTNERSHIP AND PARTNERS

1. **Partner as an agent**—S.26—Every partner of limited liability partnership is an agent of the limited liability partnership for its business. He is not the agent of other partners. There is a principal-agent relationship between limited liability partnership and a partner.

2. **Extent of liability of limited liability partnership** —S.27
   a) When limited liability partnership is not liable by partner's act? - Limited liability partnership is not bound by an act of a partner dealing with third person in the following circumstances:
   i—Absence of authority of limited liability partnership for doing a particular act and knowledge of the third person of absence of such authority or
   ii—absence of knowledge or belief that the person is a partner in limited liability partnership.
   b) When limited liability partnership is liable? - Limited liability partnership is liable to the third party for partners' wrongful act or omission in the following situations:
   i) Wrongful act or omission is during the course of business of limited liability partnership, or
   ii) When such act of omission is committed with authority of limited liability partnership.

3. **Obligation of limited liability partnership** (contractual, statutory, etc.) shall be solely the obligation of limited liability partnership.

4. The liabilities of limited liability partnership shall be met out of the property of the limited liability partnership.
   Extent of liability of partner—S.28
   i) A partner is not personally liable (directly or indirectly) for the obligation of limited liability partnership. So when limited liability partnership is exclusively liable, partner is not liable.

ii) Partner is not personally liable for the wrongful act or omission of any other partner of limited liability partnership.

iii) However a partner shall be liable personally for his own wrongful act or omission.

The combined effect of Section 27 and 28 is that partner is not personally liable for obligations of limited liability partnership though he is an integral part of limited liability partnership and shares in its profits. This Act introduces dichotomy between partners and limited liability partnership. These provisions mitigate the rigors of Partnership Act. Partner however is not exempted from liability for his own wrongful act or omission.

5. **Holding out—S.29—**
   a. Holding out is an application of rule of estoppel under section 115 of Indian Evidence Act. Sometimes when a person is not a partner in limited liability partnership, he is still liable as a partner if he is held out to be a partner. This Section is applicable in the following situations:
      i) A person by his oral or written words or by conduct;
      ii) Represents himself or knowingly permits to be represented to be a partner in limited liability partnership.
      iii) The creditors on the faith of such representation gives credit to limited liability partnership.
      iv) In the situation partner is liable to the creditor.
   Partner may not have knowledge that the representation has reached the creditor.
      Thus though not a partner, a person is liable because of his representation as a partner. He is estopped from denying the character which he has assumed. The creditor who believes on such untrue representation and suffers losses and gives credit should not suffer losses. Hence the liability by holding out.
   b. Liability of limited liability partnership due to holding out— When in the above situation credit is received by limited liability partnership as a result of such representation, limited liability partnership is liable to the extent of the credit received by it or financial benefit derived from such credit.
   c. Liability of Legal heirs— If after partner's death, business is continued in the same name of limited liability partnership or the use of that name is continued or use of the diseased partner's name is continued in the name of limited liability partnership, the legal representatives or his estate is not liable for any act of limited liability partnership after partner's death.

6. **Unlimited Liability of Fraud—S.30—**This section spells out the liability of limited liability partnership and its partners for fraudulent acts.
   i—The limited liability partnership and its partners are liable for an act carried out by limited liability partnership or by any partner with intent to defraud credits or any person. The liability is also fixed if an act is done for fraudulent purpose. The liability is unlimited for all or any of the debts or other liabilities of limited liability partnership.
   ii—If the fraudulent act is carried out by a partner, then limited liability partnership is liable to the same extent as the partner. If the act is carried out without the knowledge or authority of limited liability partnership, it is not liable.

iii—Punishment for Fraud. If business is carried it out with fraudulent intent or for fraudulent purposes, every person who is knowingly a party to such business is punishable. Punishment prescribed is imprisonment for a maximum period of two years and minimum fine of fifty thousand rupees and maximum of five lakh rupees can be levied.

iv—Compensation for loss due to Fraud. Where the affairs of the limited liability partnership are conducted in a fraudulent manner by limited liability partnership or a partner or designated partner or employee of such limited liability partnership, then a partner or designated partner or employee of such limited liability partnership, shall be liable to pay compensation to any person who has suffered loss or damage by reason of such conduct. Criminal proceedings can also be taken up under the other Laws for such fraudulent conduct. Absence of knowledge of fraud is a ground for exemption from liability for limited liability partnership.

7. **Whistle blowing**—S.31—This Section provides protection to whistle blowers. The Section is incorporated in pursuance of new legislative policy and public opinion which demands legal protection to those who assist in discovery of truth, investigation under the laws. The gist of the Section is mentioned below:

If the affairs of the limited liability partnership are under investigation and if a partner or employee provides useful information during such investigation, the Court of Tribunal may reduce or waive any penalty leviable against such partner or employee. Same protection is available when any information given by him leads to the conviction of any limited liability partnership or a partner or any employee under this Act or any other Act. No partner or employee maybe discharged, suspended, demoted, threatened, harassed, or discriminated against in the matters of limited liability partnership merely because of such whistle blowing by its partner or employee.

CONTRIBUTIONS

1. S. 32 of the Act recognizes following ways of contributions by a partner to limited liability partnership.
   a Tangible or intangible or movable or immovable property;
   b Other benefits including money, promissory note;
   c Agreements to contribute cash or property or for services.
2. Obligations to contribute—S.33—The above mentioned agreement to contribute shall be as per limited liability partnership agreement. This obligation of partner to contribute may be enforced by a creditor who extends credit to limited liability partnership on the faith of such obligation.

FINANCIAL DISCLOSURES

Chapter *VII* of the Act casts duties regarding maintenance of accounts, filing returns etc and provides punishments for failures. The duties and punishments are enlisted below.
Limited liability partnership is under a duty to....

1. Maintain proper books of accounts relating to its affairs in the prescribed manner. Accounts should be maintained for each year of existence and kept at registered office. (S.34)

2. Prepare a Statement of Accounts and Solvency within a period of six months from the end of each financial year. Statement should be in the prescribed form and signed by designated partner. This Statement needs to be filed with the Registrar within prescribed time, in the prescribed form and manner.

3. Audit the accounts of limited liability partnership as per the rules laid down.

Punishment—For failure to comply above provisions, limited liability partnership shall be punishable with minimum fine of twenty five thousand rupees and maximum of five lakh rupees. Further every designated partner of limited liability partnership shall also be punishable with fine (minimum ten thousand rupees and maximum one lakh rupees) for non compliance.

4. File an annual return with the Registrar within sixty days closure of its financial year. It should be duly authenticated and filed in prescribed form and manner. (S.35)

Punishment—For noncompliance of the above provision, limited liability partnership shall be punishable with fine (minimum twenty five thousand and maximum of five lakh rupees). For contravention of filing of return, designated partner shall be punishable with same fine under section 34.

Inspection of documents—S.36—Incorporation document, statement and returns filed u/s 34 and 35 shall be available in the office of Registrar to any person on payment of prescribed fees.

S.37—Penalty for false statement—This section penalizes submission of false statement, return or other document. To attract the penalty, document should be false in material particular and filed with the knowledge of falsity. Deliberate omission is also punishable. The person responsible for preparation or filing etc is punishable with imprisonment of maximum term of two years and fine up to five lakh rupees can also be imposed.

Powers of Registrar

1. Power to obtain information—
Power of requisition—S.38(1)—Registrar may require any present or former or designated partner or employee of a limited liability partnership to answer any question or make any declaration or supply details or particulars in writing within reasonable period.

2. Power to Summon—S.38(2)—If the person referred in the above section does not respond, Registrar has power to summon that person to appear before him or an inspector or any designated public officer to answer any such question or make declaration or supply the required details.

Punishment for non compliance—S.38 (3)—If the concerned person fails to comply the Registrar summon or requisition, he shall be punishable with fine ranging from two thousand (minimum) to twenty five thousand (maximum) rupees. Lawful excuses absolve the person from punishment.

3. Power to Destroy—S.40—The Registrar is empowered to destroy any document filed in physical or electronic form in accordance with the rules laid down.

4. Power to enforce provisions in default—S.41—This section covers two types of defaults namely default in compliance with—-
   i   Provisions of the Act/other laws requiring filing of return, accounts, document etc. or
   iii Request of Registrar to amend/correct, resubmit any document
   Registrar may direct limited liability partnership through a notice to make good the default. On failure to make good the default within fourteen days, Registrar may apply to the Tribunal for an order directing limited liability partnership or designated partner or partners to make good the default within specified time.

ASSIGNMENT AND TRANSFER OF PARTNERSHIP RIGHTS

Partner's Transferable interest—S.42—This only section in chapter *VIII* states what interests may be transferred by a partner of limited liability partnership and as a result what rights are not available to the transferee. A partner in limited liability partnership has right to share profits and to receive distributions in accordance with the limited liability partnership agreement. This right can be transferred either wholly or partially by the partner. Such transfer by itself does not lead to his dissociation with limited liability partnership or winding up of limited liability partnership. Further such transfer by itself does not give any right to the transferee or assignee of partner's interest to participate in the management of or the conduct of the business of limited liability partnership. Transferee or assignee is not entitled to access to any information relating to the transactions of limited liability partnership.

CONVERSION OF LIMITED LIABILITY PARTNERSHIP

Chapter *X* of the Act (Ss. 55 to 58) deals with conversion of other business entities to limited liability partnership and the legal consequences of such conversion.

1. Following business associations may be converted to limited liability partnership—
   a) A firm;
   b) A private company;
   c) An unlisted public company.
   Such conversion should be as per the provisions of this chapter and Second, Third and Fourth Schedule respectively.

2. Procedure of Registration— A firm or private company, or an unlisted public company has to apply for such conversion to the Registrar along with necessary documents complying the provisions of the concerned Schedule. On being satisfied as to compliance of the Act, rules and Schedule, Registrar will register the documents and issue a certificate of registration. Firm etc will be registered as limited liability partnership on and from the date specified in the certificate of registration.

   Information about conversio —Information about conversion and the particulars of newly registered limited liability partnership shall be informed by the limited liability partnership to the Registrar of Firms or Registrar of Companies within fifteen days from the date of registration.

3. Effect of conversion—Legal consequences of conversion (on and from the date specified in the certificate of registration issued under Second, Third and Fourth Schedule respectively) are enlisted below.

a) Upon such conversion, partners of the old firm, shareholders of the company converted to limited liability partnership and partners of the registered limited liability partnership are bound by the provisions of respective Schedules (mentioned above)

b) Upon such conversion, effects of conversion shall be as mentioned in the respective Schedules.

c) Limited liability partnership comes into existence by the name specified in the certificate of registration

d) All tangible (movable or immovable property) and intangible property vested in the firm or company , all assets, interests, rights or privileges relating to the firm or company, the whole of the undertaking of the firm or company as the case may be, shall be transferred to and shall vest in the limited liability partnership. Liabilities and obligations also stand transferred likewise. For such transfer no separate assurance or act or deed is necessary.

e) The firm or company as the case may be, shall be deemed to be dissolved and removed from the record of Registrar of Firms or Registrar of Companies.

WINDING UP AND DISSOLUTION

Winding up and Dissolution—S. 63—Basically there are two modes in which the existence of the limited liability partnership comes to an end viz.

1. Voluntary winding up by limited liability partnership or
2. Winding up by the Tribunal

The limited liability partnership so wound up may be dissolved.

Winding up by the Tribunal—S.64—Circumstanecs— Tribunal may wind up limited liability partnership in the following circumstances—

1. Decision of limited liability partnership for winding up by Tribunal;

2. Reduction in Number—The number of partners of limited liability partnership is reduced below two for a period of more than six months;

3. Inability to pay debts—Limited liability partnership is unable to pay its debts;

4. Anti national acts—Limited liability partnership has acted against the interests of sovereignty and integrity of India, security of state or public order;

5. Default—Limited liability partnership has committed default in filing with the Registrar the Statement of Accounts and Solvency or annual return (u/s 34 and 35) for five consecutive financial years;

6. Just and Equitable Ground—In the opinion of the Tribunal it is just and equitable to wind up the limited liability partnership.(for the meaning of the term 'just and equitable', the topic of dissolution of firm may be referred.)

LAW OF CONSUMERISM

Introduction

Prior to passing of this enactment in India, consumers as a class were a neglected section of the society. Manufacturers of consumer goods and the traders in the market were exploiting consumers. Buyers are on a weaker footing and those are mostly unorganized. An individual consumer in our society is hesitant to assert and enforce his rights. Consumers are the victims of the unfair trade practices of businessmen. In this scenario codifying law relating to consumer protection in 1986 was received like a boon. There are the other laws regulating commercial relationship between consumers and traders/manufacturers. But in those laws consumer protection is not a focul point, their interests are protected incidently. The book specifically sets out the important provisions of the Consumer Protection Act, 1986.

Chapter 41 | THE CONSUMER PROTECTION ACT, 1986

The Consumer Protection Act (CPA) came into force on April 15, 1987. This Act is a comprehensive legislation regarding consumer protection. Salient features of the Act are enlisted below.

Silent Features of the Act

This Act is a comprehensive legislation regarding consumer protection. Sailent features of the Act enlisted below.

1. The Act is benevolent piece of legislation to protect large body of consumers.
2. It has wide scope and applicability covering private, public and co-operative sectors;
3. Its main object is to promote and protect rights of consumers;
4. It recognizes class action suits. Class actions compliants enables consumer groups having same interests to seek remedies, even government can represent consumer;
5. It recognizes and confers various (statutory) rights on consumers;
6. It provides effective administrative machinery (Consumer Protection Councils) to promote and protect rights of consumer. Education and redressal are two important aspects of the Act;
7. Elaborate Three-Tier System (Consumers Disputes Redressal Agencies) to settle the consumer disputes and the incidental matters has been established under the Act; This quasi judicial machinery is empowered to give relief of compensation and penalties for non-compliance;
8. The procedure adopted by Redressal Agencies is simple, summary and speedy. It is cheap as there is no need to engage a lawyer or pay court fees;
9. Manufacturers are made accountable for defects and deficiencies;
10. The Act discourages frivolous and vexatious complaints;
11. Provisions of the Act are in addition to and not in derogation of (contrary to) the provisions of other laws.

41.1 Important Definitions

The terms used in the Act are to be interpreted as defined in section (2). Terms otherwise general have special meaning in CPA, 86.

Explanation of important terms frequently used under the Act — The explanation is based on the definitions of these terms given in the Act.

1. **Complainant (Sec. 2-1-b)** - Complainant means any of the following category and who has made a complaint under the Act –

   a. A consumer or;

   b. Any voluntary consumer association registered under the Companies Act, 1956 or under the law time being in force or

   c. The Central or the State Government or

   d. On or more consumers where there are numerous consumers having the same interests or

   e. In case of the death of consumer, his legal heir or representative.

   The term has been given wide connotation in the Act. The definition covers not only the individuals but the consumer organization also. Even the government may file a compliant to advance the cause of consumers. Consumers may have a common cause of action, but may not come together. Anybody can represent a class of such consumers and approach the court as a complaint. Public inertest litigation (class actions) for redressal of consumer grievance is entertained as a matter of routine.

2. **Complaint (Sec. 2-1-c)** - Complaint means a written allegation made by a complainant. The complaint should be relating to any of the following -

   a. Adoption of unfair trade practice or restrictive trade practice by any trader or service provider;

   b. Defects in the goods purchased or agreed to be purchased ;

   c. Deficiency in services availed or agreed to be availed ;

   d. Charging excess price i.e. in excess of the price –

   – fixed by law or displayed on the goods or any package or on the price list of the trader or under the law or

   – agreed between the consumer and the trader.

   If the price is not fixed by law or displayed as mentioned above, the price /charges is a matter settled by the parties. In that case there cannot be a complaint that price or service charges are not money's worth.

   e. Offer of sale of hazardous goods to the public (i.e. goods which are hazardous to life and safety)

   – If offer is in contravention of safety standards laid down by any law or

   – If the trader could have known with ordinary care about the dangerous nature of goods;

   f. Offer of sale of hazardous services to the public.

   Actual knowledge of the trader regarding dangerous nature of goods is not necessary. If he could have, with reasonable diligence, known that the goods are hazardous, would be sufficient ground for a complaint. The rule also applies in case of offer of dangerous services. The purpose of inclusion of this type of allegation in the definition of complaint is to protect the public/consumers from possible risks to their lives.

3. **Consumer (Sec. 2-1-d)** This is the crucial term under the Act. Analyzing the definition of the word, one can understand the concept as under.

Who is a consumer?   Following persons are included in the expression 'consumer'.
a. Buyer, buying the goods for consideration;
b. Users of goods with buyer's consent;
c. A person availing or hiring services for consideration;
d. Beneficiaries of such services with the consent of the hirer.

It would be revealed that the term 'consumer' is used in the context of sale or purchase by individuals or availing of services in the market. Payment of consideration is a must. The consideration for goods or services may be fully or partly paid or promised to be paid in full or in part or under any system of deferred payment for example, hire purchase.

Who is not a consumer? The term consumer does not include the persons mentioned below.
a. Person obtaining the goods without consideration (donee under a gift);
b. Person availing services free of charge;
c. Person-obtaining goods for re-sale or commercial purposes;
d. Person availing services for any commercial purposes.

In Gurudwara, in Langar, free catering services, food is provided. In some hospitals free treatment is given. The persons benefitting these services are not consumers.

If the goods are bought for re-sale or services are hired for commercial purposes, the purchaser or hirer cannot be called as consumer. What is emphasized is that the transaction should not be profit motivated or a part of economic activity. Person should buy a commodity for his personal use. If someone is purchasing goods and uses those in commercial activity to earn his livelihood, he is regarded as a consumer. If an individual purchases camera for his personal use, he is a consumer but a studio-owner purchasing ten cameras for selling through his shop is not covered in the definition.

Patients who are treated by doctors are consumers. Not only that, the parents of a child-patient availing doctor's services are also consumers. The term includes beneficiary of services,[113] subscriber/member of a provident fund scheme,[114] subscriber of a telephone,[115] user of electricity,[116] a person registering for lpg connection,[117] a passenger travelling in a train with ticket are held as consumers. A medical practitioner purchasing an ultrasound scanner for the purpose of his hospital is a consumer. [118]

113. *Spring Meadows Hospital v/s Harjit Ahuluwalia 1998(2) SCALE 456*
114. *Commissioner v/s Shivkumar Joshi(1999) AIR SCW 4456*
115. *District Manager, Telephones, Patna v/s Lalitkumar Bajla (1989)*
116. *Y. N. Gupta v/s DESU 1992,*
117. *Mohindra Gas Enterprises v/s Jagdish Poswal (1992)*
118. *Kodi Elcot Ltd v/s Dr. C. P. Gupta (1995)*

4. Defect (Sec. 2-1-f) - The goods should be of the following nature and should satisfy following requirements to come within the phrase.

a. Defect means any fault, imperfection, or shortcoming;

b. Such a fault etc. should be in the quality, quantity, purity, or standard.

c. Quality etc. are to be required to be maintained by or under any law or it should have been claimed by the trader or under any contract.

> The clause defines default in very general terms and states where defect should lie. If 500 ml bottle contains 470 ml liquid (any drink, oil etc.) or the goods do not possess required purity (say gold with hallmark, food item with permissible limits), goods are defective. Certain goods (eatables or drugs) should possess standard certified by marks (like Agmark, ISI mark etc.) given by approved apex associations, failing which goods are presumed to be below standard and hence defective.

5. Deficiency (Sec. 2-1-f) - This definition is more or less similar to the definition of 'defect' in goods. The word is linked with services.

a. It means any fault, imperfection, or shortcoming or inadequacy.

b. Fault etc. should be regarding quality, nature and manner of performance of service

c. Quality etc. in service is required to be maintained by or under any law or under any contract.

6. Service (Sec. 2-1-o) - Following points would elaborate the concept of 'service'

a. Service implies service of any description available to a potential user.

b. It includes the provision of facilities in connection with the following —

   Banking, financing, insurance, transport, processing, supply of electricity   or other energy, boarding or lodging or both, housing construction, amusement.

c. The section does not limit the definition to abovementioned servicees only. The list is illustrative. The services of similar kind may be covered by the Act.

d. The **term does not include** rendering of any service free of charge or under a contract of personal service. Contract of personal service covers the services rendered by employee to his employer. When the hirer of services has control over the work of the person offering services, the service is personal in nature. Services provided in private capacity is are not covered by the definition.[119] The definition applies to services rendered by the medical practitioners in private hospitals.[120] but the services provided by the Government hospitals free of charge fall outside the interpretation.[121] The definition applies to free services for maintenance of the machinery during the warranty period.[122] While it has no application to the construction, maintenance and cleaning of drain or drainage works by municipal corporation as it was held to be in

119. *A.C.Modagi v/s Cross Well Tailor(1991)*

120. *Cosmopolitan Hospital v/s Smt Vasanta P. Nair*

121. *Consumer Unity and Trust Society (CUTS) v/s State of Rajathan (1989)*

122. *Vishwa Jyoti Printers v/s Molins of India (1992)*

discharge of sovereign functions.[123] The sevices provided by the Banks, Financial Institutions, Insurance Companies, transport companies (carriage by air, road, water, goods or passanger transport) electricity distribution agencies, owners of the lodges, hotels, theatres are included in the concept of services.

7. **Unfair Trade Practice -** (2-1-r) — The idea of unfair trade practice is important from practical point of view.. The students would recollect that consumer has a right against exploitation from unfair trade practice/restrictive trade practice. The Act has taken cognizance of such unscrupulous or deceitful practices to defraud consumers and attempts to curb those practices in any possible form. The definition is inclusive in the sense that any foul practice which is unfair and injurious to consumers' interests can be prevented. Unfair trade practice is any unfair method or deceptive practice of the following nature. As per the definition, unfair trade practice should be adopted for the purpose of promoting the sale, use or supply of any goods or services. The term includes following practices—

1. Practice of making false statements (representations) which amount to —
   i) False representation concerning standard, quality, quantity, grade, composition, style or model of goods;
   ii) False representation concerning standard, quality, grade of any services;
   iii) False representation that old, second hand, rebuilt, renovated or reconditioned goods are new goods;
   iv) False representation as to sponsorship/approval/performance/characteristics of goods or services, when in fact, the goods or services do not have such approval etc..;
   v) False representation that seller has a sponsorship/approval or affiliation of another organization;
   vi) False or misleading representation concerning need or utility of any goods or services;
   vii) False warranty or guarantee of performance of any product or goods without any adequate or proper test;
   viii) Misleading warranty or guarantee of any product or goods or services or misleading promise to replace, repair an article or repeating/continuation of services;
   ix) Materially misleading public regarding ordinary/normal sale price of goods or ordinary/normal charges of services fetched or charged generally in relevant market.

2. Fake advertisements as to bargain price
Permitting fake advertisements for the supply of goods or services at a bargain price without intention to actually sell or supply at that bargain price;

3. Free Gifts Offer Schemes
   • Offering gifts, prizes or other items without intention to provide them;

---

123. *Signet Corporation v/s Commissioner of Municipal Corporation of Delhi (1997)*

- Creating an impression that goods or services are given or offered free of charge when the consideration of such items is covered in the transaction;
- Conducting any contest, lottery, game of chance or skill for the purpose of promoting the sale, use or supply of any goods or services or business interests.
- When the scheme offering gifts, prizes or other items free of charge is closed, withholding from the participants the information of final results of the scheme;

4. **Sale of dangerous goods** —Knowingly permitting sale or supply of goods or services intended to be used by consumers when goods or services do not comply safety standards prescribed by the competent authority;

5. **Hoarding or destruction of goods** — Permitting hoarding or destruction of goods or refusal to sell the goods to raise the cost of those or similar goods, same criterion applies to refusal to provide services to raise the costs;

6. **Manufacture of spurious goods** —Manufacture of spurious goods or offering such goods for sale or adopting deceptive practices in providing services. Spurious goods or services means such goods or services which are claimed to be genuine when in fact, those are genuine

To summarize, unfair trade practice includes false representation regarding goods or services, false advertisements, launching fake offers or gifts scheme for promotion of sale and thereby duping consumer community.

8. **Restrictive Trade Practice** - (2-1-nnn) -This practice has a tendency to manipulate prices or conditions of delivery of goods suited to traders' interests. Such a practice restricts the free flow of goods or services in the market. This leads to imposition of unwanted/unnecessary costs or restrictions. Restrictive trade practice includes the following :

a) Making delay (beyond agreed period) in supply of goods or providing services which leads to rise in the price; A trader treacherously waits for increase in prices, till then deliberately delays delivery and sells at enhanced prices. This harms the economic interests of the consumer.

b) Putting a condition precedent to purchase, hire or avail 'A' type of goods/services (not required by the consumer) if he wants to purchase/avail 'B' type of goods or services. Some of the gas dealers are compelling purchase of gas stove if they want a new LPG connection.

Chapter 42

CONSUMER PROTECTION COUNCILS
(Secs. 4 TO 8)

In consonance with the object of protection of consumer rights, the Act makes provisions for consumer protection Councils at central, state and district levels.

42.1 Central Consumer Protection Council - Establishment and Composition

This council is established by the Central Government. It consists of a chairman and official and non-official members. These represent interests of various sections of the society. The Minister in charge of Consumer Affairs in Central Govrnment shall be the chairman of the Central Council. Other members include Minister of State of Civil Supplies (vice-chairman), Minister of Food and Civil Supplies, Members of Parliament, Commissioners of Scheduled Castes and Scheduled Tribes, Non-Government Consumer Organizations, representatives of women, farmers. Secretary of the Department of Civil Supplies shall be the Member - Secretary of the Central Council.

42.2 State Consumer Protection Council

Establishment and Composition - The State Government shall establish the State Councils. Its composition follows the pattern of Central Consumer Protection Council. Councils consist of Chairman and official and non-official members. The members are nominated by the State Govrnment. Its objects are enlisted in Sec. 6 (Rights of consumers).

42.3 District Consumer Protection Councils.

(Sec. 8 - A has been inserted by Amendment to the Act in 2002).
The State Govrnment is empowered to establish the Councils at district level. The Collector is the ex-officio Chairman of this Council. Other members are nominated by the State Govrnment. Object of all these Councils is to promote and protect consumer rights.

42.4 Objects of Consumer Protection Councils and Rights of Consumers (S. 6)

The Consumer Protection Act provides statutory recognition to consumer rights. Object of the Consumer Protection Councils is to promote and protect the rights of consumer. These are enlisted below.

1. **Right to protection or safety**

   Right to protection or safety against marketing of hazardous goods. In this new innovative world many goods are marketed. Chemicals, drugs, engineering works, electronic goods, inflammable liquids may be inherently dangerous to handle and use by buyers. This right ensures safely from such possible risks.

2. **Right to information**

   Right to be informed about quality, quantity, purity and price of goods. The purpose is to protect the consumers against the unfair trade practices. Well informed buyer can choose articles in a better way. Buyer therefore for his satisfaction must know what he purchases. Caveat emplor (buyer beware) and right-to information are therefore complimentary. This right introduces transparency and accountability in commercial transactions.

3. **Right to choose/access**

   Right to choose the goods or services in the market. This implies right to access to commodities at competitive prices so that the consumer is not exploited. Monopoly and competition in the market are sworn enemies. Competition is desirable as it provides choice. Act encourages competition and disowns monopoly.

4. **Right of hearing**

   Right to be heard , to be represented and to be assured that consumers interests will receive due consideration at appropriate forum.

5. **Right of redressal**

   Right to be redressed against the unfair trade practice or restrictive trade practice or unscrupulous exploitation of consumers. Right of hearing and redressal are ensured by establishing consumers disputes redressal agencies. Reliefs are provided u/s 14 of the Act.

6. **Right to education**

   It implies right to the knowledge of facts affecting his judgment as a consumer. Consumers Protection Councils make efforts for spreading awareness about their rights. Nationwide seminars, symposia are organized to discuss consumer issues. Their advertisements on media channels caution consumers against frauds and unfair practices by the traders.

   At international level 'right to environment' is also regarded as consumer right but section six is silent on that.

Chapter 43 | CONSUMER DISPUTES REDRESSAL AGENCIES

One of the objects of the Act, as set out in its preamble , is to provide machinery for redressal of consumer grivances. Accordingly the Act has made provisions for a three-tier system for settlement of consumer disputes. The aggrieved consumers can seek various remedies by approaching proper forum. The Act attempts to provide a simple, inexpensive and expeditious system for remedying the infringement of consumer rights.

Consumer Disputes Redressal agencies are working at three levels. those are -

1. **Consumer Disputes Redressal Forum at District** State level known as **"District Forum"**;
2. **Consumer Disputes Redressal Commission** at State level known as **"State Commission"** and
3. **National Consumer Disputes Redressal Commission** at Central level known as **"National Commission"**

The provisions regarding their composition, functioning etc. are discussed below.

43.1 District Forum

The state government is empowered to establish the District Forum in every district. If necessary, it can also establish more than one District Forum.

a. **Composition** - Sec. --
District Forum consists of a President and two other members. Out of two, one is a woman. The President is qualified to be a District Judge and other two members appointed are persons of ability , integrity , and standing. These should have adequate knowledge or experience in dealing with problems relating to law , economices , commerce, industry, public administration etc.

b. **Jurisdiction** - Sec. 11 -
District Forum shall have jurisdiction to entertain complaints where the value of the goods or services and the compensation claimed does not exceed rupees **20 lakhs** /

(w. e. f. 15 .3.2003). Question often arises as to where to file complaint. Further the District Forum must have local jurisdiction to decide the complaint. If both the complainant and opponent reside in a district, that District Forum has the power to hear the matter. **If opponent stays outside the district,** then for local jurisdiction (for a District Forum where complaint is filed) following criterion is applied —

— Where the opponent (opposite party) or each opponent at the time of institution of the complaint, actually and voluntarily resides or carries on business or personally works for gain in the district or

— One of the opponents (in case of more opponents) at the time of institution of the complaint, actually and voluntarily resides or carries on business or personally works for gain in the district provided, permission of District Forum is obtained or the opponents outside the local limits acquisc in such filing of the complaint in that district or

— The cause of action, wholly or in part, arises in that district.

c. **Manner of filing complaint** - Sec. 12 -

Complaint may be filed by the complainant as defined earlier. It can be personally filed or sent by post. Technicalities of filing a civil suit are dispensed with and institution of a complaint is made easier.

d. **Procedure to deal with complaint** - (Sec. 13) -

Procedure on receipt of a complaint differs in view of the nature of allegations i. e. defect in goods or deficiency in service or need of testing the sample of goods. The relevant provisions are elaborated as under.

1. (S. 13-1-a) - A copy of the complaint would be referred to the opponent within 21 days from the date of its admission. The opponent would be advised to submit his explanation within a period of 30 days. The District Forum may extend this period for not more than 15 days.

2. (S.13-1-b) - The opponent may deny or dispute the allegations made in the complaint or omits or fails to represent his case, within the time allowed. The District Forum would then settle the depute by adopting the procedure mentioned below.

A) **Procedure in respect of goods requiring testing or analysis -**

When the complaint involves allegations of defects in goods, and if the defect is to be ascertained by testing or analysis following procedure is followed.

i) (S. 13-1-c) - **Sampling Goods** – The District Forum shall obtain the sample of goods from the complainant, seal it and authenticate it by witnesses.

ii) **Reference of sample to the laboratory -** The sample shall be sent to authorized and appropriate laboratory with two directions viz –

– To analyze / test the sample to know whether it is defective.

– To submit its report within a period of 45 days from the date of reference. This period may be extended by the District Forum.

iii) (S. 13-1-d) - **Cost of analysis -** Analysis requires fees. District Forum may direct to complainant to deposit fees to forum's credit to pay it to the laboratory for testing purpose. The amount thus deposited shall be remitted to the laboratory by forum.

iv) (S. 13-1-e) - **Report of Analyst** – The District Forum shall sent a copy of the report received from the analyst to the opposite party.

v) (S. 13-1-f) - Any party to the dispute may object the correctness of –

– The findings of the laboratory or

– The manner of tests or analysis adopted by the laboratory.

In that case District Forum would invite written objections of the party challenging the finding.

vi) (S. 13-1-g) - The Forum would further hear both the parties on the report and issue appropriate order pertaining to the report. Thereafter the District Forum shall pass final orders in the form of reliefs u/s 14 of the Act.

B) (S. 13-2) - **Procedure when complaint relates to goods but above procedure cannot be followed or where complaint relates to services.**

i) (S. 13-2-a) - A copy of the complaint would be referred to the opponent within 21 days from the date of its admission. The opponent would be advised to submit his explanation within a period of 30 days. The District Forum may extend this period for not more than 15 days.

ii) (S. 13-2-b) - The opponent may deny or dispute he allegations made in the complaint or omits or fails to represent his case, within the time allowed. The Distric Forum would then settle the depute by adopting the procedure mentionaed below.

iii) (S. 13-2b-1) - Where the opponent contests the claim, the District Forum would assess the evidence led by both the parties and passes the order u/s 14.

iv) (S. 13-2b-2) - Where the opponent party omits or fails to represent, the District Forum would proceed ex-party (in absence of the party) and arive at a decision on the basis of complainant's evidence.

Other provisions

1. **Dismissal for default -** (S. 13-3)
   If complainant himself fails to appear before the District Forum, the District Forum may dismiss the complaint for default or decide the complaint on its merits.

2. **Speedy Disposal -** (S. 13-3-A)
   Every complaint shall be heard by District Forum as expeditiously as possible and efforts should be made to decide it within **three months** from the date of receipt of notice by the opposite party, where goods do not require testing or analysis and if commodity requires testing or analysis, within **five months**. District Forum should not ordinarily grant adjournment except on sufficient grounds and such grounds or reasons to be recorded by the forum. Costs for such adjournment may also be granted to the other party by the District Forum.

3. **Interim order -** (S. 13-3-B)
   During the pendency of the proceedings, the District Forum is empowered to pass just and proper interim orders to meet the ends of justice.

Remedies available to consumers (Sec. 14)

The Distric Forum conducts the proceedings as per section 13 of the Act. After the conclusion of the hearing, the District Forum passes appropriate orders. The defect or defects must be proved to his satisfaction. District Forum may pass any order or issue any direction of the following nature. These are the remedies available when consumer rights are violated.

1. Removal of defects in the goods;
2. Replacement of defective goods with new goods of similar description;
3. Return of the price or service charges to the consumer;
4. Payment of compensation for the loss or injury suffered by the consumer due to the negligence of the other party. The District Forum may also inflict punitive damages if the circumstances so demand;
5. Removal of deficiency in the services in question;
6. Discontinuation of unfair trade practice and restrictive trade practice or a direction not to repeat the same;
7. Prohibition on manufacture of hazardous goods;
8. Prohibition on offer of sale of hazardous goods;
9. Withdrawal of hazardous goods from being offered for sale;
10. Prohibition on offer of services of hazardous nature;
11. Payment of an amount, besides compensation, if a large number of consumers suffer loss or injury owing to defect or deficiency; This sum should not be less than 5 % of the value of the goods or services proved as defective. The amount would be utilized for the benefit of the affected consumers.
12. Order to issue corrective advertisements to undo the effects of misleading advertisement. The cost of such corrective advertisements would be borne by the defaulter;
13. Costs of the proceedings may be awarded to the parties.

Powers of District Forum (Sec. 13- 4 & 5)

District Forum shall be deemed to be civil court for the purpose of sec - 195 and Chapter XXVI of Cr. P. C., 1973. The proceedings before District Forum are treated as judicial proceedings u/Ss 198 and 225 of I. P. C., 1908. District Forum enjoys following powers.

i) Summoning and enforcing attendance of defendant or witness, examining them on oath;
ii) Discovery and production of any document / object, material used as evidence;
iii) Reception of evidence on affidavits;
iv) Requisitioning report of analysis, testing samples from analysts;
v) Issuing commissions for examination of witnesses;
vi) Any other matter prescribed.

An appeal to State Commission

Any person aggrieved by the order of the District Forum may prefer an appeal against such order to the State Commission. The time limit for such an appeal is 30 days from the date of the order. The delay in filing the appeal may be condoned by the State Commission on showing sufficient cause. In case of appeal, the appellant has to deposite fifty percent of the amount awarded or Rs. 25000 whichever is less. Without such deposit, appeal would not be entertained.

43.2 State Commission

i) **Composition** - Sec. 16 -
State Commission consists of a Chairman and two other members. Judge of a High Court is qualified to be the Chairman. Appointment of chairman is made by the State Government in consultation with the Chief Justice of the High Court. Regarding two members, provisions are similar to that of District Forum.

ii) **Jurisdiction of State Commission** - The State Commission has original and appellate jurisdiction. The State Commission shall have jurisdiction to entertain.
   a) **Pecuniary Jurisdiction** – Complaints where the value of the goods or services and the compensation if claimed, exceeds Rs.20 lakhs but **dose not exceed Rs.One Crore** (w.e.f.15.3.2003).
   b) **Appellate Jurisdiction** – Appeals against the orders of the District Forums within the state.

iii) **Procedure followed by State Commission -**
The State Commission shall dispose off the consumer disputes (in its original jurisdiction) according to the provisions contained in sections 12, 13 and 14 applicable to District Forum. The procedure to deal with consumer complaint followed by District Forum and State Commission is thus same.

iv) **Appeal -**
Appeal against the orders of State Commission shall be preferred to the National Commission. The period of limitation is 30 days from the date of order of the State Commission. Delay in filing the appeal may be condoned by the National Commission if sufficient cause for delay is shown.

43.3 National Commission

National Commission is the apex consumer redressal agency working at national level.
i) **Composition:** The National Commission consists of —
   a) Chairman- Appointed by the Central Government in consultation with the Chief Justice of the Supreme Court of India. He must be qualified to be the judge of the Supreme Court.
   b) Four other members - Criterion for nomination of these members is the same as that of the other members of District Forum or State Commission.

ii) **Jurisdiction -**
The National Commission has both original and appellate jurisdiction. It can entertain.-

a) Complaints where the value of goods or services and the compensation if any, claimed **exceeds Rs. One crore** (w. e. f. 15.3.2003) and

b) Appeals against the orders of the State Commission.

Power to call for records and proceedings

The State Commission and National Commission have the power to call for the record and pass appropriate orders in any consumer dispute pending before lower court. This power is excercised when--

i) The forum below excercises jurisdiction when it is not vested in it, or

ii) has failed to excercise it so vested or

iii) has acted in excercise of its jurisdiction illegally or with material irregularity.

Appeal to Supreme Court (Sec. 23) –

The appeal against any order made by the National Commission in its original or appellate jurisdiction may be preferred to the Supreme Court of India. The limitation period for such an appeal is 30 days from the date of the order. Delay in filing appeal may be condoned by the Supreme Court if there is a sufficient reason for not filling the appeal within that period. The appellant has to deposit 50% of the amount ordered to be paid by National Commission or Rs. 50,000 whichever is less. The Supreme Court would not entertain appeal without such deposite in the Supreme Court.

Power and Procedure of National Commission

The National Commission shall dispose off the complaints or any proceedings by excercising powers of civil court and following the procedure prescribed by the Central Council. The National Commission may grant any relief or pass any order under Sec. 14 of the Act.

Sec. 24 Finality of orders

Every order of a District Forum, State Commission or the National Commission shall, if no appeal has been preferred against such order under the provisions of the Act, be final. (Sec. 24 A).

Limitation Period – Every complaint under this Act to the District Forum or State Commission or National Commission should be filed within a period of 2 years from the date of cause of action for such complaint. If the forum or commission is satisfied that there was a sufficient cause for not filling the complaint within the limitation period, then the delay can be condoned and the compaint may be entertained after 2 years.

Consumer Dispute Redressal Agencies

	CDR FORUM	CDR Commission Commission	National CDR
	(District Forum)	(State Commission)	(National Commission)
Established by	State Government	State Government	Central Government
Composition	President + 2 other members (maximum- as prescribed)	President + minimum 2 members (maximum- as prescribed)	President + minimum 4 members
	(one member is invariably a woman)		
Jurisdiction – Local	District	State	Nation
Pecuniary (Value of goods/ services +compensation)	Upto 20 lakhs	More than 20 lakhs upto one crore	Exceeding one crore
Appellate Jurisdiction	–	Appeals against orders of District Forum and to call for records of District Forum	Appeals against orders of State Comission and to call for records of State Comission

Part VII

Questions and hints for answers

1. Explain sailent features of CPA, 1986, TYBcom, 2013, BBM(IB) 2012.

   "The Consumer Protection Act, 1986 provides cheap and expeditious remedy to the consumers." Critically comment on the statement in the light of the provisions of Act. — PGDBM 2004, P. U.

2. Defind and explain the following terms under Consumer Protection Act, 1986. Complaint; Complainant; Defect in goods & Deficiency in services, Consumer Disputes – MBA 2003 P. U. DBM 2004. BBA 2011, BBM(IB)2013 Ans. Chapter 41.

3. Who is a 'Consumer'? What are his rights under the Consumer Protection Act, 1986? Explains. MBA 2004 P. U. (With Remedies) PGDBM 2004 P. U. (Rights).

4. State of procedure adopted by the District Consumer Redressal Forum for dealing with consumer complaints. TYBcom 2013, BBA 2013 — Ans. 43.1 (d)

5. State the provisions of the Consumer Protection Act, 1986 relating to composition, jurisdiction and working of District Forum. — Ans. 43.1 (in brief) PGDBM 2004 P. U. BBA 2012, BBM (1B) 2011.

6. State the provisions of the Consumer Protection Act, 1986 relating to composition, jurisdiction and working of State & National Commission. — BBA, 2010, TYBcom 2012, 2009 Ans. 43.2 & 43.3 respectively. MBA 2003 P. U., DBM 2005 P. U.

7. Explain the rights and remedies of Consumer under CPA, 86 - BBA 2008, BBM(IB) 2012

   Consumer protection Councils — DBM 2005 P. U.

   State Commission Councils — DBM 2004 P. U., Unfair Trade Practice

PART - VIII

THE COMPANIES ACT, 2013

Corporations have touched every walks of life. This is an age of globalization and we occasionally interact with corporate sector as it is more challenging and rewarding. Incorporated Company, being a legal person can conduct its business on a large scale with public support and under the shelter of law. Directors, managers of the company, employees there in must know the legal framework within which company's activities are confined. This part elucidates the provisions of Indian Companies Act, 1956 dealing with important aspects of company such as incorporation, its important documents, share capital and few doctrines.

The new Companies Act, 2013 has repealed the old Companies Act of 1956. The new Act is wider in scope, introduces more flexibility and minimizes government control. The Act is keen on protection of public funds and the interests of investors. Stringent penalties are provided for fraud. It relies on self regulation but at the same time provides regulatory mechanism to deal with corporate matters in more efficient and expeditious manner. Considering the scope of this part all related provisions cannot be elaborated. Topics covered incorporate the changes introduced by the new Act.

Chapter 44	CONCEPT OF COMPANY

CONCEPT OF COMPANY

44.1 Definition, Meaning and Important Features

a) Definitions of Company -

Few important definitions of the term are reproduced below.

> **Justice Lindley -** *"A company is an association of many persons who contribute money or money's worth to a common stock and employ it in some trade or business and who share the profits and loss arising therefrom."*
>
> **Prof. Haney -** *"A company is an artificial person created by law, having separate entity, with a perpetual succession and a common seal."*
>
> **Chief Justice Marshall -** *"A company is a person, artificial, invisible, intangible and existing only in the eyes of law. Being a mere creation of law, it possesses only those properties which the charter of its creation confers upon it either expressly or as incidental to its very existence."* [124]

S.2 (20) Of the Companies Act, 2013 -

> *"A company means a company incorporated under this Act, unless the context otherwise requires"*

b) Meaning -

No single definition gives essential attributes of a company. Definition under the Act does not throw light on the concept. it merely states that company incorporated under Act is a company. Each definition highlights different aspects of a company. Though it is so, company in a very general sense implies as association of individuals with a common purpose either commercial or non-comercial. Organization of persons may carry on a business with agreement

---

124. *(Ref. Trustees or Darmouth College Vs Woodword, (1819) 17 US 518*

to share profits or losses. It can be formed to promopte art, science, culture or other charitable purpose. One peculiarity which emerges from most of the definitions is its artificial existence. Company is body corporate, created by law i. e. by process of incorporation. Unincorporated associations have no place in the concept of company though their activities are very much akin to existing companies.

44.2 Special Features of a Company

Various definitions of the term and the provisions of the Act reveal following important features of a company.

i) **Incorporation -**
Company is created by registration and incorporation according to the provisions of the Act. An unincorporated association is illegal association under the Act. Company thus comes into exsitence by operation of law. Though it is so, company is a non-statution body. It is not subjected to any statutory or public duty.[125]

ii) **Artificial Personality -**
Company is a legal, juristic, artificial person created by law. Though not a natural person, it acts through dirtectors as agents. It is not a citizen and hence cannot claim rights under the Constitution or the Citizenship Act. Company can enter into transactions as private individuals.

iii) **Seperate legal entity -**
By incorporation company acquires a status of legal personality distinct and separate from its members. Unlike partnership it is not a compendious term to denote collectively its constituents, share holders. Members/share holders in a way are the owners of company or they control affairs of the company but collectively they are not described as company. Company in itself is a legal person. Atributes of separate entity are explained in succeeding paras.

Capacity to sue and be sued
As a distinct person company can sue and be sued in courts of law.

Separate Property
Like natural persons, company can acquire, own, hold, dispose of property. It can have capital, assets in its own name.

iv) **Perpetual Succession -**
Company has a perpetual succession. It never dies. Death or insolvency of its members does not affect its existence. Changes in its composition may take place (like members may come in or go out) but company continues untill wound up according to law.

vii) **Common Seal -**
Company enjoys artificial personality under its own common seal which reflects its independant life and existance. All contracts of the company are under its seal. Common

---

125. *Ramsingh V/s Fetilizer Corporation of India - (1980) 50 comp. Cas. 553.*

seal like signature, authenticates and approves company's transaction. Affixing of seal is regulated by articies of the company.

vii) **Free Transferability of Shares -**
Transferability of shares with ease is a special feature of company. Transfer of shares is goverened by articles of association and those are transferred from person to person like goods. In private company transfer is subject to few restrictions.

ix) **Separation of Ownership and Management -**
The company is owned by its members but affairs of the company are managed by Board of Directores. Employees of the compnay implement the policies of the Board. The company represents classic example of seperation of ownership from management.

x) **Limited Liability of Shareholders -**
Shareholder shares in the captial of a company. Their liability is limited to the extent of their contribution in capital in case of winding up or liquidation. Their private property is not liable for company's debts. Limited liability is the reason behind large-scale investments in corporate sector.

Termination of Existence -
The company ceases to exist when it is wound up as per the relevant provisions.

44.3 Lifting (Piercing) the Corporate Veil.

Company is a legal person distinct from its members. As an artificial person, it possesses identity separate from the members composing it. Members may come and go, company continues as it has its own life and and perpetual succession. This dichotomy has been emphasized in a leading case of **'Saloman v/s Saloman & Co.'** [126]

Facts of the case- Saloman was a boot and shoe manufacturer. He incorporated a company named Saloman & Co. Ltd and entire running business was taken over by it. Saloman and his family members subscribed to its Memorandum of Association. He and two sons were directors of that comapny. Saloman's business was transferred to the company for £ 40,000. Saloman in consideration took 20,000 shares of £ 1 each and debentures of £ 10,000. Within one year of incorporation, company went into liquidation. The unsecured creditors in their claim pleaded that Saloman had mejority of shares of company, he was managing director and company was infact under his control. They contented that company was not having separate existence, it was a sham entity, Saloman being the person who managed everything. The court **held** that Saloman & Co. Ltd. had fulfilled all the statutory requirements and hence an independant, separate personality, having legal existence distinct from its directors or members.

Once the corporate personality is established, persons forming the company or managing the company affairs are to be disregarded in the sense that there is a veil between company and its members. In many cases as a matter of fact, company and its directors, members are one. Company in reality is a group of beneficial owners of the corporate assets / property. It is promoted to benefit few individuals. Sometimes company is formed as a cloak or camoflage to

126. *(1897) AC 22*

legalize illegal, fraudulent or inproper activities or to defeat the spirit of law. In such cases it becomes necessary to lift or pierce the veil and find out the reality. Courts investigate the actual state of affairs or true relationship lifting the corporate veil. Courts have to disregard the distinctness between company and its members. To probe into the matter, comapny's legal character is ignored. The principle of lifting the corporate veil is ordinarily applied to investigate into the following matters--

Grounds for lifting corporate veil

 i) Whether compny is formed with fraudulent design or to defeat the law or to evade tax liability; [127]

 ii) Probing into legality of objects / activities of the company;

 iii) True ownership of shares and controlling power is vested, with whom ?

 iv) True relationship between holding and subsidiary company.

 v) Mismanagement and oppression by of minority shareholders mejority;

 vi) Ownership and control by enemy national or enemy country. [128]

 vi) Incorporation of company to defraud creditors, to avoid legal obligations. [129]

 vii) Number and names of the members of a company

 viii) Detection of economic offences perpetrated by shams companies. [130]

 ix) Business of the company offending public policy. [131]

Piercing corporate veil in the matters like mentioned above, may reveal propriety of incorporation and may help to safeguard the interests of the public.

127. (Re. Dinshaw Mukherji Petit's case AIR 1927 Bom 371, Delhi Development Authority Vs Skipper Construction Co. Ltd.)
128. Daimler Co Ltd. Vs. Continental Tyre and Rubber Co. (1916-17) AIIER ref 191=
129. Gilford Motors Co. Vs Horne (1933) Ch 935
130. Shantanu Ray Vs Union of India.
131. Conners Bros Vs Conners, (1974)4 AIIER 179 PC

Chapter 45 | TYPES OF COMPANIES

Concept of company can be viewed from many more angles. Accordingly companies are classified on the basis of mode of creation, liability or public participation. Various types of companies are explained as under.

45.1 Chartered Companies

Companies incorporated by special Royal Charter issued by the King or Queen are called as chartered companies. These are old companies working in Foreign Contries. Their activities are regulated by the charter. Examples - East India Company ; Bank of England, Bank of Australia.

45.2 Statutory Companies

The companies formed and governed by special Statutes / Acts are known as statutory companies. Ordinarily public undertaking companies with object of public utility are statutory companies. Where special Act is silent over a particular matter, provisions of the Companies Act would apply.

Examples - RBI, SBI, UTI, LIC, Industrial Finance Corporation of India, State Trading Corporation etc. are the companies eshtablished under the statutes.

45.3 Registered Companies

Companies registered and incorporated under the Companies Act, 1956 or the new Act of 2013 are catagorised as 'Registered Companies.' The Act, company's memorandum of association and articles of association regulate their affairs. Registered companies may again may be classified on the basis or liability as follows.

i) **Company Limited by Shares - Sec. 2(22)** - These companies are of common type in India. Companies have a share capital and the member's liability is limited by memorandum to the extent of face value of their shares. During the existence of companies or in the event of winding up, unpaid arrears of shares can be recovered from the members. Such a company may be public or private company. The name of the company ends up with the words 'Ltd.'

ii) Company Limited by Guarantee - Sec. 2(21) -

Each member in this type of company undertakes to pay a fixed amount of money in the eventuality of liquidation of the company. Such an amount is utilised for payment of debts and liabilities of the company. The amount guaranteed in such company is its reserve capital and cannot be called upon except in the event of winding up. The amount guaranteed is mentioned in the memorandum and the whole or part of it can be called upon as per the exigencies. Companies may or may not have share capital. In companies limited by guaratee having share capital, the liability of member implies liability on unpaid amount of shares and also liability on amount guaranteed by him. Non-commercial companies incorporated to promote art, science etc. are generally limited by guarantee.

iii) Unlimited Company - Sec. 2 (92) -

Company with limited liability of a member is an unlimited company. When memorandum does not mention regarding limitation on liability or memorandum with no liability clause is construed as unlimited liability. Unlimited company may be private or public. It may or may not have share capital.

iv) Private Company - Definition-5.2 (68)

The essential Characterstics of a private limited company as defined in the Act are as follows.

a) The nature of this type of company is determined by articles of the company;

b) Right to transfer shares is restricted;

c) Number of members - Maximum number of members is 200 (Exception one person company). The number of members does not include present and past employee-members of the company. 2 or more numbers holding share jointly are regarded as one member.

d) It prohibits invitation to the public to subscribe for any shares or debentures of the company.

e) The company must have minimum paid up capital of one lakh rupees or higher than that as prescribed by its articles.

The above mentioned restrictions are mandatory in case of private limited company. The words 'private limited' should be used at the end of the company's name. A private limited company may be limited by guarantee, limited by shares or unlimited companies.

v) Public Company - According to Sec.(2) (71), all companies which are not private companies are called as public limited companies. The peculiarity of public limited company may explained as under.

a) It is not a private company

b) Seven or more members should form the company

c) Maximum number of members is unlimited

d) There is no restriction on transfer of shares

e) Public is invited to subscribe to its share capital

f) Minimum paid up capital in public company should be Rs. 5 lakhs or higher than this amount as prescribed by its articles.

Public companies can be of three types based on liability of members as in case of private limited.

See the Chart for distinction between public & private company.

vi) Government Companies - Definition u/s 2(45). Government company means any company in which not less than 51 percent of paid up share capital is held by the Central Government or by any State Government. or Governments or partly by Central and partly by one or more Government, and includes a subsidiary of a Government company.

Government comapny thus is a company registered and incorporated under the Act like any other company. Majority of its shares are held by the Government. Though it is so, it cannot be called as Government. As per Supreme Court's verdict it is a 'state' under Art. 12 of the Constitution of India considering the fact that it works like an instrument of Government with public purpose. It is wound up under the provisions of the Act. It may be a private limited company. Annual report and accounts of the Government company should be placed before both the Houses of Parliament or state legislatures, as the case may be, within 3 months of the annual general meeting. The auditor of the Government Company shall be appointed and re-appointed by the Central Government on the advice of Comptroller and Auditor General of India.

vii) Foreign Company - S.2(42) - A company which is incorporated outside India is a Foreign Company. The sections regarding Foreign Company also apply to companies which -
  i) establish place of business in India after commencement of this Act (1.4.1956) or
  ii) had place of business in India before 1.4.1956 and continued to have the place within India after 1.4.1956.
  In the following circumstances a company incorporated outside India is treated as company incorporated in India.
  i) Company is incorporated outside India;
  ii) Company has established place of business in India
  iii) Not less than 50% of paid up share capital of such a company is held by one or more citizens of India or one or more bodies corporate in India.
  iv) With regard to the business in India it should comply provisions as if it is incorporated in India.

The Foreign Company should submit important documents such as its memorandum of association, articles of association, balance sheets, profit loss statements within prescribed period and also furnish information regarding principal place of business in India, registered office, country of incorporation and alterations in above documents etc.

viii) Holding and Subsidiary Company - On the basis of control of management, companies can be classified into two catagories viz. holding and subsidiary company. Where a company controls another company (subsidiary) it is called a holding company [Sec.2(46)] Such a control over another company may be exercised as follows —

- control of composition of Board of Derectors of another company; or
- controls more than half of total voting power or
- holds more than half of nominal value of equity share capital of the other company or
- It is a subsidiary of any company which is the subsidiary of some other company.

A company is subsidiary of a holding company which is controlled by holding company in above manner. These two terms therefore are relative. Both the companies are distinct, independant companies.

ix) Licenced Company or Charitable Company - Sec. 8

These companies are basically registered and incorporated for promoting art, science, commerce etc. Many organisations desire to persue non-commercial activities. Those are registered as companies under the Act provided Central Government directs registration by a licence under section 8 of the Act. Such a licence is granted in the following situations.

- An association is about to be formed as a limited company for non-business activities and
- The association intends to prohibit payment of dividend to its members and to apply profits to achieve above objects.

The company is registered as company with limited liability without addition of words 'Private Limited.' It enjoyes the privileges of limited companies and subjected to its obligations under the Act.

x) One Man Company -

Where a single person holds almost all the shares of the company, the company is known as one man company. One man company apparently appears to be contradictory but this type of company fulfills all the requirements of registration and other provisions. Both private and public companies may be one man company. One man company is usually private company.

X) One Person Company (OPC)—

Definition-S.2 (62) 'One person company' means a company which has only one person as a member'.

Only natural person can incorporate OPC. A company or body corporate or foreign company or a government company cannot form OPC. It is a private limited company and has to comply the formalities of that company.

Advantages of OPC— Such companies have been given certain relaxation under the Act. They are privileged because of fewer disclosures. Holding general meetings including annual general meeting are dispensed with. Provisions in respect of voting, proxy, quorum of general meeting are not applicable. Liability of member is limited to the extent of his capital in his company. Considering these merits, OPC is regarded as a better and beneficial form of association.

Disadvantages—Increase in the number in OPC is not possible. There is a limited scope for raising the capital. Source of the deposits are limited. The Act is silent as to the procedural formalities for conversion of OPC into a private limited company.

XI) Small Company. Definition-S.2 (85) Small company means a company other than a public company,—

i) Paid up capital of which does not exceed rupees 50 lakhs or such higher amount as may be prescribed which shall not be more than rupees 5 crore; or

ii) Turn over of which as per its last profit and loss account which does not exceed rupees 2 crores or such higher amount as may be prescribed which shall not be more than rupees 20 crores;

Provided that nothing in this clause shall apply to –

a) A holding company or a subsidiary co;

b) A company registered under section 8;

c) A company or body corporate governed by any special Act.
OPC, private company and a company other than a public company can be a small company.

Advantages of Small Company—Lesser formalities are prescribed for small company. Government is empowered to grant relaxations to such company. like lesser disclosures, only two meetings in a year. There may not be the necessity of disclosure of cash flow statement. Though not all exemptions but few can be extended to small company under the Act of 2013. Additional benefits of the status of OPC or private company can be claimed by small company. Contractual mergers are possible without the intervention of the Tribunal in small company.

Disadvantages—Relaxations are contingent upon the government policies framed time to time.
Small company is not generally discharged from liabilities of OPC or private company. Depending upon exemptions, such companies can be discharged from liabilities.

XII) Associate Company—Definition-S.2 (6)— Associate company in relation to another company means a company in which that other company has a significant influence, but which is not a subsidiary company of the company having such influence and includes a joint venture company.

'Significant influence' connotes control of at least 20 % of total share capital or of business decisions under the agreement. Thus the control or influence of one company over another is determined by the agreement.

This is a new type of company introduced under the Act of 2013. This concept finds place with a view to bring more transparency and check abuse of corporate form. Object of the Act to provide a strong regulatory mechanism and governance is reflected by making provisions for associate company. One company may have many associate companies. The company, to which other is associated, is prevented from entering into certain transactions. The accounts of associates companies should be consolidated with the accounts of associated company.

Distinction between a Private Company & Public Company

Basis of Distiction.	Private Company	Public Company
1 Definition	Sec. 3 (2) (68) - company Restriction on number, transfer of shares, prohibition on public subscription	Sec. 2 (71)-Not a private No such restrictions invitation to public to subscribe
2. Members	Minimum - 2 maximum - 200	7 Unlimited
3. Subscription to memorandum of association & article of association	By 2 members	By 7 members
4. Minimum paid up capital	Rs. 1 lakh	Rs. 5 lakhs
5. Public Investment	Public not invited to invest in shares / debentures	Public is invited
6. Commencement of business	Commencement Certificate Required	Certificate not required
7. No. of Directors	Minimum 2 Maximum - 50.	Minimum 3 Maximum - no limit
8. Directors Director's Privileges	Not retired by rotation - Can borrow funds - Cannot occupy office of profit Remuneration unrestricted	Retire by rotation Cannot borrow except with Central Govt's permission. can occupy with sanction by special resolution. Remuneration subject to law
9. Statutory meeting, reports	Not mandatory	Mandatory
10. Quorum for meeting	2 members (subject to articles of association)	5 members
11. Special privileges	Enjoys certain privileges	No such privileges
12. Index of members	No need to maintain	Must be maintained
13. Transfer of shares	Restricted	Freely transferable

14. Share warrant	Cannot be issued	Can be issued
15. Deferred shares	Can be issued	Cannot be issued
16. Appeal agaist refusal to transfer shares	Right to appeal not available	Appeal to Central Government can be preferred
17. Restriction on Managerial remuneration	No restrictions	Total managerial remuneration should not exceed 11% of net profits.

Chapter 46 | INCORPORATION OF A COMPANY

Company is a company 'formed and registered' (incorporated) under the Act. Company takes birth and enjoys legal status as an artificial person by the process of incorporation. Incorporation therefore, assumes significance. Incorporation however is an extensive affair considering the time spent, documentations and number of formalities. Procedure for incorporation and its effects are discussed below.

Procedure for Incorporation

1. **Application for 'name' of the company**
   The promoters have to apply for approval of the company's proposed name. The application in the specific format, is to be made to the Registrar of Companies alongwith prescribed fees. This provision is made to avoid similarity of names of companies and possible misleading of the public.

2. **Mode of forming a company**
   For the formation of an incorporated company any 2 or more members of a private company or any 7 or more members of a public company should subscribe their names to memorandum of association and articles of associations of their company and comply with other provisions of the Act relating to registration and incorporation.

3. **Procedure for Registration**
   Application for registration in specific format should be made to the Registrar of the State alongwith prescribed fees and following documents--
   -- memorandum of association, articles of association, agreement of appointment of manager or managing director, if any, list of directors (alongwith their consent to work as directors) and declaration as to compliance of provisions, and rules regarding registration.

4. **Satisfaction of Registrar as to compliance**
   The office of the registrar scrutinizes the documents supplied alongwith application. If the registrar is satisfied that the procedure as to registration is complied with, he shall enter the name of the company and other documents in the register kept fot the purpose.

5. **Certificate of incorporation and its significance**

The Registrar issues certificate of incorporation in the name of the company. Company is born and its life commences on the issuance of certificate. Certificate of incorporation is a conclusive proof of the compliance regarding registration of the company. It is an evidence of the matters precedent, incidental to registration, fact of existence of a company as a body corporate. Validity of such a certificate cannot be called in question. This certificate however will not serve to legalise otherwise illegal objects / business of a company.

6. **Commencement of Business**

For a public company to start its business, 'certificate of commencement' issued by the registrar is necessary. Private companies can start their business directly after certificate of incorporation is obtained.

7. **Pre-incorporation Contracts**

The contracts entered into by the promoters prior to the formation the company are called as pre-incorporation contracts. Company as such can neither enforce nor bound by such contracts. But Sec. 15 and 19 of the Specific Relief Act, 1963 give certain remedies for enforcements of contracts by or against the company provided of course, the company ratifies the pre-incorporation contracts.

8. **Consequences of incorporation**

Refer point no 5 & 6 - Consequences of incorporation may be briefly stated as under-
  i) Company assumes legal personality;
  ii) It is independant & distinct from its members;
  iii) It enjoys perpetual succession;
  iv) It can commence business directly (private company) or after obtaining commencement certificate (public company)
  v) It can enter into contracts.

Chapter 47 | MEMORANDUM OF ASSOCIATION & ARTICLES OF ASSOCIATION

While incorporating a company, two important documents are required to be stamped, registered and filed with Registrar of Companies. The nature, contents and importance of these documents is discussed below.

47.1 MEMORANDUM OF ASSOCIATION

a) *Definition :*

'Memorandum' is defined under section 2 (56) of the companies Act, 2013 as

> *"Memorandum means Memorandum of Associations of a company as originally framed or as altered from time to time in pursuance of any provisions of previous company laws or of this Act."*

Other Definitions :

> **Lord Macmillan** - *"The purpose of Memorandum is to enable the shareholders, creditors and those who deal with the comapny, to know what is its permitted range of activities."*
>
> **Lord Cairns** - *"The Memorandum of associations of a company is its charter and defines the limitations of the powers of a company."*

b) Objectives and importance of Memorandum

Memorandum is one of the most important documents of a company which speaks about constitution, objects and activities of the company. It lays down the framework within which company functions. Company cannot go beyond that framwork. It sets out range of its activities and defines the powers of the company. Powers under Memorandum cannot be exceeded otherwise the act or transaction would be ultra-vives and void. Memorandum has two effects -- An affirmative when it lays down the ambit and extent of powers within which company has liberty to act and in the negative - that nothing shall be done beyond the scope. Memorandum of association is a public document and serves to inform the public, creditors, shareholders and outside world the state of affairs of the company, risk involved in dealing with it or its prospects. Memorandum is a charter governing the company. Company cannot be registered without this basic document.

c) Form of Memorandum

Various forms of memorandum are provided in Schedule I in different tables. Table A, B, C, D, E contain Memorandum for company limited by shares, company limited by guarantee without and with share capital and unlimited companies with or without share capital. The memorandum should be printed, divided into paragraphs, numbered consecutively and signed by each subscriber. Their addresses, occupation, designations in the company should be given in memorandum of association.

d) Contents of Memorandum of Association

Memorandum of Association is a document containing various clause in paragraphs furnishing basic information about the company. The memorandum gives details about name, office, object, capital structure, liability of the company.

1. Name Clause

The name of the company is to be approved by the Registrar of companies. It should not be similar to the names of other existing companies or undesirable or prohibited by the Central Government. Name and address of the company should be affixed outside the premises. In case of limited liability, 'Limited' or 'Private Limited' should be added to the name of the company.

2. Registered Office

A company should have a registered office on which notices, communications can be sent. Memorandum should specify the address and mention the State in which its registered office is located.

3. Object Clause

This clause assumes significance as it delimits the area of functioning of a company. Objects enlisted in the Memorandum should be --

-- Main objects;

-- Incidental or ancillary (supporting) objects necessary for fulfilment of main objects

-- Other objects of the company

The subscribers and creditors know about objects of the company and take an informed decision as to investment in the company. Validity of company's activities can be tested by this clause. When main objects fail, the company may be wound up by court's order.

4. Capital Clause

This clause should make a mention of authorised or nominal share capital of a company having share capital. Number of shares (with their kinds and values) in which share capital is divided should also be specified. In case of company limited by guarantee, amount guaranteed by each member should be mentioned. Shares taken by each subscriber to the Memorandum should be written against their names in Memorandum.

5. Liability Clause

Memorandum should state that the liability of members is limited if it is a company limited by guarantee or by shares. Memorandum should emphasize that in a company limited by guarantee, each member undertakes to contribute to the assets of the company in the eventuality of winding up to the extent of amount covered by their guarantee. The amount for the payment of debts and liability of the company, costs, charges, expenses of the winding up and adjustments of the rights of contributors.

6. Subscription or Association Clause

As previously stated, in case of private company minimum two and in public company minimum seven persons should subscribe to the Memorandum. Their subscription, (signatures) is to be attested by atleast one witness. (Each of the subscribers to the Memorandum should take at least one share.)Association clause in specific format should express desire of the subscribers to form the company and a commitment to take the number of agreed shares.

47.2 Articles of Association

a) Definition, Meaning and Nature

Definition - Sec. 2 (5) --

> *"Articles mean articles of association of a company as originally framed or as altered from time to time in pursuance of any previous companies law or of this Act."*

This definition, like the definition of memorandum of association dose not clarify the concept of article of association . The articles the regulations for the internal management of the company. These are the rules and regulations for the internal affairs of a company. Memorandum of association sets out the framework beyond which a company cannot traverse. Article of association sets the guidelines for conducting the business internally, within the framework. Articles, in importance, are subordinate to the memorandum.

Public company limited shares may or may not have Articles. But in the case of an unlimited company or a company limited by guarantee or a private company limited by shares, articles of association shall be signed by subscribers and registered with memorandum of association . It shall be printed, divided into paragraphs numbered consecutively. Articles should be signed by subscribers of memorandum of association and attested by atleast one witness whose address designation and occupation should be recorded.

b) Contents of Articles

As stated earlier articles are meant for internal management of the company affairs. They regulate relations of the members inter-se and relation between members vis-a-vis company. Articles must mention the number of members with which it is registered in case of unlimited company and company limited by guarantee.

Articles ordinarily contains the rules regarding the following —

i) Share capital & it alteration ;
ii) Calls, payment, transfer, lien, forfeiture of share certificates, warrants;
iii) Pre-incorporation contracts, ratification and execution thereof;
iv) Conduct and proceedings of meetings of company & Board of Directors;
v) Qualifications, appointments, powers, remuneration etc of directors;
vi) Borrowing powers, arbitration clause;
vii) Voting rights of members, regulation of voting;
viii) Audit, Accounts;
ix) Dividents, Reserves;
x) Winding up of company

In case of private limited company, the articles should provide for restriction on tranfer of shares, limiting number of members peculiar to that type of company. Articles should not affend any provision of the Act. Articles inconsistent with the Act are inoperative. If articles are silent on any matter, that matter is regulated by model articles. Model forms of articles in various types in schedule I are given below

Tables for model of Articles

Table for model Articles	Type of Company
F	Limited company having share capital
G	Company limited by guarantee without share capital
H	Company limited by guarantee with share capital
I & J	Unlimited company with or without share capital respectively

47.3 Doctrine of Ultra-Vires

Meaning

Literal meaning of 'Ultra-vires' means **'beyond powers or authority'**. When a comapany engages into any act which is beyond its power or authority, the act is ultra-vires the company. The ultra-vires acts, transactions, contracts are **void and inoperative.**
When company's acts are ultra-vires?
Acts which are within company's authority or power are called **'intra-vires'**. Such acts bind the company as against third parties. Act are said to be intra-vires when authorised by

i) Main objects, objects incidental;
ii) The Statute, the Companies Act.

Transactions, ventures beyond the scope of memorandum of association or the Act are regarded as ultra-vires. Acts which are not fairly and reasonably incidental to main objects are also ultra-vires.Doctrine of ultra-vires has been laid down in a landmark judgement in **Ashbury Railway Carriage and Iron Co. Ltd. vs Riche.**[132]

132. (1875) - L R 7 H L

Facts of the case : Company's object's were to manufacture, sell, lend or hire railway carriages and wagons and all kinds of railway plants, to carry on the *business of machanical engineers and general contractors* including allied activities. Company entered into a contract with Riche to finance the construction of a railway line in Belgium. The contract was ratified (approved) by the mejority of the shareholders of the company. Company later repudiated the contract. Riche claimed damages for alleged wrongful cancellation on the ground that contract was well within powers and objects of the company as company was doing the *business of 'general contractors'*.

Ruling : The court (Lord Cairnes) held that contract to finance the construction of railway line was ultra-vires the company. The phrase 'general contracts' was not given wide cannotation to include financing, though a railway line. The court further held that ultra-vires act is void - ab-initio (null and void from the beginging) and hence cannot be ratified. Once an act is void being ultra-vires, it cannot be made 'intra-vires, by ratification, estoppel, laches (delay), acquiscence.'

Company's act ultra-vires the Act - Any act in contravention of the Company's Act or exceeding authority under the Act is also void. Payment of divided out of capital, reducing share capital without complying provisions is ultra-vires the Act and hence ineffective.

Legal consequences of ultra-vires acts —

As stated earlier, ultra-vires acts are void-ab-initio. Such transactions are infructuous, inoperative creating no rights and liabilities. Those are not binding on the companies. Neither company can be sued nor it can sue on such acts. Court can grant injuction (prohibition) order restraining company from doing ultra-vires acts. Acts which are not fairly and reasonably incidental to main objects are also ultra-vires.

Acts ultra-vires the articles but intra-vires the memorandum - Not void-- such acts can be ratified by the company altering articles.

Director's acts / transactions - His acts ultra-vires his powers but intra-vires the articles can be subsequently adopted by the company. If director's acts are ultra-vires articles, such acts also can be given post-facto sanction. But director's acts ultra-vires the memorandum cannot be legalized in any manner.

A. Doctrine of Constructive Notice and Indoor Management.
Doctrine of Constructive Notice
Memorandum of association and articles of association of a company are filed and registered with Registrar of Companies. These are public documents. These are open and accessible to every person. Anybody can inspect those documents. It is therefore presumed that public has notice of such documents. Outsider or shareholder dealing with company is deemed to have notice of contents of these documents. He is presumed to have read and understood the contents and as such presumed to have 'constructive notice' of these documents. This doctrine of constructive notice is subject to an important *exception in the form of doctrine of 'indoor management'* which is explained below.

B. Doctrine of Indoor Management

Company is an artificial person. It acts through directors, agents. Manytimes directors purport to act as per Memorandum of association of a company and apparently within their authority but not according to the procedure or internal regulations. Doctrine of indoor management in such situations validates the acts of director protecting third party's interests.

According to the doctrine of constructive notice, any person dealing with the company is presumed to know memorandum of association or article of association but he is not bound to verify whether internal affairs of the company are conducted as per the articles of the company. Public documents are open for inspection but procedural compliance by company is not open for inspection. According to the doctrine of indoor management, a party dealing with company is entitled to assume that internal proceedings or domestic affairs are carried out in accordance with internal rules and regulations. He is supposed to know the contents of memorandum or article of association but not supposed to know the irregularities or non-compliance of formalities under articles. There is no presumption of notice of irregularity in company's affairs as against a third party.

Doctrine of indoor management was recognised and applied **Royal British Bank v/s Turquand,** known as **'Turquand Rule'**[133]

As per articles of the company the directors could borrow and give a bond to third party if authorised by a special resolution. The directors issued a bond to one Turquand without passing necessary resolution. The court held that the company was bound by the bond. Absence of actual authority was not an excuse for the company. Turquand was entitled to assume that such a resolution was passed. If the directors have powers and authority to bind company but certain formalities (preliminaries) are not complied before exercise of that power, the third party has a right to assume that directores are acting lawfully in all respects.[134] Company cannot escape liability under a transaction by showing some irregularity in compliance. It would be revealed that doctrine of constructive notice protects company while this doctrine protects third parties vis-a-vis companies. This doctrine is subject to following exceptions.

Exceptions

1) Knowledge of irregularity

Where a person dealing with the company has knowledge of irregularity (actual or constructive) of internal affairs affecting his transaction, the doctrine does not apply.

2) Ultra-vires acts

Where the dealing (act) is ultra-vires the memorandum of association, it is void-ab-initio hence it cannot be validated.

Ruben v/s Fingall Ltd.[135] Secretary of a company forged the share certificate and issued to a share holder under company's seal. As forgery conveys no title, the holder has no right on that certificate.

---

133. *177 (1856) 25 L. J. Q.*
134. *Premier Industrial BankVs Carlton Manufacturing Co. Ltd [(1909) K B 107)*
135. *1906 A C 439 H L*

3) Act outside apparent authority

When the act is, on the face of it, beyond the apparent authority of officer of a company, third party is not protected. An accountant of a company sold company's property. This transfer was held to be void as the purchaser ought to know that normally accountant has no authority to transfer company's property.[136]

4) Act beyond agent's authority

Company is not bound by the an act of its agent committed by exceeding his authority.

5) Negligence of third party

If a third party had the means of discovering the truth and in suspecious circumstance he could have revealed irregularities by making inquires, he would not be protected against company.

---

136. *Anand Behari Lal V/s Dinshaw and Company. AIR 1942 Oundh 417*

Chapter 48 | PROSPECTUS OF A COMPANY

Many times prospectus of companies is published in the newspapers. Public companies issue prospectus and invite the public to purchase shares and debentures. Prospectus is an informative document projecting the soundness of the company. It sets out prospects on which potential investors form opinion and take decisions as to investment in a company. Financial background, its undertakings, future programmes, nature of investment with risk factors are highlighted in the prospectus to induce the investors to subscribe.

48.1 Definition and Meaning

Sec. 2(70) of the Companies Act, 2013 defines prospectus as

"a prospectus means any document described or issued as prospectus and includes a red herring prospects, or shelf prospectes or any notice, circular, advertisement or other documents inviting deposits from the public or inviting offers from the public for the subscription or purchase of any securities of a body corporate."

From the definition, it reveals that following documents are including in the term —
  i)   Document described or issued as a prospectus
  ii) Red herring prospectes or shelf prospects
  iii) notice, circular, advertisement or other document inviting the members of public to deposit, subscribe or purchase securities in a company.
  Prospectus thus is a document aimed at securing capital by issue of shares / debentures.

Salient Features of Prospectus

1. **Written & signed document**
    Prospectus is a written document dated and signed by proposed or existing directors of the company or authorised agents. (5.26)

2. **Issued by public companies**
    It is issued by public companies and not by private companies.

3. **Invitation to the public**

   Important feature of the prospectus is that it is an invitation to public to offer for purchase of shares securities. Legally speaking it is an invitation to section of the public, selected members, etc. Communication to one party or private communication is not a prospectus. An invitation to relatives of family members or friends of the company management would not be regarded as prospectus.

4. **Contents of Prospectus - (Sec. 26)**

   A prospectus shall state the matters specified in Part I of the Schedule II and report specified in Part II of the schedule II (Subject to part III of Schedule II)

5. **Dating and Registration (Sec. 26)**

   Prospectus issued by intended or existing company must be dated. That date is deemed to be the date of its publication. It must be registered as per the provisions of company law.

6. **Deemed prospectus - (S.25)**

   It is also called as prospectus by implication. Any offer of sale of shares to the public shall be deemed to be prospectus. According to Sec. 26, any document containing offer of shares or debentures for sale shall be prospectus and all the provisions of prospectus shall apply to it also. Any document though not called as prospectus will be construed as prospectus.

Shelf prospectus

S. 31. (1) —Any class or classes of companies, as the Securities and Exchange Board may provide by regulations in this behalf, may file a shelf prospectus with the Registrar at the stage of the first offer of securities included therein. Shelf prospectus shall indicate a period not exceeding one year as the period of validity of such prospectus. This period shall commence from the date of the first offer of securities under that prospectus. In respect of a second or a subsequent offer of such securities issued during the period of validity of that prospectus, no further prospectus is required.

(2) A company filing a shelf prospectus shall be required to file an information memorandum containing all material facts relation to new charges created, changes in the financial position of the company as have concurred between first offer of securities or the previous offer of securities and the succeeding offer of securities and such other changes as may be prescribed with the Registrar within the prescribed time, prior to the issue of a second or subsequent offer of securities under the shelf prospectus.

Provided that where a company or any other person has received applications for the allotment of securities along with advance payments of subscription before making any such change, the company or other person shall intimate the changes to such applicants. If they express a desire to withdraw their application, the company or any other person shall refund all the monies received as subscription within fifteen days thereof.

(3) Where an information memorandum is filed, every time an offer of securities is made under sub-section (2), such memorandum together with the shelf prospectus shall be deemed to be a prospectus.

Explanation—For the purposes of this section, the expression "shelf prospectus" means a prospectus in respect of which the securities or class of securities included therein are issued for subscription in one or more issues over a certain period without the issue of a further prospectus.

Red herring prospectus S. 32.

(1) A company proposing to make an offer of securities may issue a red herring prospectus prior to the issue of a prospectus.

(2) A company proposing to issue a red herring prospectus under the sub-section (1) shall file it with the Registrar at least three days prior to the opening of subscription list and the offer.

(3) A red herring prospectus shall carry the same obligations as are applicable to a prospectus and any variation between the red herring prospectus and prospectus shall be highlighted as variations in the prospectus.

(4) Upon closing of the offer of securities under this section, the prospectus stating therein the total capital raised, whether by way of debt or share capital and the closing price of the securities and any other details as are not included in the red herring prospectus shall be filed with the Registrar and the Securities and Exchange board.

Explanation—For the purpose of this section, the expression "red herring prospectus" means a prospectus which does not include complete particulars of the quantum or price of the securities included therein.

48.2 Registration of Prospectus - Sec. 26

The rules relating to registration of prospectus are summarized below.

i) First of all a copy of prospectus duly signed by every person named as director or proposed director or a company should be delivered to the Registration of Companies before its publication.

ii) The copy of prospectus delivered to the registrar should be accompanied by written consent of auditor, legal advisor attorney, solicitor, banker or broker of the company, experts to file prospectus, director's copy of underwriting agreement etc.

iii) Unless such a copy is delivered as above before its publication, prospectus shall not be issued to the public.

iv) The Registrar shall register the documents on being satisfied that requirements have been complied with.

v) The prospectus shall be issued within 90 days of the delivery of the copy for registration.

vi) If a prospectus is issued without delivery of the copy in the registrar, the company and every person, knowingly a party to the issue of the prospectus, shall be punishable with a fine from 50,000 rupees to 3 lakh rupees.

48.3 Statement in Lieu of Prospectus - Sec. 70

This term is self explanatory. Where a public company raises capital by private arrangement and not by public participation, prospectus may be dispensed with. When the prospectus of a company is not issued but shares are to be allotted, statement in lieu of prospectus should be registered.

a) **When required ?**
   When -
   i) Company having a share capital does not issue a prospectus or
   ii) Company has issued a prospectus but has not proceeded to allot shares offered to the public for subscription.

b) **Delivery to Registrar -**
   The statement in lies of propectus must be delivered to the Registrar for registration at least 3 days before the allotment of shares or debentures. Without delivery and registration, company cannot allot shares / debentures.

c) **Signed Document -**
   This statement should be signed by every person named therein as director or a proposed director or by his agent duly authorised in writing to sign.

d) **Form & Contents -**
   Part I & II of Schedule III prescribe the form and contents (particulars & reports) of statement in lieu of prospectus.

e) **Statement in lieu of prospectus -**
   Statement in liew of prospectus should also be delivered and registered when a private company is converted into a public company. Form and contents would be as prescribed in Part I Schedule and reports set out in Part II Schedule IV and of the Act.

48.4 Liability for Mis-Statement in the Prospectus

Prospectus of a company induces the investors to invest in its ventures through shares and debentures. Members of the public take a decision to invest fund based on the information given in the prospectus. If the prospectus contains incorrect, or false data or information, the people are misled. To safeguard the interests of the public against possible fraud, the Act holds the company liable for misstatement in prospectus. The prospectus should depict honest picture of company's ventures. It should give a true state of affairs of the Company's activites. The Company and its authorised persons / experts would be responsible for making false, wrongful statements or for failure to disclose important aspects which may affect the investor's decision as regards purchase of shares etc.

a) **Meaning of Mis-Statement -**
   Mis-Statement includes the following acts or omissions
   i) Untrue (false) statements
   ii) Misleading statements or statements producing wrong impression.

iii) Omission of facts or

iv) Conceatment of material facts.

According to Sec. 51, a statement would be deemed untrue if -

i)   Statement is misleading in form and contest in which it is included (in prospectus) and

ii) Omission from a prospectus of any matter calculated to mislead.

The prospectus must contain accurate information. Mis-Statement can be either a false statement made positively, intentionally or negligently made incorrect statement. Failure to disclose material facts or active concealment thereof is also a mis-statement 180. [See **Derry v/s Peek** in the chapter on Fraud]

Liability for making mis-statement entails two types of liability i] Civil liability and ii] Criminal liability. Remedies available on these two types of liabilities are discussed here under

b) Civil Liability (Remedies) For Mis - Statement- S.35

1) Rescission of Contract

(See. Rescission of contract in U/S 19 A of the Contract Act)

Rescission means repudiation or cancellation of contract. Purchase of shares is a contract with company and if company defrauds or misleads the purchasers' contract can be cancelled at the opinion of purchaser. He has to relinquish shares and return the money with interest.

Conditions for rescission - Allottee of shares must prove the following -

i)   Statement was of fact and fact was material.

ii) Statement was 'mis-statement' (a positive statement or omission or concealment.)

iii) The allotee acted upon it. The allottee / purchaser has to apply to the court for relief of rescission. Rescission would be granted if action is taken

- Within reasonable time;

- before commencement of winding up proceedings. Acceptance of dividend destroys this remedy.

2) Damages for fraud - If the mis-statement in prospectus amounts to fraud, the Company is liable to pay damages to the purchaser. The purchaser has to surrender shares before suing the company for damages. (Derry Vs Peek).

The purchaser has to prove the conditions mentioned in rescission and in addition he has to prove that -

i) company acted fraudulently;

ii) he acted upon mis-statement and suffered losses.

The above remedies are available against the company as such.

3) Compensation - Where a person suffers losses / damages due to mis-statement in prospectus, he is entitled for the compensation from the persons liable. Mis-Statement may be wilful or innocent.

4) Liability for non-compliance of Sec. 26

Director or other persons are responsible for non-compliance or contravention of S. regarding matters to be disclosed or reports to be set-out in propectus. They have to pay compensation to the agrrieved for contravention of S.

Persons responsible for mis-statement (Sec.) -

i) Every director at the time of issue of prospectus

ii) Every director named as director in prospectus

iii) Every promoter of the company

iv) Every person authorised to issue prospectus

5) Defences in Civil Liability - following defences / justification can be taken up by the above persons in order to absolve himself from liability for mis-statement.

i) Issue of prospectus without his consent or knowledge and he gave public notice when he knew about such an issue or

ii) Withdrawal of consent as director and issue of prospectus without his consent or authority or

iii) Withdrawal of consent after the issue but before allotment & the fact of public notice given by him;

iv) Reasonable ground of belief in the truth of statement and in fact he belived to be true.

v) Statement was made by an official or is an official document.

vi) Statement was a fair summary or copy of an expert's reports.

6) Experts' Liability for Mis-Statement

Prospectus incorporates or rather based on experts opinions and comments. Experts should make responsible statements regarding company's affairs. They are equally liable for incorrect reports, valuation, assessment or untrue statements. An allottee of a share can successfully maintain an action against experts for damages or loss sustained by their mis-statements. Compensation under Section is recoverable from experts.

7) Defences available to experts

Experts can plead and prove following justifications in an action for damages.

i & ii) First two defences u/sec. already discussed. or

iii) He was competent to make statement and had reasonble gorund for belief in its truth and did infact believe in truth or

iv) Report was fair and correct representation of statement or

v) Statement was a correct copy of or a correct and fair extract from the report or valuation.

1) Criminal Liability (Sec. 34 and 36)

Mis-statement in prospects attracts penal liability under section of the Act- Whoever authorises misstatement in the public issue is punishable with --

i) imprisonment of minimum 6 months 2 maximum 10 years.

ii) minimum fine equal to amount of fraut or maximum fine up to 3 times such amount.

iii) both imprisonment and fine

2) Procuring investments by fraud - Sec. 36 - Whoever fraudulently induces another to enter into an agreement —

i) with a view to acquire, dispose off, subscribe for or underwriting shares or debentures

or

ii) purpose of which is to secure profit to any of the parties from the yield of shares or debentures or by reference to fluctuation in the value of shares or debentures, is punishable as follows

i) imprisonment upto 5 years or

ii) fine upto 10,000 or both

This offence covers making false, misleading or decepting statements knowingly or negligently inducing others to enter into above type of agreements. Attempt to commit offence is also punishable.

3) Defences in criminal liability

Defences in criminal liability are enlisted below -

i) Statement was not significant

ii) There was a reasonable ground for belief in the truth of the statement and that was in fact believed to be true

4) Defence for an expert

Defence which can be pleaded in civil liability at no. (i) to (iii) discussed earlier can also be pleaded in criminal liability.

Meaning

Capital of a company, raised by issue of shares is called as 'share capital'. It affords as a source of funds for the company. Capital through shares may be raised while forming a company or afterwords for expansion of its business. Capital structure implies division & sub-division of authorised capital into shares of different denominations / kinds. Share capital is the total face value of the shares in a company. Only company limited by shares and incorporated with share capital can build up share capital.

49.1 Classification of Share Capital

Share capital is classified as under

1) **Authorised capital**

   Authorised capital is also known as 'Nominal or Registered or Total Capital' of the company. It is the capital with which a company is registered. It is mentioned in the memorandum of association of the company and the company therefore cannot raise capital beyond that amount unless memorandum of association is modified to that effect.

2) **Issued Capital**

   To commence the business, a company may not require entire amount of nominal capital. As per requirement a company issues shares & raises certain capital called as 'issued capital'. Obviously issued capital is less than or equal to authorised capital.

3) **Subscribed Capital**

   The entire issued capital may not be subscribed by the purchsers. Part of the issued capital subscribed by the public is known as 'Subscribed Capital.' Subscription is in the form of applications (offer) to purchase shares.

4) **Called-Up Capital**

   Company may not require at one time all the subscribed capital. In stages it may be called up. the Capital which company calls upon subscribers to pay is called as 'called-up capital.'

5) Uncalled Capital

The part of the subscribed capital which is not called-up is 'Uncalled Capital.' Thus the remainder of the subscribed capital is described as uncalled capital.

6) Reserve Capital

Where the share holders agree by a special aresolution that either full or part of the uncalled capital shall be called up only on liguidation, that capital is called 'Reserve Capital. Company cannot call up this capital during its life time. Such a capital can neither be mortgaged nor charged.

7) Paid-Up Capital

The capital actually paid up by the subscribers is termed 'paid-up capital.' Despite the calls to pay as per applications, subscribers may not pay. Thus the entire amount of money may not be actually paid by the subscribers.

E-COMERCE
INFORMATION TECHNOLOGY ACT, 2000

The Preamble of the Act sets out the objectives of this new legislation. The chief objective of the Act is to recognise the electronic transactions and facilitate the electronic filing of documents with the government agencies. This Act gives effect to the Model Laws on 'Electronic Commerce' adopted by the United Nation's Electronic Commission on International Trade Law. The enactment aims at promoting efficient delivery of Government services by means of reliable elctronic records and to amend Reserve Bank of India Act, 1934, Indian Penal Code, the Bankers Books Evidence Act, 1891 and The Indian Evidence Act, 1872.

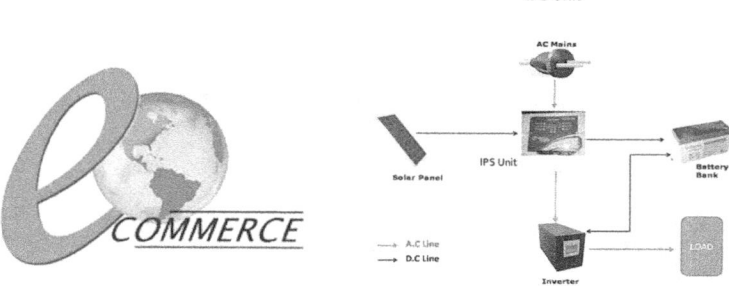

Chapter 50 | IMPORTANT DEFINITIONS UNDER THE ACT

The definitions u/s 2(1) the Act are reproduced below. These key terms may be referred for better understanding of the topics covered.

S.2 (1)

(d) **"Affixing digital signature"** *with its grammatical variations and cognate expressions means adoption of any methodology or procedure by a person for the purpose of authenticating an electronic record by means of digital signature;*

(g) **"Certifying Authority"** *means a person who has been granted a license to issue a Digital Signature Certificate under section 24;*

(h) **"Certification practice statement"** *means a statement issued by a Certifying Authority to specify the practice that the certifying Authority employs in issuing Digital Signature Certificates;*

(i) **"Computer"** *means any electronic, magnetic, optical or other high-speed data processing device or system which performs logical, arithmetic and memory functions by manipulations of electronic, magnetic or optical impulses and communication facilities which are connected or related to the computer in a computer system or computer network;*

(l) **"Computer system"** *means a device or collection of devices, including input and output support device and excluding calculators which are not programmable and capable of being used in conjunction with external files and output data, that performs logic, arithmetic, data storage and retrieval, communication control and other functions :*

(q) **"Digital Signature Certificate"** *means a Digital Signature Certificate issued under sub-section (4) of section 35;*

(t) **"Electronic record"** *means data, record or data generated, image or sound stored, received or sent in an electronic form or microfilm or computer generated micro fiche;*

(v) **"Information"** *includes data, text, image, sound, voice, codes, computer programmes, software and database or micro film or computer generated micro fiche;*

(x) **"Key Pair"**, *is an asymmetric crypto system, means a private key and its mathematically related public key, which are so related that the public key can verify a digital signature by the private key;*

(zc) **"Private Key"** *means the key of a pair used to create a digital signature;*

(zd) **"Public Key"** *means the key of a key pair used to verify a digital signature and listed in the Digital Signature Certificate;*

(zg) **"Subscriber"** *means a person in whose name the Digital Signature Certificate is issued.*

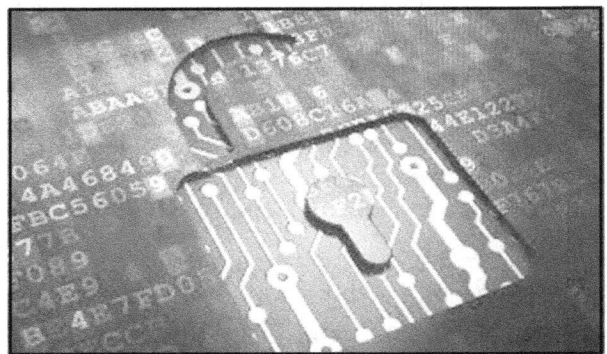

Chapter 51

DIGITAL SIGNATURE

51.1 Definition (Sec. 2.(1)(p))

> *"Digital Signature" means authentication of any electronic record by a subscriber by means of an electronic method or procedure in accordance with the provisions of section 3;*

Digital signature in simple terms means authentication of electronic record. Signature in ordinary sense means approval or adoption of the contents above it. This approval or authentication is made by means of electronic method or procedure laid down in Sec. 3 of the Act.

Authentication (Procedure) of Electronic Records (Sec. 3)

1. The subscriber may autheticate an electronic record by affecting his digital signature.
2. Authentication is done by the use of 'asymmetric crypto system' and 'hash-function' By these two processes initial e - record is transformed into another e - record. These two terms have been explained under the Act as follows.

Asymmetric crypto system [Def. U/s 2(1) (f)]

"asymmetric crypto system" means a system of secure key pair consisting of a private key for creating a digital signature and a public key to verify the digital signature;"

Hash - function [Explanation to Sec. 3(2)]

Hash - function means "an algorithm mapping or translation of one sequence of bits into another, generally smaller, set known as "hash result" such that an electronic record yields the same hash result every time the algorithm is executed with the same electronic record as its input making it computationally infeasible –

a) to derive or reconstruct the original electronic record from the hash result produced by the algorithm;

b) that two electronic records can produce the same hash result using the algorithm;

3. Any person by the use of a public key of the subscriber can verify the electronic record.

4. The private key and the public key are unique to the subscriber and constitute a functioning key pair."

Authentication by digital signature involves following steps to be followed by sender of information. —

i) Sender has to Perform hash function on the message to be sent to the receiver. Result of hash function is 'message digest'

ii) Encrypting the result (message digest) can be done with private key.

iii) Appending resulting digital signature to the message.

Steps for verification of message by receiver —

i) Decrypting the digital signature with public key to get a message digest.

ii) Performing same hash function on the message received (Result would be the message digest)

iii) Comparing / matching these two results (message digest) obtained by hash function and decryption.

If the results corrospond or found to be same, the digital signature is verified.

1) Any person with the use of public key can verify the electronic record.

2) Private key and public key constitute a functioning pair and are unique to the subscriber.

3) Sec. 5 of the Act recognizes digital signature, electronic record or information be authenticated by digital signature which is affixed in the prescribed manner.

Functions of Digital Signature

Digital signature serves following purposes

i) **Confidentiality** - Digital signature ensures confidentiality of the transaction - Transaction remains a private affair.

ii) **Integrity** - Digital signature helps to preserve integrity in the sense that data information passed is not tampered, document is sent unaltered.

iii) **Authenticity** - The sender of the message is identified.

iv) **Non-Repudiation** - The sender cannot repudiate or terminate the transaction. Denials or unilateral alterations are prevented.

Identity and authentification leaves no scope for impersonation or forgery of the document. Digital signature protects the sender from false denials or claims. Legal requirements as to writing, originality genuiness of the documents are also fulfilled by the use of digital signature.

51.2 DIGITAL SIGNATURE CERTIFICATES

Chapter VII (Sec. 35 to 39) contains the provisions regarding digital signature certificates which are briefed as follows.

1) **S.35 - Application for digital signature certificates**

   Application for digital signature certificate may be made by any person to Certifying Authority. Application should be in prescribed format and accompained by fees and 'Certification Practice Statement' (as defined u/s 2-h of the Act). The Certifying Authority after considering the application and certification practice statement may grant digital signature certificate. While granting certificate the Certifying Authority has to ensure that -

   - Subscriber holds private key capable of creating digital signature and
   - Applicant (subscriber) holds private key corrosponding to public key;
   - Public key can be used to verify digital signature.

2) **S. 36 - Certification by Certifying Authority**

   While issuing digital signature certificates, the Certifying Authority will certify compliance of the provisions of the Act, Rules etc, publication of digital signature certificates, accuracy of the information in digital signature certificates. He will also certify what he has to ensure u/s 35.

3) **S.37 - Suspension of Digital Signature Certificate**

   Certifying Authority has power to suspend digital signature certificates either on the request by subscriber or his agent or in public interest. Before suspension, he has to serve a notice to subscriber u/s 39 (In case of suspension for a period more than 15 days). Suspension should be communicated to the subscriber.

4) **S.38 - Revocation of Digital Signature Certificate**

   Certifying Authority may revoke the digital signature certificates in the following cases —

   i) On the request by subscriber or, his agent or

   ii) Death or insolvency of subscriber; or

   iii) Dissolution of firm or winding up of company or

   iv) False representation or concealment of material fact in digital signature certificates or

   v) Non-compliance of provisions of Act, Rules, Regulations or

   vi) Subscriber's private key or security system is compromised affecting digital signature certificates's reliability.

   Procedure - Notice of revocation should be sent to subscriber and then only decision by Certifying Authority would be taken. Notice of revocation should also be published in the repository specified in digital signature certificate.

Chapter 52 | ELECTRONIC GOVERNANCE

ELECTRONIC GOVERNANCE

We have noticed that in many cases law or Govenment authorities require a particular information or matter in writing and signed by the concerned person. Members of the public do file returns, submit various forms with Govenment agencies which issue licenses or permits. Record evidencing transactions also needs preservation. In all such cases of legal requirement, this Act permits the generation, preservation, acceptance, issuance, use etc. of electronic record in stead of papers or documents. By making provisions in this chapter, this Act provides legal recognition to electronic records, digital signatures, electronic methods of preservation and publication of any information or material. The relevant provisions are discussed below.

1. **Legal Recognition of Electronic Records**
   (S.4) - If law requires any information/matter in writing, (typewritten or printed) that requirement is deemed to have been complied if such information or matter is -
   a) made available in e-form and
   b) accessible and usable for subsequent reference.

2. **Legal Recognition of Digital Signatures**
   Sec. 5 of the Act approves and permits authentication of any information or matter by digital signature wherever signing is necessary by law. The digital signature should however be affixed in the prescribed manner.
   Sec. 4 & 5 supercede existing law as to necessity of writing and signing a document.

3. **Use of electronic records and digital signature in Government and its agencies (Sec. 6)**
   Sec.6 of the Act permits filing the following activities in electronic form -
   - filing any form, application, or any document with Government offices;
   - issue or grant of any license, permit, sanction or approval by the Government authorities;
   - Receipt or payment of money
   The Government is empowered to prescribe rules regarding manner of filling, creation of documents, issue of licenses etc and payment of fees or charges in eletronic mode.

4. Retention of Electronic Records (Sec. 7)

Where any law requires retention of information, documents etc. the requirement is satisfied if that information is preserved in electronic form. Such retention in electronic form should follow the following conditions. —

— Information should be accessible, usable for a subsequent reference.

— Original format of generation of information should be retained ;

— Electronic record should have details for identification of origin, destination, rate and time of dispatch or receipt of such e-record.

5. Publication of rules etc. in Electronic Gazette — (Section 8)

Permits publication of any rule, regulation, order, by-law, notification in electronic gazette as well as in conventional official gazettes.

Acceptance of document in electronic form - Not a Right

Sec. 9 clarifies that no person has a right to insist Government or officer to accept, issue, creat, retain or preserve any document in electronic form - Sections 6, 7 and 8 are permissive in nature and they do not confer a right to accept any document in electronic-form.

Chapter 53

ELECTRONIC RECORD

Attribution, Acknowledgement and Dispatch of Electronic Record

1. **Attribution – S. 11**

   In the following circumstances, an electronic record is attributed to the originator if it is sent by —

   a) Originator

   b) Originator's agent appointed in respect of e-record

   c) Information system is programmed by originator to operate automatically.

2. **Acknowledgement of a receipt – Sec. 12**

   When form or mode of acknowledgement is not agreed between originator and addressee, acknowledgement may be given in the following way –

   a) any communication by addressee (automated or otherwise) or

   b) Implied receipt i.e. conduct of addressee showing receipt of e-record.

   If between them, receipt of acknowledgement is necessary to makes electronic record binding, then e-record shall be deemed to have been never been sent by the originator if acknowledgment is not received. Where receipt of acknowledgement is not necessary to make e-record binding, where acknowledgement is not received, the originator may give a notice to the addressee stating the time for sending acknowledgement. If within that time acknowledgement is not received, originator may again give notice to the addressee treating that e-record has never been sent to him.

3. **Time and place of dispatch of e-records - Sec. 13**

   a) Dispatch of e-record occurs when it enters a computer resource outside the control of the originator.

   b) The time of receipt of an electronic record shall be determined as follows, namely —

   1) If the addressee has designated a computer resource for the purposes of receiving electronic records –

   i) receipt occurs at the time when electronic record enters the designated computer resource; or

ii) if the electronic record is sent to a computer resource of the addressee that is not the designated computer resource, receipt occurs at the time when the electronic record is retrieved by the addressee;

2) if the addressee has not designated a computer resource along with specified timings, if any, receipt occurs when the electronic record enters the computer resource of the addressee.

iii) An electronic record is deemed to be dispatched at the place where originator has his place of business, and is deemed to be received at the place where the addressee has his place of business.

The above provisions are subject to the agreement between the originator and the addressee.

iv) The provisions of sub-section (2) shall apply notwithstanding that the place where the computer resource is located may be different from the place where the electronic record is deemed to have been received as stated in (iii) above.

Secure E-Records and Secure Digital Signature

1. **Secure E-Records** – Sec.14 States that where any security procedure has been applied to an electronic record at a specific point of time, the record is treated as secure e-record from such point of time to the time of verification.

2. **Secure Digital Signature** – According to Sec.15, a digital signature shall be presumed to be a secure digital signature where, by applying agreed security procedure it can be verified that (when it was affixed) digital signature was found to have following attributes.
   - Digital signature was unique to the subscriber;
   - Digital signature was capable of identify the subscriber;
   - Digital signature was created in a manner or using means under the exclusive control of the subscriber. The digital signature is linked to e-record in such manner that alteration of e-record would invalidate Digital Signature.

Security Procedure – By Sec.16, the Central Government is empowered to prescribe security procedure. The Government has to consider commercial transaction including following matters
   - Nature of commercial transaction;
   - Standard of sophistication of parties in view of their technological capacity;
   - Volume of similar transactions engaged in by other parties;
   - Cost of alternative procedures;
   - Procedure adopted in similar type of transaction.

Chapter 54 | REGULATION OF CERTIFYING AUTHORITIES

54.1 Controller of Certifying Authorities – (Sec. 17)

Controller is the important authority under the Act. He is working in the supervisory and controlling capacity. He lays down the standards for maintaining database, certifies public keys and determines contents of digital signature certificates. He is supposed to ensure secrecy and security of digital signatures. Provisions regulating these aspects are elaborated below.

a) Appointment

The Central Government is empowered under the Act to appoint Controller of Certifying Authorities. Deputy and Assistant Controllers may also be appointed by the Government. The Controller shall discharge the functions assigned under the Act and would work under the control and direction of the Central Government.

b) Functions of Controller

Sec.18 of the Act enlists the functions of the controller which are as follows –

i)   Exercise of supervision and control over Certifying Authorities;

ii) Laying down standards to be maintained by Certifying Authorities and their duties.

iii) Certifying public keys of Certifying Authorities, specifying form and content of digital signature certificate and key

iv) Specifying following things ...

Qualifications, experience of staff of Certifying Authorities.
- Manner of dealing with subscribers by Certifying Authorities.
- Conditions for conducting business by Certifying Authorities.
- Contents of documents/materials, advertisement (written, printed) used in respect of digital signature certificates and public key.
- Form and manner of maintenance of accounts by Certifying Authorities.
- Terms and conditions of appointment and remuneration of auditors.

v) Facilitating the establishment of any electronic system by a Certifying Authority and regulation of such systems.

vi) Maintaining a data base containing disclosure record of every Certifying Authority and making it accessible to public.

vii) Resolving conflict of interest between Certifying Authorities and their subscribers.

c) **Duties of Controller — Sec. 20**

1. The controller shall be the repository of all digital signature certificates issued under the Act;

2. For the purpose of ensuring secrecy and security of digital signature, the controller shall —
   — Make use of hardware, software and procedure that are secure from intrusion and misuse.
   — Observe the standards prescribed by Central Government.

3. The controller is obliged to maintain a computerized database of all public keys. Such database and keys should be made available to the members of public.

54.2 License to issue Digital Signature Certificates

Sections 21 to 26 of the Act deal with issue, renewal, suspension and revocation of licence to issue digital signature certificates. The provisions are explained below.

Procedure for obtaining License –

a) **Application for License – S. 21**

Application for license to issue digital signature certificate may be made by any person to the controller. The applicant has to satisfy the criteria as to qualifications, expertise, manpower, financial resources and other infrastructure facilities as prescribed by the Central Government.

The application in specific format should be submitted along with fee (upto Rs.25000) and following documents –

i) Certification practice statement

ii) Statement of indentification of the applicant.

iii) Other documents prescribed by the Central Government (S.22)

b) **Grant of License – S. 24**

The controller after considering the application and accompanying documents may grant the license or reject the application. Before rejecting the application he has to give reasonable opportunity to applicant to explain his case.

The license shall be valid for a period prescribed by Central Government and would be subject to terms and conditions as specified by the regulation. It is a non-transferable and non-heritable document. (Sec.21)

c) **Renewal of License – S. 23**

License can be renewed by making application in specific format along with fees (maximum Rs.15000). The application should be made 45 days before the date of expiry of the period of validity of the license.

d) Revocation of license – S.25

The controller has power to revoke the license of a Certifying Authority on the following grounds. **Grounds of Revocation –**

i) Furnishing incorrect or false information in the application for license or its renewal.

ii) Failure to comply with terms and condition of license.

iii) Failure to maintain standards laid down by Controller u/s 20 of the Act.

iv) Contravention of the provisions of the Act, Rules or Regulations or order thereunder.

Procedure for Revocation – Order of revocation of license should be made only after giving a reasonable opportunity of hearing and conducting inquiry in the matter.

e) Suspension of License – If there is a cause to believe that any ground of revocation exists, the controller may suspend the license pending completion of inquiry ordered by him. If suspension is for a period exceeding ten days, then show-cause notice to Certifying Authority should be given before suspension. During suspension period, Certifying Authority cannot issue digital signature certificates.

Public notice of suspension or revocation

S. 26. The controller has to publish a notice of suspension or revocation of license in the database maintained by him. Such a database with notice shall be made available through a website accessible round the clock.

54.3 Duties of Certifying Authority

Sections 30 to 34 of Chapter VI of the Act cast certain duties on Certifying Authority Those are enumerated below —

a) Duty to follow certain procedures
Sec. 30 – Every Certifying Authority is required

i) To make use of software, hardware and procedure, that are secure from unauthorised intrusion and misuse;

ii) To provide a reasonable level of reliability in its services. Services should be able to accomplish intented functions.

iii) To follow security procedures assuring secrecy and privacy of digital signature.

iv) To observe the standards prescribed by regulations under the Act.

b) Ensuring compliance by employees

S. 31. Every Certifying Authority has to unsure that its employees comply the provision of the Act, Rules, Regulations in the course of their employment / engagement.

c) Display Licence – S. 32 – Every Certifying Authority has to display its licence at a prominent place of the premises where business is conducted.

d) Disclosure by Certifying Authority – S. 34 – Every Certifying Authority is under a duty to disclose the following things —

– Its digital signature certificates (with its public and private key);

– Notice of suspension or revocation of its digital signature certificates issued, if any;

– Any fact materially and adversely affecting the reliability of digital signature certificates issued by it.

If by any event or situation, integrity of its computer system is materially and adversely affected or the conditions of grant of digital signature certificate are affected, the Certifying Authority should inform the person who is likely to be adversely affected by such event. In the alternative he should follow the procedure specified in Certification practice statement to overcome such an event.

Legal Issues in E-Commerce

' Internet is seen as a kind of Wild Wild West landscape....It is a virtual world of lawlessness.' Clifford Gregory, Senior VP,(Security Solutions), IONIDEA

E-commerce eliminated the need o the people to physically transact the business. Internet dispenses with the middlemen. There is no need of sore houses.Computer and electronic devises like mobiles are being used to deceive the people and to commit various cyber crimes. Shoppers are moving towards, smaller stores, e-commerce. Extent of financial frauds is invisible now but it is apprehended that it would assume serious proportions in the days to come. Criminal complaints are filed against online stores. Consumers are trapped in alternatives. Book, household articles, electronic instruments are sold online. Even drugs and medicine without prescriptions are available online. With the onslaught of ecommerce following legal issues have emerged.

1. Customers /buyers are less sophisticated, less educated and fall prey to unscrupulous practices of traders. Ordinary people are not aware of I.T. Act of 2000.

2. Admissibility and acceptability of computer generated documents is a major legal barrier for e-commerce enforcement in spite of I.T. Act of 2000. Origin, accuracy, retrieval and visual display of the data still pose problems in evidence as to existence of contract;

3. E- notices-Authenticity, fact of dispatch, acknowledge of receipt of e-notice seems to be complicated in legal parlance as notice has a great legal significance;

4. Jurisdictional Issues—In e-contracts place of formation of contract, place of delivery assume importance as those factors determine as to which court has the power to decide the disputes between contracting parties. In the virtual world, without geographical boundaries, jurisdiction of the court is a big hurdle in enforcement of laws;

5. Cyber insecurity creates a fear psychosis among the consumers who are focal point on e-commerce. There is no adequate legal protection to e- consumers either under C.P.A.,1986 or I.T.Act 2000;

6. Authentication of trading parties; Innocent subscriber may be made liable by fraudsters;

7. Infringement of intellectual property, contents, advertisement infringement has financial repercussions;

8. Lack of standard e-payment infrastructure.

9. Taxing e-commerce transactions is complicated due to jurisdiction, identity of taxpayers.

10. Damage, theft of valuable confidential information; direct financial losses on account of fraud, mischief are common.

These issues are illustrative. E-commerce has tremendous advantages. It has a big business potential which cannot be undermined in the digital world. E contracts should be made technically safer. E-literacy of consumers may minimize risks. Strict vigilance by law may curb cyber crimes. Amendments in I.T. Act 2000, C.P.A., 1986 providing more protection to consumers may boost e-commerce. Ethical standards should be evolved and adopted by the consumers and online stores.

PART IX

Questions and hints for answers

1. What is 'Digital Signature' ? Explain in brief the provisions relating Digital Signature Certificates. ✓ Ans. Chap. 51.1 and 51.2

2. What is 'Digital Singature'? How it can be created and verified ? How digital signature certificate is obtained ? Explain with reference to the law contained in Information Technology Act, 2000. MBA - 2004 PU (Chap. 51)

3. State the provisions relating to 'Electronic Governance' contained in the Information Technology Act, 2000. ✓ Ans Chap. 52

4. Explain the duties of Certifying Authorities under the IT Act 2000. MBA - 2004 P. U. ✓ Ans Chap. 54.3

5. How licence to issue Digital Signature Certificates is obtained? When it is suspended and revoked ? Explain. ✓ Ans Chap 54.2

6. Write an explanatory note on "E-Governance" in the light of provisions of Information Technology Act, 2000. MBA - 2005 – PU Chap. 52.

   E – Records – MBA 2004 PU

PART - X

INTELLECTUAL PROPERTY RIGHTS

PATENTS, COPYRIGHTS, TRADE MARKS and DESIGNS

INTELLECTUAL PROPERTY –

Property implies any kind of interest, right, advantage with respect to subject matter of property. Intellectual property originates from human intelligence. It is the fruit of intellectual endeavor. It emanates from human creativity, innovative tendency. Inventions, works of literature, artistic works, music, films, designs, computer programmes are all intellectual property as those are the produce of mind. Patents, copyrights, designs, trademarks are the species of intellectual property. Intellectual property needs protection of law. Whoever creates something out of his intellectual labour must be able to commercially exploit it. The creator should get economic benefit of what he develops. Economic incentive is necessary for new ideas, inventions as they contribute in the progress of the country. Patents, trademarks, copyrights or designs fetch huge value in the market. Intellectual property, therefore, requires protection of law. Ownership in these rights is controlled, regulated through various laws. Ownership is also restricted in the interests of the society. This chapter defines and analyses the conepts of selected intellectual property. Their registration, assignment, term is not within the scope of this chapter.

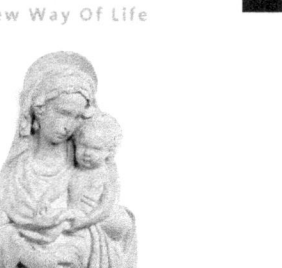

WIPO

Introduction and Background—

Intellectual creativity has gained significance as a property worldwide. Recognizing commercial element of IPRs (Intellectual Property Rights) and the benefits derived by exploitation of various forms of IPRs and the need to protect these rights, various international agreements have been executed in the last two decades of 19th century. Paris Convention of 1983 followed by Berne Convention of 1886 are the milestones in the development of IPR legal regime for the protection of Intellectual Property. Paris Convention emphasizes equal treatment to nationals of member states as far as protection of their IPRs and advocates Uniform Rules and minimum protection for industrial property rights of the creators whether own nationals or nationals of member states. Berne Convention governs copyrights issues.

WIPO (World Intellectual Property Organization) is seen as a significant development towards protection and promotion of IPRs at international level and it is known for its remarkable contribution in the development of IPR jurisprudence at global level. WIPO is the specialized agency of United Nations established by the Convention signed in 1967. WIPO has 188 members and its Headquarter is at Geneva.

Objectives of WIPO— Objectives of WIPO are enlisted below.

1. Promotion of protection of intellectual property at international level through cooperation of their member states and collaboration with international organization;
2. Ensuring administrative co-operation among the unions;
3. Harmonizing domestic intellectual property legislation, rules and procedures with other member states;
4. Making provisions of services for international applications for IPRs;
5. Exchange of information on intellectual property;
6. Providing legal and technical assistance to developing countries;
7. Facilitating the resolution of disputes of IPRs;
8. Making use of information technology for storing, accessing and using valuable information relating to IPRs.

Organs of WIPO

WIPO has to discharge its functions and execute the programs in the field of IPR. Following organs are available to WIPO to carry out its activities.

1. **General Assembly -** This comprises the members of the Union, i.e. the member states who are parties to the Convention establishing WIPO. Upon nomination by Coordination Committee, Director General is appointed by General Assembly. Director General has to follow the instructions of General Assembly as his reporting authority. Half of the member state constitutes the quorum of General Assembly and each member has one vote.

2. **Conference -** This organ is composed of the state parties to the Convention. These state parties may not be the members of the union.

3. **Coordination Committee -** This Committee is comprised of the state parties to the Convention which are the members of the Berne Union or Paris Union or both. Preparing

draft agenda of General Assembly and draft programs and budget of the Conferences is its prime function. It is an advisory body for the Unions in administrative and financial matters.

4. **International Bureau** - International Bureau is the Secretariat and representative of the WIPO. Director General is the chief executive of WIPO. His term is for a minimum period if six years. Director General looks after internal and external affairs of Bureau.

5. **Worldwide Academy** - for dissemination of IPR information. Academy is constituted by WIPO recently to fulfill its objective of spreading awareness about IPR worldwide.

Programs and Activities of WIPO

Following are the Programs and Activities of WIPO...

1. **Development of Commerce** - Use of Internet digital technology is inevitable. Intellectual property rights subsist in various facets of internet technology. Realizing this vital linkage, well back in 1999, WIPO implemented work programs for protection of proprietary rights of creators of works like music, films, knowledge and the internet.

2. **Assistance in Computerization** - Developing countries do not have adequate internet technology resources to manage and administer their intellectual property resources. WIPO has designed computerization programs for developing nations for acquisition of internet technology resources to direct their administrative procedures for management and administration of their own human and material form of IP resources.

3. **Education and Training Programs** - WIPO has undertaken comprehensive literacy and training programs for officials dealing with intellectual property and its enforcement. WIPO also conducts such programs for native people having traditional knowledge and user groups for appraisal of the value of intellectual property and methodology for more beneficial use of traditional knowledge and thus creating more economic assets out of such use. Programs under this head are conducted at national and regional levels.

4. **Advisory Programs for Revision of Laws** - WIPO member states are obliged to amend their laws in IPR regime in pursuance of TRIPs agreement. WIPO has designed programs for rendering advice and providing expertise for revision of national laws to bring harmony with international norms and standards regulating IPRs.

5. **Financial Assistance** - WIPO programs provide financial assistance to its needy member states for participation in its activities and meetings specially meant for facilitating adoption of international norms and practices in IPR regime.

6. **Collective Management of Copyright** - Developing and the least developed countries need sophistication for management of IPRs, particularly copyrights, for better use and to gain more benefits of advanced techniques. Keeping this aspect in view, WIPO had designed a special program to promote collective management of copyright owned by authors, composers, artists etc.

7. **Application of international norms** - Progressive development and adoption of international norms and standards has resulted in effective and better protection of IPRs globally. WIPO is administrating eleven treaties which recognize certain IPRs and lay down standards for international protection.

8. **Activities of Worldwide Academy -** As stated earlier this Academy is established for dissemination IPR related information. For conducting training etc, policy planners, advisors, development managers are its target groups. Nature of its activities is given below.

I— Use of modern public access media for dissemination IPR related information;

II— Use of distance learning centers having internet facility;

III— Devising novel teaching and training techniques for literacy;

IV— Providing learning modules and materials suited to specific client.

TRIPs AGREEMENT

Uruguay Round (UR) is the eighth round of multilateral trade negotiations (MTNs) held under auspices of GATT. The special feature of the UR was the inclusion of trade in services, in intellectual property, investment measures etc. Controversial outcome of the UR was the agreement on Trade Related Aspects of Intellectual Property Rights. IPR are "information with commercial value'. International community started recognizing that proprietary rights subsist in new ideas, inventions and creative expression. Such creative work deserves property status. Community thought that knowledge producers, owners of creative work should be given right to exclude others from access to or use of the protected subject matter. IPRs denote and include patents, copyrights, trademarks, geographic indications, trade secrets, industrial designs.

The members of WTO are the members of TRIPs. Prior to TRIPs agreement different domestic rules in different nations existed for regulation of IPR regime and their enforcement. There was no harmony in these national laws to govern IPRs world wide. TRIPS is an international agreement administered by the World Trade Organization (WTO). TRIPS agreement introduced intellectual property law into the international trading system for the first time. It lays down minimum standards of regulation for many forms of intellectual properties.. TRIPs has created inter-governmental framework for enforcement of IPRs on international plane. TRIPs requires member states to provide minimum standards for protection and enforcement of all IPRs irrespective of country of origin. Those include catagories mentioned below. TRIPs provides for enforcement procedures, remedies, and dispute resolution procedures. Ultimate aim of this agreement is to boost economic relations among the nations through facilitated trade IPRs.

Objectives of TRIPS Agreement

The Objectives of TRIPS Agreement can be enlisted as follows—

1. To minimize distortions and remove impediments in international trade to promote effective and adequate protection of IPRs and to insure that the procedures and the measures for enforcements of IPRs do not hinder legitimate trade in IPRs;

2. To lay down standards and principles regulating availability, extent and use of IPRs;

3. To provide a multilateral framework of principles, rules and disciplines governing international trade in counterfeit(fake/duplicate) goods;

4. To devise a mutually supportive relationship between WTO and WIPO and other organizations working in international trade;

5. To meet the special needs of the least developed countries regarding maximum flexibility

in the domestic enforcement of laws and regulations so as to enable those to have a sound and viable technological base;

6. To provide effective and appropriate means for enforcements of provisions of TRIPS agreement in view of the inconsistencies and disharmony in various legal systems at national level;

7. To lay down multilateral legal procedures to settle the disputes involving IPRs trade issues;

8. To lay down multilateral effective and expeditious legal procedures for prevention and resolution of inter governmental disputes.

Categories of IPRs covered by TRIPs Agreement

Ss. 1 to 7 of Part II of the TRIPS agreement enlists following categories of IPRs—

1. Copyrights and Related Rights
2. Trademarks
3. Geographical Indications
4. Industrial Designs
5. Patents
6. Layout designs of Integrated Circuits
7. Protection of Undisclosed Information

All these categories of IPRs are explained in more details at the appropriate places in this part of the book.

Specifically, TRIPS requires WTO members to provide <u>copyright</u> rights, covering content producers including performers, producers of sound recordings and broadcasting organizations; <u>geographical indications</u>, including appellations of origin; <u>industrial designs</u>; <u>integrated circuit layout-designs</u>; <u>patents</u>; <u>new plant varieties</u>; <u>trademarks</u>; <u>trade dress</u>; and undisclosed or <u>confidential information</u>. Today TRIPS remains the most comprehensive international agreement on intellectual property rights.

1. PATENTS — Definition and Meaning

Patent as a concept originates in Great Britain. The queen used to grant 'Letters Patent' to its subjects. It connotes royal prerogative to grant monopolies i.e. exclusive right to make use, exercise and vend inventions. Patent generally means a privilege, property, authority or a grant by a Government to a person. Patent is an intellectual property and the patentee has right to sell, grant license or assign patented property. Indian law relating to patents is contained in the Indian Patents Act, 1970 as amended by Patents (Amendment) Act, 2005.

Definition of Patent—Section 2-(m) of the Act defines patent as—' *patent means a patent for any invention granted under the Act* '. Patent is thus granted to an invention and it is defined in terms of invention. It therefore becomes essential to know 'invention' to understand the concept of patent.

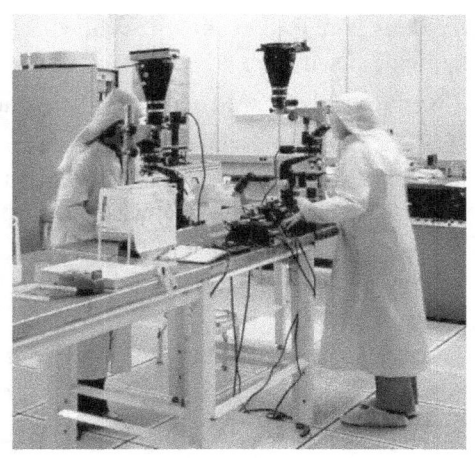

Salient features of Patent

a) **Invention** — Definition of the term given in section 2(j) of the Act reads as ' *invention means a new product or process involving an inventive step and capable of industrial application.*'

Following important features of invention can explain the concept of patent.

Important features of invention. —

1. It is a new product or process;
2. Such a product or process must involve ***inventive step***—The term 'inventive step' has been defined as—

   "inventive step means a feature of an invention *that involves technical advance as compared to the exiting knowledge or having economic significance or both and that makes the invention not obvious to a person skilled in that art ".*
3. Invention must be ***capable of industrial application.*** According to S. 2 (ac), — *'capable of industrial application ' in relations to an invention means that the invention is capable of being made or used in an industry."*

b) **Patentable Invention**—From these definitions, characteristics of patentable invention can be developed. Those are—

   i. *Newness—Novelty*—Whatever is already known to the public or which is of common knowledge cannot be an invention and hence cannot be patented. Something which is newly created, developed can be rewarded with a patent.
   ii. *Usefulness—Utility*—Invention must have utility value. It must be capable of being applied in industrial or manufacturing process. The society must get benefit out of an invention. Commercial or economic importance is attached to the patentable invention.
   iii. *Non-Obviousness*—Invention to be patentable should not be obvious to the person knowledgeable in that subject. For an ignorant person every new thing is like invention. Therefore the test of obviousness depends upon the person skilled in the art.

c) **Inventions Not Patentable** – Sections 3 and 4 of the Act enlist the invention those are not patentable. In fact S.3 states what are not inventions. Those are given below.

1. Invention, which are frivolous or contrary to natural law;
2. The use or commercial exploitation of invention is against public order or morality or it is harmful to human beings or animals, or plants or environment; cloning though remarkable invention, still regarded as harmful to mankind.
3. Mere discovery of a scientific principle or of any living thing or non-living substance in nature;
4. Mere discovery of a new form without improvement of efficacy of new property or new use of known substance or mere use of a known process without resulting in a new product;
5. Obtaining a substance by mere admixture of components and bearing the properties of components in aggregate or a process producing the same substance;
6. Mere arrangement or rearrangement or duplication of known devices;
7. A method of agriculture, horticulture, process for the medicinal, surgical, curative, diagnostic, therapeutic or other treatment of human beings or process for a similar treatment of animals;
8. Plants and animals other than micro-organisms but including seeds, varieties and species, an essential biological process for propagation and production of plants and animals;
9. A mathematical or business method or a computer program per-se or algorithms;
10. Literary, dramatic, musical, artistic, cinematographic works and television production (which are registered as copyrights)
11. Method of performing mental acts or of playing games, presentation of information, traditional knowledge;
12. Invention relating to atomic energy.

Types of Patents—Patents can be of two kinds—1- Product patents and 2- Process patents. Product patents may be granted for a machine, apparatus, article or any newly invented substance. If the product is the invention, it is a product patent. A mobile handset, car, a pen may be patented as a product patent. Process patents are available for any novel manner, method or an art. Drugs, medicines, chemical substances are the results of a chemical procedure and in such case the process of making may be regarded as process patent. For medicines and chemicals product patent can also be granted. Indian law does not recognize certain product patents clarified in the non-patentable inventions.

Patents of Addition

Process of invention is never ending. The main invention (which is registered with 'complete specification'/description) may be improved. This improvement or addition to the subsisting patent may also be registered. Patents of addition are the patent for improvement or modification of the main patent. A substance may be produced by combination of known components but with a new process or a more useful or more economical process. This can be treated as a new or useful improvement. Sometimes the same result can be obtained in a better, more expeditious or economical manner. Improvement may be an addition, omission or alteration to get a better performance. Patent can be granted for such a better process. On the contrary, by the same procedure an entirely new product with different components may be obtained which is worth a patent of addition. Modification implies an alteration without radical transformation. An improvement is change, retaining features of original invention. For registration of patent for addition, improvement should independently be an invention as defined.

A patient has to be registered by the true and first inventor. The patent thus registered is available for certain number of years (called, term of patents). During this period the owner can sell assign, grant, and license it to others by accepting royalty. Without owner's consent, no other can use the invention. Unauthorized use is an infringement of patents and action can be taken against violators under the Act.

Rights of Patentee

Following rights are conferred on patentee under Indian law of patents—

Right of Exploitation

1. In product patent, patentee has exclusive right to prevent third parties from making, using, offering for sale or selling such product. Import of patented product in India can also be prevented. (S.48)

2. In process patent, patentee has exclusive right to prevent third parties from using that process or to prevent from offering for sale or selling or importing the product in India, obtained directly by the patented process. (S.48)

   S.48 clarifies that use etc. of product or process patent in above manner by the third parties is possible with the consent of the patentee.

3. Rights of Co-owners of Patents—S.50— When a patent is granted to two or more persons, each co-owner has a right to equal undivided share in the patent. However sharing in the patent can be modified by agreement between co-owners.

4. Right of Grantee or Proprietor— Where there are two or more grantee or Proprietor of a patent, each of those is entitled to a right under S.48 for his own benefit without accounting to the other grantee or proprietor. When there are registered grantee or proprietor, license under the patent shall not be granted and share in the patent shall not be assigned by one without other's consent. This provision is subject to S.51 and an agreement to the contrary. (S.51 empowers the Controller of Patent to give directions as to sale, lease of patent or grant of licences under patent, upon application made to him by one of such grantee or proprietor) If patented article is sold by one of such grantee or proprietor, the purchaser has a right to deal with the article as if he purchases it from sole patentee.

5. Patent is treated like movable property and the rules of ownership and devolution of movable property are applicable to patent.

6. Assignment etc…s. S.68—Patentee can assign a patent or share in a patent or mortgage, or give its licence or create any other interest in the patent like other properties. However for validity of such transfers, a written agreement with all the terms and conditions as to rights and obligations must be signed and executed.

7. Power of registered grantee or proprietor —S.70— Registered grantee or proprietor of a patent shall have power to assign, grant licences or otherwise deal with the patent. They can give effectual receipts for any consideration for any such assignment etc..

8. Right to Surrender Patent—S.63—Patentee has a privilege to offer to surrender his patent. The Controller has adequate powers to accept the offer and revoke the patent.

9. Right to Duplicate Patent-S.154-If a p is lost or destroyed, applicant can get duplicate of the p. Application has to be made to the Controller in the prescribed format along with the fees. If non production of p is accounted for to the satisfaction of the Controller then also duplicate can be obtained.

10 Remedies in case of Infringement of P—Ss.104 TO 110—Infringement (violation) of p is a serious issue. Suits may be filed for various remedies like injunction, damages for the loss caused due to violation or account for profits made by infringement. The court may also order the seizure, forfeiture or destruction og the infringing goods or materials and implements. This right to take proceedings is also available to the exclusive licencee as the patentee in respect of any infringement. Remedies may be granted considering the loss suffered by the licencee or the profits earned by infringement. Holder of a compulsory licence u/s 84 has a right to seek an injunction to prevent violation if the patentee fails to take legal action within prescribed time.

Term of Patent—S.53 The term of every patent granted (After the commencement of the Patents Amendment Act, 2002) shall be twenty years from the date of filing application for the patent. If on the date of commencement of the Patents Amendment Act, 2002, term of any existing patent has not expired and such patent has not ceased to have any effect, that patent also has the term of twenty years from the date of filing application for the patent.

Term of patent in case of International applications filed under the Patent Co-operation Treaty designating India, shall be twenty years from the international filing date accorded under the above Treaty.

Expiry of the Term—A patent shall cease to have effect on the expiration of the period prescribed for the payment of renewal fees and if such fee is not paid within that prescribed period or extended prescribed period. On cessation of patent right due to non-payment of renewal fee or on expiry of the term of the patent, subject matter covered by the patent shall not be entitled to any protection.

Term of Patents of Addition—S.55 Term of patent of addition would be equal to that of the patent for the main invention or such period of the term as has not expired and shall remain in force during that term or until the previous cesser of the patent for the main invention. Section clarifies that if the patent for the main invention is revoked under this Act, on the request of the patentee, the Court or the Controller may order that the patent of addition shall become an independent patent for remainder of the term for the patent for the main invention. Afterwards, such patent continues in force as an independent patent.

2. COPYRIGHTS

The regime of intellectual property rights covers different forms of rights enjoyed in the produce of mind. Things flow from the exercise of brainpower. For example, ideas, inventions, literary work are the results of the process of intellectual endeavor. Copyright is asserted in respect of product of human intellect, skill, labor. Copyright is a bundle of rights in some work of art, music, etc. Right consists in publication, reproduction of the work. It is a right to prevent piracy of one's work. Copyright is available to the *form of expression of an idea and not to the idea itself.*

Because of the technological development and accessibility of new devices, the 'copying' has become easy. To protect the interests of the creator, and to prevent piracy, the Indian law on copyright i.e. Copy Rights Act, 1957 with amendment in 1994 makes the provisions for registration and term of copyright, its infringement and the remedies after violation. The scope of this chapter permits only the conceptual understanding of the copyright.

COPYRIGHTS—Definition and Meaning

The concept of copyright is contained in section 14 of the Copy Rights Act. This section enlists certain acts, which can be performed in respect of certain works. Copyright is a right to do those acts permissible by the nature of work. Subject matter of this right are —-*literary, dramatic, musical, artistic work, sound recording, cinematographic films and computer programs.*

Copyright is an exclusive right to do the following acts—
1. Reproduction in material form the literary, dramatic, musical, artistic work and computer programs;
2. Issuing copes to the public of literary, dramatic, musical, artistic works and also copies of films, cassettes and computer discs containing computer programs;
3. To sell or hire copies of literary, dramatic, musical work, films, cassettes and computer disk containing computer programs;
4. Translation of literary, dramatic, musical work and computer programs;
5. Communication of artistic work, work of sound recording and films etc. to public;
6. Performing literary, dramatic, musical work in public;
7. Adaptation of literary, dramatic, musical, artistic work and also of computer Programs;
8. Making cinematographic films of literary, dramatic, musical work.

Subject Matter of Copyright
Some of the key terms pertaining to the subject matter of copyright require explanation.

1. **Liberty Work** – Literary work needs labor, skill, judgment and capital. Copyright subsists in literary work. A literary work provides information or may give pleasure of literary enjoyment. Literary work normally is presented in written or printed form. A novel, commentaries, poem, notes are the common illustrations of literary work. Authors, publishers enjoy copyright in literary work. The literary work may not possess literary talent or merit. The railway timetable, telephone directories, tourist manual, stock exchange quotations have been treated as literary work.

2. **Dramatic Work** – Author of dramatic work is entitled to copyright in such work and its adaptations. It includes any piece of recitation, choreographic work, scenic arrangement, acting form reduced into writing. Dramatic work does not include cinematographic films.

3. **Musical Work** – Musical work exists in the original music and its notations. A song is a literary work while musical composition given to it is musical work. Adaptations of musical work in orchestra or with other instruments deserve copyright if these involve sufficient intellectual creation.

4. **Artistic Work** – Artistic work includes painting (art by colors on a surface), sculpture (casts, models), a drawing (a diagram, map, chart, plan) ,an engraving (etching, woodcuts, lithographs, carving figures on the surface), work of architecture and artistic craftsmanship, photograph. Cinematographic film is visual recording of moving images and reproducing it by a process or device.

5. **Cinematographic Film** – Cinematographic film is rapid projection by cinematograph. A video film is also included in cinematographic films.

6. **Computer Programs** – Computer programs recorded on any storage device, a disc, tape is treated as literary work. Copyright subsists in computer programs, software.

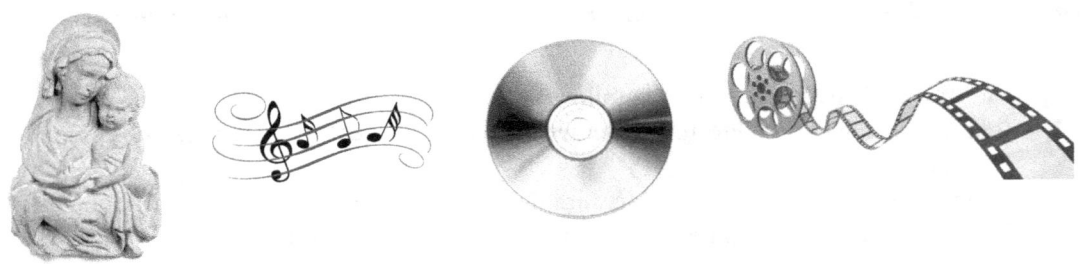

Rights of the Copyright Owner

S.14 of the Act explained earlier enlists the activities which can be undertaken by the owner of copyright by way of right and that are the very concept of copyright. Apart from those facets of copyright, the owner has following rights,

1. **Acts u/s 14**—Right to do all the acts in respect of subject matter of copyright enlisted in S.14, elaborated earlier;

2. **Positive right of exploitation**—The owner of copyright has right to exploit himself or give a liecnce to others to exploit as per S.14 in consideration of royalty.

3. **Negative right of prevention**—By the very nature, copyright is a negative right in the sense that the owner of copyright can prevent others from exploiting his creation without his consent;

4. **Right of Assignment—S. 18**—Owner of copyright may validly assign the existing work either wholly or partially. Future work may also be assigned but assignment would be effective only when the work comes into existence. Assignee of copyright is treated

as the owner of copyright. Assignment may be subject to limitations and may be for the whole of the term of copyright or part thereof.

5. **Right to grant Licence—S.30—**Owner of copyright is entitled to grant a licence of any interest in existing copyright in writing and signed by him. Licence of future work may also be granted but grant would be effective only when the work comes into existence.

6. **Owner's control over copyright Society—S.36—**Copyright society shall be subject to the collective control of the owners of copyright. The owner of copyright has right to regular, full and detailed information regarding all activities of copyright society in relation to the administration of their copyrights. Owners' approval is necessary for its procedures of collection and distribution of fees and for utilizations of fees for other purposes.

7. **Broadcast Reproduction Right—S.37—**Every broadcasting organization has a special right known as 'broadcast reproduction right' in respect of its broadcast. The broadcasting organization has remedies for infringement of this right in case of rebroadcasting, sound or visual recording of broadcast, reproduction or selling or hiring to the public of such sound or visual recording of broadcast without licence of the owner of broadcast. Broadcast reproduction right subsists until twenty five years from the beginning of the calendar year next following the year in which the broadcast is made.

8. **Performer's Right—S.38—**Performer has a special right to be known as the 'performer's right' in relation to his performance. This right subsists until fifty years from the beginning of the calendar year next following the year in which the performance is made.

9. **Resale share right in original copies—S.53-A-**Author (first owner) of painting, sculpture or drawing or of the original manuscript of a literary or dramatic work or musical work has a right to share in the resale price of such original copy or manuscript. To claim the right, the resale price should exceed ten thousand rupees and this right is available notwithstanding of assignment of copyright in such work.

10. **Rights in case of Infringement—** The author of copyright has following rights/remedies if his copyright is infringed—
    i. Right to recover the infringing copies unsold;
    ii Right to the price of copies sold;
    iii Right to file a suit for injunction, damages, accounts and profits.

11. **Translator's right—** The translator has a right in the work translated. He is however not entitled to reproduce or publish the translation without the consent of the author of original work.

12. **Moral rights of the owner of copyright—** Above mentioned rights have economic dimensions. Besides these general or economic rights the owner of copyright has following 'moral rights' in respect of his subject matter. These can be claimed independently of copyright and even after assignment either wholly or partially.
    i. **Right of publication—**He has liberty to publish the work i.e. he may or may not publish;

    ii **Right of paternity**—Author owns credit for his work wherever displayed, used etc..

13. **Author's special rights u/s 57**—Author of work shall have right to—

    a authorship of work;

    b restrain or claim damages for any distortion, mutilation, modification of said work which is prejudicial to his honour or reputation. This distortion etc. should be done before the expiry of the term of copyright and this right is not available in respect of adaptation of a computer programme. These rights can be claimed by the legal heirs of the author.

Term of Copyright

Ss. 22 to 29 state the term of copyrights in various forms of subject matter. Nature of copyrighted work and the term is as under.

1. **Published literary, dramatic, musical and artistic work**
   (other than photograph)—Published within lifetime of author——Until 60 years from the beginning of the calendar year next following the year in which author dies;

2. **Anonymous and pseudonymous work**— Literary, dramatic, musical and artistic work (other than photograph)—Published anonymously or pseudonymously——Until 60 years from the beginning of the calendar year next following the year in which the work is first published;

3. **Posthumous work**—Literary, dramatic, musical work or an engraving in which copyright subsists at the date of death of the author but which has not been published before that date—- Until 60 years from the beginning of the calendar year next following the year in which the work is first published;

4. **Photograph**—Until 60 years from the beginning of the calendar year next following the year in which the photograph is first published;

5. **Cinematographic Films**—Until 60 years from the beginning of the calendar year next following the year in which the cinematographic film is published;

6. **Sound Recording**—Until 60 years from the beginning of the calendar year next following the year in which the sound recording is published;

7. **Government Works**—Where the government is the first owner—Until 60 years from the beginning of the calendar year next following the year in which the work is first published;

8. **Works of Public Undertaking**—Where the public undertaking is the first owner—Until 60 years from the beginning of the calendar year next following the year in which the work is first published;

9. **Works of International Organizations**—To which S.41 applies— Until 60 years from the beginning of the calendar year next following the year in which the work is first published.

3. TRADE MARKS

Businessmen, traders or manufacturers very often carry on their business under some name, may be that of their family, city or any other unique title of their choice. The purpose is to identify their product in the market. Such names give distinct mark to the goods. Trademarks describe the goods, their quality, distinguishing those from other competitive traders. Trademark is a visual symbol indicating trade origin either in name of the person or organization. For example, Philips, Murphy, Reliance, Bata etc. Trademark is viewed as intellectual property. It contemplates monopoly right to trademarks and prohibits rival traders from using it. Unscrupulous traders may use other's reputed trademark and promote their substandard goods in the market. Such spurious goods dupe the consumers. Selling one's product in other's trademark is a wrong of 'passing off'. The trademark law protects the trademarks and prohibit passing off. Trademarks Act, 1999 has replaced old enactment, Trade and Merchandise Marks Act, 1958.

The concept of trademark embodied in the Trademark Act, 1999 is discussed below.

TRADE MARKS — Definition and Meaning

Section 2(zb) of the Act defines DefoFTM. The essentials of the concept emanating from the definition are given below.

1. *Trademark is available for goods and services.* Goods means movable properties, consumable, household articles sold in the market. Old Act did not provide trademark for services but now the services could also have trademark. According to S.2 (z), service means service of any description available to a potential user. The term includes provision of services in industrial or commercial matters, banking, financing, chit-funds, insurance, communication, conveying of news or information and advertising, entertainment, amusement, construction, repair, real estate, transport, storage, material treatment, processing, supply of electrical or other energy, boarding, lodging.

2. *Trademark is a 'mark'.* Mark includes device, brand, heading, label, ticket, name, signature, word, letter, numeral, shape of goods, packing or combination of colours or any combination thereof. (Definition u/s2-m of the Act) Thus the phrase 'mark' is of wide interpretation and anything, which can identify the product, can be called as trademark.

3. *Graphic Representation and Distinciveness*— Mark must be capable of –

—Being represented graphically i.e. graphic representation of goods or services;

—Distinguishing goods or services of one person from those of others i.e. distinctiveness is the important feature of trademark. Distinctiveness makes the consumers to choose the goods easily. Distinctiveness may be inherent or acquired. Get up or packing of articles can be distinct in itself. Article comes in the market with that unique and original and inherent mark, say, a wrapper of a chocolate. Distinctiveness may be acquired through long use, invented use, words, device or mark. By prolonged use, the words do not become descriptive but suggestive of quality. McDowell's 'm' is short, appeals to eye.

4. *Mark includes*—shape of goods, their packaging and combination of colours, certification trademark and collective mark.

'Package' implies a case, box, container, covering, folder, receptacle, vessel casket, basket, wrapper, label band, ticket, reel, frame, capsule, cap, lid, stopper and cork (definition, u/s 2-q).

Certification Trademark—Such a mark is registerable under chapter 10 of the Act in the name of the proprietor of the certification trademark. This mark is certified by the proprietor in respect of origin, material, and mode of manufacture of goods or performance of services, quality, accuracy and such characteristics, which bring distinctiveness to the proprietor's goods/services.

Collective Mark—The members of an associastion of persons can obtain this mark. The association is the proprietor of the collective mark.

In this Act reference to trademark shall include reference to certification trademark and collective trademark.

Rights of Trademark Holder

Trademark holder of a registered trademark has following rights—

1. **Right to Exclusive Use**—Registered proprietor has exclusive right to use the trademark in relation to the goods or services for registered trademark;

2. **Right to Assign**—Registered proprietor of trademark can validly transfer the trademark by way of licence or assignment. Registered user however cannot assign or transmit trademark. By these two Right registered proprietor can commercially exploit the trademark ;

3. **Right to seek correction of error**—Registered proprietor can apply for correction of errors in the register in respect of name, address or description of registered proprietor. He can seek deletion of any entry of any goods, services;

4. **Right to seek alteration of registered trademark** — Registered proprietor can apply to the Registrar for permission to add or alter the trademark in any manner without substantially affecting original features of trademark;

5. **Right of registered proprietor to take legal action**—Trademark holder can seek remedies like injunction (to prevent making, applying the trademark and its abuse), damages (for the loss sustained due to violation of trademark) or a suit for accounts and

profits (gained out of wrongful use of trademark). He can also ask for delivery of infringing articles.

6. **Right of registered user to take legal action**—Registered user has a right to initiate legal proceedings for infringement of trademark;

Domain Names

Meaning—Large section of the community is using internet for e- commerce. There is a vast virtual market place for business transactions. Trading parties may not personally know each other. But identity is essential to form contracts or otherwise transact with each other. Domain names serve the purpose of establishing online identities of transacting parties.

Resource on the internet has its own address (URL). Domain name is a part of this address assigned to each computer or service on the internet. In simple words, domain name is the address of the business personalities on the network. Domain name is the complete description of the party on the internet site. It has host name, sub domain and domain. These parts are shown by dots. '.com' is the last part of domain name known as 'Top Level Domain' (TLD).

Legal Status Domain names—Domain names are treated as trademark. Indian courts have recognized domain name as trademark and protect as such. Pronouncements in *Yahoo! Inc.* v/s *Akash Arora* [78 (1999), Delhi Law Times,285], *Rediff Communications Ltd.* v/s *Cyber Booth and Another* [AIR 2000 Bom 27], *Satyam Infoway Ltd.* v/s *Siffynet Solutions Pvt. Ltd.* [(2004) 6 Section 145] are illustrative judgments in which domain names has been protected as IPR. More the use of internet, more are the occurrences of imitations, piracy and passing off. This concept and the law are evolving.

4. DESIGNS

The Designs Act, 2000 deals with the proprietary rights in designs. This new Act has repealed the Designs Act, 1911 recognizing the international standards for industrial designs as per the TRIPS agreement. Design is a species of intellectual property right and it is protected and regulated by the above Act. Consumers purchase goods not only by the utility or quality but also by their appearance. The purchasers are attracted by design of an article. Considering the importance of outward appearance of objects in attracting customers, the manufacturers also use such designs and try to increase the sale. For example, design of a new car, camera, and bottle of soft drink. Design is the result of creative efforts having artistic and functional attraction. It helps to distinguish and identify the product. Design improves the utility value of the object. Design that way has enormous value in the commercial world. It is a powerful corporate tool. Design has goodwill and can be profitably used by the traders. The originator of the design has a monopoly right in the design and can exclude others from using it as in patents or trademarks.

DESIGNS— Definition and Meaning—

According to S.2 (d) of the Designs Act, 2000, design should have some shape, configuration, pattern, or ornamentation or composition of lines or colors. Following are the **essential characteristics/requirements** of registerable design.

1. *Design is applied to articles/objects*—The subject matter of design is an article. Article itself is not design. Design represents article. Typical shape of a motorbike, furniture, toys, shoe would explain the applicability. It can be applied in any form to an object. It must be incorporated in the article itself. It can be two dimensional on a piece of paper/textile or three dimensional in nature in the form of a shape or configuration. Coca-cola bottle has a three dimensional design. Design is an applied art. It is applied through industrial process. Functional designs which exclusively make the article work or function are not to be registered.

2. *Visual Appeal*—Design is always addressed to an eye and are said to be judged solely by the eye. Design catches the eye of a consumer in the marketing world. Peculiarity of design lies in its striking or distinct appearance. This visual test rules out the functional consideration of a design. Appearance is the gist of the design. Articulation of design is a creative activity, which gives ornamental or formal appearance to the product.

3. *Novelty and Originality*— Design to be registered should be new or original. The sources of a design may be natural objects or other object commonly seen elsewhere. The drawing should however be in a new fashion. Design should involve a new pattern or ornament.

4. *No previous publication*—The design should not be previously published in India. Publication is not defined in the Act. Publication implies that the design is made available to the public or disclosed or shown to the members of public. Design should not be part of what is already known to the public or exploited.

To claim the right in the design, it should be registered under the provisions of the Act of 2000.

Rights of Design Holder

Rights of Design Holder are enlisted below.

1. **Right upon registration**—Registered design is nothing but 'copyright in design'. Registered proprietor of design has exclusive right to apply the design to the article.

2. **Term of copyright in design**—The copyright in the design subsists for ten years from the date of registration. On application it can be extended for five years. Maximum term of design is fifteen years.

3. **Right to restore lapsed design** —After initial period of ten years, if proper steps are not taken design lapses. Application for restoration of lapsed design can be filed. However if it should be shown to the satisfaction of the Controller that failure to pay the renewal fee was unintentional and there was undue delay in applying, design may be restored.

4. **Piracy of Registered design and Right of Legal Action**—Infringement of registered design is called as piracy. Piracy may be in the form of unauthorized application, fraudulent

imitation of registered design or importing and selling articles without owner's consent. Design Holder can seek remedies like injunction (to prevent making, applying the design and its abuse), damages (for the loss sustained due to violation of copyright) or a suit for accounts and profits (gained out of wrongful use of copyright in design). He can also ask for delivery of infringing articles.

5. GEOGRAPHICAL INDICATIONS

Very recently a German company has obtained trademark of 'Khadi' for its 'Khadi Nature Products'. It is learned that IPR Association of Indian Producers has claimed 'geographical indication' for 'Khadi'.

It is observed that certain goods are marketed under geographical names. Those geographical names have earned good will in the market. The names indicate geographical area and good are very much associated with such titles. The geographical names indicate place of origin and also the quality, chief attributes, peculiarities of the goods.

Illustrations of geographical names—Basamati Rice, Kolhapuri Chapples, Tirupati Laddu, Darjeeling Tea, Nagpur Orange, Paithanee Saree, Scotch Whiskey etc.

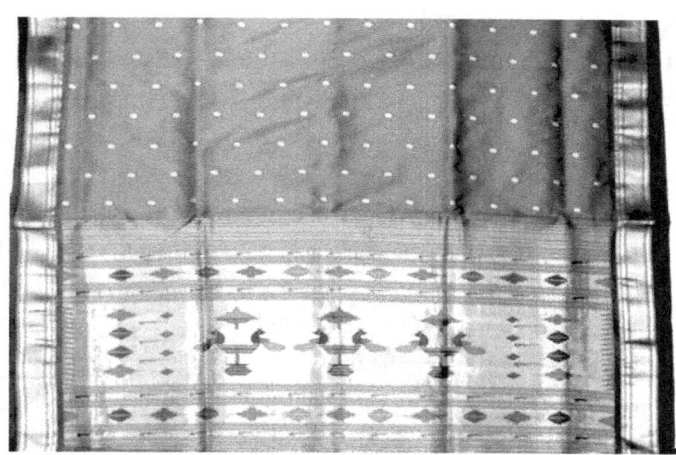

Certain goods are cultivated only in particular locality or naturally found in a region or manufactured traditionally by local people. These goods possess special taste, fragrance and quality. Indigenous goods produced or cultivated have value as medicine/ drug or food (Turmeric, Neem) Geographical indication appeals the customers. The geographical names have gained popularity, reputation and economic importance like trademarks. Sometimes goods without any association with geographical territory are sold under reputed geographical names. Those indicate falsely the geographical association to pass off and boost the sale, may be of substandard goods. By this abuse of geographical indication, the people are duped. Hence the need was felt to protect geographical names of the goods.

At international level attempts were made to protect geographical indication. Madrid Convention, Lisbon Agreement (1958), TRIPS agreement embody provisions to protect geographical indication internationally. Indian Parliament has passed Geographical Indications of Goods (Registration and Protection) Act, 1999 for registration and protection of geographical indication.

Definition, Meaning and Concept of Geographical Indication—

Definition u/s 2(e) of the Act—'geographical indication' in relation to goods means an geographical indication which identifies such goods as agricultural goods, natural goods, or manufactured goods or originating or manufactured in the territory of a country, or a region or locality in that country where a given quality, reputation or other characteristics of such goods is essentially attributable to its geographical origin and in case where such goods are manufactured goods, one of the activities of either the production or of processing or preparation of the goods concerned takes place in such territory, region or locality, as the case may be.'
To understand the concept better, definitions of following terms are reproduced.

Goods— Definition u/s 2(f) 'goods' means agricultural, natural or manufactured goods or any goods of handicraft or of industry and includes foodstuff';

Indication— Definition u/s 2(g) 'indication' includes any name, geographical or figurative representation or any combination of them conveying or suggesting the geographical origin of goods to which it applies'..

Important Features of Geographical Indication—Perusal of above definitions leads to following features of geographical indication—

1. Geographical indication identifies or associated essentially with goods;
2. Geographical indication is available to agricultural, natural or manufactured goods. It is also associated with goods of handicraft or industry goods and foodstuff;
3. Geographical indication can be obtained for the goods originating or manufactured in the territory of a country, or a region or locality in that country where a given quality, reputation or other characteristics of such goods is essentially attributable to its geographical origin;
4. If geographical indication is to be acquired for manufactured goods hen one of the activities like production or processing or preparation of the goods concerned should take place in such territory, region or locality;
5. Geographical indication includes any name, geographical or figurative representation or any combination of them conveying or suggesting the geographical origin of goods;
6. If geographical name does not indicate the name of a country, region or locality of that country, still that name is considered as geographical indication if the name relates to a specific geographical area and it is used upon or in relation to particular goods originating from that country, region or locality as the case may be.[Explanation to S. 2(e)]

Other aspects of Geographical indication—

7. Geographical indication needs to be registered under the Act for its protection. Any person, manufacturer or producer or organization can apply for geographical indication to the Registrar of Geographical Indication. Initial registration is valid for ten years and can be renewed for additional period of ten more years.

8. Registered user of geographical indication has exclusive right to use the geographical indication in respect of the concerned goods;

9. In case of infringement of geographical indication one can prefer remedies like injunction (to prevent abuse), damages (for the loss sustained due to misuse) or a suit for accounts and profits (gained out of wrongful use of geographical indication) or can seek infringing labels and indication for destruction.

10. Penalties and punishment for falsifying and falsely applying geographical indication and applying false geographical indication are provided under the Act which may be fine ranging from fifty thousand to two lakh rupees or imprisonment from six months to three years.

11. The objective of the Act is thus to prevent the misuse of the geographical indication and protect the interest of the consumers, manufacturer preserve the honor of that geographical area.

6. CONFIDENTIAL INFORMATION AND TRADE SECRETS

It is said that all great work is the result of great ideas in the mind. World community has now acknowledged that proprietary rights subsist in ideas and information. When a person generates ideas or knowledge then he only should be allowed to use it and others should not disclose that information without his consent. If the special information is the result of intellectual exercise, then it should be kept secret. Information could be personal, commercial or technical. Confidentiality and secrecy has gained importance in the competitive business world. Business houses, trading communities have sensitive information which outsmarts others and hence has commercial value. If such knowledge or information is not protected, there are chances of misuse by unauthorized exploitation. Confidential information, knowledge and trade secrets, therefore, are recognized as class of IPRs.

Concept of Confidential Information and Trade Secret —

There is no standard and precise definition of confidential information (synonymously called undisclosed information). Following points may be noted in connection with such information or trade secret —

1. This type of information is kept confidential as it has economical value and commercial advantage in the competitive business world;

2. Confidential information is accepted as a kind of IPR and may be invisible, intangible;

3. Confidential information which can be sold and purchased is generally described as trade secret;

4. Owner enjoys it in confidence or shares in confidence;

5. Employees who handle the trade secret during their course of employment are under express (as a term of contract of employment) or implied duty of fidelity(duty to be loyal or faithful to employer), even former employee is under obligation not to divulge secret information of the company which he served;

Confidential information is a trade secret or not generally depends upon nature of information, employment, employer's view of secrecy etc;

Illustrations of confidential information or trade secret — Information regarding manufacturing process, raw materials, sources of material used, technical drawings, product plans,/ costing, research reports/data formula, program device etc is treated as undisclosed information. Even it includes business model, financial aspects of business, administrative procedures, methods, training modules, technique or process affording cutting edge advantage over competitors. Reports of pharmaceutical, agricultural or chemical products are significant trade secrets. Sometimes information generated is a valuable source as a foundation of a patentable invention or industrial design capable of being registered as such but in fact not registered as a patent or industrial design. This information not materialized into any IPR is also trade secret.

Legal Protection to Confidential Information and Trade Secrets—WTO, TRIPs agreement contain provisions to protect confidential information to encourage honest commercial practices. Under these agreements member states are obliged to protect undisclosed information. Under common law, information held in confidence should not be disclosed and the person would be guilty of breach of confidence. Judicial decisions hold the same view. In absence of express statute, common law principle or judge-made law is to be followed. In India so far there is no separate law to deal with the confidential information or trade secret. Indian courts have protected secrecy under the provisions of Indian Contract Act, 1872 or the Specific Relief Act, 1963 following principles equity and firmness. In view of this there is an urgent need for legal framework to regulate and protect confidential information or trade secret.

7. TRADITIONAL KNOWLEDGE

Introduction—We are living in the world of knowledge. In this information age knowledge is the power and source of wealth. Knowledge is now accepted as property and internationally recognized as IPR like patents etc. knowledge may be created or possessed by an individual and he can use it to the exclusion of others. But a community or local people may have knowledge passed on by generations and they continue to use it by tradition. This type of knowledge is tradition based and created, owned and managed by a particular community. Obviously then traditional knowledge has historical references. Indian scripts, folklore, Aurveda reflect tradition based knowledge passed on to present generation. Modern music composers are exploiting tribal tunes and film producers are displaying villege culture. Indigenous people from time immemorial know the methods of exploitation and conservation of biodiversity. World community has realized the significance of traditional knowledge and attempt has been made to shape this knowledge into a kind of IPR.

Concept of Traditional Knowledge (TK)—There is no universally accepted definition of traditional knowledge. WTO prefers the term in the context of tradition based inventions, discoveries, artistic, scientific works, undisclosed information and tradition based creations and innovations which are being applied in various fields. Generally traditional knowledge is not embodied in documents but transmitted orally from one generation to the next one and pertains to people of particular territory. Civilization, urbanization, scientific and technological developments have no bearing on such knowledge though field of knowledge may evolve, adapt and improvise.

Fields of Traditional Knowledge and Economic Dimensions—Medicines, heath care, biodiversity, agriculture, textile, environment, music, dance, arts, crafts, culture in general etc. are the illustrative area where traditional knowledge is evident. Tribal communities know the specific medicinal uses of plant varieties like Neem, Turmeric, Tulsi, They also know the harvesting practices. Aurveda is the treasure of traditional knowledge. World is celebrating 'Yoga Day'. Yoga is the classic example of traditional knowledge. One would realize that those people who possess it should be allowed to exploit it commercially. It is a fact that multinational companies, manufacturers are exploiting this knowledge and earning huge money. Hence justice demands that indigenous people should be given share in the benefits by the use of traditional knowledge.

Legal Framework for Protection of Traditional Knowledge—WIPO and UNESCO recommend model laws to protect folklore. Convention on Biological Diversity of 1992(CBD) is a milestone in the protection of biodiversity and tradition based knowledge. Doha Declaration of 2001 emphasized correlation between WTO, TRIPS agreements to effectively provide a framework for guarding the interest of local community. In India there is no independent law to protect traditional knowledge. Some of the other laws viz. laws relating to patents, copyright, geographical indications do indirectly protect the traditional knowledge. Bio-Diversity Act of 2002 (following the recommendations of CBD) provides for ' sustainable use' of components of biodiversity and fair and equitable sharing of their benefits with local people. In a significant development, the Protection of Plant Varieties and Farmers' Rights Act, 2001 aims at protection of farmers' rights in traditional knowledge. Conceptually these two laws expressly recognize ownership of traditional knowledge with indigenous people.

$$\boxed{\textbf{PART - XI}}$$

Chapter 55	**LAW OF ARBITRATION AND CONCILIATION**

THE ARBITRATION AND CONCILIATION ACT, 1996

Concept of Alternative Dispute Resolution (ADR)

In old days disputes among the villagers were settled by senior and respected members of the community commonly called as 'Panch' who held so called 'Panchayat'. People instead of going to the court preferred old practice of Panch/Panchayat. The phrase 'Alternative Dispute Resolution' (ADR) means a system of some alternative to regular litigation. Settlement of disputes through judicial proceedings has inherent limitations. Legal procedure is complicated and costly. Unreasonable delay in decision making causes harassment of litigants. Delayed court proceedings result in loss of money, time and energy to vindicate genuine claims. Alternative to this cumbersome process is always desirable. The concept of ADR aims exactly at that. It contemplates dispute resolution through alternative means, alternative to litigations/suits in civil matters. ADR includes Arbitration and Conciliation. The existing system of Lok Adalats under the Legal Services Authorities Act, 1987 (as amended in 2002) is based on ADR. The Arbitration and Conciliation Act of 1996 incorporates and gives effect to ADR.

Advantages/merits of Arbitration/ADR

1. Arbitration is the chief method of ADR;
2. ADR adopts expeditious procedure, and delay is avoided. Advocates are neither prohibited nor bound to be allowed; It saves time and money of the litigants;
3. Parties have freedom to frame own rules of procedure. Simple, streamlined procedure, appeal to parties. There is a procedural flexibility as to time, place, rules, laws, oral hearing;
4. Fair and impartial trial is conducted by independent tribunal with judicial framework;
5. No unnecessary technicalities are found and elaborate provisions of Civil Procedure Code, 1908, Indian Evidence Act, are not applicable;
6. Arbitral award is final and binding, enforceable as decree of civil court;
7. Arbitration is successful in disputes like commercial trade disputes, building and construction, shipping industry(generators), labor management…
8. In commercially sensitive matters privacy and confidentiality is maintained ;
9. Arbitrators are persons of choice hence satisfaction in settlement of disputes.

Background of the Act

This Act has repealed the Arbitration Act of 1940. The Act follows recommendations of General Assembly and UNCITRAL (United Nations Commission on International Trade Law) Model Law on International Commercial Arbitration in 1985 and UNCITRAL Conciliation Rules in 1980. It incorporates unified legal framework for fair and efficient settlement of disputes arising out of International Commercial relations.

Act has been passed with following objectives —

1. —Consolidation and amendment of law relating to—
   —Domestic arbitration,
   —International commercial arbitration,
   —Enforcement of foreign arbitral awards.
2. —To define the law relating to conciliation and incidental matters.

Salient Features of the Act of 1996

1. **Comprehensive Legislation** — The Act deals with domestic, international or inter-state arbitration. Provisions of the Act suit foreign investors. Framework for conciliation is provided. That way it is a self contained code. Law and procedure of arbitration and conciliation is given in detail.

2. **Procedure** — Detail procedure for conduct of arbitration and conciliation is provided, maintaining freedom to adopt own procedure. Application of CPC, 1908 is optional.

3. **Courts interference is minimized** —. No judicial authority shall intervene in arbitration proceedings except where it has been so empowered by the Act. (S.5)

   This provision ensures liberty of arbitrator/parties in regulating conducting arbitration proceedings.

4. **More powers to Arbitrator** — S. 16 of the Act bestows better competence to arbitral tribunal to rule on their jurisdiction. Interim measures can be ordered by arbitrators.

5. **Introduction of conciliation proceedings** — Parties can resort to newly introduced concept of conciliation for resolving pending or future disputes.

6. **Arbitral award is final and conclusive** — Arbitral award does not require reference to or confirmation of civil court.

7. **High Court' Powers** — The Act empowers Chief Justice of High Court to appoint arbitrators when appointment by parties fails.

8. Grounds for challenging awards have been made more specific;

9. More powers on arbitrators are conferred to interpret and correct its award.

10. Obstacles in ADR are removed; Environment favorable to ADR is evident.

ARBITRATION —

S. 2(1) (a) of the Act defines arbitration as, 'arbitration means any arbitration whether or not administered by permanent arbitral institution'. This definition does not elucidate the concept of arbitration. It can be explained as, 'settlement of disputes and difference relating to civil matters between parties in a judicial manner, by the decision of one or more persons called, arbitrators, appointed by the contending parties, without having recourse to law.' Arbitration has following features—

    i — Settlement of disputes or differences;

    ii — Dispute relates to civil matters in contrast to criminal matters;

    iii — The manner of resolving the dispute is judicial in the sense that basic principles of fairness, objectivity, justice are followed;

    iv — Deciding authority is called arbitrator/s who are appointed by the contending parties themselves;

    v — Subject matter of differences of arbitration cannot be resorted to court of law, that means the jurisdiction of the civil court is ousted.

The concept would be more elaborated by arbitration agreement.

Arbitration Agreement - S.7

Arbitration is an old method of settling civil disputes between parties by reference of the dispute to a third person. The third person is called an arbitrator. He should be an independent and impartial one. Arbitration is preferred to the usual civil courts because resolution of disputes by arbitrator is quick, inexpensive and by a simple procedure. Arbitration thus is a **domestic forum** and not a court. Arbitrator however works like a court.

Arbitration agreement is necessary for determination of disputes through arbitration. S.7 of the Act defines arbitration agreement as –

'an agreement by the parties to submit to arbitration all or certain disputes which may have arisen or which may arise between them in respect of a defined legal relationship whether contractual or not....'

Essentials of Arbitration Agreement –

The arbitration agreement must be valid and enforeable. It should satisfy following essentials under Arbitration Act.

1. **Form of Arbitration Agreement** – Arbitration agreement must be in writing. Terms of the agreement must be in writing. It could be a formal document executed between the parties. But such a formal document is not compulsory under the Act. It may be a separate agreement or a clause or a term in principal agreement.

2. **Presumption of agreement in writing** – Such an agreement is presumed to be in writing if –

    a) an agreement is contained in a document signed by the parties;

    b) an agreement is evident in exchange of letters, telegrams, telex or any other means of telecommunication. By this standard, electronic messages could be an evidence of a written agreement. Such a communication/correspondence must be a record of agreement to refer.

    c) exchange of statement of claims and defense between the parties elsewhere can also be treated as agreement in writing. However it should be clear from exchange that an agreement is alleged to be in existence by one party and not denied by the other.

Thus in absence of express agreement, it can be gathered from other documents or writings. Normally parties like companies insert an arbitration clause in their main agreement.

3. **Agreement is to refer dispute** – Agreement should be to refer present or future disputes to arbitral tribunal. Existence of dispute is the crux of the whole arbitration agreement. If there is no dispute, arbitration agreement will be inoperative. Dispute may be subsisting or it may arise in future. Reference can be made only when the dispute actually arises.

4. **Subject matter of arbitration agreement** – Definition makes it amply clear that disputes under reference must be out of a defined legal relationship whether contractual or not. Generally disputes of civil nature may be referred to arbitration. Criminal matters cannot come under arbitration as that would defeat the purpose of prosecution.

   Matters which can be referred to arbitration - Disputes relating to money, property, damages out of breach of contract, personal rights between the parties (validity of marriage, maintenance to spouse/wife, terms of separation between husband and wife), claims barred by limitation, compensation for defamation etc.

   Matters which cannot be referred to arbitration - Criminal matters/disputes, insolvency or testamentary (claims under a will or validity of a will) matters, questions covered by petition for divorce or restitution of conjugal rights, public trust matters...

5. **Legal consequences/effects of arbitration agreement** – When there is an arbitration agreement, the disputes covered under that cannot be taken up before ordinary courts. Arbitration agreement is an exception to 'An agreement in restraint of legal proceeding - void' under S.28 of Indian Contract Act. Hence it is perfectly valid. If the subject matter of a civil suit is within the scope of arbitration agreement, the court can stay the suit on verifying original arbitration agreement between the same parties.

ARBITRATION PROCEEDINGS

Provisions (Ss. 18-43)

1. **S.18 - Equal Treatment of Parties** – The arbitrator (arbitral tribunal, hereinafter, 'tribunal') is under two obligations.
   a) to treat all parties with equally;
   b) to give full opportunity to each party to present his case.
   The principles of natural justice demand that equality and fair hearing should be followed during arbitration proceeding. The tribunal stands in place of a judge. He should not discriminate the parties on any ground. The parties should be permitted to present relevant documents, witnesses and offer arguments. The right of hearing extends at all stages of arbitration proceeding.

   Rules of Procedure for conducting arbitration -

2. **S.19 – Procedure to be followed** – Arbitral tribunal is not bound to follow the usual procedure in civil matters laid down in Civil Procedure Code, 1908 or Indian Evidence

Act, 1872. However tribunal should not ignore principles of natural justice and fair play. The parties may decide the procedure for conducting arbitration proceeding. If parties do not agree on the procedure, the tribunal may follow procedure which it feels proper. Arbitral institutions have standard procedural rules which can be adopted.

Law Applicable for arbitration in India – S.28

a) For 'domestic arbitration', disputes would be decided according to substantive law for the time being in force relating to the dispute.

b) For 'international commercial arbitration', the parties may designate the law. i.e. Indian Law or foreign law. In case of disagreement, the tribunal is free to decide the matter under any appropriate law including trade, usage customary law...

3. **S.20 – Place of Arbitration** – The parties are free to determine the place for arbitration proceedings. In case it is not fixed, the tribunal can decide the place which would be convenient to both the parties. For consultation amongst members, inspection of documents, goods, property, hearing of experts, witnesses, parties, convenient place may be decided by the tribunal.

4. **S.21 – Date of Commencement of Arbitration Proceedings** – Date of commencement may be fixed by the parties, if not, the date of commencement would be the day on which the other party receives the request for reference of the dispute to tribunal.

5. **S.22 – Language of the Arbitration Proceedings** – Unless otherwise agreed by the parties, the tribunal shall determine the language used during the arbitration proceedings. Normally it would be English. Translation of any document in language used in the arbitration proceedings can be made available to the parties.

   After settling above preliminary matters, the party (claimant) may serve a written notice to the other party (respondent) for referring the dispute to tribunal. Arbitration proceedings begin when respondent receives the notice of reference.

6. **S.23 – Statement of Claims and Defense** – The claimant has to file statement of claims before the tribunal. Statement of claims is to be filed within the time agreed upon by the parties or fixed by tribunal. Statement of claims is like a plaint/suit/petition stating facts supporting claim, allegation, cause of action, issues, prayers/reliefs etc. Respondent should submit his statement of defense to claim. Statement of claims and defense is normally accompanied by the documents relied upon. Amendment to statement of claims and statement of defense or addition by way of supplement (joinders, rejoinders) during arbitration proceedings is possible.

7. **S.24 – Hearing** – The parties may agree not to hold oral hearing. In absence of that understanding, the tribunal may hold oral hearing for presentation of documents or arguments or he may consider only documents and materials as evidences and conduct the proceedings. The tribunal has to serve sufficient advance notice of the oral hearing or of written proceedings to the parties. Fair hearing entails that each party should get the copies of the evidences (documents, materials, reports, information) relied upon by the adversary.

8. **S.25 – Effect of default of a party** – This provision is subject to the agreement to the contrary. If the claimant fails to submit statement of claims within the time, the tribunal shall terminate the arbitration proceedings. But if respondent fails to submit his defense, tribunal shall proceed ex-parte. If the party fails to attend oral hearing, the tribunal may continue ex-parte and make an award.

9. **S.29 – Decision Making by Arbitrators** – After the completion of arbitration proceedings, the tribunal arrives at a decision.
   Following are the possibilites –
   i) Decision on merits on entire Dispute – If there is more than one arbitrator, the decision of the majority would prevail (Subject to agreement between the parties.)
   ii) Decision on question of procedure – Here also the decision of the majority would prevail. The parties however may authorise the presiding arbitrator to pass a decision on question of procedure.

   Termination of Arbitration Proceedings – If there is no majority for a decision (i.e. all members of tribunal are of different opinion), and continuation of arbitration proceedings that way becomes impossible and unnecessary, the tribunal may terminate the arbitration proceedings under S.32(2)(c)

10. **S.30 – Settlement** – During the arbitration proceedings, tribunal may encourage settlement by mediation, conciliation. If the dispute is settled by this persuasion, the award would be drawn in terms of settlement terms and arbitration proceedings would be terminated.

11. **S.31 – Award** – Award (Arbitral award) is the final decision of the tribunal. It is final and binding on all parties to reference. It is like a decree of a civil court and no confirmation is needed by the court. As such an award is enforceable directly.

Form and contents of Award –

Award should be in writing. Signatures of majority of all members of tribunal are sufficient. The award should be speaking i.e. a reasoned decision. However the award may not give reasons if parties agree or if it is based on settlement agreement. Award must state date and place of arbitration proceedings. Signed copy of award should be given to each party.
Interim award may be passed and remain in force till final award is passed. Unless otherwise agreed, for monetary award, tribunal imposes interest @18% p.a. from the date of award till actual payment. Unless otherwise agreed, award shall specify the amount of costs, party to pay, who is entitled to receive the costs and manner of payment.

Corrections etc. in Award

There is a possibility of clerical or typographical or computational or similar errors in award. To correct such mistakes, request in the form of application may be made to the tribunal within 30 days from the receipt of the award. The party should also send a notice to the other party regarding such correction. Request may also be made for interpretation of a specific point in award or a part thereof. If requests are justified, the tribunal shall make necessary corrections or provide interpretation within 30 days from the receipt of request. Suo motu corrections of above types may also be effected by tribunal within 30 days from the date of award. Unless otherwise agreed, parties may apply for additional award. If justified, tribunal may make additional award within 60 days from the request.

CONCILIATION

Conciliation: Definition and Meaning

Old Arbitration Act of 1940 had no provisions for conciliation. This Arbitration and Conciliation Act of 1996 has a set of express provisions (Ss. 61 to 81) dealing with Conciliation. The new Act has followed the Conciliation Rules adopted by the UNCITRAL of 1980.

Conciliation or mediation is an informal process for negotiated settlement of disputes. Conciliation contemplates amicable settlement of disputes. Disputant parties themselves arrive at a solution in a friendly and cordial atmosphere. The role of conciliator is very important because he creates a conducive atmosphere for decision making by the parties. Conciliator improves communication between the parties, brings them together and explores the potential for negotiations and peaceful settlement. Decisions in controversial matters are taken in fair and free atmosphere. Conciliator is authorized by the parties to mediate between them. Conciliator is not an arbitrator, he does not decide, he is only a facilitator. No award is passed in conciliation proceeding. He endorses the settlement agreement and forwards it to the arbitrator for an award based on such agreement.

S. 61 of the Act states that Part III to applies to conciliation of disputes arising out of legal relationship, whether contractual or not and to all proceedings relating thereto. Conciliation method of ADR can be resorted to the differences out of legal relationship for example, matrimonial relationship or near relationship, sacrament or contractual.

Conciliation Proceedings

1. **Commencement**—S.62—Both parties must agree to settle the dispute through conciliation. Any party may send written invitation to the other to conciliate. Conciliation commences when the other party accepts the invitation. The acceptance should be given within 30 days from the receipt of invitation. If no reply is sent within 30 days or the other party expressly rejects the invitation, there will be no conciliation.

2. **Appointment and number of Conciliator** — Parties may appoint one (sole), two or three conciliators. Maximum no of conciliator is three. In absence of consent as to two or three conciliator, one is invariably appointed. The term conciliator refers to a sole, two or three conciliators as the case may be. If sole conciliator is provided, parties should name him. In case of two, each party may suggest name of one conciliator. In case of three, each may appoint one and both, by consent, may appoint third conciliator. If conciliators are more than one, they act collectively.

3. **Procedure for Conciliation**—Ss. 65 to 73—
   i) Submission of Statement, Documents etc — The conciliator may request each party to submit a brief written statement regarding dispute in general, issues involved along with the documents, evidences relied upon by them. Copies of these would be supplied to each party either by the other party or by conciliator.

ii) The role of the conciliator is to assist parties to arrive at an amicable settlement of disputes. He should follow natural principles of objectivity, fairness and justice. He should act in an independent and impartial manner. Rights and obligations of parties, background of the dispute and trade usages should be given due consideration.

iii) Manner of Conciliation Proceedings—Conciliator may decide the manner of conciliation proceedings.The parties are free to decide the place for conciliation. If not fixed by them, conciliator would decide the place for consultations. Conciliator may have discussion on dispute with parties separately or jointly and for that he may communicate orally or in writing. Institutional or personal administrative assistance may also be sought in conciliation proceeding at the instance of parties or by conciliator. The parties should attend the meetings, provide needed material, evidence and cooperate with the conciliator.

iv) Suggestions for peaceful settlement may be made by the parties of their own or on invitation by the conciliator. Conciliator at any stage of the proceeding may propose a settlement. If he feels the possibility of settlement acceptable to both the parties, he should formulate the terms of the possible settlement and send it to the parties for their observation.

On receiving observations from the parties, he may reformulate the terms of the possible settlement and submit it again to the parties for their deliberations. As a result, if parties reach a settlement, they may draw and sign a written settlement agreement. Conciliator may also assist them in drawing up this agreement. Conciliator has to authenticate the settlement agreement which shall be final and binding on the disputant parties.

Legal significance of Settlement Agreement— Settlement Agreement duly signed and authenticated by the conciliator is having the same effect as an award passed by the arbitrator u/s 30 and it treated as a decree of the civil court enforceable u/s 36 of this Act.

v) Termination of Conciliation Proceedings —S.76- -In the following circumstances the conciliation proceedings come to an end. (Reasons and date of termination is given) —
   a) —Signing the settlement agreement by the parties (from date of agreement);
   b) — Written declaration by the conciliator that conciliation efforts cannot be further justified (from date of declaration);
   c) —Written declaration by one party to the other party and conciliator that conciliation proceeding are terminated. (from date of declaration);
   d) —Written declaration by both the parties addressed to conciliator that conciliation proceeding are terminated. (from date of declaration).

4. **Miscellaneous Provisions —**

   a) Confidentiality—S. 75—Parties are obliged to keep confidential all matters relating to conciliation proceedings including settlement agreement. However disclosure can be made for enforcement and implementation of award.

b) Restriction on preferring other preoceeding—S.77—During continuance of conciliation proceedings parties cannot resort to arbitral or judicial proceedings (except when those are necessary for enforcement or preservation of rights.);

c) Cost –S.78—Conciliator shall determine the costs of conciliation proceedings. Costs should be reasonable and relate to the following—

— Fees and expenses of conciliator and witnesses called with parties' consent;

— Expert advice sought by conciliator with parties' consent;

— Administrative assistance sought by conciliator;

— Other expenses incurred in connection with conciliation proceedings and settlement agreement;

— Normally costs are born by the parties equally. Settlement agreement may mention otherwise.

d) Conciliator not to act as arbitrator—S. 80— Conciliator is prevented to act as an arbitrator or counsel or representative of a party in any arbitral or judicial proceeding in respect of conciliated dispute. With parties' consent this restraint can be removed. He cannot be called as a witness in such proceedings.

e) Non admissibility of evidence—S.81—Following things cannot be relied upon by parties as evidence in any arbitral or judicial proceeding—

— Views and suggestions or admissions made by party during conciliation proceedings ;

— Proposals made by the conciliator;

— Fact of willingness to accept such a proposal by one party..

LEGAL TERMINOLOGY

	Legal Term	Meaning
A	Absolute	Complete, final, perfect
	Absolute acceptance	Acceptance without any condition.
	Absque	Without
	Abstinence	Holding back from doing something
	Accomodation Bill	A bill of exchange to a person who has not received its value.
	Accord	An agreement between two or more persons.
	Acquiescence	Agreeing quietly
	Act of God	Act of nature, vis major
	Action	A legal demand of a man's rights, a suit
	Actionable Claim	Claim which can be satisfied by legal action
	Ad infinitum	Without limit, to infinity, endlessly
	Adjudication	Judicial decision, process of adjudicating
	Affidavit	A statement of oath
	Aggrieved Party	Affected party
	Alien Enemy	Foreign National of Enemy Country
	Annuity	An annual payment
	Apparently	Outwardly (appearance)
	Appellant	A person who files an appeal in higher court to change decision of a lower court
	Apprentice	Beginner or Learner
	Arbitration	Settlement of dispute by the decision of an arbitrator (a person chosen to decide a dispute)
	Assent	To agree
	Assertion	Declaration
	Asylum	A refuge to sufferers from mental disease
	Attorney	A person appointed to act for another in business transactions or legal matters.

B	Bailment	Handling over.
	Bias	Prejudice, a leaning of mind, prepossessions, inclination, bent of mind, special influence that sways mind
	Bonafide	In good faith, without fraud or unfair dealing
	Breach of Contract	Non performing contractual terms
C	Case Laws	Law established by precedents, i.e. earlier decisions of courts
	Cause of Action	Reason of a case in court or ground of a legal action
	Civil	Non criminal, relating to private relations
	Civil Suit	Suit of civil nature
	Claim	Formal request or demand
	Coercion	Persuade or restrain by force
	Cogent Evidence	Convincing proof
	Collateral transactions	Secondary or substitutional transactions
	Compensation	Reimbursement in money
	Competent	Capable, Able
	Concealment	Keep secret
	Concept	General notion
	Consensus ad idem	Meeting of the minds of the parties in full & final agreement
	Consensus ad item	Two parties agree upon the same thing and in same sense
	Consent	Be willing to allow
	Contemplate	To intend or to think
	Convict	Person undergoing imprisonment as per final decision of court
	Cyber	Computer used process
D	Damages	Monetary compensation
	Decree	Formal judgment or decision, Formal expression of an adjudication conclusively determining rights of parties
	Defendant	One who defends a suit
	Destitute of legal effects	Without legal effects
	Detain	keep in custody or lock-up.
	Detriment	Harm, injury, loss
	Discretionary	With freedom to decide, to decide as one thinks fit.
	Disguise	To conceal by changed appearance
	Dominance	Influence
	Duress	Coercive circumstances
E	Elucidate	Explain
	Embody	Include, comprise
	Emptor	Buyer
	Encumbrance	A liability burdening property
	Enforceable	Which can be given effect to by law.

	Entitle	Give a title or right to —
	Equitable	Valid in equity, may not be in law
	Equity	Fairness, Honesty
	Evidence	Proof
	Exhaustive codes	Comprehensive laws
	Exorbitant	Grossly excessive
	Express	Distinctly stated
	External Manifestation	External demonstration or display
	Extinguish	To render an obligation or a right void
F	Fame sole	Female as an independent person
	Fiduciary Relation	Relation of trust and confidence
	Forbearance	Patience, Tolerance, Control
	Forbid	Refuse to allow a thing or a person to have a thing
	Forum	A court or a tribunal
	Fraud	Intentional mis-statement
	Frivolous	Silly or of little worth
G	Gratis	Without a reward
	Gratuitous	Free of charge, without legal consideration
H	Held	Decided by court
I	Illusory	Unreal
	Immunity	Freedom from obligation, penalty
	Implied	It is one, which is inferred from the acts or conducts of the parties or course of dealing with them
	Inadvertently	Carelessly or Unintentionally
	Inception	Beginning
	Indemnity	To compensate
	Infringe	to break or violate
	Injunction	Order of the court to do or not to do-something (i.e. act)
	Issue	A point of fact or law to be decided by a judge
J	Judgement	Final decision of the court
	Judicial Precedent	Earlier decisions (binding)
	Jurisdiction	Power to hear and determine a case
L	Legal Consequences	Result under Law
	Legal Obligation	Obligation which binds person to do something
	Legal Relation	Lawful relation
	Litigation	A law suit, To litigate - to go to law
	Lunacy	Madness or Insanity
M	Malice	Wrong motive, bad intention
	Merger	Absorption in another, of a right, action
	Misrepresentation	Represent wrongly or give a false idea

N	Negotiable	Capable of being passed,- transferred
	Nudum Pactum	Naked agreement
	Null	Without any consequence, with no legal binding
	Nullity	Invalidity
O	Obligations	Binding power, duty under law
P	Plaint	Petition or Suit
	Plaintiff	One who files a plaint (petition or suit)
	Precedent	Previous binding decision of superior court.
	Prejudice	Injury or harm.
	Prima Facie	On face of it
	Privity	Nearness of relationship in contract
	Presumption	The act of presuming, take for granted
	Profess	To declare openly
Q	Quantum Meruit	As much as earned or deserved or merited
	Quash	To annual, make void, nullify
	Quasi Contract	Relation similar to contracts
	Quid pro quo	Something in return, something for something
R	Ratifications	Post facto approval or confirmation
	Rebuttal, To rebut	To negative the theory of other party, refutation, contradiction
	Recognisance	A bond binding a person to do particular act
	Recompense	Reimbursement
	Redress	Remedy
	Remedy	Remove anything undesirable, Rectify, solutions through law, legal or equitable relief
	Repudiate	Disown, reject, refuse dealing, deny, refuse to discharge an obligation
	Rescission	Cancellation, Repudiation.
	Restitutio in integrum	Restoration to the original position
	Restitution	Restoration (Return)
	Restraint	Under control, keep in check, restriction.
	Revoke	To withdraw
	Rule of Estoppel	Not allowed to deny earlier position
S	Seclusion	Away from society
	Set off	Claim for debt or damages set up by a defendant against plainfiff
	Spring	Arise, Appear
	Subsists	Which exists
	Subtle	So delicate or precise as to be difficult to decide
	Suffice	Satisfy
	Suo moto	Of one's own motion

	Susceptible	Likely to be influenced or harmed by a particular thing
T	Taint	To spoil
	To cease	To stop, to brings to an end.
	To Forbear	Retrain, Keep away from
	To sue	To begin a law suit
	Tort	Wrong
	Transgress	To sin or to do wrong, to exceed limit
U	Uberrima fidei	Most abundant faith
	Unjust enrichment	Obtaining benefit, money at the expense of other in an unfair manner
	Ultra - Vires	Beyond powers (in the law of corporations)
	Unconscionable Bargains	The bargain in which a man of ordinary prudence would not enter into
	Usage	Well known, customary and uniform practice in a business or profession
V	Vague	Unclear
	Valid	Good in Law
	Vendor and Vendee	A seller and a buyer
	Vis-à-vis	opposite of or facing to
	Vis major	Irresistible force of nature
	Vitiates	Make less good or effective
	Void	Empty, Vacant, without force, meaningless
	Void-ab-initio	Void from inception (from beginning)
W	Witness	Confirming evidence, Testimony

SELECTIVE BIBLIOGRAPHY

- **Ramchandran V. G.** – *Law of Contract In India* (1983) — Eastern Book Company, Lucknow.

- **Avtar Singh** – *Law of Contract* (2005) — Eastern Book Company, Lucknow.

- **Mulla** – *The Indian Contract Act & Specific Relief Act* — Tripathi M M Publications.

- **Chada P. R.** - *Business Law* (1999) — Galgotia Publshing Company, New Delhi.

- **Kuchhal M. C.** *Business Law* (2005) — Vikas Publishing House Pvt. Ltd.

- **Bulchandani K. R.** *Business Law for Management* (2006) — Himalaya Publishing House.

- **Gulshan S. S. & Kapoor G. K.** - *The Sale of Goods Act & Partnership Act* Business Law (2005) — New Age International Publishers, New Delhi.

- **Desai S. T.** – *Law of Partnership* (1964) S C Sarkar & Sons Pvt. Ltd., Calcutta.

- **Avtar Singh** : Company Law : Eastern Book Company, Lucknow.

- **Datey VS**–Elements of Company Law : Tax......

- **Bhashyam & Adiga** – *The Negotiable Instruments Act* — Law Weekly (1956) Madras.

- **Khargamwala** on The Negotiable Instruments Act (O P Faizi) Butterworths 2003

- **P. Narayan** – *Intellectual Property Law* Eastern Law House - New Delhi-2000

- **Krishna Kumar** – *Cyber Laws* (2000) : Dominan Publishers & Distributors; New Delhi.

- **Dr. Sreenivasulu NS** –Intellectual Property Rights (2007) Regal Publications, New Delhi.

- **Salil K. Roy Chowdhari & HK Saharay** – (1996) Kamal Law House, Calcutta.

About the Author

Prof. Dr. Kulkarni Shashikant Narayanrao

B.Sc LL.M. SET, PDGHE, Ph. D. (Environmental Laws)

Associate Professor, HOD, Department of Business Laws

B.Y.K. College of Commerce, Nasik (Maharashtra)

Total teaching experience as a Law Lecturer in Pune & Nashik for more than 30 Years;

Publications
  i) **Books-**
   1) Laws Regulating Business—Diamond Publications, Pune
      ISBN-978-81-8483 -024-8
   2) Labour Laws (co-author) Nirali Publications, Pune
      Two more books are under publication.
  ii) Nine **Research Articles** published so far with ISSN and ISBN Numbers.

Other curricular and extracurricular activities—

- Former Member Board of Studies, Business Law Board of Pune Universty
- Former Chairman/Member of Syllabus Revision Committee for T.Y.B Com, BBA, FYB.Com, S.Y.B.Com & M.Com ;
- Resource Person for Human Rights in Virtual Learning Program of YCMOU, Nasik, Department of Computer Science, Physics, University of Pune;
- Visiting faculty for MBA, MMM, DBM and MAMCJ for 15 years. Panel member for GDPI in MBA admission process for five years;
- Occasionally write articles in newspapers on law subjects;
- Guest faculty/Resource Person in other colleges and reputed institutions in Pune & Nashik
- Recognized as a Ph.D. Guide of North Maharashtra University, Jalgaon in Law (Ph.D. by Research) under the faculty of law and in Business Law of Pune University; PG Teacher in Law subjects…..